He always knows the nightmare for what it is.

Even if the scenes that preceded it—getting hammered at a bar with drinking buddies he hasn't seen in years or sitting in a strange classroom, taking a final exam in a subject he knows nothing about—seem real at the time, the spell is broken every time the screen door slams.

Vincent jerks upright. He is sitting on a faded brown couch, one leg tucked under him and the other dangling over the side. Slowly, inevitably, he turns his head toward the door, knowing he will find Bella there, struggling with two overstuffed grocery bags. His heart pounds while he waits for her to speak.

"Were you sleeping?" Her tone is accusatory.

What Vincent should say is "I must have dozed off." But the nightmare, while a thief of reality, is not a true memory and is perhaps worse than the actual moment of tragedy because he knows what will come next.

He knows, and he is powerless to stop it.

Books by David Michael Williams

Tales of Altaerra

Magic's Daughter

The Renegade Chronicles

Rebels and Fools

Heroes and Liars

Martyrs and Monsters

———————

The Soul Sleep Cycle

If Souls Can Sleep

If Sin Dwells Deep

If Dreams Can Die

Available at Amazon.com

If Souls Can Sleep

David Michael Williams

ONEMILLIONWORDS

If Souls Can Sleep is a work of fiction. Names, characters, places, and incidents either are products of the author's imagination or are used fictitiously. Any resemblance to actual persons, living or dead, business establishments, events, or locales is entirely coincidental.

ONEMILLIONWORDS

Inquiries can be directed to info@david-michael-williams.com.

First published by One Million Words, LLC, Wisconsin, USA

First printing, January 2018

ISBN 978-0-9910562-8-6

Written by David Michael Williams (david-michael-williams.com)

Cover art copyright © 2018 by One Million Words, LLC

Cover design by Mary Christopherson (mary.design)

Author photograph by Jaime Lynn Hunt (jaimelynnhunt.com)

If Souls Can Sleep is dedicated to my friends and comrades-in-arms in the Allied Authors of Wisconsin, whose critiques make me a better writer and whose encouragement is much appreciated.

Soul sleep, more properly known as psychopannychism, is the belief that the human soul is uncomprehending during the time between bodily death and resurrection on Judgment Day.

"The virtuous man is content to dream what a wicked man really does."

Plato

Prologue

Vincent stumbled through the hospital's unexpectedly automatic door. A sudden blast of heat burned his bloodshot eyes.

The antiseptic air made his skin twitch, his stomach roil. Though he hated hospitals on principle, he knew his nausea had more to do with a belly full of whiskey. All those hard-fought months of sobriety, wasted.

But am I drunk enough?

Vincent batted the thought aside and focused on walking a straight line to the elevators. When he spotted a policeman leaning against the information desk, he nearly lost his nerve.

Not a real cop. He doesn't even have a gun.

Keeping tabs on the middle-aged security guard out of the corner of his eye, Vincent performed his best impression of a model citizen as he crossed the lobby and waited for the elevator. Fortunately, the guy seemed more interested in flirting with the young brunette behind the counter than scrutinizing visitors.

The elevator opened, and he hurried in, letting out a big breath as his view of the rent-a-cop was replaced by the shiny metal door. His relief was short-lived, however, when he considered what lay ahead.

Leaning against the elevator's faux wood paneling, he wished he had some liquid courage left. If he had brought a bottle with him, he would've emptied it fast.

But there was nothing fast about the elevator. Why the hell wasn't it moving? Panicked thoughts about the sly security guard and a master control panel disappeared when he realized he had never pressed the button for the floor he wanted.

Focus, damn it!

He jabbed a finger into the number three. The elevator's sudden acceleration tightened his stomach. When the door opened, he took a few steadying steps onto the long-term patient observation ward. The vegetable garden.

As much as he wanted to avoid contact with hospital staff, he knew he'd never be able to find his destination without help. He had visited his brother only once before, and that was eight months ago. The day Danny went into a coma.

Vincent wiped his brow with the back of his hand, smearing sweat into his wild tangle of hair. He resisted the urge to rub his eyes as he approached the front desk.

A middle-aged woman with artificially blond hair and wearing a frumpy brown pullover looked up.

He forced his mouth into what he hoped would pass for a smile. "Hi, I'm, ah, looking for Danny..." He cleared his throat. "...*Daniel* Pierce. Can you tell me what room he's in?"

The woman—Suzanne, according to her nametag—regarded him warily. Her nose twitched, and he wondered if the stench of booze could ever be mistaken for cheap aftershave.

"Mr. Pierce doesn't get many visitors," she said. The statement might have been an offhand comment or an accusation. "What is your relation to the patient?"

"I'm his brother. *Half*-brother, actually."

The receptionist's eyebrows arched. "You're Vincent. Eve's other son."

He winced.

Eve's other son...Cain.

"Yeah, I'm Vincent. Wait a minute. She's not here, is she? My mother, I mean."

"No, not yet." Suzanne glanced at her watch. "Mass won't be over for another hour or so. You'll have to sign in."

She pushed a clipboard toward him, and he scribbled his name on the line. It felt like signing a confession.

"It's Room 307," she said when he returned the clipboard. "Down that hall and take a left."

Vincent dropped the pen and walked away. While watching his feet to make sure they did what they were supposed to, he almost collided with a big, grim-faced man in scrubs. Vincent muttered an apology and continued down the corridor. His pulse quickened with each number. 301, 302, 303...

The door to Room 307 was open. He paused at the threshold.

Daniel Pierce lay on his back, a tightly tucked blanket covering his lower half. His red hair, usually an untamed mass of curls, had been cut short and combed. He looked pale, but then again Daniel always looked pale. Were it not the hospital gown and the many tubes connecting him to the bedside electrical devices, Vincent might have believed his brother was just sleeping.

He is *sleeping. Asleep and then some.*

Without realizing it, Vincent had entered the room and walked up to the bed. Looking down at Daniel's peaceful expression, he remembered the last argument he had had with their mother, who was still waiting for a miracle. But Vincent had sided with the doctors, trusting facts over faith.

Daniel was a hopeless case. He would never wake up.

Vincent would make sure of it.

People always said "pull the plug," but there were a lot of wires and tubes. If he cut the wrong ones, would it alert the staff before he found the right one? Was it as easy as just yanking the power cord out of the electric socket? He couldn't afford to make any mistakes. There was no such thing as a second chance.

He reached a hand inside his pocket and grasped something small and cold. Still staring at his brother's face—he half expected the intense blue eyes to open or the lips to curl into a smirk—he brought out the jackknife and opened it. The click echoed inside his skull.

Vincent held out the knife, his arm trembling. He wondered what would be quickest. Slashing the throat? Cutting his wrists? Plunging the blade into Daniel's heart, vampire style?

The thought was so ridiculous he laughed out loud. Then he doubled over, gagging and gasping for air. Seconds later, the dry heaves subsided. When he righted himself, the room was spinning, but all he could see was Daniel as a kid, playing with Matchbox cars and reading comic books. A teenager, snitching cigarettes from their mother's purse. A young man, holding his newborn niece for the first time.

Clementine...

Tears streaming down his face, Vincent took a deep breath and whispered, "I'm sorry."

Chapter 1

He always knows the nightmare for what it is.

Even if the scenes that preceded it—getting hammered at a bar with drinking buddies he hadn't seen in years or sitting in a strange classroom, taking a final exam in a subject he knew nothing about—seem real at the time, the spell is broken every time the screen door slams.

Vincent jerks upright. He is sitting on a faded brown couch, one leg tucked under him and the other dangling over the side. Slowly, inevitably, he turns his head toward the door, knowing he will find Bella there, struggling with two overstuffed grocery bags. His heart pounds while he waits for her to speak.

"Were you sleeping?" Her tone is accusatory.

What Vincent should say is "I must have dozed off." But the nightmare, while a thief of reality, is not a true memory and is perhaps worse than the actual moment of tragedy because he knows what will come next.

He knows, and he is powerless to stop it.

Even if he could change the script and overcome the cold hand of dread keeping him silent and rooted to the couch, it would be too late because the horrible thing has already happened.

"Where's Clementine?" Bella asks.

He scans the room, hoping, praying, *begging* to see a pair of black pigtails peeking up from behind the coffee table or a telltale lump under the afghan on the rocking chair. The nightmare will not be swayed, however. Bella walks past him and dumps the brown bags onto the dining room table, spilling one of them in the process.

"Clemmy? Where are you, baby?" she calls.

They notice the open bathroom door at the same time. Some sadistic force, perhaps the nightmare itself, compels Vincent to finally leave the couch and follow her into the bathroom. Bella's scream comes right on cue. Helpless to stop himself, he steps through the doorway.

Clementine's bare feet stick out of the tub, her little toes pointing toward the ceiling. Bella has not started crying yet. In that forever instant, there is only silence as a rubber duck, Clementine's favorite toy, floats atop the pink-tinged water.

Vincent gasped and blinked frantically against the darkness that harbored the image of his dead daughter. Kneeling on his bed, which was nothing more than one mattress stacked on top of another, he groped through the black air until he found the string for the overhead light.

With a click, the room burst into existence around him. He fell back onto his bed. Staring up at the crisscrossing cracks in the ceiling, he listened to the sound of his breathing until his pulse no longer pounded in his ears and the pressure in his chest eased into a dull ache.

I used to wake up sobbing like a baby. Maybe someday the nightmare won't even wake me up. Maybe someday I won't even remember that I had it.

Knowing he would never be able to fall back to sleep— that was one thing that hadn't changed in seven, almost eight years—Vincent sat up again and looked at the clock. 9:44. In the morning? No, the little dot of light was next to "p.m." But what exactly did that mean?

The third-shift lifestyle still messed with his mind after almost a year. It took him a full minute to piece it together. He had gone to bed just after noon and hadn't set the alarm because he had off tomorrow—*today* off. Today and to-morrow.

He got out of bed and put on an old pair of jeans that were lying atop one of the piles of clothes. A sorry-looking black T-shirt was the sole contents of the dresser. He pulled it over his head. Since none of his socks were even close to clean, he condemned his bare feet to the cold hardwood floor. Stifling a yawn, he opened his bedroom door.

The living room light was on. He was not alone.

"Oh! Hey, Vincent. We didn't wake you, did we?"

For once, his roommate was not in his recliner. Instead, Jerry sat on the long, stumpy couch—dubbed "the Low Rider" by a former resident—next to a young woman sporting a lip ring and lots of cleavage. Jerry's eyes were wide with concern. She smiled sheepishly.

"No, no," Vincent said. "I didn't even know you were out here."

The girl stared at him. He ran a hand through his hair, trying to diagnose by touch how bad a case of bed head he had.

A fine first impression…or do I know her?

"Good," Jerry said. "We were being extra quiet. Even turned the volume down all the way." He gestured at the TV with the hand that wasn't holding a joint.

Vincent turned in time to see a woman in skimpy attire leap up from the sand to spike the ball over the net.

"You're watching volleyball?" Vincent asked.

Jerry shrugged. "Paish used to play in high school. And I'm watchin' 'cause…well…look at them!"

I have *met her.*

Paish, short for Patience, was Jerry's dealer. Vincent had been home when she paid a visit more than a month ago. "Made a delivery" was probably more accurate, since she had left soon after the transaction. "Schwag," "nugs," "steamrollers"—Jerry and Paish had spoken a different language. She seemed friendly enough, but Vincent hadn't said more than hello and goodbye to her. According to Jerry, they were just friends.

She played volleyball. Just like Bella did.

Jerry passed the joint to Paish, who took a long drag. The smoke escaped from her mouth in a slow, steady stream. When she leaned forward for the ashtray on the coffee table, Vincent was afforded an unobstructed view down her shirt. Her puffy eyes met his.

"Do you want to hit this?" she asked.

The question caught him completely off guard. "What?"

She held the joint out to him. "Do you want a hit?"

Clearly, the expression "hit this" meant something different in Druggie Speak than the slang Vincent was used to. For a second, he had thought she was making a far more intimate offer. Embarrassed, he could only stammer and shake his head.

Before he could make more of a fool of himself, Jerry said, "Vincent doesn't get high. I don't think he drinks either."

"Well, aren't you a good boy?" Paish said to Vincent. She handed the joint back to Jerry.

"I try," Vincent replied, forcing his eyes not to stray south of hers. He cleared his throat. "I'm going to jump in the shower."

He retreated from the living room. Passing through the kitchen, he heard Paish say to Jerry, "Your roommate is kind of cute."

Vincent smirked to himself. He supposed he should be flattered. Jerry had said she was a student at UW–Milwaukee, which meant she was younger than both of them, maybe by as much as a decade. She was pretty, though bleach-blond highlights and pierced lips weren't his cup of tea. And then there was the recreational drugs use.

Standing in front of the toilet, he was half-amused, half-ashamed to find that he was getting hard.

Must be a side effect of abstinence.

Vincent flushed and washed his hands, glancing up at the mirror. He wouldn't be mistaken for an undergraduate, but he didn't look the worse for thirty years of wear. He was reasonably tall, somewhat dark, and closer to handsome than hideous. Maybe Paish found his dark, sleep-tousled hair charming. Maybe she liked half-Hispanic guys.

Or maybe she was just stoned.

If the divorce were done with, would I have flirted back?

He pulled back the shower curtain and gasped.

Two little legs and a rubber duck.

Vincent staggered back to the toilet and focused on not puking. After several minutes spent staring into the rust-stained bowl, beads of sweat sliding down to his neck, he finally looked at the bathtub again. Of course, it was empty.

By the time he stepped into the tub, all thoughts of sex had vanished. Thanks to outdated plumbing, the shower-head spat out an unsteady trickle of lukewarm water. He barely noticed.

His hair dripping false tears down the sides of his face and once more wearing the faded black T-shirt and jeans, Vincent ventured back into living room. He made a beeline for his bedroom but stopped when he saw Paish was gone.

"She works in the morning," Jerry explained from the comfort of his mustard-colored recliner. "Man, I'm glad I don't work weekends."

Hand on the doorknob to his room, Vincent said, "I thought you didn't like hanging out with college students. Or is it common courtesy to schmooze with your supplier?"

"Whuh? Paish? She's the shit. A bit of a tease sometimes, but what's wrong with that?"

Vincent went into his room. He picked up two matching socks off the floor and slipped his tennis shoes on over them.

"And I got nothing against college students," Jerry said from the next room. The closed door hardly muffled his roommate's voice at all. "I told you I never wanted to *live* with one ever again. Too many bad experiences."

Vincent ran a comb through his slick hair a few times before returning to the living room.

"Did one of them nark on you or something?" He hoped his tone came off as more curious than condemning. Jerry had been upfront about his drug use from day one, and aside from the not-quite-campfire reek of marijuana, Vincent couldn't complain about his roommate.

"Naw," Jerry said, his eyes glued to the volleyball game. "But my last roommate…a philosophy major from Waterford…threw a big party that got busted. I was damn lucky none of the cops found my stash. Anyway, college kids never have any money. When they're not moochin' your food, they're moochin' your weed."

"Well, that's something you don't have to worry about with me." Vincent paused. "I'm going for a walk."

Jerry suddenly stood up, and for a moment, Vincent

feared the big guy was going to invite himself along. Instead, his roommate went to the pantry and retrieved a bag of potato chips. On his way back to his threadbare throne, Jerry said, "Alrighty. I'll probably crash soon. See ya tomorrow."

"See ya."

Vincent was halfway out the door, coat in hand, when the phone rang. Something made him stop.

"Hello?" said Jerry with mouth full of chips. "Oh, just a sec."

Vincent turned around. Jerry held the phone against his chest. "It's for you. I think it's your mom again."

Christ.

"Tell her she just missed me."

"Dude—"

Vincent shut the door and pounded down the hallway stairs. He refused to feel guilty about ditching his mother, but he did regret leaving Jerry to deal with her. For all of his foibles, Jeremiah Weis was a good guy. He also was the closest thing Vincent had to a friend.

More than a dozen bars called Milwaukee's East Side home, and most of them were within walking distance of the apartment. The bulk of them lined Brady Street, which was one block from home.

Vincent went in the other direction.

Chapter 2

The door slammed, and Vincent jerked upright.

He braced himself for what would follow—the relentless nightmare's retelling of the worst moment of his life—and even turned to where he knew Bella would be grappling with the grocery bags.

But it wasn't Bella lingering in the doorway.

Vincent stared uncomprehendingly at a figure covered head to foot in a frayed gray garment. Long sleeves dangled down past the man's hands, and a hood hid his face entirely. The stranger was a dead ringer for the Grim Reaper, sans scythe.

And Halloween is still a month away.

The tang of smoke tickled Vincent's nose. An open fireplace on the opposite of the room sent shadows dancing on bare wooden walls. The dozen or more people gathered around small, square tables spoke quietly, their indistinct words punctuated by the crackling of roasting logs and the clinking of cups against the hard tabletops.

Vincent knew a bar when he saw one, even if this one looked like something ripped from the pages of a history book.

The other customers all wore period costumes—tall boots, heavy leather cloaks and other drab garments whose colors were lost to the dim lighting. One bushy-bearded man even had a sword strapped to his back.

Where the hell am I?

Vincent stood up. The strange scene blurred, and he lost his balance. On his way back down to the bench, his thigh hit the table in front of him. Something made of metal clattered to the floor. The empty mug came to a stop a few feet away from the table.

"Easy does it, man!" yelled a squat man with patchy red beard facial hair from behind a long counter to Vincent's right. "You've quaffed enough spirits to topple a giant. Take it slow!"

Vincent's mind was spinning. It had been months since he stepped into a bar. How could this have happened?

He struggled in vain to remember how he got there—wherever it was. As far as he knew, there weren't any Renaissance-themed festivals in Milwaukee, and the nearest Medieval Times was in Illinois.

"What is this place?" he asked the bartender. He nearly didn't recognize his own hoarse voice.

The short man barked a laugh. "No more ale for you, friend!"

Before Vincent could reply, the ghostly, cloaked stranger swept past his table and approached the bar. From his seat a few feet away, Vincent saw that the dark gray fabric was tattered in places. A ring of what might have been moisture discolored the bottom few inches of the coat. Vincent caught a whiff of something earthy.

"What'll ya have, friend?" the bartender asked. His mouth smiled, but his eyes did not.

The stranger had a good half-foot on the bartender. Vincent expected to hear a loud, ominous voice. Instead, he had to strain to make out the whispered words.

"I am…looking…for someone."

The bartender grunted. "Most folks who come to my outpost are lookin' to warm up with a fire and a stiff drink. Names are not Orson's business. Coins, on the other hand…"

Vincent thought the bartender—Orson?—was fishing for a bribe, but the hooded stranger didn't take the bait.

"A traveler told me the man I seek lives in this village and frequents your tavern," said the soft, raspy voice. "Do you know of the one called Valenthor?"

Orson's frown deepened. "Mayhap I do. A piece of silver might aid my memory."

"Please, sir." The billowing sleeve shot out, and a pale hand closed over the bartender's wrist. "I have no money. Your kindness—"

Orson wrenched his arm away. His heavy brows reduced his beady eyes to slits. Vincent expected him to slug the other guy.

After several tense seconds, Orson muttered, "Kindness is rarer than a pretty whore in the frontier lands. But fortune smiles upon us both. That is Valenthor sitting right behind you. He has drank his fill this night, and like you, beggar, he has no money to his name. Why don't the two of you take your leave, hmm?"

When the stranger turned to find Valenthor, Vincent did too. Although none of what was happening made any sense him, he was caught up in the act. If nothing else, it was easier to watch the show than worry about how he had fallen off the wagon. He wondered if the guy with the sword was Valenthor. It sounded like a warrior's name.

"Wake up, Valenthor. You have a visitor." The bartender was looking at Vincent.

So was the stranger.

"Me?" Vincent braced himself against the table and slowly pulled himself up. He winced as the floor teeter-tottered beneath his feet. "You must be mistaking me for somebody else."

Orson scowled. As for the stranger, all Vincent could

see was a pointed white chin. Everything else was lost within the sagging hood.

"I have come so far to find you, Valenthor."

The half-whispered proclamation, coupled with the Grim Reaper getup, gave Vincent goosebumps.

"My name is Vincent, not Valenthor." He looked to Orson for help, for an explanation, but the bartender didn't so much as blink. Vincent was suddenly aware that the other customers were staring too.

I gotta get out of here.

Keeping the table between himself and the stranger, Vincent moved as quickly as he dared toward the door.

"Wait!" The stranger's voice had gone up a notch in volume as well as pitch.

Now Vincent wasn't so sure it was a man after all. Reluctantly, he stopped.

The stranger came closer. "You do not look how I had expected, but I am certain it is you."

"What do you want from me?" Vincent demanded.

"I need you to return with me to my homeland."

"What homeland? Why me?"

"Because you are the Chosen One."

His own laugh caught him by surprise.

That's the best you can come up with? Even for a cheesy restaurant, that's really lame.

Long, slender fingers clutched Vincent's arm. "Please, Valenthor! My people are in danger. You must fulfill the prophecy, or the forces of darkness will conquer all nations."

Vincent wasn't listening anymore. Without quite realizing what he was doing, he reached out and pushed back the hood to get a better look at the stranger. His eyes lingered for a moment on the oversized eyes that were too green and glittery to *not* be wearing contact lenses. Then he took in the smooth, porcelain skin and prominent cheekbones. Her honey-blond hair spilled down a long, flawless neck.

She was damn gorgeous, in spite of her pointy ears.

A shared gasp filled the room.

"Ye gods, it's an elf!" someone shouted.

"Don't let her escape!" Orson cried.

Vincent couldn't make sense of the other customers' hate-filled expressions. Almost all of them were on their feet. The big bearded man unsheathed his sword and stomped across the room.

The look of sheer terror on the woman's face stole Vincent's breath.

Supermodel looks and real acting talent to boot. She should be filming in Hollywood, not doing improv in this dump. Oh well, might as well play along.

"Leave the…uh…damsel alone!" he shouted.

But the swordsman kept coming, and his blade looked awfully sharp for a prop. Vincent stepped in front of the woman, not at all certain what he was supposed to do next. His foot came down on the tin cup that had rolled off his table earlier.

His legs flew out from under him. He fell in slow motion, affording him just enough time to realize that while he wasn't experiencing the recurring nightmare about Clementine, he was dreaming nonetheless.

He woke up the instant before his head struck the worn, wooden planks.

Vincent stumbled into the living room. The light from the tall, slightly tilted lamp stabbed at his eyes. Jerry's lava lamp was on too, but the TV was off. He gave no more thought to his roommate as he plopped down onto the Low

Rider.

Head in hands, he stared at the hardwood floor and tried to put reality back together.

His confusion slowly faded as he mentally replayed the ordinary events of yesterday. A wave of relief washed through him when he realized that he had not, in fact, given into the temptation to drink. But he had been drunk in the dream, and it had felt very real. All of it had.

Except for the nightmare about Clementine, Vincent almost never remembered his dreams. He doubted he would soon forget the medieval tavern—or the elf with the sparkly green eyes.

The rattling of silverware snapped him back to the real world. The sound of running water immediately followed. Jerry was home, and he was doing dishes.

He repressed the absurd impulse to run back into his room. It had been a while since Vincent had washed any dishes, but then again he couldn't remember the last time he cooked. Maybe not since Clementine died. He figured half of his paycheck went to the sub shops, pizza places, and a certain greasy spoon on Farwell.

Jerry's voice drifted into the living room, "I wouldn't take it too hard. You're probably just an easy target, ya know?"

Company? He waited for a second voice but then saw the phone was missing from its dock on the desk. Vincent had been grateful when Jerry offered to share the landline with him, but now that he had his own cell, Vincent wondered why Jerry didn't trade the cordless relic for a true mobile phone.

Maybe he's strapped for cash. Who knows how much he spends on weed?

"Hey, no problem," Jerry said. "I'll let him know you called…sure…buh-bye."

Vincent uttered a wordless greeting, as Jerry walked into the room and hung up the phone.

"Oh, you're up! You missed your mom again."

Vincent shrugged. "I'm sure it's nothing important." His thoughts caught up with him suddenly. "Wait, were you just talking to her now?"

"Uh-huh." Jerry folded his arms. The perpetually cheerful man's lips twitched into something resembling a frown. "I know it's none of my business, but maybe you should call her back."

"Why's that?" Vincent asked, trying to sound nonchalant.

"'Cause she's worried about you, man."

Too bad.

"I'm just sayin'—"

"You had it right the first time, Jerry. It's none of your business." He got up from the couch, skirted the coffee table, and headed for his bedroom. He opened the door, but stopped suddenly. "Wait a minute, what exactly did my mother tell you?"

Jerry opened his mouth, but no words came out.

Vincent's stomach did a somersault. Jerry knew…

"I'm really sorry about your dau—"

"Don't!"

Trembling, Vincent entered his bedroom. His thoughts were a blur as he got dressed. He felt rage boiling beneath the surface, but he pushed it down. He didn't want to think about Jerry's conversation with his mother. He didn't want to think about anything.

When Vincent returned to the living room, Jerry was still standing there. He brushed his shaggy blond hair out of his eyes. For once, the light blue irises weren't bordered by crisscrossing red spider webs. The whites were glossy with gathering tears.

Something inside Vincent exploded.

"The least you could've done is invite my mom over and get her stoned first," Vincent snarled. "The old Evangeline would've been all too happy to stay all night...smoking, telling stories...whatever *else* you wanted."

Pale-faced and wide-eyed, Jerry managed to utter a single, quiet word: "Dude."

"But let me guess," Vincent said. "She didn't get around to telling you about her days as a druggie. Or that she used to be a slut. No, I'm betting she didn't tell any stories about *her* days as a neglectful parent, did she?"

Jerry scrambled out of the way as Vincent stormed past him and out the front door. He was half a block away from the apartment before he realized he had forgotten his coat. He didn't care. The autumn wind cooled his feverish skin.

She had no right to tell Jerry.

Vincent stood at the corner of Brady and Arlington for several minutes. He was barely aware of the passersby—a group of college kids, a pair of stout elderly women speaking Russian, a panhandler who wisely did not to ask Vincent for charity.

The neighborhood contained as motley a collection of residents as Vincent could imagine. A haven for misfits. Down the street, he could make out the red script lettering of the neighborhood drugstore.

Across the street was a high-dollar lounge where yuppies happily pissed away their money on overpriced martinis. To his right, past the Italian restaurant, was a bar for the blue-collar crowd. The jukebox always played classic rock. Farther down, there was a small building that boasted an array of beers from around the world. Young scholars and would-be Bohemians flocked to the outdoor seating in summer.

Vincent had never been to any of them, but at the moment, he wasn't feeling at all picky.

Working-class watering hole, it is.

Heart pounding, Vincent hurried over to it, stopping at the bottom of the steps. A neon sign promising a refreshing light pilsner on tap beckoned him.

She had no right to tell him about Clementine. How does she expect me to move on with my life if I can't escape the past?

He rested his hand on the doorknob. The sounds of drums, electric guitar, and voices trying to talk above the music pushed through the closed door. He already could smell the cigarette smoke, taste the satisfying sting of whiskey on his tongue.

Then Vincent was running back down Arlington Street, past the apartment building, and to the familiar roads lined with houses, a church, and a school. The words of Orson, medieval bartender, echoed in his ears:

"No more ale for you, friend!"

Chapter 3

The rhythmic crunch of snow beneath his shoes was the only sound in the universe. The houses flanking the endless street stood dark and still. No headlights, no traffic sounds. The world slept.

But not Milton.

A blanket of clouds wrapped the sky in impenetrable twilight.

When was the last time I saw the sun or moon?

Milton pulled back his right coat sleeve to look at his wristwatch, but the glass was fogged, blurring the position of hands and numbers alike.

He plunged his hands deep into his coat pockets, even though they weren't at all cold. He supposed they must be numb.

I've been walking for so long. I need to get warm.

Even as the thought surfaced through the haze of fatigue, a bus stop appeared in the distance. Milton quickened his pace, feeling more alert than he had in ages. A layer of ice obscured the route number and any hint of a destination. It didn't matter.

As long as I keep moving, I'll stay ahead of them…ahead of…

An inhuman growl, followed by a long, high-pitched shriek, shattered the silence. Milton spun around, muscles tense, to confront whatever terrible beast had stolen up on him. The dragon in his mind's eye dissolved as the bus screeched to a stop beside him.

His sigh of relief escaped on a puff of steam.

The door folded open, and the entire frame of the vehicle dipped closer to the ground, almost as if the vehicle were genuflecting. The gesture would have felt more welcoming without the mechanical hiss that accompanied it.

Milton stepped up and deposited a few coins into the metal receptacle, not bothering to look at the driver, who, in turn, offered no greeting. The bus suddenly lurched forward, forcing Milton to take a few unintentional steps down the aisle. Rather than fight the momentum, he performed the awkward dance past rows and rows of empty seats until he reached the back of the bus.

"The woods are lovely, dark, and deep," said someone from across the aisle.

Milton jumped in spite of himself. Hadn't the bus been empty?

A young man wearing blue jeans and a hooded sweatshirt sat sideways in the seat, knees against his chest. Reddish-brown curls peeked out from under the hood. He gave Milton a lopsided grin.

Milton looked away from the piercing blue eyes.

"They say there's always one crazy person on every city bus," the young man said. "I'm sure glad you showed up."

Milton reluctantly turned back to him. "I'm sorry?"

The young man took a drink from a silver beer can that Milton hadn't noticed before. "If there's always a crazy person on the bus, and I was the only one here, then that would make me crazy. But now that you're here." He waited a few seconds and then scoffed. "Never mind. Obviously, it was a bad joke."

His gaze never left Milton as he raised the can to his

lips again. "I'm DJ. Who are you?"

Milton opened his mouth but stopped himself just in time.

What if he is one of them*?*

DJ laughed. "A little shy, huh? Or maybe just socially inept. You remind me of a teacher I had in high school. Mr. Kenneth Furrows. All us kids called him Kenny. Mind if I call you Kenny?"

"Ah, I suppose not."

DJ's uneven smile widened. "Are you a teacher?"

What's with all of the questions?

"No," Milton replied. DJ waited expectantly. "I mean, I'm not a teacher anymore. I'm…I'm between work right now."

Why did I tell him that? Just face forward, Milton, and maybe he'll shut up!

Milton smiled politely and looked away. He turned to the window for a distraction, but the world outside the bus had become a black abyss. Acting as a mirror, the glass broadcast the interior of the bus, revealing a stubble-cheeked, heavy-lidded version of Milton. The transparent reflection of DJ, still staring straight at Milton, took another drink of beer.

"Are you OK, Kenny? You look like shit."

Milton gritted his teeth. "I'm fine. I just haven't slept in a while."

"You're not a teacher, but I bet you have a ton of books lying around your house," DJ said. "Stacks and stacks of 'em, right?"

Milton sighed, rubbed his eyes, and looked over at his unwanted companion. "You sure think you know a lot about me."

"Am I right?" DJ asked. "About the books?"

Milton tried to picture his home, but no matter how

hard he concentrated, the image remained hopelessly blurred.

How long have I been gone? How long have I been running?

"Seriously though," DJ continued, "you should try to get some sleep. I heard you'll go nuts if you miss too many nights in a row."

Sleep deprivation can cause blurred vision, depression, general confusion, hallucinations, and, yes, psychosis.

"How long have you been awake, Kenny?"

"That's none of your business."

DJ emptied the beer can into his mouth, coughed, and wiped his lips with the back of his sleeve. "How about I guess how long it's been, and you tell me if I'm too high or low?"

"Are you insane?"

DJ closed his eyes and laughed quietly. "No, *you're* the crazy one, remember? Of course, I never said there was only *one* crazy person per bus. We both could be out of our minds."

The young man scooted closer to Milton, planting his gray-white tennis shoes on the floor between their seats.

"The problem with you," DJ said, "is that you don't just go with it. There's this guy...he rides the 30 and hands out suckers to all the girls on the bus. Nice guy but kinda creepy.

"And there's this big black woman who, out of no-where, will start shouting and swearing. Damn near pissed my pants the first time she did it. Funny thing is, I think she's yelling at her own reflection in the window."

Milton edged away from DJ and looked at the back of the seat in front of him. He considered getting off at the next stop, but now that he was on the bus, his exhaustion had caught up with him. Feeling more tired than ever, he feared he would nod off while waiting for the next bus.

If nothing else, DJ, inebriated though he may be, is keeping me awake.

"All the good crazies have gimmicks," DJ continued. "But you, Kenny…for all I know, you're just a run-of-the-mill weirdo."

"For all you know," Milton muttered.

"I got it!" DJ shouted.

Milton regarded the young man with alarm. DJ's bright blue eyes burrowed into him.

"You can't sleep because you're so damn paranoid. You think the whole world is out to get you."

Milton glared at him, trying to decide whether to be angry or afraid.

DJ crossed his arms. "Am I wrong, Kenny?"

Milton hesitated, then sighed. What was the worst that could happen?

"I don't think 'the whole world' is out to get me," he snapped. "But I am on the run. They've been following me for days…maybe weeks."

"Who?"

A voice in the back of his mind cautioned him against trusting DJ, but he ignored it. He had to tell *someone*, even if that someone was a stranger he would never see again. Or perhaps because of it. Milton took a deep breath and turned toward DJ.

"They work for the government…CIA, I believe," he all but whispered.

DJ gasped. "Do they wear suits and dark glasses?"

"I…I can't be sure. It's been a while since I…"

Across the aisle, DJ's lips curled back into his customary smirk.

"You're mocking me, aren't you?"

"Can you blame me?" DJ retorted. "Conspiracy

theorists are a dime a dozen. You're probably on your way to the copy shop to print out your manifesto."

"I don't have a manifesto! I'm just trying to stay alive!"

DJ let out a great yawn and reached both of his arms up in a long and exaggerated stretch. Milton noticed for the first time that the front of DJ's sweatshirt was marked up with what looked to be whiteout. The imprecise lines formed the silhouette of a wolf, its toothy mouth agape.

Milton stiffened.

The wolf…it means something…

Crossing his arms again, DJ asked, "So what's this vital information you have that the government will stop at nothing to recover?"

Swallowing his fear, Milton replied, "Oh…nothing that would interest you, I'm sure. Like you said, it's probably all in my head."

DJ frowned. In a voice low and soft, he intoned, "But I have promises to keep."

"What did you say? Are you quoting something?"

"Come on," the young man drawled. "One lunatic to another…what's your secret, Kenny?"

"For the love God, my name is *Milton*, not Kenny!"

DJ's grin reappeared. The lights inside the bus flickered, and somehow DJ looked older.

"How, exactly, do you intend to prevent the end of the world, Milton?"

He was on his feet in an instant. "Who said anything about the end of the…hey, what's that on your hand?"

Without breaking eye contact, DJ raised his forearm and rolled up his sleeve, revealing a tattoo of a grayish green snake. "Do you like it?"

The serpent, the wolf—Milton knew were important, but he couldn't piece it together. Lethargy coated his brain like sludge, but the two images filled him with a sense of urgency he couldn't ignore. He tried in vain to mask his terror.

DJ chuckled. "You can't run forever, old man."

Milton yanked hard on the cord and was halfway to the front of the bus when he heard DJ shout, "And miles to go before I sleep."

When the bus jolted to a stop, Milton scrambled down the stairs and almost slipped on the icy pavement. He spun around, expecting to find DJ following him, but as the bus pulled away, he saw DJ through the window.

Their gazes locked. DJ's lips moved, and Milton knew the young man was repeating the last line of the poem: "And miles to go before I sleep."

Milton waited for the bus to be swallowed up by distance and darkness before resuming his hike. His only destination was a direction far from the bus route, far from DJ. He turned at the first corner he encountered.

Unable to sort through the chaotic flashes of thoughts and memory, he concentrated instead on keeping his eyes open and ignoring the lulling cadence of his snow-crunching footsteps.

They can't catch me if I never stop.

If I never sleep.

Chapter 4

The screen door slammed—except there was no door.

Lying on his stomach, Vincent stared uncomprehendingly at the metal bowl clattering to a stop against the cold floor a foot from his face. He propped himself up on an elbow and inspected the bowl's sloppy brown contents. The stench twisted his insides. He was on the verge of pushing away the mystery meal when he noticed the wall of bars.

I'm in jail?

A revelation lurked on the fringe of his memory. He had been somewhere else a moment ago, but the more he tried to grab onto that thought, the farther it receded.

He sat up and groaned. The sudden pounding in his head felt a lot like a hangover, but he didn't remember getting drunk.

I don't remember getting arrested either. How the hell did I end up here?

Vincent cradled his head in his hands and winced when his fingers found what felt like a doorknob protruding from the back of his skull.

Must have hit my head. That would explain the memory loss.

"Valenthor."

The whispered word sent a chill down his spine. Half-crouching, he turned around to confront his cellmate, but all he found was a shapeless pile of material crumpled up in the dark corner. He squinted, trying to make sense of what he saw.

Vincent stifled a gasp as the blanket creature situated itself into a more or less upright position. There was an opening near the top, but even deeper shadow hid the thing's face.

"Stay back!" Vincent scrambled away from the monster until his back hit the bars.

"Thank the holy Ancestors!" The creature's tone was warm and feminine, not the deep, guttural voice a demon. "I feared you had departed for the next world."

A memory started to surface—a beautiful woman in a bar—but then the shadows closed in again.

He carefully climbed to his feet. "'The next world'? What's that supposed to mean?"

"I thought you were…dead." She pronounced the last word strangely, like she was testing it out for the first time. He couldn't identify her accent, but she definitely was a foreigner.

"Why are we in jail? What happened?" he asked.

The woman shifted, causing her hood to slide back a little, revealing a narrow chin. "Caution, Valenthor. We are not alone."

Vincent tore his gaze away from the exposed pale skin and looked around the small cell. Aside from them, a single mattress that looked like it was made of straw, the soup bowl, and a rusty bucket that might have been a makeshift toilet, the space was empty. He peered through bars but found no sign of someone lurking in the dimly lit hallway beyond.

"You must have good eyes because I don't—" He choked on his words and spun around to face the woman.

Her eyes!

Everything came back to him then. The big, unnaturally

green eyes. The high cheekbones. The pointed ears.

Everyone in the bar was coming at her. I tried to stop them but fell flat on my ass.

An eerie sound interrupted Vincent's reverie. It was only when he saw the knight emerge from what must have been a doorway down the hall that he realized he was hearing the creaks of metal scraping against metal.

"It hath been told that the Fair Folk see the night as though it were day. Forsooth, yon she-elf proves the legends speak truth," the knight said.

The stingy light of the windowless room managed to glint off the knight's sword. Vincent took a few steps back.

"Hail, Valenthor of the Three Rivers," the knight said in a booming baritone that belied his tall, thin frame. "Long has it been since fortune smiled upon thee."

"No arguments there," Vincent replied. "But for the last time, my name's not Valenthor. I'm Vincent Cruz. I've never even heard of Three Rivers."

The visor of the knight's bullet-shaped helmet was open, providing Vincent with an unobstructed view of the man's fierce frown. The deep furrows suggested his captor was older than Vincent, in his forties at least. However, the thick, dark mustache showed no hint of gray.

"How came thee to be familiar with the she-elf?" the knight demanded.

"I'm *not* familiar with her." Vincent glanced back at the huddled figure, feeling a pang of guilt as he added, "She came up to me in the bar, asking for my help. I'd never seen her before in my life."

"Yet by the landlord's report, she asked for thee by name," the knight said.

"The *wrong* name!"

The knight's steely eyes widened. His jaw clenched.

"Playing the fool will not save thee. Thy refusal to cooperate, compounded with thy enduring fondness for inebriation, puts thee in a precarious position."

"Is that right?" Vincent muttered.

"Verily!" The word echoed down the corridor. The knight took a steadying breath. "Surely thou knows the penalty for conspiring with the enemy."

"I am no enemy of thine!" the elf shouted.

Vincent spun around in shock. He almost couldn't believe that the delicate creature was capable of such vehemence. She pulled herself up to her feet, using the mildew-speckled wall for support. For the first time, Vincent wondered what abuse she might have suffered after he lost consciousness in the tavern.

The elf pulled back her hood, her face full of defiance. "Ever have the Fay strove for peace between our people, and yet—"

"Be silent, ye dagger-eared demon, lest I tear out thy tongue!" the knight roared and raised his sword.

Vincent took a step toward the knight and stepped on the bowl of slop, almost losing his balance. He slammed into the bars with more force than he would have liked, causing the knight to fall back in surprise.

"What's your problem anyway?" Vincent asked, passing off his blunder for bravado. "Do you get off on threatening defenseless women or something?"

The knight straightened up. "Either the ale has pickled thy brain, or tragedy has made thee as vulgar as a bastard."

"Fuck you."

The knight moved so quickly that Vincent didn't realize the danger until the butt of the sword collided with the bridge of his nose. Then he found himself falling into a black expanse where no thoughts could survive.

*   *   *

Vincent struggled in the darkness. Tangled in his sheet, he fell to the floor with a thud. He frantically freed himself from the fabric's stranglehold and turned on the bedroom light. The sight of plain white walls and scattered clothes calmed him a little but couldn't replace the memory of the cold jail cell, the iron-clad captor, and his alleged co-conspirator.

Vaguely aware that his door was buzzing from a loud, throbbing noise from the living room, he pulled on a long-sleeved T-shirt—the same one from yesterday?— and approached the faded wood-framed mirror he inherited from his mother back when he moved in with Bella.

Sweat, not blood, coated his unusually waxen features. He gingerly touched this nose, but there was no pain.

The sword...it felt so real.

The blasting sound from beyond the door abated for a moment, only to return just as strong as before. Vincent glanced back at the bare mattress, not knowing what he expected to find there, before opening his bedroom door. Jerry nearly jumped out of his recliner when he saw him.

"Damn, dude. You scared the shit out of me!" He scrambled over to the stereo and stopped the music. "Sorry 'bout that. I didn't think you were home."

Vincent shrugged off the apology. "Don't worry about it. I'm not sure if it was the music that woke me up, but if it did, I should be thanking you."

"A nightmare?" Jerry asked, plopping back down in his not-quite-gold throne.

"Something like that."

The ensuing silence was louder than the music had been. Nearly a week had passed since their argument, and Vincent was tired of tiptoeing around.

"Look, Jerry, about the other day…I'm sorry I was such an asshole," he said before he could talk himself out of it. "I just…I don't like talking about the past. I guess I'm trying to start over, you know?"

Jerry licked his lips and smiled weakly. "No worries, man. Let's just forget about it."

More silence.

"So…" Vincent leaned against the doorframe, faking a comfortable pose. "When did you start listening to heavy metal, anyway?"

Jerry's full-on dopey grin made its first appearance of the night. "Actually, Hypnogaja is hard rock, not metal. And, *yes*, there is a difference. It has to do with the sing-ing-to-screaming ratio."

Vincent, who hadn't bought music since Kurt Cobain died, nodded stupidly.

"Metal is probably about the only genre *not* represented in my music collection," Jerry said. "I can groove to just about anything. But I can put something else on if you want, or we can watch TV. You don't usually have off on Friday nights."

"What?" Vincent asked, confused by the segue. At once, he realized he had no idea what time it was.

Christ, don't tell me I overslept!

A glance at the clock confirmed it. 9:37 p.m. Two and a half hours late. Vincent made a beeline for his bedroom and snatched up the clock on his dresser. The alarm was set for the usual time, but it was switched to off.

He returned to the living room and asked, "Did you hear my alarm go off before?"

Jerry shrugged. "Just got home."

Vincent cursed under his breath. He reached for the phone but thought better of it. Darlene, the supervisor from hell, never missed a chance to bust his balls. Not at all eager for another verbal battle, especially after his encounter with the imaginary knight, he decided to give Darlene the weekend to cool down.

"Need a ride to work?" Jerry asked.

Vincent shook his head. "No, thanks. They'll just have to find some other sucker to push the broom tonight."

Considering the dreams I've been having, maybe a sick day isn't too much of a stretch. The nightmares about Clemmy always feel real because that all really happened. But these new dreams...they're so damn vivid!

Jerry's voice wrenched his attention back to the present. "You look like you got a lot on your mind."

Vincent hesitated. On one hand, he wanted to keep the lines of communication open. On the other, he didn't want his roommate to think he was losing his mind. Vincent chuckled inwardly.

Jerry has probably seen stranger stuff while stoned than my subconscious could ever cook up.

"It's probably nothing," Vincent said, moving to the Low Rider, "but I've been having the strangest dreams lately."

Sharing the two-part adventure of elves, knights, and a case of mistaken identity took only a few minutes. Looking down at his hands while he spoke, Vincent said, "Then I got pissed at the knight and called him a bully...or something like that...and he hit me with the dull end of his sword. Pretty messed up, huh?"

He stole a glance at Jerry, who had remained silent throughout the story. Jerry, his face scrunched up in an expression of extreme concentration, leaned back in his chair, pulled a joint out of the breast pocket of his Hawaiian shirt, and lit up.

From behind a cloud of smoke, Jerry asked, "What do *you* think it means?"

Vincent forced a laugh. "How should I know? I mean, they're just dreams. They don't have to mean anything …right?"

Jerry took another puff. "Yeah, but, they gotta come from somewhere. Did you watch *The Lord of the Rings* lately?"

"I've never seen any of those movies," Vincent answered.

"And you don't read books about elves?"

"I can't remember the last time I read a book, let alone one filled with fairytales."

Jerry scratched at his mop of sandy blond hair. "This isn't really my field of expertise. I mean, I played D&D in high school, but these days I'm more of a sci-fi guy. Hey, are you sure this chick was an elf? Vulcans and Romulans have pointy ears too."

"Everyone called her an elf," Vincent said. "Anyway, there was no technology around. The jail cell was straight out of the Dark Ages, not part of a spaceship."

Jerry set the joint in the ashtray. "We should do some research."

Before Vincent could ask for clarification, Jerry got up and walked into his room. A few seconds later, he returned with a laptop Vincent had seen only once or twice before and set it on the coffee table.

Vincent moved closer to the computer, leaving room for Jerry, who sat down and clicked a key to banish the psychedelic screensaver. The flashy colors were replaced by the image of a remarkably average-looking naked woman reclining, her legs spread farther apart than Vincent would have thought possible. The woman smiled invitingly at the camera. Vincent blushed and looked away.

"Uh…sorry 'bout that," Jerry mumbled and quickly

opened a new browser window. "So...what was the name everyone kept calling you in the dream?"

Vincent felt ridiculous repeating it, but Jerry looked at him expectantly. "Valenthor," he said with a sigh.

Jerry typed the word into a search engine.

"Ninety-one results," Jerry said, "assuming that's the right spelling."

Vincent shrugged. He was about to ask Jerry exactly what he expected to find when Jerry started humming to himself.

"Hmm...let's see here." Jerry clicked the first link. "This looks like some kind of fantasy game message board...a user profile...hmm...he...or she, I s'pose, is twenty-two and lives in Santa Cruz. That's weird."

"What?" Vincent asked.

"Your last name is Cruz, right?"

Vincent rolled his eyes.

"What else do we got?" Jerry went back to the search engine and clicked on the second link. The two of them skimmed the new profile, which appeared to be part of a comic book-themed forum. According to the stats, Valenthor the Silent was a fifteen-year-old male. He had never left a comment on the site.

Further exploration of the web revealed a number of online fantasy game sites. Sometimes Valenthor was a first name and other times, a last name. In one instance, he was a troll.

"These probably aren't all the same person," Jerry said after a while. "Could be Valenthor is just an easy name to come up with. It certainly sounds fantasy-ish. But there doesn't seem to be any famous books or movies or any-thing with a character named Valenthor."

Leaning back on the couch, Vincent said, "So my sub-conscious made it all up. Maybe you should look for a website on dream interpretations."

First I'm getting drunk, and then I'm stuck in a jail cell. Do I really want Jerry copiloting the journey into my psyche?

"Never mind," Vincent added hurriedly.

Jerry might not have heard him. Completely consumed by the task at hand, he said, "We're out of our element. Time for a new tactic."

Jerry clicked back to the search engine and began typing.

Vincent leaned forward and watched Jerry type "master of all things fantasy" into the search field. "What are you doing?" he asked.

"There are millions of geeks out there, and thanks to the internet, we can capitalize on their otherwise useless knowledge."

Two clicks later, they found themselves at yet another message board. Jerry scrolled through the thread. Vincent was about to make a snide comment about a wild *elf* chase when they found a rather substantial post containing the exact phrase from Jerry's search.

Vincent laughed out loud. "Someone actually calls himself Master of All Things Fantasy? Had you heard of him before or something?"

"Naw," Jerry said, grinning ear to ear. "Thought it was worth a shot though. Now let's see if he knows his shit."

Shaking his head, Vincent pushed himself up off of the Low Rider. "I'm gonna pass. Sometimes weird dreams are just weird dreams." He found the remote control wedged down in the cushion of Jerry's recliner and turned the TV on. "But do let me know if the Master of All Things Fantasy knows anything about jailbreaks."

Chapter 5

Vincent turned off the vacuum cleaner and was overcome by silence.

Florescent lights looked down on a maze of cubicles equipped with computers, binders, inboxes, outboxes, family photos, and the occasional knickknack suggesting the some drones who occupied the offices by day had an iota of personality. Calendars crammed full of multi-colored scrawling were also a common component of the dusty desktops.

Cleaning up after the cretins who worked in Milwau-kee's tallest building—he supposed it qualified as a sky-scraper—afforded Vincent a lot of time to think. When the others were working on the opposite end of the floor or taking "lunch" together, he felt like the only living soul left on the planet. Being left alone with his thoughts was one of the drawbacks of being a janitor.

That and dealing with the flush-optional mentality of some guy on the fifth floor.

Those corporate types weren't all bankers, but Vincent liked to imagine the lot of them as rich snobs who went home to the condos lining Lake Michigan or palatial homes in the snootier suburbs to the north. In his musings, they all were wealthy, but never happy.

And if they thought their shit didn't stink, well, he knew otherwise.

As the early-morning minutes ticked away, he lost

interest in his imaginary adversaries. The sad fact was he needed them. If no one made any messes, he'd be out of work, and if those long months of living with his mother had taught him anything, it was that a crappy job was better than no job.

His coworkers—an army of flunkeys under the command of Darlene Sanders, a forty-something woman who was wider than she was tall and who hated everyone but men most of all—counted the seconds to morning. But Vincent hated the dawn, when his thoughts invariably turned inward.

The virgin rays streaming through the floor-to-ceiling windows touched the deepest recesses of his mind, casting light on the moment when it all went wrong. If Clementine hadn't died, he and Bella would still be living together as man and wife. He wouldn't have gotten a DUI and lost his license along with his old job of driving truck. If Bella hadn't kicked him out, he wouldn't have had to move in with his mom and learn that they were still incompatible after so many years.

If I hadn't let my own daughter die, I never would have become such a loser.

Clementine…

Vincent jerked upright. Dripping sweat and fighting for air, he pushed the memory out of his mind, but he felt the nightmare pulling at his thoughts like an undertow, determined to drown him in despair. The darkness around him only added to his disorientation.

He rubbed his eyes and flinched when his hand grazed the side of his nose.

"I treated your injury. With naught but water and the cloth of my cloak, I could do little more than wash away the blood," the woman kneeling beside him said.

No, not a woman. An elf.

"Thanks," he mumbled, carefully tracing the slope of his nose. The skin was hot and swollen, but everything felt in place. The knight's sword hadn't broken any bones.

A vague memory tugged at him, something about sunlight shining into a tower, but Vincent shrugged it off. He had more important things to think about, like getting away from their violent captor.

"So much for knights being noble." Vincent glared through the bars, silently daring the jailer to return.

"The hour grows late," the elf said. "Sir Angus will not soon return."

Vincent turned to face her, leaning against the bars until the cold metal caused him to shiver. "You know that bastard's name?"

Despite the dim light in the cell, he had no trouble seeing out the elf's white face. When her thin eyebrows drew together, the furrows stood out like cracks in china.

"When Sir Angus used that word, you became angry. And now you say it of him. What does it mean?" she asked.

"What word? 'Bastard'?"

She nodded timidly.

"Um, technically, it's what you call a man who never knew his father," he said.

The confusion creasing the elf's expression deepened. "You are the son of a widow then?"

Vincent grunted in amusement. "Not exactly. My mother never married, and my father didn't stick around long after I was born." After a few more seconds of silence, he added, "Maybe there aren't any oops babies where you came from."

Blank stare.

"Don't elves have...accidents?" he asked, exasperated.

Her stunning green eyes seemed to double in size.

"Right," he said. "It's not exactly...gentlemanly...to suggest a guy's mother slept around."

Vincent paced the perimeter of the cell that measured no more than a handful of steps in any direction.

I didn't do whatever the knight is accusing me of, but he'll never believe me. I have to find a way out of here.

"You spoke while you slept," the elf said quietly.

"Eh?" He wrapped his fingers around the bitter-cold bars and pulled until his biceps burned from the strain.

"You repeated a single word again and again," she said, "in between your cries of anguish."

A nightmare? What possibly could've been worse than being trapped in here?

A shadow of memory clawed frantically at the edges of his mind but failed to find purchase.

"Mayhap it was a name," the elf said.

The air grew very cold—colder than the bars had been.

No...

The elf spoke rose to her feet. "Before he departed, Sir Angus mocked your attempt to defend me. He declared you could never be anyone's champion because you are a slave to intoxicating drinks."

"Is that a polite way of calling me an alcoholic?" Vincent joked, but he couldn't bring himself to smile.

"Sir Angus said once upon a time you were heralded as hero among your people, but then the gods of men took the life of your child—"

"Stop!" Vincent's voice echo off the walls. He clenched his eyes closed. The tightness in his chest stole his breath.

"The name you call out in your dreams," she persisted, "is it your daughter's?"

"Please!"

"Valentine," she whispered.

What?

Vincent's eyes shot open. She stepped closer, her cheeks painted with the shiny path of tears.

"I share in your sorrow, Valenthor," she said.

He took a step back, shaking his head. "My daughter's name isn't…*wasn't* Valentine. It's…"

Panic squeezed his racing heart as he struggled to come up with the name.

"Can you not see, Valenthor? My Ancestors and your gods have brought us together. You yearn for a new purpose and a righteous cause. My people need a champion, a savior—"

"For Christ's sake, stop calling me Valenthor!"

She recoiled, her eyes widening in alarm. He didn't care. The elf's dilemma, Sir Angus's attitude, even the claustrophobic jail cell—nothing mattered except remembering the real name of his dead little girl.

"We must escape," the elf said, drawing closer.

"Stay away from me!" he screamed and backed into the hard stone wall. He was so close to remembering, but every time he opened his mouth to say the name, all he came up with was "Valentine."

She reached out to him. "If we do not flee, they surely will kill us both."

Valentine…Valentine…Valentine…no, no, no!

She took his trembling hand in her own. "I will save you, Valenthor, so that you can save the world."

Vincent made a halfhearted attempt to wrench his hand away from her, but her touch seemed to have sapped all of his energy. He fought against the dizziness, closed his eyes to block out the spinning room.

God help me, what is her name?

"Rest now," the elf whispered. "Very soon, you will need your strength."

Clementine!

"Well, I don't know who Clementine is, but for your sake I hope she likes her men unemployed."

Someone loomed over Vincent. Because of the morning light pouring in from the tall windows overlooking the lake, he could make out only a short, wide silhouette.

Even if he hadn't recognized his boss's squat shape, there was no mistaking her disdainful voice.

"Darlene, I'm *so* sorry!" Vincent scrambled to his feet, wiping the drool off his chin. He almost wished he was back in the medieval prison. "I'm not sure what happened, but I promise it'll never happen again."

"Damn right it's never gonna happen again 'cause your ass is fired."

Vincent, who had been reaching for his vacuum, flinched.

Oh God, this can't be happening.

Holding back the sea of emotions swelling inside of him, he said, "Please, Darlene, I need this job."

"'Please, Darlene' *nothing*. Two weeks ago, you don't bother showin' up, and now I find you napping on the clock. Uh-uh. Two strikes, and you're out 'round here. If this job is too damn hard for you, I'm sure I can find someone else who's up to the challenge."

Darlene punctuated her lecture with a tilt of her head and then waddled away.

"Hey, wait!"

She silenced him with a glare and crossed her arms, nearly losing them beneath a layer of flab. "Uh-uh, Vincent. I never liked your attitude. Always acting like you was doing us a favor by bein' here. Well, no thank you, Mr. Cruz. Hand over your keycard and get the hell out."

For a moment, he couldn't move. He wasn't about to give her the satisfaction of watching him grovel, especially since it wouldn't do any good. She had been gunning for him from the start and had never missed a chance to tell him exactly what she thought of him. There was nothing he could say to appease her.

Looks like the loser loses again.

He slapped the keycard into her pudgy palm and stomped over to the elevator. His pulse was still pounding in his ears when he reached the empty street corner outside.

"Goddamn it!"

The lifeless buildings around him gave no reply. Somewhere nearby, a bus groaned. Otherwise, the city was silent. Vincent rushed past the bus stop. Twenty blocks stretched between the skyscraper and his apartment, but he couldn't stomach the thought of being around anyone right now, even strangers on the bus.

The autumn air felt cool against his feverish skin. He was walking so fast his breaths came in frantic, shallow gulps. However, he couldn't outpace his thoughts.

You did it again, Vincent. How many times can one guy screw up?

A black luxury sedan drove past, heading in the direction of the tower. Vincent pictured Monopoly's Uncle Moneybags sitting behind the wheel, on his way to count stacks of gold coins.

How am I going to pay the rent? I have nothing. I'm just killing time until I die.

How he wished he had died that day instead of Clemmy.

Why didn't I drain the tub? If only I'd just let her take her rubber duck into the living room? If only I had stayed awake...

And why the hell did Bella have to go grocery shopping so damn early that morning when she knew I had been driving half the night before?

Vincent shook his head, laughing helplessly. He had wandered down that road many times before, alternating between blaming himself and Bella, his not-yet-ex-wife. There was no point to it. Nothing would change. He couldn't undo what already was done.

Valentine.

The word popped into his head out of nowhere, refueling his anger. It was ridiculous to blame the fairytale dream for losing his job. And yet, he had never nodded off at work before, not even back when he had first started and had had the queen of all hangovers. He didn't even remember feeling sleepy.

The dream sucked me in again, only this time I was awake when it happened. Maybe I really am Valenthor. Maybe we all become somebody else when our brains shut down for the night.

Or maybe I'm going nuts.

No rational explanations came to him in the hour it took to get home, but as he inserted his key into the front door, Vincent felt certain of one thing. If he was to have any chance of living a normal life, he was going to have to figure out what was really going on in his head.

He heard the phone ringing from out the hallway, shoved open the apartment door, and picked up the receiver before the answering machine—an archaic contraption, to be sure—could intercept the call.

Maybe Darlene changed her mind!

"Hello?"

There was a pause. "Vincent?"

He almost laughed. It was the perfect end to a perfect day.

"Hi, Mom."

Chapter 6

Vincent dropped his keys onto the kitchen table and leaned against one of the chairs. Cradling the phone between his shoulder and ear, he waited for his mother to speak.

"I thought I was going to get the machine. I didn't expect you to be home so early," she said.

Did you call the landline, hoping you could have another chat with Jerry while I was at work?

He took a deep breath, holding in the accusation. He pulled his cell out of his pocket, turned it on—Darlene had a strict no-phone policy—and rolled his eyes when the display informed him that he had one missed call and one message from his mother.

"Do you have off today?" she asked, her tone pleasant, unconvincingly upbeat. He tried to picture the person on the other end but couldn't reconcile the clashing images of the girl who had refused to be a mother when he needed one and the woman who insisted on being one now that he didn't.

Vincent doubted he ever would know the real Evangeline Pierce.

Since there was no right answer to her question, he said, "Must be your lucky day." Another stretch of silence. "Is everything OK?"

"Oh, I'm fine," she replied. "I was just checking in…planning to leave another message."

He bristled at the implication. "I've tried to get back to

you, but you're never home."

"I'm never home when you return my calls on Sunday morning," she corrected. "I come home from church every week to find a message from you on my machine. Coincidence?"

Vincent opened the refrigerator, offering up a silent plea for cold beer. A container of creamer and a twelve pack of Mountain Dew shared the otherwise empty top shelf. He was half disappointed, half relieved that God still wasn't answering his prayers.

He slammed the door shut, rattling the bottles of condiments in the door.

"I'm not the only one playing phone tag," Vincent said. "You just said you didn't expect me to be home right now."

She sighed into the phone, and he almost felt guilty.

"I don't want to argue with you," she said. "I'm genuinely glad you picked up. It's been forever since you and me talked."

That's because we don't have anything to talk about.

"I've been thinking about you a lot lately, Vincent. About the arguments we had when you were living here. How angry you were...and...and everything."

Vincent waited, scowling.

"I've been praying a lot about it."

Here we go...

"And what did the Almighty have to say?" he snapped.

Another sigh. "There's so much distance between us. I understand why you couldn't stay, but I really hope we can still have some kind of relationship. We both know that I never got the hang of this parenting thing, but I'm doing the best I can. With Danny in the hospital, you're the only family I have."

Any sympathy he might have had vaporized at the mention of his half-brother.

"With Danny in the hospital." More like *"with Danny being a vegetable" or "with Danny as good as dead."*

But he wasn't about to rekindle that fight.

"I worry about you, Vincent," she said at last. "Like I said, I've been thinking a lot lately…about us. Then I had this dream about you last night. I had to call to make sure…I don't know…"

Vincent didn't realize he had been pacing until he stopped. "A dream? What kind of dream?"

"You were in some kind of trouble, I think. I don't really remember, but I woke up with this horrible feeling."

For a fraction of a second, he considered telling her everything—the strange dreams *he* had been having, how he had just lost his job, how frightened he was about what was happening in his head.

Instead, he said, "You don't have to worry about me. I'm doing OK."

"Have you spoken to Bella lately?"

He opened the fridge. Still no beer.

"Sorry, Mom, but I'm going to have to let you go. I have some errands to run, and then I'm going to get some shuteye."

"Shuteye"?

"All right. But if you need anything…anything at all…please let me know." It was the voice of the reformed Evangeline in his ear, but in his mind's eye, Vincent saw young, rebellious Evie.

So many promises, all of them broken.

"I will," he lied.

"I love you."

"You too, Mom."

He let his feet take him into the living room, deposited the phone on the desk, and slumped down in Jerry's recliner. Thinking of nothing, he stared out the window, where dying leaves dropped one by one to the ground.

Vincent opened his eyes. A faint glow above the neighboring rooftops hinted at morning's demise and the inevitable triumph of evening over afternoon. The overcast sky flooded the apartment with shadows. Fierce winds sent leaves flying in all directions. With each gust, an unearthly moan crept through the invisible spaces between the porch door and its frame.

Shivering in spite of the apartment's overactive Old World radiator, he reached for the lamp next to the recliner. He stretched his arm until he found the switch and then nearly fell out of the chair when the light came on.

A few feet away, Jerry sat on the Low Rider, hunched over the coffee table, holding a massive sub sandwich with two hands.

"Mmmf," Jerry said, his mouth full of food.

Once Vincent was sure his heart wasn't going to explode, he asked, "Why are you eating in the dark?"

Jerry chewed for a few more seconds, swallowed with a grimace, and said, "Didn't want to wake you."

Jerry lifted his cup, and there was no sound of shifting ice cubes. Vincent recalled a ganja-induced rant about how paying for cups full of frozen water represented everything that was wrong with America.

Straw still in mouth, Jerry asked, "Were you having The Dream?"

Vincent sighed. "Not just now, but you'll never guess what happened at work today."

As Jerry attacked the formerly foot-long sandwich, Vincent summarized his unexpected journey into Valenthor's world while wide awake and the conversation with his pointy-eared cellmate. Because Evangeline had spilled the beans about Clementine, Vincent skipped over the part about Valenthor's having had lost a young daughter.

He couldn't, however, omit the fact that he got fired.

"Damn, that sucks." If Jerry was at all concerned about how Vincent would pay his half of the rent and utilities, he was kind enough not to bring it up. "So...the elf chick wants to break out of jail because she thinks the knight is going to kill both of you. And she still wants you to save her homeland."

"That about sums it up," Vincent muttered.

"Do you know what you're supposed to do to save Elf Land?"

Vincent shook his head. His stomach was rumbling at the sight of Jerry's ever-shrinking sandwich, which made him realize he hadn't eaten anything all day. Not that any of the food in the house was his.

I should go to the grocery store and buy a lifetime supply of ramen. Gotta start rationing what little is left of my savings.

"Well," Jerry said, popping the bit sandwich into his mouth, "doesn't sound like there's anything new to report to the Master."

Vincent rolled his eyes. He wasn't sure how many times Jerry had emailed the Master of All Things Fantasy since first making contact two weeks ago, but Vincent had gamely tried to answer the questions Jerry relayed from him:

"How tall is the elf?"

"Hard to tell. She's always wearing a cloak and tends to crouch a lot."

"But she's not tiny...not like a Keebler elf or anything, right?"

"No, she's actually tall for a woman, I think. But she's shorter than me."

"Does she know magic?"

"Not that I know of."

"Hmmm. And she speaks English?"

"Yes."

"Is she a princess?"

"I don't know. It's not like she's wearing a crown."

"Does Valenthor wear a green hat or wield a boomerang?"

Apparently, there was no shortage of elf maidens and warrior heroes in the fantasy genre. While the name Valenthor rang no bells with the Master, he—or she—wasn't ready to rule out the possibility that Valenthor was a forgotten follower of King Arthur, an obscure warrior from Middle-Earth, or the legendary hero from any number of video games.

Vincent had little hope Jerry and the Master would discover anything worthwhile. How could they? Even if they stumbled upon some reference that proved Vincent's subconscious was stealing details from the real world, it wouldn't explain how or why it was happening.

Meanwhile, Vincent kept his own theory to himself because he couldn't face his growing fear that on top of his many other problems, his brain was dividing into two different personalities.

As long as I remember I'm Vincent, not Valenthor, I'll be OK.

Jerry swallowed the last bite of his sandwich and leaned back with a satisfied groan. "We need more information. The name of the city...or, better yet, the world. If nothing else, you gotta get the elf's name."

"It doesn't work like that," Vincent said. "When I'm in The Dream, I won't remember we had this conversation.

I'll know my real name, and sometimes I realize that I don't belong there, but that's about it."

"But isn't it kind of weird that you don't know her name yet?" Jerry asked. "You are stuck in a cell together."

Vincent dropped his heads in his hands. "I guess so. Maybe. What difference will any of it make?"

"Well, for starters, we might get an idea of what you need to do next."

"This isn't a game, Jerry! I don't want to do anything next. I just want these dreams to stop!"

Jerry took his paper plate into the kitchen and tossed it into the garbage. His voice carried from the other room. "Fair enough, but maybe the only way to stop them is to reach the end of the story...in which case the Master is a good person to have in our corner. He says he's read almost every fantasy book ever published."

I can't deal with this anymore.

When Jerry came back into the living room, Vincent stood up, relinquishing the recliner back its rightful owner.

"I need a distraction," Vincent said. "I just want to...I don't know...*do* something...have a little fun for once and forget about...everything!"

Jerry half leaned, half sat on the arm of the recliner and almost lost his balance. "What do you wanna do?"

No, Vincent, keep it together.

Vincent chuckled dryly. "I'd suggest we invite some friends over, but honestly, Jerry, you're the only friend I've got these days."

"We can have a little get together," Jerry said. "I know plenty of people who don't need an excuse to have fun. We can order some food, listen to some tunes, and get distracted."

I deserve this.

"I'll give Paish a call," Jerry said. "I know for a fact she doesn't have classes tomorrow. No one besides clueless freshmen enroll for classes that meet on Fridays. What do you say?"

Vincent almost asked Jerry if he'd ever gone to college. Instead, he said, "Sure, Paish seems nice."

This is a mistake.

Jerry grinned and reached for the phone. "I'll give her a call. I'm almost out of weed anyway."

Vincent forced a smile.

At this point, what do I have left to lose?

Chapter 7

Vincent clicked through the half-dozen channels over and over again. He barely saw the parade of sitcom actors, newscasters, and revolutionary products that promised to make life easier and happier.

Jerry was out "picking up supplies," but Vincent had volunteered to stay at the apartment in case Paish and her friends arrived before he returned. Never mind that their guests had to catch a bus from UWM and that the nearest liquor store was only a couple of blocks away.

"Anything in particular you want me to get?" Jerry had asked. "My treat."

"No…just whatever," Vincent had replied quickly.

As though not making the choice myself absolves me…

Sitting on the edge of the Low Rider, hammering his foot against the hardwood floor, he tried to focus on the evening traffic report, but the aerial shots of slow-moving vehicles only reminded him that while hundreds of other people were driving home from work, he had no job.

He turned off the TV and started flipping through one of Jerry's *Maxim*. Instantly, he was aware of the sound of someone coming up the side door. He spun around on the couch, craning his neck to get a clear view of the building's only communal entrance, just in time to see the door slam shut.

Vincent came into the kitchen at the exact moment Jerry opened the apartment door, but he could think of nothing to say other than, "Hey."

"Greetings and salutations." Jerry set a case of Milwaukee's Best on the kitchen table. From a tall paper bag, he produced a two-liter of cola and a bottle of whiskey. "You strike me as a whiskey guy."

Jerry set the liquor on the table and put the beer and soda in the fridge.

"Works for me," Vincent muttered.

Let's get this over with.

"I'll start with a beer, though," he added.

"Ah, the Beast." Jerry handed a can to Vincent and then took one for himself. "Even more vicious when it's warm."

Vincent cracked open the can but just stared at it.

Am I really going to do this? All those months of sobriety down the—

"Down the hatch!" Jerry took a few gulps and wiped the white foam away with his sleeve.

Vincent raised the can to his lips. The skunky smell alone made him lightheaded.

Sorry, Clemmy. I've failed again.

He took a long drink. The nearly forgotten but instantly familiar taste lingered on his tongue. He didn't fall to floor, dead. The world didn't end.

He smiled and took another drink.

They both were on beer number two when the doorbell buzzed—a loud, horrible noise that never failed to scare the shit out of Vincent. Jerry went down to open the side door while Vincent waited in the kitchen. He leaned against the refrigerator, but the pose felt phony. He polished off the rest of his beer and was reaching for another one when Jerry returned, trailed by three guests.

"Anybody want a beer?" Vincent asked.

"Or if you want something a little stronger…" Jerry

gestured at the table. Four shot glasses formed a semi-circle around the whiskey bottle. Lost souls worshiping at the foot of an idol.

Paish approached the fridge. "I'll have a beer."

A turquoise barrette held her bangs up to one side. Vincent thought that maybe she had gotten a haircut but didn't ask.

"You're Vincent, right? I'm Tara," a small young woman with light blond hair said. "I'll also have a beer please."

Both of the girls wore hoodies, but their difference in taste was immediately apparent. Paish's sweatshirt was a solid dark gray, while Tara's was pink and brown and studded with rhinestones. Paish's jeans were snug and featured several small factory-supplied holes. Tara's were at least two sizes too big, a fashion statement that reminded Vincent of his brother's skater phase as well as his subsequent gangster stage.

The final guest—a hefty, dark-haired guy with baggy pants and a long wallet chain—made a beeline for the whiskey.

"Who wants to do a shot?" he asked.

"No way, Marc," Paish said. "That stuff kicks my ass."

Jerry also declined.

Tara set her beer on the counter. "Why not? Let's get this party started!"

Vincent thought that one shot might be enough to start and *end* the party for the petite woman.

"How about you?" Marc asked, turning to Vincent.

The question kickstarted Vincent's pulse. For a moment, he could only stare dumbly at the bottle. Keenly aware of everyone's eyes on him, he cleared his throat and said, "Sure, why not?"

"Right on," Tara chirped.

Vincent watched Marc filled a third shot glass. He had never seen the set before. Each glass was adorned with a big-headed bird in a different stage of drinking—from thinking to having an idea to guzzling down a bottle of liquor to lying legs-up on the floor. Marc handed him the last one. Vincent considered the bird's X-shaped eyes.

"Not planning on being a good boy tonight, huh?" Paish asked slyly.

Before he could answer, Marc shouted, "Cheers!"

I deserve to feel good for once.

He pounded the shot. The fire that flowed down his throat and into his veins made him feel alive.

Tara coughed and stuck her tongue out.

"How about another one, T-dawg?" Marc asked.

Tara, eyes watering, shook her head. "Maybe later."

Marc turned to Vincent. "Whaddaya say?"

"I'm game."

As Marc filled the two glasses, the others moseyed into the living room. Vincent downed the second shot, and a happy fog drifted into his mind. He closed his eyes and basked in the buzz.

"That's what I'm talkin' about." Marc grabbed a beer and went into the living room. Vincent followed, whiskey in tow.

Jerry was already settled in his recliner, and since Vincent was the last one out of the kitchen, the couch had been claimed by their three guests. No vacancy.

"You can sit on my lap," Paish offered.

"I'll grab a chair from the kitchen," he replied. "But thanks for the offer."

When he returned, Jerry was handing Paish some money. He took a moment to examine the leafy contents of a Ziploc baggie. At last, he took a big, satisfied sniff. Tara, perched with her legs tucked under her on the opposite end of the couch as Paish, rolled a joint.

"What's up with the pinner, T-dawg? Do you want to get high or what?"

"Shut up, Marc," Tara scolded with a smile.

Vincent wondered if the two of them were dating. He hoped so.

"It's always so hot in here," Paish said to Jerry. She pulled her sweatshirt over her head, nearly removing her blouse with it. She pulled her blouse back down, but not before Vincent caught a glimpse of her pierced navel.

I take back all the bad things I said about those radiators.

Jerry surveyed everyone on their music preferences. Vincent hadn't heard of any of the undergrads' suggestions and promptly stated that he was cool with whatever. He laughed as the small talk about bands evolved into smack talk. Through context clues, Vincent worked out that Tara and Paish had met freshman year, and he was pretty sure Tara and Marc had lived in the same dorm. Whether the two of them were a couple remained unconfirmed.

When the joint came around to him, Vincent was a little tempted to take a hit. Part of it was that he didn't want to look lame, but more than that, he wanted to feel good.

In the end, he couldn't bring himself to do it. Drugs—even small-time stuff like marijuana—always reminded him of his mother, a former addict, and his father, who had cut out just before Vincent's memories kicked in. Then there was Danny...

He did another shot of whiskey, clinking glasses with Marc, and made the most of his vantage while leaning over the coffee table. He almost didn't care if Paish caught him checking her out. The low-cut shirt had been designed specifically to complement cleavage. And hers definitely was worth showcasing.

Patience McFadden wasn't as pretty as Bella, but she was sexier or, at least, more provocative. A wardrobe that emphasized her curves. The lip ring that hinted at a rebellious streak. A thong that made an appearance every time she reached for the joint from Jerry.

Nothing wrong with looking. We're all adults here.

"What are we listening to?" Tara asked. Her eyes looked sleepy, and her lips her fixed in a perma-smile.

"Of Montreal," Jerry said.

"I'm really digging their sound," Tara confided. "Good stoner music. Are they from Canada?"

"Band names don't *mean* anything." Paish played with her barrette, repeatedly snapping it open and closed. Finally, she stuffed it in her pocket and let her hair fall over one eye. "It sounds a little like disco. Not in a bad way, though...just reminds me of the '70s or something."

Jerry chuckled. "It *reminds* you? You weren't even alive in the '70s!"

Marc took a deep drag off of the joint and started coughing, spewing out puffs of smoke. He swallowed a mouthful of beer and said, "They're not bad, but I'm not a fan of synthesizers."

"Why not?" Paish asked.

"I don't know. Fake drums are like...like fake tits. The real things are so much better."

Paish adjusted her bra. "No argument here."

Everyone laughed at that. Somewhere around midnight, Marc had the idea to play a drinking game with a deck of cards. Throughout the game, Paish fired more than a few suggestive comments Vincent's way, and he flirted right back. Why not? It was all in good fun.

Later—how much later, Vincent couldn't say—Tara lay passed out on the couch. In the kitchen, Jerry and Marc searched for munchies and waged an earnest debate about what the number nine would be called if numbers had names like people.

"Nathan," Marc asserted. "It's totally Nathan."

"No...no..." Jerry droned. A few seconds later, he shouted, "Lenny!"

The two of them broke into uncontrollable laughter.

Beside him on the couch, Paish giggled. "Those two are fucked *up*." Glancing over at Tara, who was breathing loudly though not quite snoring, she asked, "What time is it anyway?"

Vincent squinted at the blurry blue-green mess that should have been the clock. He blinked a few times, and the shapes settled into something recognizable.

"3:07," he replied. "You have somewhere to be?"

"No," she said, standing up. "I'm just wondering how much longer I'm gonna have to wait before you make a move."

Vincent tried to say "huh" and "what" at the same time. It came out "wha-huh?"

"Just thought I'd cut to the chase." She strolled, almost stumbling, over to the doorway of his room. She turned back and smiled mischievously at him.

A voice from somewhere far away shouted warnings about the nine-year age difference and the fact that he was still married. Meanwhile, Paish crossed her arms, which caused more freckled flesh to peek up from her low-cut shirt.

Barely married...

No sooner had he closed the door than the two of them were pressed together, kissing frantically. Her lip piercing felt strange against his mouth, but not in a bad way. He reached a hand up under her shirt while devouring her neck.

After another couple minutes of mutual groping, he felt her hand brush against the front of his pants. She pulled at the button and unzipped his fly.

"Why don't you have a seat?" she asked, tugging his waistband down to his knees.

Vincent sat back on his bed and watched Paish pull off her shirt, then reach back for the clasps of her bra. He removed his shirt too, suddenly wishing his gut didn't look so chubby. On a whim, he reclined back, resting on his elbows. The position somewhat lessened the beer-belly effect.

Then Paish, naked from the waist up, leaned over him, and *his* body was the last thing on his mind.

"Told you they're real," she said, cupping a considerable breast in each hand and squeezing. She leaned in, kissing him on his lips…neck…chest…lower. Slowly, teasingly, she flecked the tip of her tongue, bringing him to full attention. Vincent closed his eyes and let out a long sigh.

At first, he didn't think anything of the room's spinning. After all, drinking a quarter of a bottle of whiskey and countless cans beer had a way of messing with the scenery. But then he could no longer feel the warm wetness of Paish's mouth. When she spoke his name, it was as though her voice were drifting from a great distance away.

"Vincent? Are you OK?"

He tried to answer but couldn't. The room, the bed, Paish—everything was gone. There was only darkness.

From miles away, from across the vacuum of space, Paish said, "Hey, wake up!"

Vincent wanted only to obey, but he was too busy falling into nothingness.

I drank too much. Son of a bitch, I'm passing out!

"Wake up. Please wake up!"

Paish's voice sounded louder now but different.

"You must wake up, Valenthor!"

Not again! Not now!

The elf stood with her back to him, arms outstretched and palms pressed flat against the stone blocks of the cell's back wall. The capacious sleeves of her gray cloak had fallen back, exposing pale, slender arms. Hair the color of honey flowed down her to the small of her back. It was the first time he had seen her without the hood.

Vincent pulled himself up onto one elbow. The vague feeling of annoyance that had followed him from whatever dream he had been having fizzled away as he strained to hear her whispers. The long blond tresses seemed to ripple in an unfelt breeze, occasionally covering the peculiar points of her ears.

His breath caught in his throat when a white glow washed over her. She appeared to be bathed in moonlight despite the wall of stone separating her from the sky. The sight was so eerie he couldn't have called out her name even if he knew it.

Slack-jawed, he watched as widening circles of light spread from her fingertips along the rough surface of stones. Her voice grew louder and more passionate with every syllable. The words meant nothing to him, but the hairs on the back of his neck prickled. When the ground began to tremble, he finally stood up and took a tentative step toward her.

Her final word was a cry of anguish or elation. She spun around. For a moment, the glow of false moonlight lingered in her eyes, and she didn't seem to recognize him. Then, once more in a whisper, she said, "We must flee."

She managed two steps toward him before her knees

buckled. Vincent dove forward, scooping an arm under her neck before her head could hit the floor.

"Hey, are you OK?"

She didn't answer. Eyes closed, body limp, she might have been dead except for the slight rise and fall of her chest. He adjusted his hold and pulled her up against him. His face mere inches from hers, Vincent thought he had never seen a woman so beautiful.

The ground shook again, and the rumble was underscored by a loud crack. When the dust settled, he saw that a crisscross of deep fissures marred the far wall precisely where the elf had touched it. Smaller fractures continued to spread outward like a wayward spider webs.

"What fell sorcery hath yon demon wrought?"

Vincent spared a quick look at Sir Angus, who stood on the other side of the bars. "A damn good question."

A giant chunk of wall fell to the floor, leaving behind a dark hole the size of a human head. A second later, two larger pieces crashed down. Sir Angus swore and called out for someone to bring the keys. Glowering at Vincent, he unsheathed his long, thin sword.

"Entertain not the notion of escape, Valenthor!"

Vincent knew he had an important decision to make and not a lot of time to make it. He could stay and surrender to the ornery knight or risk his own life by making a run for it.

He suddenly hated the elf. If not for her, he would be back at the tavern, drinking. She had gotten him arrested in the first place, and now, after starting a jailbreak, she was forcing him to finish the job on his own. As if to emphasize the thought, more rubble dropped from the hole in the wall. The chilly night air caressed his face. He took a deep breath and tasted freedom.

I don't owe her anything.

The jingling of armor or keys grew louder. Several more stones toppled to the floor.

But I don't want her to die either.

Heart pounding, he carried the elf over to the hole in the wall. She was far lighter than he expected, considering she wasn't much shorter than he. Carefully but quickly, he pushed her through the gap. He was forced to yank out several loosened stones before he could squeeze after her.

No sooner had he extricated himself than Sir Angus's helmeted head appeared on the other side of the hole.

"Halt!"

A metal-covered hand reached for Vincent, but he pulled back beyond reach. Sir Angus tried to climb through the hole. His armor scraped noisily against the stone before catching against the jagged edges. Wedged firmly in place—half in, half out of the cell—the knight growled in frustration. With some effort, Sir Angus reversed directions and pulled himself back into cell.

Vincent, with the elf draped over his shoulder, was already running.

Chapter 8

A blanket of dreary clouds covered the sky, choking out the sparse light of either dawn or dusk. Smoke swirled up from the chimneys of the houses on either side of the empty dirt road. All was quiet—except for the shouts erupting from around the jail.

Vincent, though already breathing hard, didn't dare stop. Even if he stumbled upon a serviceable hiding place for him and the elf, it would only be a matter of time before Sir Angus and his men found them. From the look of the single-story, bare-wood buildings around them, the settlement was likely a village, not a true city.

I have to keep moving. Maybe I'll get lucky, and there'll be a forest outside of town.

"Ho!"

He heard the cry at the same time as he saw its source—a man wearing a long coat trimmed with light brown fur running straight at him. Even from a distance, Vincent could make out his small ax and round shield.

Shit.

The paths between houses were dark and narrow. God only knew if they led anywhere. Beyond the watchman was open expanse, the obvious way out of town. If he could get past the soldier, he would be home free.

But between the elf in his arms and the stitch in his side, there was no chance of going around the watchman without a confrontation. Vincent set his unconscious companion on the ground and frantically searched for a weapon. He grabbed the first thing he found, a hammer with a long handle leaning against the side of a nearby building, just as the watchman arrived.

"Pray do not be a fool, Valenthor," he said between clenched, yellow teeth. "This cannot end well for you."

Vincent snorted. "Yeah, well, I wouldn't know what to do with a happy ending."

Here goes nothing.

He swung the hammer with all of his strength, hoping to lay the man out with one lucky hit. But the watchman raised his shield even as he thrust the spiky tip of his ax at Vincent's abdomen. The hammerhead smashed the shield into splinters and kept going, which made the watchman pitch sideways. The jab of the ax went wide but not completely off target.

Son of a—

Vincent suddenly adjusted his footing and twisted his body. The wicked point whizzed harmlessly past. Without pausing, he thrust the other pole end of the hammer into the watchman's sternum. The man stumbled back a few steps, gasping for air. Vincent followed through with another powerful swing, connecting with the arm that had held the shield but now hung uselessly at his side.

The watchman landed face-first onto the dirt road and did not move.

How in the hell did I do that?

"Valenthor!"

At the sound of Sir Angus's voice, he turned and assumed a defensive stance, ready to confront the knight. Sir Angus was not alone, however. Four knights flanked him, two on each side. Vincent inspected his adversaries with a calm clarity that belied his racing pulse, taking note of their weaponry, bearing, potential weaknesses.

Sir Angus did not demand his surrender. His fate was sealed. The knights would surround him and kill him. Through dumb luck, he had overpowered the watchman, but it would take a miracle to dispatch five warriors on his own.

In the distance, a wolf howled.

Never thought it would end like this. If there's an after-life, I'll see you soon, Valentine.

Balancing the heavy hammer on his shoulder, he said, "Come on then. Let's get this over with."

Two of the knights exchanged a look of uncertainty. Another shuffled his weight from one leg to the other. But Sir Angus charged, sword raised high.

Reacting purely on instinct, Vincent gripped the hammer's long handle with both hands and lifted it above his head. The sword hacked into the wooden shaft and stuck fast. Vincent gritted his teeth as the impact sent a jolt of pain through his arms. Before Sir Angus could pull his sword free, Vincent kicked him square in the chest and sent both him and his long sword sprawling.

Vincent followed up with a wide swing of the hammer. The nearest man backpedaled, easily avoiding the arc. Meanwhile, the other three spread had spread out and were already closing in. There was no time to regain his balance, no way to block their blades.

Valentine…

Inexplicably, one knight pitched forward, slamming into his nearest ally. Both men crashed to the ground. One of the remaining two knights turned to confront the new threat, but before Vincent could get a look at his rescuer—perhaps the elf had woken up and cast a spell?—Sir Angus and the final knight rushed him.

The hammer whooshed through the air and struck its target, smashing the unknown knight's breastplate and breastbone beneath. As the man dropped to the ground with a groan, Vincent's attention was already fixed on Sir Angus. The knight's sword lashed out again and again.

Somehow Vincent stayed one step ahead, ducking, darting, working his hammer in small circles to deflect the blade. The evasive maneuvers took a toll, as every second stretched beyond reason. Vincent's limbs ached. His lungs burned. After what felt like an hour of desperate combat, Sir Angus got the better of him.

One moment, the blade was coming in high and then, at the last second, low. With the hammer poised to block from above, Vincent couldn't bring the weapon down fast enough. He leaped backward to avoid getting skewered. The sword grazed his side, tearing his flimsy shirt and flesh alike.

Yelling through the pain, Vincent put all the strength he had left into a clumsy counterattack. Sir Angus saw it coming and sidestepped the blow. The heavy hammerhead would have passed through empty air, except Vincent had adjusted his hold on the hammer. As predicted, the handle end moved much faster than the heavy hammer end would have—and faster than Sir Angus could react.

The hardwood shaft struck the knight's helmet with a hollow clang. Three heartbeats later, Sir Angus's eyes rolled back in his head, and he crumpled to the ground.

Vincent spared a moment to wipe the sweat from his brow before confronting more enemies. But there were none to confront. The three remaining knights lay scattered about the street, unmoving, possibly dead. Standing over one of them was a tall figure in a brown cloak. Beneath his hood was a round, wooden mask.

Dark, empty sockets bore into him. The wolf's cry sounded closer this time.

"Who…who are you?" Vincent asked breathlessly.

The other man tapped a long, gnarled staff against one of his boots.

Is that *what he used to defeat those knights…a stick?*

"'Tis not the time for questions. The true enemy draws nigh." The mask muffled the man's voice, not garbling his words, but granting them a grating tone. "Retrieve thy Fay friend and follow me."

Vincent took a couple of steps toward the elf and then stopped. Clutching his warm, sticky wound, he said, "I don't think I can carry her."

"But thou must."

"Why?"

The unsettling sound from behind the mask might have been a laugh. "Because thou art the hero."

The masked stranger moved swiftly down the empty road. Valenthor, once more bearing the weight of the elf, did his best to keep up. He concentrated on putting one foot in front of the other and tried not to worry about what would happen if they encountered more watchmen. Up ahead, the gate lay open, abandoned.

He was too tired to even wonder why.

The elf, who had seemed so light at first, grew heavier with each passing minute. Adding to his burden was the hammer, which he refused to discard. His gait was awkward, and the wound in his side protested with every step.

From a few paces in front of him, his mysterious guide glanced back at him repeatedly, regarding him from behind the expressionless, owl-like mask. Valenthor didn't have to see the man's face to sense his impatience. He neither stopped nor slowed after they had left the confines of the town.

As the grueling hike stretched into eternity, Valenthor's

thoughts faded into a vague awareness of his surroundings. It wasn't until the man in the mask finally came to a halt that Valenthor truly saw the forest around them. Indeed, the small glade was an island lost in an unending sea of trees. Up above, a sliver of a moon and handful of stars pierced the gloomy sky.

Valenthor gently lowered the elf to the dew-kissed grass and then collapsed beside her, shivering.

"So cold..." he muttered through chattering teeth.

The man in the mask knelt beside him. "You have lost a lot of blood," he said, gingerly exploring Valenthor's injury with fingers wrapped in leather. He reached for something inside his coat.

"Will you to tell me your name now?" Valenthor asked weakly. He almost didn't recognize his own voice.

"Call me Locke." He held out a small bottle filled with a dark, murky liquid. "Drink this. It will assuage your pain and restore your vigor."

Valenthor pulled out the cork and downed the contents in one swallow. It tasted like vinegar mixed with—

Jägermeister?

—anise. He coughed until the burning in his throat faded.

"Why did you save me...save us?"

The wooden mask remained motionless for a moment. "We have enemies in common."

"Sir Angus and his men?" Valenthor asked.

Locke scoffed. "Forsooth, the knights. Among others."

Valenthor pulled himself into an upright position. He tensed, waiting for the pain to lance through his ribs, but numbness had settled over his body. Locke's drug seemed to have the same effect on his mind. All he wanted to do was close his eyes and surrender to oblivion. Instead, he studied the elf, looking away after several minutes of watching the swell of her chest rise and fall.

"Do you know who she is?" he asked Locke.

"I have my suspicions."

When Locke didn't expound, Valenthor said, "She has uncanny abilities…magic."

"Naturally."

Valenthor licked his dry, cracked lips. His tongue felt too big for his mouth, and the cold was already a distant memory. A fog was gathering in his head. He pushed it away.

"Why do you wear a mask?"

Locke rose from his haunches and drove the end of his staff into the ground. It stood on its own, a lone sapling in the glade. "Wherefore doth anyone don a mask? I must have something to hide."

Valenthor might have pressed the point, but he knew his senses would soon leave him. "My name is Vin—"

"Valenthor of the Three Rivers," Locke provided.

"Actually…" The thought fled his mind, and Valenthor shrugged inwardly. His eyes closed, he said, "We owe you our lives, Locke."

The disturbing laugh came again. "Forestall the end of the world, and your debt will be forgiven."

Vincent lay perfectly still in his bed. The throbbing in his head ticked away the seconds. Memories of last night popped into his severely dehydrated brain at random intervals. That first shot with Marc. Playing cards and more drinks. Jokes that lost their luster in the light of day. Talking to Paish about politics, of all things. The softness of her freckled breasts.

Many pieces of the evening were blurry at best, but he recalled every aspect of The Dream with startling clarity.

He wondered which was worse, reliving the sins of last night or reflecting upon the insanity that was the continuing adventures of Valenthor.

Was that my punishment for falling off the wagon and fooling around with Paish? Is The Dream itself payback for letting Clementine die?

He thought he might be sick, but deep breaths kept his stomach in check. At least Paish had not spent the night in his room. He figured she had either left for home last night—early that morning, actually—or she had crashed on the couch. The thought of facing her kept his back glued to the bedspread until his bladder finally threatened to rebel.

Slowly, he sat up, got to his feet, and walked over to his bedroom door. He opened it warily and let out a long sigh when he saw the empty living room. Jerry's door was closed, but Vincent knew he would be at work.

On the one hand, having the apartment to himself brought some relief. On the other, he didn't necessarily like being alone with his thoughts. Or his guilt.

I need help.

He wandered into the bathroom. The sight of the rust-stained toilet made his stomach quiver. He repressed the nausea, finished his business, and went to the kitchen for some water. Cup in hand, he then headed for the couch but stopped suddenly in front of the desk. On impulse, he pulled open the top drawer and took out an out-of-date phonebook, which he took with him to the Low Rider.

He opened to the yellow section, searching the categories for inspiration.

There has to be someone out there that can help me figure this out. My stoner roommate and his self-professed expert on fantasy just aren't cutting it. And God knows I can't help myself.

Vincent flipped through the pages but harbored little hope of finding a professional who specialized in crazy, life-stealing dreams. But then, he spotted a name he knew and decided it must be a good omen.

Unless I want to share my mind with Conan's lesser-known cousin, what choice do I have?

Chapter 9

A silent wind pelted Milton's face with icy snowflakes. He knew he ought to be cold, but he couldn't feel much of anything. Was the numbness a side effect of prolonged exposure to the elements, he wondered, or another symptom of his exhausted brain?

The freezing air hadn't dulled his other senses, however. Ever since he had gotten off the bus, still feeling on edge from facing DJ and his peculiar questions, Milton heard his pursuers' footsteps echoing through the alleyways. Shadows crept along the never-ending line of streetlights behind him. Several times he had stopped to confront them, to fight or to surrender.

To end the charade once and for all.

But no one answered when he shouted into the dead, frosty night. And when he stopped to investigate the side streets and small spaces, he found only the silhouettes of garbage cans and misshapen shrubs.

Milton refused to be lulled into a false sense of security. He knew his enemies were out there—if not on his heels, then lingering farther back, waiting for Mother Nature to do their dirty work for them.

Stifling a yawn, he trudged through an ankle-deep carpet of snow. There was no heat to be found. The storefronts and apartment buildings around him were lightless and lifeless. He wondered if there was an all-night diner nearby, wondered where in the world he was. But no matter how hard he tried, he couldn't reach any memories to explain how he had come to be there.

It's as though that part of my mind is hibernating. Too bad I can't afford to wait until spring to figure out who, exactly, is after me.

DJ had said something about the end of the world—right before telling Milton he couldn't run forever. Was DJ caught up in the conspiracy? He didn't want to believe it. If nothing else, DJ was too young to be in the CIA. But even more disconcerting than the boy's words was the wolf on his sweatshirt and his snake tattoo.

Those images represent the enemy. They symbolize a threat.

Milton knew he was close to a revelation, but the more he focused on the wolf and serpent, the further the truth retreated. In the distance he heard someone laugh. Or was it the cry of a crow?

"Why can't I remember?" The words left his mouth with a stream of steam.

They must have tampered with my brain. I discovered what they were up and managed to escape, but not before they locked the secret away in my mind. They'll stop at nothing to find me...to keep me from telling the world about their sinister plot to—

Milton opened his eyes wide and gasped. The street was gone, replaced by a large room lined with lab equipment. He lay on a table. A man with a high forehead and gray-green eyes stared grimly down at him. The man wore a white coat.

In his white-gloved hand, he held a syringe.

Then the white glove was gone, replaced by a dark fist clutching a sword.

Milton pitched forward, nearly falling to the pavement but catching a hold of a snow-covered bench. The cold metal sent a jolt through him, wrenching his thoughts back to the present. Sitting down, he tried to hold onto the face of the man with the bleak gray-green eyes, but already the vision was fading. Staring blankly at the whitewashed landscape, he forgot what was in the man's hand and then forgot the hand entirely.

Before the memory was lost entirely, he whispered a single, stray word: "Odin."

As though in answer to a password, a door opened in his mind. Milton closed his eyes, eager to explore a memory that hitherto had been hidden from him. Before he could cross the threshold, however, the door slammed shut.

He knew only an instant of despair before his thoughts were whisked away to another place from another time.

Milton sits in a soft armchair with a bold floral pattern. His fists clenched, he says, "You crossed a line, William!"

Across the room, a windowless parlor adorned with an unbelievable variety of spoons, a man of Japanese descent crosses his arms. He meets Milton's accusing gaze with a relaxed, almost bemused expression. A ghost of his charming smile glints in his dark eyes.

"And which line might that be, Milton?" The man's tone is steady. Polite. Professional. It only fuels Milton's indignation.

"For starters, you invaded someone's thoughts without permission," Milton replies. "And to make matters worse, you shared your exploits with the entire group without even consulting your fellow officers first. Don't you think the rest of them are going to try it now too?"

William Marlowe reaches for a goblet of red wine and takes a dainty sip. He's the only one in the room wearing a suit, the only member of the Lucid Dreaming Society who would ever think to wear a tie to a meeting.

"Why shouldn't they try it?" William asks mildly.

"Because it's reprehensible!" Milton shouts.

To his left, sitting on a sofa—covered with the same big, red roses as Milton's chair—a woman clears her throat. "Let's all just take a breath, and we can discuss the ramification of William's discovery."

"The four of us should have done that *before* bringing it before the full Society," Milton snaps, glaring across the room at William. "Or, better yet, *before* our vice president attempted something so dangerous."

"Be that as it may…" Annette says, her Southern drawl making "may" sound more like "my." "We have an opportunity to talk about it now. Can I get you some more tea, Milton?"

Milton tears his eyes away from William's, glances at the nearly empty mug, and says, "No, thank you."

Annette smiles warmly. She's a big woman, her girth occupying all of one cushion and a fair portion of the neighboring one. Her wavy brown hair is pulled back into a long ponytail. She has a pretty face but wears too much eyeshadow. Her penchant for gaudy jewelry is outmatched only by her generosity.

"Maybe you should start at the beginning, William," Annette suggests.

At the other end of the couch, the fourth LDS officer chews on a pencil, intently studying the blue shag carpet. Milton wonders if he is even listening. Cormac hates meetings at Annette's house because he can't smoke. Milton considers reminding Cormac that the role of secretary includes taking notes but then thinks maybe this conversation would be better kept off the record.

"Certainly, Annette." William sets his wineglass down

on a coaster made out of needlepoint. "We already know that naturals can find one another in their dreams, creating a shared dream experience. Members of the LDS have been doing that with varying degrees of success for many months." His eyes meet Milton's for an instant. Turning back to Annette, he adds, "We also know it is possible for naturals to visit non-naturals in their dreams, as with Janet and Keith."

"Janet and Keith are members of the Society," Milton interjects. "They let us in willingly."

William continues as though he didn't hear him. "The next test, obviously, would be to learn if naturals could enter the dreams of non-naturals who did not expect him or her to show up."

"An unsuspecting victim," Milton mutters.

"Milton." Annette speaks his name with a tone usually reserved for a fidgeting child. To William, she says, "And you were successful?"

William shrugs and reaches for his wine. "I already told the Society exactly what happened. While drifting off to sleep and, then, while in a dream state, I focused on the subject..." He clears his throat. "...on the woman who cleans my condo. There was initial resistance...an unconscious reaction, I'm sure...but she did not seem surprised to see me. I had predicted as much. She knows me, after all."

Cormac looks up for the first time. "What do you suppose would've happened if she *didn't* know you...like if you disguised yourself or something?"

"Only one way to find out, I suppose," William replies cheerfully.

Milton scowls. "He crossed a line. Am I the only one who sees that?"

"But, Milton, isn't that the point of the Lucid Dreaming

Society?" William asks. "Didn't we come together to break through the barriers of modern science…to penetrate the deepest reaches of human understanding?"

Milton rolls his eyes. "Damn, that's poetic, Will."

"Language!" Annette scolds, adjusting a gold broach perched atop her ample bosom. Three bejeweled owls watch Milton warily.

"I'm sorry, Annette, but it is our duty, as officers, to develop guidelines for the members of the Society, not only for their own good, but for the good of a public that is unaware of our existence." Milton takes a steadying breath. "We must pass a motion banning the intrusion into the dreams of non-members."

Cormac grunts and removes the mangled pencil from his mouth. "That's a bit hasty, yeah? Besides, normal folk won't be the wiser. They'll think it's all part of the show, just another crazy dream."

"That's not the point!" Milton shakes his head, as much out of disgust as to clear his thoughts. "And what if you're wrong, Cormac? Think of what harm would befall the Society if the world's first impression of naturals, we seemingly ordinary human beings who were born with such an extraordinary ability, is that we are bunch of voyeurs…or worse!"

Cormac shrugs and resumes gnawing on the pencil.

William leans forward. His fingers are steepled. His elbows rest on his knees. He's in full-blown psychologist mode. "Encountering people in their dreams is not unlike running into them on the street. So long as we adhere to the ethics that govern us in the waking world, we have nothing to fear."

Milton notices that William always says "waking world," not "real world," as most other LDS members do.

"In the real world, there are police to punish those who

violate the law," Milton says. "In the dreamscape, we have an unfair advantage. Who will ensure that we don't sacrifice our morals in this pursuit of knowledge?"

William doesn't miss a beat. "We are good people, Milton. We watch out for one another."

"The Society is a family," Annette adds. "And as you pointed out, it's our job, as officers, to keep everyone safe…naturals and non-naturals alike."

Milton winces. It doesn't surprise him that Cormac, who always struck him as something of a brute, is siding with William Marlowe. But he had hoped Annette would understand the hazards that surely lie ahead if LDS members started dropping into the dreams of friends, loved ones, colleagues…

Annette smiles warmly at Milton. She isn't stupid, he thinks, just hopelessly naïve.

"Without rules, we condone anarchy," he says to her, but his words are directed at William.

"We all swore an oath to behave ourselves and to be discreet," William says. "By thinking up new rules, we needlessly limit our potential."

"Snooping around other people's subconscious seems like a big detour on the road to self-discovery," Milton argues.

Annette claps her hands once, drawing everyone's attention. Dimples frame her big smile. Though Milton is angry with William, he imagines himself smacking the grin right off her face when she says, "Let's vote on it, shall we?"

Cormac says, "Nay," without hesitating, followed immediately by William. Annette appears to consider the issue for several seconds before throwing in with the others. Now Milton feels like *he* was slapped in the face.

The discussion turns to what Annette, the Society's

president, should say to the other LDS members so that they exercise caution if they attempt to enter a non-natural's dream. In the end, Annette decides she will remind everyone that unseemly behavior is grounds for immediate expulsion from the Lucid Dreaming Society, at the officers' discretion.

Milton hardly hears the conversation anymore. And when Annette finally gives William an obligatory reprimand for not sharing his discovery with the officers first, Milton doesn't bother to chime in. Breathing evenly in spite of his pounding heart, he can't decide which is more frustrating, that William got his way again or that he didn't see this crossroads coming a long time ago.

The meeting ends, and Cormac is the first to leave, an unlit cigarette pressed between his lips. Annette clears Milton's teacup and William's goblet. Milton tries to follow Annette out of the parlor, but as he walks by, William takes him by the elbow. Clenching is teeth, Milton reluctantly faces the man.

William's dark eyes have softened. There's no sign of the subtle smirk. "No hard feelings…"

"No good will come of this, Will," Milton declares. "Mark my words."

William stares at him, expression blank, for a moment. With a perfectly level tone, he asks, "Are you angry because I introduced dream drifting to the others or because, in doing so, they now believe William Marlowe was the one who discovered it, and not Milton Baerwald?"

The distant grumble of a large vehicle made Milton jump up from the bench. He squinted through the curtain of thick flurries and saw pale, yellow headlights farther down the street. Muscles tensed, ready to spring into action,

Milton watched the lights grow steadily larger.

I fell asleep, and now they found me!

Paralyzed with fear, Milton allowed himself a moment to consider the jumble of images and impressions swirling in his mind. A familiar place…lots of spoons…red roses …red wine…old friends…or were they foes? He tried to fight through the haze, but the dream slipped away.

Freud theorized we forget our dreams to prevent conflict between the conscious and unconscious. We protect ourselves without even trying.

As the headlights drew closer, he saw they belonged to a city bus. He sighed in relief. His enemies had not found him. On the contrary, providence had presented him with a chance to get warm. As he waited for the bus to arrive—by sheer luck he had fallen asleep at a bus stop—Milton wondered how long he slept and how narrowly he had escaped hypothermia. He stepped onto the bus, rubbed his cold, colorless hands together and surveyed the rows of seats.

The bus was empty, except for a young man sitting way in the back.

"Milton!" DJ called, smiling widely and waving him over. "How's my favorite nut job?"

Chapter 10

Leah Chedid was exhausted, had been tired all day, but as she lay in bed, motionless and cocooned in absolute darkness, her brain showed no signs of relinquishing its hold on consciousness.

Since she couldn't slow—let alone stop—her racing thoughts, Leah tried to wear them out by focusing her mental energy on mundane memory exercises. Yet even after she had conjured up the names of all of her elementary school teachers and remembered nearly all of her third-grade classmates, she was not any closer to sleep.

She wasn't surprised. Such cognitive retraining techniques seldom worked for her.

It's like my mind knows I'm trying to trick it...like I'm too smart for my own damn good.

The sleep mask kept her from checking the clock, so she didn't know how long she had been lying there, wrestling with sleeplessness. However, Leah, an insomniac for almost all of her life, was confident more than two hours had passed since she had finally forced herself to go to bed at midnight.

The strategy of staying up so late in hopes of outmaneuvering insomnia was a no-no. So was lying in bed awake for hours out of sheer stubbornness.

With a sigh of defeat, she kicked off the blanket and began fiddling with her wrist restraints. There was always a moment of panic. In the second or two it took to activate the release, she imagined that, at last, the restraints malfunctioned. She would scream for help until her throat was raw. The neighbor from downstairs would break down the door and discover her, bound and blindfolded, and would mistakenly conclude she was the victim of a sex game gone wrong.

Which was better than the alternative. If no one would hear her, and she would be trapped in a sensory-deprived state for days.

Better to die of embarrassment than from thirst and starvation.

Thankfully, whoever had designed the S&M restraints cared only about the appearance of helplessness. After the first satisfying click, she freed her right hand and then used it to assist the left with opening the other cuff. She pulled off the sleep mask and removed her earplugs. On principle, she triggered the release on restraints around her ankles before letting herself look at the clock.

3:07 a.m.

Damn...even worse than I thought.

After twenty to thirty minutes, she should have left her bed to read more of that horrifically dry article from *Sleep Research Online* or turned on the television or engaged in any activity other than allowing her mind to run rampant for hours. But being an expert on sleep disorders didn't mean she had mastered hers.

Leah stood up and arched her back until it cracked. As she left her bedroom, she pointedly ignored the treadmill in the corner, which wasn't difficult because it was covered with clothes. After a stop at the bathroom, she went to the kitchen. It was a routine she knew well: eat a small snack, watch some TV, and return to bed for another go at it.

If I'm lucky I get, what, four hours of sleep before I

have to get up for work?

Something pressed against her leg, and Leah smiled in spite of herself.

"Fancy meeting you here," she said.

The Persian cat tilted her flat face up at Leah and meowed.

"You're not getting any milk, Emira."

"Meow."

Leah was about to remind the cat that, like most felines, she was lactose intolerant, but there was no use repeating it. She was a cat, for one thing. And if by some miracle Emira did understand English, she was obviously willing to risk the consequences of indulging in her favorite treat.

Speaking of indulging...

Against her better judgment, Leah opened the freezer. A quart of double-fudge brownie ice cream greeted her.

Sure, Leah, eat some sugar at three in the morning. Brilliant idea.

"Meow."

She glanced down at Emira, whose big, coppery eyes bore straight into her heart.

"You probably think I'm the biggest bitch. You know I have the power to give you what you want and can't understand why I don't."

"Meow."

Leah opened the refrigerator and took out the carton of skim milk.

"You win, girl. One of us ought to have what she really wants."

As Emira contentedly lapped up her liquid treat, Leah opened the cupboard and grabbed the peanut butter. She reached for the bread but stopped. The magnesium in peanut butter had calming properties. The bread was just extra carbs.

Peanut butter jar in one hand, spoon in the other, she headed for the living room. A quick search revealed the remote jammed between two cushions. She might as well have left the TV off, though, considering her choices. *Law & Order*, *Sanford and Son*, a show that looked like a video game, plenty of infomercials—television had no love for the nocturnally challenged.

At last, she decided on a documentary about timber wolves. A specialist of some sort explained that while the wolf was often maligned in the European tradition, Native American myths portrayed it in a more positive light. On screen, a black wolf with blue eyes padded through snowy woodlands.

Leah popped a heaping spoonful of Skippy into her mouth and wondered why she had been thinking about old teachers and classmates.

It was the alumni magazine that got my mind on about the past. Aldrich made another breakthrough in his research, got another grant, and published his findings in yet another journal.

I should be happy for him. He's a good person, and he deserves it. I shouldn't be jealous.

Thinking of Aldrich Iwate, whom she had dated throughout grad school, had taken her mind down the avenue of what had become of her other college friends. Were they making names for themselves? Rich? Married?

Not that Leah wasn't doing well for herself. She had a good job and lived comfortably. One of these days she'd buy a condo, in spite of her father's insistence that a house was better. She liked her job. She was making a difference, albeit on a smaller scale than Aldrich was.

As for a family, well, it's not like she wasn't trying. Was it her fault that none of her recent boyfriends were marriage material—or even boyfriend material, for that matter? But she wasn't desperate enough as to let her sisters play matchmaker, not when they used such dangerous descriptions as "respectable" and "witty" to describe the ubiquitous friend-of-a-friend.

Emira jumped up onto her lap and meowed. Leah scratched her behind the ears, evoking an immediate purr.

Memories from UW–Madison had segued into thoughts about friends from farther back. I lost track of so many people after high school. Whatever happened to the friends who helped me survive adolescence...Jeanie, who wanted to play French horn in the Chicago Symphony Orchestra ...Carrie, who lost her virginity at fourteen and instantly became the expert on all matters sexual...or Bella Stark? I wonder if any of them ever wonder about me?

She laughed at herself. Emira's ears perked up.

Why am I worrying about any of this? Thirty is too young for a midlife crisis.

On TV, a thin ribbon of clouds floated past a big, yellow moon. The scene was accompanied by wolf cries. Leah watched the documentary for a while longer, only half paying attention to the narrator's explanation of why wolves howl. She felt her thoughts drifting, her eyelids drooping.

It was dangerous to fall asleep on the couch, unrestrained, but she didn't care. The short trek to her bedroom could jinx everything, and she needed to squeeze in a few hours of sleep before work. She couldn't afford to burn another sick day.

The last thing she heard before sleep's sweet embrace was the narrator's description of a condition that causes a person to believe he or she can transform into another animal, such as a wolf.

*   *   *

By noon, Leah was ready to call it a day. She could barely keep her eyes open, and the left side of her face had been throbbing ever since she woke up to find herself on the floor in the hall, her alarm chirping insistently from the open bedroom door.

Her drive to work was more a series of impressions than a memory. Her morning got a little better, thanks to the magic of Starbucks, but as the hours dragged on, concentrating on her patients' problems became increasingly difficult. When yet another coworker asked about the colorful bruise on her cheek, she pretended not to hear the question.

That was reckless of me. I was lucky all I got was a contusion.

Alone in her office, she stared uncomprehendingly at her computer screen. After five yawns in as many minutes, she shut the computer down, grabbed her coat, and locked the office door behind her.

Taking half of a sick day is better than a full one, I guess.

Leah barely slowed as she walked past the receptionist. "I'm feeling unwell and will not be back this afternoon, Ellie. Please cancel my appointments."

"But, Dr. Chedid, there's someone here to see you now."

"What?" Leah reluctantly returned to the front desk. It took all of her willpower not to glare at Ellie, a fresh college grad who alternately came off as confident or arrogant, depending on the amount of sleep Leah had under her belt. "There was nothing on my calendar."

"I was just about to call you," Ellie said. "That man over there says he needs to see you right away. I told him we don't do walk-ins, but he asked for you by name. He said he's an old friend of yours."

Leah scanned the waiting room. There was only one male in the group, and he didn't look familiar. She was on the verge of telling Ellie that he would have to make an appointment like everyone else, when the man looked up, and their eyes met. Leah cursed inwardly.

So much for a stealthy escape.

The man jumped up from his seat and hurried over. "Leah! Hi! Sorry to barge in like this, but I need your help."

He looked to be about her age. Dark stubble covered his cheeks, and he stank of sweat. But he looked sincere and wasn't altogether unhandsome, despite his disheveled hair and red-rimmed eyes.

A fellow insomniac?

Her expression must have conveyed her confusion because he added, "Of course you don't recognize me. It's been, what, twelve years? I'm Vincent Cruz. We went to high school together."

Leah swallowed a gasp.

I whiled away the wee hours of the morning pondering old classmates, and one of them happens to walk into the clinic today? Too weird.

"Oh, right...Vincent. Yeah...it's been a while," she stammered. "Good to see you again, but to be honest, I was on my way out. I'm not feeling—"

"Please, Leah...*Doctor*...I don't know where else to go. I just lost my job, and if I can't get control of this...this..." He took a breath. "I think I'm losing my mind."

She glanced at the door beyond Vincent, catching a glimpse of freedom through the glass panels. But instead of making a mad dash, she smiled at Vincent and led him back to her office.

You get five minutes, buddy.

Inside her office—which was neither big nor small and featured framed art that was colorful enough to break up the monotony of the monochrome walls without being too much of a distraction—Leah motioned for Vincent to take a seat in one of the empty chairs. She shut the door behind them and took her place on the other side of the desk.

Typically, Leah began consultations by asking patients to describe their symptoms and followed by going through a list of stock questions about sleep environment, family history, and so forth. Under the circumstances, however, Leah felt she should say something to break the ice with the boy who sat behind her in U.S. history class.

Before she could think of a suitable comment, Vincent said, "I found your name in the phonebook by dumb luck. I'd have thought you'd be living on the East Coast or something, not still in Milwaukee. You always seemed so smart back in high school."

Leah didn't know what to make of the backhanded compliment, so she answered with the truth. "I suppose I haven't found any reason to leave Wisconsin. My parents and sisters all live around here. What about you?"

"Me?" Vincent gazed up at the ceiling. "I guess it's like you said. I don't have any reason to leave. Then again, I don't really have any good reasons to stay either."

What is that supposed to mean?

"So…are you married?" he asked.

"No, are you?" she asked with a curtness that surprised her. She told herself that it was the lack of sleep and the throbbing bruise that made her feel so impatient.

Vincent shifted in his chair. "Yes, technically I am. I married Bella Stark a few months after we graduated. But we're separated now. The divorce papers will probably come any day now."

Leah felt her mouth pop open and quickly closed it.

Bella Stark!

The two of them had become best friends shortly after Bella's family moved to Shorewood in third grade. Leah and Bella drifted apart during freshman year of high school, joining different cliques. Leah became a brainiac, while Bella spent her free time with her volleyball team-mates. Leah remembered hearing a rumor senior year that Bella was pregnant, but it was hardly appropriate for her to ask Vincent about that.

Does he even know I was good friends with his estranged wife, way back when?

"I'm sorry to hear that, Vincent." Clearing her throat, she added, "We should talk about why you're here."

Vincent ran a hand through his oily hair and looked down at his knees. "It's going to sound crazy, but I've been having these dreams…really messed up dreams."

"What makes them 'messed up'?"

Still not meeting her eyes, he said, "For starters, I'm always somebody else…but that's not the strangest part. The Dream keeps going on. Not every night, but more and more lately, I find myself back in the same story, picking up where the last dream left off. And the last couple of times it happened, The Dream pulled me in."

"Pulled you in?"

He nodded. "That's why I got fired. I was at work, wide awake, and then I was in The Dream. My boss found me sleeping on the job, and that was that."

She asked him a series of questions about his symptoms, jotting down his answers and mentally ruling out night terrors, sleep paralysis, hypnogogic hallucinations, and a handful of other disorders.

"Do you think it's narcolepsy?" he asked.

She finished writing "psychological?" and said, "It's possible. Are you tired now?"

"A little, but I'm also hungover."

Leah nodded, wrote the word "alcohol."

That explains the red eyes…and the smell.

"Do you often feel tired during the day?" she asked, maintaining the professional tone she had perfected in the four years she had been working at the clinic.

"I worked third shift, so I'm used to sleeping whenever I have to."

Leah made a note about inconsistent sleep patterns. "Human beings are diurnal. Staying up all night can disrupt the body's natural biorhythms. When was the last time you were 'pulled' into the dream?"

"Last night."

She leaned back in her chair. "After you had been drinking."

Vincent's eyes narrowed. "Yes, but I was stone-cold sober all the other times."

"Are you taking any prescriptions?"

"No."

"Do you use street drugs?"

"No."

"How often do you drink?"

"I don't drink…except for last night." He rubbed his forehead. "Can't you just hook me up to a machine to see if my brainwaves are scrambled or something?"

Yeah, just let me take a catnap first, and then I'll give you a tune up.

Leah smiled politely. "That would be a bit premature." She set the pen down and folded her hands. "Sleep science doesn't extend into the makeup of dreams. The feeling you have of getting pulled into dreams is puzzling, but as for analyzing the dreams themselves, you might consider making an appointment with a psychotherapist—"

Vincent stood up suddenly. "I don't do shrinks. Thanks

anyway, Leah. Sorry to have wasted your time."

He turned to leave.

Maybe it's for the best.

"Hey, wait a minute!" she said before she could stop herself.

Vincent turned around.

What am I doing?

"Maybe your condition is something I treat professionally, but if not, perhaps I can help, as a friend. I would like to hear more about your dreams. Would you be interested in meeting for lunch tomorrow?"

An emotion rippled across Vincent's face, but she couldn't identify it.

"Sure, that would be great," he said at last.

As they made the arrangements, Leah wondered what possessed her to set aside a precious Saturday afternoon for a work-related obligation. She continued to stare at the door after he left, momentarily forgetting her exhaustion as she tried to decide if she were helping Vincent as a favor for an old friend or out of some secret hope that he had a disorder worth writing about.

Then Leah laughed.

My first lunch date in months, and it's with Vincent Cruz. Sorry, Mom. I must be allergic to marriage material.

Chapter 11

Vincent sat up slowly, bracing himself for the hangover headache that had haunted him since that morning. The pain, however, had faded into a dull throb. His mouth was dry, and his tongue tasted like something he might have cleaned out of the fifth-floor restroom back at the bank tower.

Back when he had a job.

At least I didn't have The Dream during that last nap. Thank God for small miracles.

He rose from the Low Rider with a groan and went into the kitchen. He spotted Jerry's keys on the table. Next to them was a job application for the City of Milwaukee Department of Public Works. The line of light under Jerry's bedroom door suggested his roommate was inside, likely changing out of his smelly, garbage-stained uniform.

Vincent took one last look at the job application before going to the refrigerator. Inside, one lonely can of Milwaukee's Best stared back at him. No milk. No soda. It was either tap water or some hair of the dog. He reached for the beer.

Might as well get rid of it.

He took his first gulp as Jerry came out of his room.

"Oh, hey," Jerry said. His gaze landed on the can.

"Sorry, it's the last one."

Jerry took a glass out of the cupboard and filled it with water from the sink. "That's OK. I got my own little pick-me-up waiting." He flashed Vincent a goofy grin.

Vincent followed Jerry into the living room. Once in his recliner, Jerry unrolled a sandwich baggie and sifted through the dark green stuff inside with his index finger. His brow furrowed.

"Damn, we smoked a lot last night." His smiled returned as suddenly as it had left. "But it was fun, right?"

Vincent had to admit that it had been fun—right up until the end. Too much fun, in fact. Thinking of the whiskey shots and foreplay with Paish, he wished he had never agreed to host the get-together.

"Yeah, it was a blast," Vincent said with as much enthusiasm as he could muster. "I'm paying for it today, though."

"No hangovers with weed," Jerry said cheerfully.

I was more than hungover this morning. I must have still been a little drunk to show up at that sleep clinic. It almost seems like a dream...except if it had been, Leah would've had pointy ears.

"So, what happened with you and Paish?" Jerry asked.

Vincent took a long swig of beer, stalling. "What do you mean?"

"You know what I mean! Marc and I were talking in the kitchen, and when we came back in here, Tara's passed out, and you and Paish are in your room with the door closed. I'm not askin' for the dirty details or anything..."

Vincent relaxed a little, relieved that Paish hadn't gone back out into the living room to report how he had fallen asleep while they were fooling around. She must have stayed in Vincent's room for the remainder of the night and left with her friends in the morning after Jerry left for work.

Vincent wondered if she felt half as humiliated as he did.

"Yeah, we had fun," Vincent muttered, hoping his suggestive smile would defer further questions. It didn't.

"Are you going to call her?" Jerry asked.

"I don't know. Maybe," he lied.

Time to change the subject.

"I had another dream last night, and it was a doozey."

Jerry placed the freshly rolled joint in his mouth and lit it. "What happened?"

Vincent told Jerry about the jailbreak and the battle with the knights, though he didn't linger on the latter. His stomach soured whenever he thought of what he had done—what *Valenthor* had done—to the soldiers.

None of it was even real, so why do I feel so guilty?

Enthralled, Jerry forgot to smoke as he listened. Ash dropped from the end of the joint onto his pants, but he didn't notice until Vincent finished talking.

"That Locke guy really saved your bacon, huh?" Jerry said. "But you took out a few knights by yourself. That's pretty badass."

Vincent shrugged. "*Valenthor* is bad ass. Those weren't my bulging biceps, and that wasn't me swinging that hammer." He brought the beer up to his lips but then thought better of it. "I just wish I knew why I keep going back there."

Jerry stood up, absently brushing the ash off of his pants. After a quick puff, he set the joint on the edge of the ashtray, walked into his room, and returned with the laptop.

"We'll figure it out," Jerry said. "You made some progress this last time."

"What do you mean?"

"You got a name...the name of a main character. The elf's name would have been better, but we'll take what we can get, right?" Jerry typed something on the keyboard and looked up, frowning. "Is it L-O-C-K, like a lock and key?"

"How should I know? I didn't ask him to spell it!" Vincent knew he should be grateful for Jerry's attempt to help with The Dream. He just wished the guy wasn't having so much fun doing it.

Several seconds later, Jerry said, "Google isn't turning up anything, but...oh, wait...the Master is online. Maybe he can help."

"Wonderful."

Vincent stared at the silver and blue beer can, but his thoughts were back in The Dream as Jerry used instant messaging to update the Master of All Things Fantasy. At the moment, pondering the mysteries of Valenthor's world was preferable to sorting out his problems in real life.

I have to figure out The Dream first. That's Issue Number One.

Jerry's exhaled of a stream of smoke. "He's got a few new theories."

Vincent leaned forward. "Such as?"

"Well, for starters, he's pretty convinced that the elf chick is a priestess because she can use magic. I'm not really sure how a priestess is different from a wizard, but...oh, he says she might even be a high priestess. She's definitely someone important in her society, probably a princess. And he says there's a thirty-five percent chance that the two of you will fall in love."

"What? How did he come up with that statistic?"

"I don't know. He's read a lot of books, though. Maybe he's come up with some kind of formula." Jerry took another hit off the joint. "It makes sense if you think about it. Valenthor is a single guy, right?"

Vincent didn't correct him. He had never told Jerry that Valenthor also had lost a daughter. Vincent didn't know if Valenthor's wife was alive or not—or if he had even been married at all—but he had his suspicions. Not wanting to touch upon the details that so closely paralleled his own miseries, he waited for Jerry to continue.

"And the elf wants you to save her homeland. You have a journey ahead of you. Stuff could happen along the way."

Vincent chuckled dryly. "Except now I've got a third wheel."

Jerry laughed too. "Yeah, well, maybe the Master can shed some light on why the masked man came out of nowhere."

Jerry started typing again, using one finger on one hand. It was slow going.

"So," Vincent began tentatively, "does the Master have any idea *how* this is happening to me?"

Jerry gave a look that might have come off as pensive, were it not for his puffy eyes. "How could he? His specialty is fantasy fiction. As far as he's concerned, I'm giving him bits and pieces of a story. I think he thinks I'm an amateur writer or something."

Because if he knew the truth, he'd think I was crazy and stop returning your emails. Why don't you think I'm crazy, Jerry?

Vincent said, "So the Master only knows half of the story?"

"Not exactly," Jerry said, still plinking away on the laptop. "I told him that you…a character named Vincent …becomes Valenthor when he dreams. He told me that the concept was interesting but not really a new one. There have been a handful of fantasy series about people from the real world getting sucked into other dimensions. Let me pull open that email…

"Here we go. He wrote, 'One of the more popular examples of this formula is Stephen King's *Dark Tower* series, in which characters from several time periods are drawn into a fantasy world steeped in Old West themes, a realm that touches upon the settings and characters of many of King's other books. Matters get complicated, however, as King introduces alternate Earths, and at one point the protagonists even visit King in the supposed real world in order to get him to finish writing the series. They call that metafiction.

"'Other examples include *The Chronicles of Thomas Covenant, the Unbeliever* by Stephen R. Donaldson, *The Spearwielder Tale* trilogy by R.A. Salvatore, and *War of the Flowers* by Tad Williams. The latter involve an average Joe visiting the faerie realm, which is a device that predates the Arthurian legends.'"

Jerry stopped talking for a second, then added, "The Master just IM-ed that the knights probably will continue to track you guys and that the elf will wake up in a couple of days...or chapters...oh, and that you shouldn't trust Locke. Hmm, he's spelling it with an E at the end. Anyway, he says Locke might have saved your life because he wants to use you and/or the elf for his own purposes. Locke might even be in league with your enemies, and by taking him with you to the elf's homeland, you'll be giving him easy access to whatever he's after."

Jerry's eyes scanned the computer screen. "He says that the mask means Locke is hiding something."

"No shit. He told me as much himself."

Jerry went on, unperturbed, "If you can get his mask off, there's a ninety percent chance you'll discover he's evil."

Again with the statistics?

"And what about the other ten percent?" Vincent asked.

Jerry typed the question. A moment later he said, "'If Locke is not one of the enemy's lieutenants, he's probably being coerced somehow. If he is not a spy, he has his own agenda, which can only complicate the plot. It would be rather dull if Locke turned out to be an all-around good guy because that would reduce him to nothing more than a deus ex machina'…whatever that means. 'In any event, Locke surely is someone the hero has met before. He might even be a relative.'"

The jarring buzz of the doorbell made both of them jump. Vincent leaned over the couch to look down through the window at the side entrance.

"Who is it?" Jerry asked.

"I think it's…shit, it's my mom. And she saw me."

Vincent crushed his beer can with unnecessary force and stomped past Jerry, who hastily extinguished his joint in the ashtray.

"We still have some spray in the bathroom, right?" Jerry asked.

Ignoring him, Vincent tossed the beer can into the garbage on his way to the door. He took his time on the winding stairway. When he reached the bottom, his mother waved to him through the cloudy glass window.

We look nothing alike.

Evangeline was fair-skinned and blond. She had passed down her blue eyes to Daniel. Vincent, on the other hand, had his Hispanic father's dark features. God only knew what else he had inherited from Señor One-Night-Stand. Schizophrenia, maybe?

Vincent understood why so many men had found his mother to be beautiful, though there were times when her weariness made her look much older than forty-seven. Then again, she had always seemed older than really she was to him. Even in his earliest memories, she was a grown up, though everyone else surely had seen a teenager with a baby.

He pulled open the door and said, "Hi, Mom."

She smiled back, but it didn't show in her eyes. Picking nervously at her frayed brown gloves, she said, "I was in the neighborhood and thought I'd try to catch you before you left for work."

"You caught me," was all Vincent could think to say.

"Can I come up?"

"Yeah, of course," he said and turned back the way he had come.

When he opened the apartment door, an vanilla fist hit him in the nose. Jerry leaned against the refrigerator, trying to look casual. Vincent could see the top of the air freshener bottle poking out of the sink.

Smooth, Jerry. Real smooth.

"This is Jerry, my roommate," Vincent said. "You two have talked a few times on phone, if I recall."

"Nice to meet you in person, Mrs. Cruz," said Jerry.

It's Pierce, not Cruz. And she's never been missus anything.

"Please call me Eve. It's nice to meet you too, Jerry."

An awkward silence filled the kitchen. Jerry excused himself with an unintelligible mumble and retreated into the living room. Evangeline pulled a chair back from the rickety kitchen table and sat down. Her slight frown brought out the wrinkles that framed her mouth like parentheses.

"I know you're not going to want to hear this, Vincent, but I had another dream about you...and...I just had to see you." There was no humor in her laugh. "I even left work so I could come here and make sure you were OK. I'm not saying they're premonitions or anything, but..."

Vincent felt the color drain from his face. He took a seat next to her at the table. "What was the dream about?"

For a moment, she just stared at him, probably shocked

that he would want to hear more, considering one of their biggest fights had been about a dream in which, she claimed, an angel had spoken to her. But Vincent had to know if there was a connection between her recent dreams and The Dream.

Finally, she said, "Nothing really happened. It was more like images...of you...with your hands covered in blood."

Vincent's nausea had nothing to do with the hangover. He couldn't recall if any of the dead knights' blood had literally spattered onto Valenthor's hands, but in a meta-phorical sense, he felt the weight of what Valenthor had done on his conscience.

"You haven't done anything, have you? Not planning anything...?" Evangeline asked.

The enormity of what his mother was implying hit him like a punch in the gut. "Are you asking me if I'm going to kill somebody?" His laugh sounded like it came from someone else. "I'm not the son who shoots cops!"

She started to cry, and Vincent suppressed the urge to throw the table across the room. He hated himself for getting his hopes up.

Sorry, Mom, but I have my own insanity to attend to. You should have checked your religious madness at the door.

He took a few deep breaths.

"I'm sorry. I shouldn't have brought that up. It's a shame what happened to Daniel, but I'm not like him, Mom. I'm not in any trouble."

Not any trouble that you would understand.

She wiped her eyes with the knitted gloves. "I know you two boys are very different. But you are alike too. I believed Danny when he told me that everything was OK because that's what I wanted to hear."

Vincent opened his mouth to protest, but Evangeline pressed on.

"I know. You warned me he was up to something, and deep down I think I knew he was making his money illegally." She reached for his hand. "Can't you see I don't want to make the same mistake twice? I was blind before, and it nearly cost Danny his life."

It did *cost him his life! When will you see that Daniel is gone for good?*

"If God is giving me a second chance—"

Vincent pulled his hand away. "I am not a drug dealer. And I'm not going to kill anybody. I know my life has been in the dumps lately, but I'm doing the best I can."

He forced his eyes to meet hers.

After a couple of seconds, she smiled slightly. "Well, please let me how I can help. I know you don't like it when I butt in, but I could talk to Bella—"

Vincent held up a hand. "Bella doesn't want to be married to me anymore. Neither of us should have to beg her to take me back. Anyway, I'm trying to look forward now, not back."

Evangeline's smile was even sadder this time. "But we can't forget the past, Vincent. And as much as we might like to free ourselves from painful memories, we can only endure our hardships with God's help."

Vincent blinked away the stinging in his eyes. He knew she kept photos of Clementine on the walls of her apartment.

She still considers herself a grandma, even if I've stopped thinking of myself as a dad. She visits her grave too...probably right after her trips to see Daniel at the hospital. Mom doesn't give up on people. Even though there's zero chance Bella and I will get back together, she believes we could have a happily-ever-after.

Does that mean her faith is just another form of denial?

Evangeline stood up. "I should probably go. Maybe you could come over for supper one of these nights. We can order Chinese and play cribbage."

"Yeah, good idea." Even as he said it, he knew it wouldn't happen. He had moved out of her apartment following a fight about whether Daniel should be kept on life support, but the truth was Vincent had been looking for an excuse to leave ever since he had gotten there. There were too many memories haunting the place.

Maybe the same thing happened with Bella too. Maybe I wanted her to kick me out so we wouldn't have to remind each other of what we once had.

Vincent walked his mother to the door, said goodbye, and locked it behind her. He stood there for a couple of minutes, looking down at his hands and thinking about his mother's dream.

He thought of the Master's warning about Locke and betrayal, and he smirked.

Funny how it never occurred to Mom that the blood on my hands might be my own.

Chapter 12

Leah thought she heard something over the hiss of the blow dryer. She clicked the switch to off and listened to what turned out to be her phone. The ring tone, an electronic interpretation of Meredith Brook's "Bitch," identified the caller as Sister Number Two.

Still clutching a hairbrush, she sprinted from the bathroom, nearly tripping over the viola case, which *someone* had left propped up in the hallway. She stumbled into her bedroom and flipped open the phone, intercepting the call a split second before it went to voicemail.

"Hello?"

"Are we screening our calls now?" The voice on the other end sounded a lot like Leah's—as well as the other two Chedid sisters'—but the attitude was all Zaina's.

"No," Leah replied indignantly. "You just have the knack of calling at the worst possible times."

Zaina's laugh was a low hum that came in three staccato bursts. "So you finally found a new boyfriend? I'll call back in a couple of minutes."

"Har, har." Leah awkwardly cradled the cell between her shoulder and ear. She used a combination of brush and fingers to tame her dark hair. "Actually, I'm running late for a lunch thing."

"With a guy?"

Leah sighed. "Aren't you a little old to be thinking about sex all of the time?"

"Not too old, just too *married*," Zaina said without missing a beat. "That's why I'm forced to live vicariously through my little sister's wanton escapades."

Leah reached for her perfume but then thought better of it. "You must be talking about Bekah because I've got nothing to report on that front. I'm meeting an old friend...actually, he's a friend of a former friend."

"But he *is* a *he*."

"*He* is research," Leah insisted.

"Cute research?"

"Is this why you've been trying to get a hold of me, Mrs. I-Never-Leave-a Message...to harass me? Because if that's the case, I really will start screening my calls."

Leah heard what sounded like a car horn, followed by a stream of curses that would have put a sailor to shame. "Goddamn buses think they own the road!"

"I hope my nephew isn't in the car with you, hearing you swear up a storm." Leah opened the closet door and sifted through the mountain of footwear.

"I'm calling," Zaina said, "because Adina wants to throw a surprise party for Mom and Dad's anniversary. November third...two weeks from today. Can you make it?"

One shoe on, one shoe off, Leah hopped over to a calendar hanging on the wall. "Yeah, I'll be there. Just send me the details, OK? I really have to let you go now. I'm running late."

"Fine, fine," Zaina said. "Enjoy your date."

"Bite me."

Leah hurried over to the table in the corner, where Vincent greeted her with a clumsy standing gesture.

"Sorry, sorry!" she said breathlessly. "Believe it or not,

I'm late for lunch because I overslept. Then my sister called just as I was walking out the door." She sat down in a chair across from him. The tang of curry tickled her nose. "I hope you weren't waiting long."

Vincent sat back and crossed his arms. Those dark bangs, which had framed red-rimmed eyes yesterday, now were combed to one side. His flannel shirt was only a little wrinkled.

"Don't worry about it. I live a couple blocks away. It took me all of five minutes to get here. Anyway, you're the one doing me a favor by coming here."

Leah smiled and reached for a menu. When he had suggested meeting at an ethnic restaurant, she had wondered if it was a courtesy of some kind. It wouldn't have been the first time someone mistook her for being Indian, even though her skin was olive, not brown.

Of course, there wasn't a plethora of Lebanese restaurants in Milwaukee…

"So…you live on Farwell?" she asked as she scanned the list of entrees.

"No, I'm right off Brady Street on Arlington. In an apartment. I've had the buffet here before. It's pretty good."

She set the menu on the table. "The buffet it is, then."

She wanted to ask if he lived alone. Or had he and Bella separated because Vincent found someone new?

He said he was expecting divorce papers soon. I wonder what he did to deserve them.

A Middle-Eastern waitress came to take their order and then directed them toward the steaming smorgasbord. Leah didn't have to be told twice. She spooned generous portions of chicken pakora, lamb curry, and poori onto the warm plate. She had slept through breakfast, but her appetite was wide awake now, thanks to the blend of exotic aromas wafting up from the buffet table.

It's not a date, so why bother with the whole salad-and-water routine?

When they got back to the table, the conversation centered on the food. After a stretch of silence, it became clear to her that Vincent wasn't going to delve into his problems unprompted.

"How did you sleep last night?" she asked, glancing up from her nearly empty plate.

He took a drink of soda. "Pretty good, considering."

"And your dreams?" she asked.

"Normal...if there's such a thing as a normal dream." He continued eating.

This was a mistake.

After several more seconds, Vincent cleared his throat. "I'm sorry. This isn't easy for me. I probably *should* see a shrink, like you said, but it didn't do any good when Bella and I...not to mention I don't have a job, let alone health insurance, to pay for it."

"Forget about psychiatrists, Vincent. Just tell me when you first started having trouble sleeping."

He stopped eating and fixed her with a stare sharp enough to cut overcooked kabob. She chewed slowly, refusing to look away from the unnerving intensity of his eyes.

"I suppose it really started eight years ago, right after my daughter drowned in the bathtub. She was three."

Leah stopped chewing.

"I kept having the same dream over and over, finding her in the bathtub... I was supposed to be watching her." His eyes grew shiny with unspent tears. "I'd given her a bath that morning, but I didn't drain the tub. Hell if I know why. I'd gotten in late the night before. Bella was grocery shopping at the time...don't know why she couldn't have waited until later, why she couldn't have let me sleep longer. I was driving truck back then. Seems like ages ago…"

Leah forced the flavorless wad of food down her throat. Before she could interject, Vincent continued.

"I'd just gotten back from a job…a long drive…the night before. I'm not even sure what time she woke me up. I'm sure it wasn't as early as it seemed, but I was obviously exhausted because I dozed off after Clementine's bath. She must've been reaching for Webster, her rubber ducky. Clementine loved ducks."

He stopped abruptly and rubbed a sleeve across his eyes.

"Oh, Vincent." She tried to blink away the blurriness but failed.

Looking down at his half-eaten lunch, Vincent said, "I've heard that a lot of couples who lose a child don't make it. Bella and I were OK before the accident, I guess, but after Clemmy died…"

"Vincent, I am so sorry." Leah set her fork down, her appetite a distant memory. "So then the dreams started?"

He nodded. "Almost every night in the beginning. I'd wake up drenched in sweat, shaking. And Bella would wake up. I could tell that, after a while, she really resented that. Like I was doing it on purpose. Or maybe she chalked it up to a guilty conscience. She never said so, but I know she blamed me. Which is fine, since I blame me too."

Vincent wasn't the only one wrestling with guilt. Leah had come to this meeting in hopes of studying—and capitalizing on—the poor man's condition. Her one-sided competition with Aldrich suddenly seemed very petty, compared to Vincent and Bella's suffering.

I also came here to see if I could help him.

"Grief can have strange effects on the brain," she said

at last. "At what point did you start feeling yourself getting 'pulled' into the dream?"

He poked at a pile of rice. "I don't get pulled into *that* dream. Two or maybe three weeks ago, I stopped reliving that terrible day. Come to think of it, it was the day after my last nightmare about Clementine that I first found myself in the new dream...the recurring story-dream that cost me my job...and my sobriety."

Vincent jerked, and Leah thought it was a reaction the mention of his drinking, until he said, "Sorry...my phone is on vibe." He pulled a cell out of his pocket, pressed a button, and said, "Hello?"

His eyes widened, and Leah, already tensed, held her breath.

After a few seconds, he said, "Yes, I'm here. I just wasn't expecting to hear from you." His eyes met Leah's. "So, how have you been, Bella?"

Leah had gone on dates with some creeps over the years, but as far as she knew, she had never been the other woman. It didn't matter that she wasn't interested in Vincent in that way. Bella didn't know that.

Please don't mention me, Vincent.

"Uh-huh," Vincent said.

Leah looked around, wishing she could swap places with anybody else in the restaurant. She spotted a statue of the elephantine god Ganesha across the room.

I'll give you a peanut if you help me out here.

"I appreciate the call, but I'll tell you what I told my mother yesterday. I'm not in any trouble. I'm sorry she got you worked up too, but—"

Leah assumed Bella had cut him off, but just as she looked back across the table, the phone dropped from his hand, and his eyes rolled back in his head. He tumbled out of his chair and onto the floor.

"Vincent? Oh, God…"

Instantly, she was kneeling beside him, hunting for a pulse. She let out a relieved sigh when she found it. The rising and falling of his chest were slow but even. His eyes were closed. No signs of a seizure. By all appearances, he was asleep.

Could it be as simple as narcolepsy after all?

A buzzing noise drew her attention to the phone, which had landed under the table. She picked it up and held it to her ear.

"—you still there, Vincent? Hello? Hello?"

It didn't sound like the Bella Stark of her Shorewood High days, but the phone's tin-can effect might have had something to do with that, not to mention the blatant concern in Bella's voice.

An early memory of her mother literally catching her elbow-deep in the cookie jar came unbidden to Leah's mind. She nearly hung up, but at the last second she realized how cruel that would be. Bella deserved an explanation.

Leah said, "Um…hello…sorry, but something's come up. Vincent will have to call you back."

Before her onetime best friend could fire off a question, Leah ended the call.

So much for an explanation…

For the first time, she noticed the waitress and a man dressed in white standing over her. She dropped Vincent's phone into her pocket.

"What has happened?" the man asked, his bushy eyebrows forming a dark V.

"Narcolepsy," she said. "He'll be all right."

Neither of the employees budged. Was that skepticism she saw in the look they exchanged?

Well, it's not food poisoning, if that's what you're

worried about.

The other people in the restaurant stared and muttered. Leah's cheeks reached a temperature usually reserved for her third glass of wine. She shook Vincent's shoulder gently and then a little harder, repeating his name again and again. She thought she heard him moan, but otherwise, he didn't stir.

I should call an ambulance.

Instead, she took some money from her purse and handed it to the waitress, who, finally snapping out of her trance, took it. To the bearded man, she said, "I'm a doctor. Can you help me get him out to my car?"

The man's frown said no, but he must have decided that removing unconscious customers from the dining room was better for business than standing around scowling. He gave a curt nod and pulled Vincent up with a grunt. Leah ducked a shoulder under Vincent's other arm, and the two of them half carried, half dragged Vincent out of the restaurant, adopting a method that Leah could think of only as *Weekend at Bernie's* style.

Once she was sitting behind the wheel of her Camry, she took a couple of slow breaths. In the passenger's seat, Vincent sat with his head resting against the window, his breath fogging the glass. He wasn't snoring per se, but his breathing had the audibility of someone in a deep sleep. She reached over to fasten his seatbelt and put her own on.

The voice of reason, which sounded suspiciously like her father, urged her to drive straightaway to St. Mary's Hospital. The car started with a satisfied hum. After merging into the one-way traffic, she took advantage of the first side street to do a one-eighty, heading north.

Do the right thing, Leah.

She almost screamed when Vincent turned suddenly in his seat. She glanced over and saw a grimace of pain on his face. God only knew what nightmare his brain was brewing up.

If it's narcolepsy, there's no need to take him to the hospital, especially if he doesn't have insurance.

A familiar song wafted up from inside her purse. Eyes on the road, she fumbled about the depths of the bag until her fingertips grazed the glossy finish of her phone.

"Zaina," she said into the receiver.

"Just thought I'd call in case you needed an out for your not-date," her sister replied. "You can tell what's-his-name that Jordan fell down a well or something."

"Cute."

"Well, how *are* things going? You can talk in code if he's sitting right there," Zaina said.

No need for that!

"Um," Leah mumbled. For a moment, St. Mary's Hospital could be seen outside the passenger-side window. Then it was gone. Half-digested Indian food performed a little dance in her stomach. "I'll tell you all about it later."

Zaina laughed suggestively. "Good luck, girl. And if you take him home, be safe!"

Chapter 13

Sunlight on his face, birdsong in his ears, Valenthor fought against a wave of disorientation. He opened his eyes and stared futilely at a patch of cerulean sky ringed by tall treetops. In an attempt to shrug off sleep's lingering hold, he rolled onto his side.

His dew-soaked clothes and the morning chill clung to his body. He shivered, then gasped, as he sat up. Memories of the elf's magic, their flight from captivity, and the ensuing battle resurfaced with the sudden sting in his side.

Gritting his teeth, he pulled up his tunic and gently prodded the crusty red line that crossed three ribs. To his surprise, the pain was a mere echo of the previous night's misery. The wound—caused by Sir Angus's sword, he recalled—had closed hours ago. The bright red blood staining his fingers had faded to a dull brown overnight.

"You sleep like the dead," said a muffled voice.

Valenthor flinched and winced again when the sudden movement pulled at the wound. Locke sat straight-backed against a looming oak several feet away. It was no wonder Valenthor hadn't noticed him before. Locke's brown cloak appeared to be an extension of the rough bark; his mask's eyes, a pair of knotholes.

"I was dreaming," Valenthor said as soon as the idea occurred to him. He thought for a moment, but the details of the dream evaporated. All except for one. "I think I was talking with my wife."

"Your wife is dead," Locke stated.

"What difference does it make?" Valenthor demanded, bracing himself against a fresh pain in his chest. "It was but a dream."

Locke rose and walked over to him. He had the speed and grace of youth, but at the same time, his movements seemed carefully measured, belying a degree of discipline that came only with experience.

Valenthor reminded himself that the man defeated three armed knights with naught but a quarterstaff.

Looking down at him, Locke said, "The gods have been known to share their wisdom through dreams. Might you recall what your wife said?"

Although annoyed by the request—if the gods were real, he wanted nothing to do with them and their cruel ways—Valenthor tried to return to the scene in his mind. "I think…I think she was concerned for me. I assured her that I was safe and well."

The same unsettling sound from yesterday reverberated against Locke's mask. Valenthor decided it was surely a laugh.

"Then you lied to her," Locke said. "The enemy passed quite near our camp at the break of dawn. Verily, our peril grows greater whilst we remain here."

"You believe Sir Angus still searches for us?"

Locke's nod was a slight dip of the mask. "That one is a slave of duty. Moreover, he seeks vengeance. Such men would sooner be separated from their manhood than their honor. However, the defenders of the realm are a lesser concern by far. They follow us by finding the natural signs of our passing, but the Jötunn possess other methods for tracking us."

"The Jötunn?"

"Aye, it was giants, not men, who nearly discovered

us," Locke said. "If the gods smile upon us, our foes will find each other first...and the fewer from either side to survive that confrontation, the better!"

Valenthor considered Locke's words, confusion furrowing a brow slick with sweat in spite of the late autumn air. "What do the giants want with us?"

"'Twas not happenstance the Jötunn were so near a human settlement at the time of your escape. Mayhap they had been following the elf whilst she ventured westward. Else, an agent amongst the townsfolk informed them of her presence, and they hastened to her."

Valenthor glanced where the elf lay curled up on the ground, wrapped in the ill-fitting cloak. She had asked him to save her people from the forces of darkness—the Jötunn?

"Did she wake while I slept?" he asked Locke.

"No. Whatever incantation she performed to free you from the prison has taken a toll on her body and mind. I pray she stirs before the morrow. We cannot afford for her to hinder our pace when we set out once more."

Valenthor spun around to face Locke. "Surely remaining here another day would be folly! We were lucky the giants missed us the first time. If they should return..."

Locke scoffed. "Nay, Valenthor, luck had nothing to do with it. Forsooth, the Fay are not the only ones with knowledge of the gods' mysteries."

Valenthor eyed the man warily. "You are a sorcerer?"

Scoff. "The she-elf demonstrated a mastery over the natural elements of this world. My talents are more subtle, a style more suited to stealth and secrecy."

"Pray tell, what style is that?" Valenthor asked.

"Deception."

"If he is not a spy, he has his own agenda..."

One of Locke's hands shot out, and Valenthor flinched.

Embarrassed, he accepted the proffered hand and braced against the pain in his side as Locke pulled him to his feet. From his new vantage, Valenthor noticed a complex symbol carved into the trunk of the tree Locke had been leaning against.

"The enchantment will protect us for a while longer," Locke said. "During that time, you will regain your strength. I will obtain food, but you would do well to clean your wound. A small stream lies beyond that bend."

Valenthor nodded. He found it difficult to look into the cavernous holes of Locke's mask. Had the man been horribly scarred during a battle? Had he suffered a deformity since birth?

His eyes dropped from the smooth wood of the mask down to a pendant that served as a clasp for the cloak. The onyx disk was engraved with the silhouette of a wolf's head encircled by a serpent eating its own tail, a discomforting image to be sure.

Valenthor turned away from his peculiar companion. "You are certain the Jötunn are pursuing the elf?"

"The giants hate all of the gods' creations, but none more so than the elves," Locke said. "Rarely do the Jötunn venture this far east. If they plan to lay siege to the lands of the Fay, then it is another sign the final prophecy shall soon be realized."

The wind howled through the trees. Valenthor shivered. "Final prophecy?"

Scoff. "I have heard tell how the great Valenthor turned his back on the gods after they took his wife and daughter from him, but even those without faith know of the Last War...when men, elves, giants, and the gods themselves will meet on the battlefield one final time."

"She...the elf...believes I am the Chosen One from a prophecy," Valenthor said. "Do you?"

He half expected to hear that raspy laugh again, but when Locke spoke, his tone was unnervingly sincere. "If I did not, you would be dead."

Locke's words echoed in Vincent's thoughts as he lay prostrate on a couch he didn't recognize, staring up at a ceiling he'd never seen before.

He sat up slowly, expecting a flash of pain in his side. It didn't come. Likewise, the moisture on his chin wasn't dew.

Of course not! I'm not Valenthor. I've never been in a real fight, let alone killed anyone. Valenthor, the elf, that creepy Locke guy...they're all an invention of my subconscious, whatever that *says about me.*

Alone, confused, Vincent took in the unfamiliar living room. He had woken up in some unusual places before he quit drinking, but usually the morning-after experience always included a splitting headache and nausea. He felt fine, except for his inability to remember where he had been before waking up as Valenthor with Locke and the elf in the clearing.

Self-consciously, he flipped the pillow drool-side-down and got up to take a look around. One thing was clear from the start. Whoever's place it was didn't hurt for money. All of the furniture looked new, and the flat-screen TV was about three-times the size of Jerry's. The view outside the windows revealed he was on the second floor of a large apartment building. He didn't recognize any of the cars in the parking lot or the adjacent houses.

Across the room, framed photographs hung on the wall. He was halfway to them when he crossed paths with a brown-and-black cat. The two of them stopped in their tracks, observing each other for several seconds, until

Vincent conceded defeat in the staring contest and stepped around the animal.

The first picture was a portrait of a middle-aged couple in fancy clothes. The second one showed four women squeezed onto a couch, wearing what appeared to be genuine smiles. Vincent was just thinking of how much they all looked alike and that they could be sisters when he recognized the one on the end as Leah Chedid.

Their conversation at the Indian restaurant and then Bella's phone call came back to him in a rush.

"Hello?" he called. "Leah?"

No answer. Feeling very much like an intruder—the ball of fluff was still eyeballing him—Vincent made his way around the apartment. The more ground he covered, the more anxious he felt. After checking the kitchen, a bedroom, and what turned out to be a closet, he came upon another door, one that was open slightly.

"Hello?" he said again, pushing the door timidly. "Is anybody…oh!"

Vincent tensed. Inside, someone stood in front of a bathroom sink. "Sorry. Didn't mean to barge in."

Leah didn't respond. She grabbed a handful of hair, pulled it away from her head, and with her other hand, cut a crooked line through the long black strands with a scissors. The strange act, combined with her continued silence, made his skin crawl.

"Leah?" He almost whispered her name.

She combed her fingers through the hair on the back of her head, formed a fist near the ends, and pulled so hard that her head jerked back. Her other arm had to bend at an awkward angle in order to bring the scissors back to the taught fibers. Vincent flinched as the blades clipped the hair at a severe angle.

"Hey, what are you doing?"

As he hurried to the sink, he caught her reflection in the mirror. The first thing he noticed was the makeup smeared all over her face. The second was that, even as she reached for more hair, only the whites of her eyes could be seen beneath the half-closed lids.

What the hell is going on?

When she brought the scissors up for another pass, Vincent seized her by the wrist. She made a half-moaning, half-whining noise and pulled away from him. Her unrestricted hand yanked at her hair even harder.

"Stop that!" He took her other hand too, trying to get her to release the clump of hair and the scissors at the same time. She was stronger than he expected.

"…won't know me like this…" she slurred.

"Leah, wake *up!*"

The hand that had been holding her hair went limp in his hand. At the same time, she pushed forward with the scissors. Vincent swore and quickly withdrew his hand as the blades whirred past him. Leah's other hand popped back up again. The scissors went to cut the hair that wasn't there and met her fingers instead.

She squealed but didn't drop the scissors until he slapped it out of her hand. Her knees gave out, and he managed to slip an arm around her, slowing, if not stopping, her fall to the floor.

Leah started to fight him, swiping blindly at him. Vincent called her name over and over, shaking her as best he could while avoiding her attacks. When her bloody palm struck him in the chin, Vincent slapped her back.

Her eyes opened, and for a moment she didn't move.

"Leah, you were…sleeping, I think. You cut yourself."

She regarded him groggily. Then the pain in her hand must have kicked in. She shot upright, gaped wide-eyed at the trail of red running down her arm, and gasped.

Vincent stayed sitting on the floor. As Leah rinsed hair and blood from her hand, he tried to make sense of what had just happened. He knew he was awake, but somehow the struggle seemed more like a dream than anything that had happened to Valenthor.

Leah screamed.

His body reacted to the startling sound by jumpstarting his heart and pumping his limbs full of adrenaline. But all his weary mind could conjure up was *now what?*

Leah gazed, horrified, into the mirror. The fingers of her uninjured hand trembled as they picked through the uneven strands of hair. Then she bowed her head and closed her raccoon-like eyes.

Vincent, paradoxically tense and numb, watched inky tears flow down her cheeks.

Chapter 14

No matter what Leah did to try to hide them, the uneven strands of hair spilled out from under the bright red Badgers cap. The sight of her disheveled, puffy-eyed reflection in the mirror nearly convinced her to attempt to salvage the horrible haircut right then and there.

But she had already scrubbed the makeup mess off of her face and rinsed the hair off of her neck. Further grooming would have to wait because, as much as she wanted to, she couldn't forget there was a guy in the next room waiting for her.

Waiting for some answers.

She turned away from the imposter in the mirror, steeled herself with a deep breath, and left the sanctuary of her bedroom. She found Vincent slouched in Emira's recliner. He offered her an uneasy smile. Then she saw his gaze sweep over her hat—a long-forgotten souvenir of a college fling—and nearly lost it all over again.

"It's not that bad," Vincent said. "Short hair is in these days."

Leah doubted the veracity of the statements. Even if every supermodel on the planet was sporting pixie cuts, which they weren't, *she* wouldn't have jumped on that bandwagon. She had flirted with short hair a few years ago and hated how the new 'do instantly transformed her round features into a fat face.

It'll grow back, girl. Pull yourself together.

"I don't think your cat likes me very much," Vincent said.

From a far corner of the room, Emira glared at him. Leah smiled in spite of herself. "That's because you're in her chair."

"She should have said something then."

She felt the smile fade from her lips. "I appreciate you trying to cheer me up, but I owe you an explanation."

"Look," he began, "I'm the one who came to you for help. As long as you didn't drug my food so you could bring me back to your place and kill me, I'm willing to forget about what just happened...unless you *want* to talk about it."

Her thoughts jumped back eons to the scene at the Indian restaurant. "One moment, you were talking to...talking on your phone, and the next, you were on the floor, out cold. I probably should have taken you to the hospital, but all the evidence indicated you were only asleep. I must have dozed off in that chair while waiting for you to wake up..."

She took a big breath.

"Which wouldn't have been a problem, except that I suffer from an extreme form of rapid eye movement sleep behavior disorder." He stared blankly, so she continued. "When most people sleep, their brains paralyze the majority of the muscles in the body. It prevents them from acting out their dreams. However, a very small percentage of the population lacks this motor inhibition, which can lead to twitching or sleep walking—"

"Or sleep grooming," Vincent provided. When she didn't laugh, he added, "Sorry. So is that why you became a sleep doctor? Because you have this...disorder?"

She nodded. "RBD is most commonly diagnosed in men in their late fifties or early sixties. I've shown symptoms since I was seventeen, and I suffered from insomnia long before that. Naturally, I wanted to know more about what was causing my brain to malfunction. I started researching RBD and other parasomnias in high school. I guess I never stopped."

"There's no cure?" Vincent asked.

Leah sighed. "In most cases, RBD can be treated by various medications, but nothing seems to work for me, at least not in the long run. So I take precautions. For some reason, people with RBD tend to act out negative dreams, which is why I use restraints that prevent me from leaving my bed and injuring myself."

"Then it's my fault that you nearly cut off your hand with a scissors," Vincent said, frowning. "If I hadn't been here, you wouldn't have fallen asleep in the living room."

Leah glanced down at her hand, where the rhythmic throbbing of her pulse surged beneath a bandage. The wound burned like a son of a bitch. "No, Vincent, it was my own damn fault. I've been careless lately. I got this bruise on my cheek because I didn't use the restraints. In fact, if you hadn't been here, things could have gotten much worse."

"Wouldn't the pain have woken you up?" he asked.

She shrugged. "Possibly. But like I said, my RBD skews toward the extreme. Sometimes I don't know anything happened until I wake up and find a broken window or get strange looks from all of my neighbors because I was screaming in my sleep all night."

Judging from the long silence that followed, not to mention the uncertain expression on his face, Vincent was at a loss for words.

He's probably wondering why he didn't make a run for it when I was cleaning up in the bathroom. Now he's trying to devise a tactful way to escape the crazy woman's

125

apartment.

Finally, he sat up straight in the recliner, looked her in the eye, and said, "That was a valiant effort, Dr. Chedid, but as strange as your disorder sounds, whatever is wrong with me takes the cake. At least *you're* not passing out in restaurants so your subconscious can play Dungeons & Dragons."

As he described The Dream, Leah forgot about her own embarrassment and might have forgotten about the accidental makeover entirely were it not for the nagging pain in her hand. She didn't dare interrupt him with questions. Somewhere inside Vincent, the cork had been popped, and all of the thoughts that had been bottled up flowed freely. He talked very quickly, and she did her best to digest the bizarre tale.

At last, he said, "It turns out Locke also thinks I...*Valenthor*...is the Chosen One. I'm not sure what happened next because then I woke up here in your apartment."

Several seconds slipped by in silence. Leah opened her mouth to say something—she didn't know what—but Vincent added, "The weird thing is that every time I go back there, I'm more and more Valenthor. In the beginning, I knew I was really Vincent Cruz and that I didn't belong in that world. Now it's like I don't have any of my real memories in the dream."

"If you aren't aware it's a dream, it's not a lucid dream anymore," Leah said.

"OK. Sure. But they still feel pretty damn real." He sighed. "So...what do you make of it? Have you ever heard of anything like this?"

Leah hadn't yet answered the first question to herself, but she had no difficulty with the second one.

"Never." She paused, choosing her words carefully.

"The parallels between your life and Valenthor's can't be coincidental. There might to be some logical explanations as to why certain themes have found their way into your dreams."

"Like what?"

"Well, both you and Valenthor have a daughter. And back at the restaurant, you said you used to have recurring dreams about her...about your girl—"

"Clementine."

"—about Clementine. You're obviously dealing with a lot of grief, Vincent. You also said your marriage is in trouble. In The Dream, that manifests itself as Valenthor's wife being dead. And you just lost your job. It must feel like the world is crashing down around you, but when you sleep, you become Valenthor, the Chosen One, destined to save the world."

Vincent flashed a cynical smile. "So you're saying because I'm a loser in real life, I have to play the part of hero in my dreams?"

Leah shook her head helplessly. "I don't know. But even Valenthor isn't a hero yet. That knight, Sir Angus, made it sound like Valenthor has fallen from grace, turning to the bottle for comfort." She thought she saw him wince. "But Valenthor has been given a chance to redeem himself. Maybe it means your subconscious is looking for a way to get *your* life back in order."

"You make it sound so simple," Vincent muttered. "But even if I'm losing my mind because of grief, that doesn't explain why I'm falling asleep in the middle of the day."

"The narcoleptic effect is puzzling," she conceded, "but the brain has been known to shut down in times of extreme stress. You *were* talking to Bella when you passed out at the restaurant."

Vincent picked at something on his sleeve. "It can't *just*

be stress. There has to be something else going on."

"Such as?" she asked. "You don't think there's really a Valenthor somewhere out there, do you?"

"Of course not! But, Jesus, my mind can't be that fragile. I can't be *that* pathetic."

Leah noticed her fists were clenched. She flattened her palms on her knees. "Were you hoping I would come up with some complicated mental illness? I told you before I'm not a psychologist. If you're in the early stages of multiple personality disorder...or whatever they're calling it these days...I couldn't diagnose it."

"But you do think I'm going nuts."

She crossed her arms and took a deep breath. "What do you want me to say, Vincent? What exactly do you expect from me?"

"I want you to *cure* me! This has to stop!" He shot to his feet. "It's great that Mr. Medieval Warrior has a shot at saving the day, but I can't fix my own life as long as I have to deal with this damn dream."

Maybe Valenthor needs to complete his quest in order for the dream to end and for you to come to terms with what has happened in your life.

OK, that does *sound oversimplified.*

"I don't think you're crazy," she said quietly, gesturing for him to sit down again. "I'm just processing what you told me. I still think that a psychotherapist might be better equipped to help you, but I'm willing to take a stab at it."

Vincent's deep blue eyes searched her face for a moment. A corner of his mouth lifted, then, as he said, "Thanks...but did you have to use the word 'stab'?"

The tension slipped from the room, and Leah smiled too. "We should start with a sleep lab study. We're generally pretty busy, so it might take some finagling to fit you into the schedule."

And then there's the billing...

"Just let me know when," he said. "I'm unemployed. I've got nothing but time."

"I'll call you this week," she said. "In the meantime, stay away from alcohol, nicotine, caffeine...anything that might affect your body chemistry. And considering you can fall asleep anywhere at any time, you might want to stick close to home."

"Great. I'll be able to catch up on my soaps." He stood up slowly and put on his coat. "Here's to hoping for a good week...for both of us."

She followed him across the rooms, stopping beside the small table that was home to her keys and unopened mail. "Let me give you a ride home."

"No," he said quickly. "No, thanks, I mean. I've inconvenienced you enough. Public transportation will do just fine."

After an uncomfortable exchange of goodbyes, Leah locked the door and went back to the couch. Emira had already reclaimed her chair. She stared accusingly at Leah.

"Don't look at me like that."

Emira's copper-colored eyes didn't waver.

"He's just an old friend...of sorts. Anyway, he's not encroaching on your territory."

The cat didn't look convinced.

"And who knows? There might be a way I can help him and my career at the same time."

Leah inspected the gauze wrapped tightly around her hand. A faint red stain had blossomed in the center of her palm.

God knows I can't seem to help myself.

*　　*　　*

Vincent scooted over as far as he could in his seat, pressing up against the cold glass of the window. The bus was only about half full, so he supposed he should take it as a compliment that the newest passenger—an overweight white guy with a scraggly gray/black beard—chose him as a seatmate.

What was that Danny used to say about the weirdos on the bus?

When they were kids, he and Daniel had depended on the Milwaukee County Transit System to take them anywhere they couldn't walk, since their mother never owned a car. A diligent parent might have been leery of letting her young sons travel halfway across the city on their own, but no one had ever accused Evangeline of being overprotective.

As older brother, Vincent had been responsible for mapping out the route and, as their mother never failed to remind him, keeping an eye on his little brother. There were times when Vincent, a mere two years older than Daniel, wondered who was going to keep an eye on *him*.

It was Daniel who had made a game out of finding the creepiest person on the bus. Laughing at the junkies and shifty-eyed strangers made them all seem less scary. Vincent suspected the jokes were made for the benefit of his big brother, not himself, because Daniel Joseph Pierce had been born without fear. Or so it seemed.

Vincent wondered if the little wisecracker had worn a smile the day he shot that cop and took a bullet for his trouble.

"There's always one crazy person on the bus." That's what he used to say. Well, Danny boy, I might just take the cake this time.

He replayed his conversation with Leah in his mind. Was it possible that losing Clementine had knocked a screw loose? What was the alternative? He couldn't really be transforming into a medieval warrior in some other dimension.

As the city swept past his window, Vincent tried to focus on something else—Leah's strange sleep disorder, for starters—but his thoughts always returned to her comment about minds taking extreme measures when coping with stress.

What's the real reason I think Leah is wrong? Why couldn't losing Clemmy have had such a devastating impact on me? Is it because it took eight years for me to snap or because mediocre dads don't have the right to have a breakdown when they lose a kid?

Maybe I'm afraid I'm getting exactly what I deserve.

Vincent sniffed and wiped a sleeve across his nose, earning him an unappreciative look from the fat man next to him. Vincent's stop was several blocks away. He pulled the cord anyway.

Chapter 15

The sight of DJ sitting in the back of the bus, smiling broadly, stopped Milton mid-step. He considered fleeing, but then he involuntarily pitched forward as the bus renewed its tireless tour of the city.

I wanted a confrontation. Looks like I'll get it.

Heart pounding, his snow-crusted shoes sliding across the smooth floor of the aisle, he slowly made his way to the only other passenger on the bus. He ignored DJ's wordless invitation to take the seat across from him.

"Why are you following me?" Milton demanded. He glared down at the young man, but DJ's crooked smile never faltered.

"Me follow you? That's rich." DJ leaned in and whispered, "In case you didn't notice, I was here first. Why are *you* following *me*?"

Milton shook his head. He had nearly forgotten how infuriating DJ could be. "It can't be a coincidence. I don't know how you got ahead of me—"

"Ahead of you?" DJ scoffed. "This is the same route I always ride. The last time we met was two stops up from where we are now. You're going in circles, man!"

Milton's shoulders slumped, and when the bus made a fast right turn, he didn't fight the inertia, falling into the vacant seat beside DJ with a thud.

"That's impossible," he whispered.

"Maybe you should buy a map," DJ said. "Or you could

tell me where you're trying to go. I know this city like the back of my hand."

To emphasize his point, DJ raised his left hand. The baleful stare of the snake tattoo met Milton's own red-rimmed eyes.

"Where am I going? I'm running away from you and your friends!" Milton shouted, unable to look away from the peculiar tattoo. Not a viper or a cobra. The serpent's broad face and thick body looked more like a prehistoric creature than the sleek, sinuous species typically chosen for emblems of rebellion.

DJ sat up a little straighter. "Shows what you know, old man. I don't have any friends anymore, just family."

"But…but the last time I saw you, you threatened me," Milton argued.

DJ scratched the red stubble on his chin. "Did I? Oh, you mean 'You can't run forever'? I was just pointing out a fact. And even if you could run forever, why would you want to?"

Milton didn't know what to say. At the time, he had been so convinced DJ was one of his enemies. Maybe he was harmless after all.

"But wait," he said, suddenly remembering more of their prior conversation. Was it a coincidence that his thoughts seemed clearer when he was with DJ? "You said something about the end of the world…"

DJ rolled his eyes. "Lucky guess?" Milton's body language must have conveyed his skepticism because DJ added, "I'd figured you for a schizophrenic. Delusions of persecution…everyone is out to get you…the government is evil, so you have to expose the sinister plot. Blah blah blah."

"I'm not crazy," Milton said.

"Maybe you are, and maybe you aren't. I'd be happy to

make a diagnosis. Why don't you tell me how you got into this mess in the first place?" DJ pulled his sweatshirt's hood up over his messy hair and slid closer to the aisle. "Who is really chasing you and why?"

Milton searched DJ's face for signs of treachery, but if there was anything sinister lurking beneath the eager expression, the boy hid it well. To Milton's surprise, he truly wanted to tell the boy everything, to unburden himself from the terrible secrets—if he could only remember them.

I just need more rest…more time…

"C'mon, Milton," DJ prompted. "Don't be such a bore."

Something about that last word tugged at Milton's weary mind, but he lost the thought before it could even be born.

What do I have to lose? If DJ is one of them, he already knows the truth.

"Like I told you before, I believe the CIA is involved." Milton shivered in spite of the bus's toasty interior. "Their scientists are doing horrible things…meddling with our minds."

"How?"

"Dreams!" Milton blurted, surprising himself with the force behind the word. He closed his eyes and once more saw the balding man in a white lab coat.

"But why mess with people's dreams?" DJ asked.

Milton rubbed his eyes with the palms of his hands and stifled a yawn. "I…I'm not sure."

"Wake up, man. This is important!" DJ snapped, hastily adding, "Unless you really are delusional."

"No…no…" Milton reached for the answers, but the truth was buried somewhere deep. The snowstorm outside had nothing on the tempest raging inside his brain. "To get into people's thoughts," he said at last.

DJ jumped up. "Mind reading? Really?"

"Yes...I think...but that's not the whole of it...I just can't...can't seem to..." He yawned again.

DJ crouched down, his face inches from Milton's. "*Where* are they doing this?"

"Here."

"Here?" DJ growled in disgust. "Here is nowhere! What kind of an answer is that?"

Milton closed his eyes again. He could almost see a picture in the darkness. The laboratory. The man with gray-green eyes. The syringe. The sword.

"Odin," Milton whispered.

"What did you say? Milton? Don't you dare fall asleep!"

Milton barely heard DJ over the voice in his head—*his own* voice.

"Odin is chief god in the Norse pantheon. He is associated with wisdom, magic, prophecy—"

A different voice chimed in:

"And battle and death."

Someone grabbed Milton by the shoulder and shook him. He opened his eyes, expecting to find the man with the high forehead and lab coat. But it was only DJ. Or was it? The man crouched beside Milton resembled DJ—certainly the bright blue eyes were the same—but the intensely serious look on his face aged him by a decade or more. The man's bloodshot eyes were wide, expectant.

DJ's sweatshirt was gone, replaced by a black leather jacket. Milton glanced down, searching for some sign of the wolf. He gasped. Something dark and wet was dripping from a hole in the front of the jacket. The metallic scent of blood assailed him.

Milton scrambled away until his back was against a

window. Then he must have blinked because the wounded man was gone, and young DJ was back.

"Easy there, Milton." DJ stood in the aisle, draping a hand over the back of the seat in Milton's row and his other over the one in front of it. Standing squarely between Milton and escape. The crudely drawn wolf head was at eyelevel.

"Were…were you bleeding just now?" Milton asked.

DJ replied with a question of his own. "Who is Odin?"

Tires squealed from somewhere nearby, and Milton jumped. From the aisle, DJ turned to the rear window of the bus and quickly looked away when a bright light flooded into the bus. Milton thought they were too bright to be headlights. He turned in his seat, craning his neck to see—

"Get down!" DJ yelled, taking cover in the opposite row of seats.

Ignoring the warning, Milton peered into the painfully bright light. The vehicle behind the bus was too big to be a squad car or even the black sedans government agents always drove in the movies. It appeared to be a large van.

And it was getting closer.

Milton dove down onto the seat at the exact moment that the van's grill struck the bus. Pieces of glass poured down on him, cutting into his hands and the parts of his face he couldn't cover.

Oh God, they've found me. They've finally come for me!

The van's motor roared angrily through the glassless hole in the back of the bus. Judging by the sound and the blur of streetlights in the remaining windows, both the van and the bus were accelerating. Milton wondered why the bus driver didn't pull over.

Something tugged at Milton's leg, and he kicked out in

sudden panic.

"Ouch! Damn it, Milton. It's just me," DJ said. Half of his face was whitewashed with artificial light. "Looks like you're not crazy after all. Now move to the front of the bus. Go!"

Milton did as he was told, cringing when his movements sent glass shards clattering across the floor. He dared to glance at road behind them. The van was a little farther back, but it was picking up speed, its tires sending clumps of snow spraying in its wake.

As Milton pushed past DJ, he saw the young man remove a silver pistol from the back of his waistband. Their eyes met.

"What can I say? I have enemies too," DJ said with a shrug before firing at the approaching vehicle. Over his shoulder he cried, "Get going!"

The bus started to sway from side to side, skidding on the slick road. Milton was forced to grab onto each seat in succession to keep his balance. Another gunshot. He focused on the big broad windshield ahead, though he had no idea what he was going to do when he reached the front of the bus.

How ever did I get here? I'm a scientist, not a—

He halted halfway to his destination and repeated aloud, "*I'm* a scientist!"

The next bang was far too loud to be DJ's gun. The bus pitched sharply to the side, flinging Milton forward into a sideways, bench-like seat. He thought, for one maddening moment, that the van had fired a cannon at them, but then all he could do was hold on as the bus started to spin.

He felt the crash in every nerve of his body. Even after the bus's momentum was absorbed by whatever it had struck, everything kept swirling around and around. Milton closed his eyes, as much as to shut out the nauseating spectacle as to retreat from reality.

"Hey, wake up." DJ gave Milton a shake. "That van spun out a little farther up the road."

Milton accepted the young man's hand and was pulled to his feet. All he could manage to say was "Who?"

"That's what I'd like to know," DJ muttered, frowning. "These guys play by their own rules."

DJ half guided, half pushed Milton to the door of the bus. There was no sign of the driver. The folding door was already open. Since the front, right wheel was suspended a foot or more off the ground, he and DJ were forced to jump down.

Milton numbly took in the crash scene. The bus had struck into the side of an old business building. One of the pillars, having snapped in half, rested horizontally in a self-made trench on the top of the bus. A clock, which must have been attached to the building, now lay in the street. From where he was standing, the clock's face appeared to contain only eights.

Farther down the block, the van's driver-side door opened. A tall man stepped out.

"Time for you to start running again." DJ raised his arm, and a loud crack rent the still night.

The tall man didn't flinch. A spark on the side of the van revealed DJ's aim to be off by a good three feet.

Milton turned and ran, but after a few steps he stopped. DJ hadn't budged. "Come on, boy!"

DJ shook his head and aimed again at the slim driver, who was walking purposefully, if not swiftly, toward them. "I'll buy you some time."

Milton started to argue, but the tall man shouted the word "bore."

No, not "bore." Borr!

His thoughts started to swim, but his concentration

shattered when DJ started firing again. Bullets whizzed past the long-legged man, hitting the van and the street but not the intended target.

"Son of a bitch," DJ spat.

Suddenly, a bright light poured down from the sky, bathing the van in blue-white light. For a fraction of a second, Milton caught a glimpse of a gray, eight-legged horse painted on the side of the vehicle, but then the spotlight swept over to DJ Milton shielded his eyes. He heard the unmistakable staccato of a helicopter propeller.

Standing between him and the tall man, DJ fired at the sky until the gun was empty.

DJ turned toward Milton, smirking. "Well, it was worth a shot." He chuckled. "Get it? 'A shot'? Guess I'll catch you later, Milton."

Before Milton could reply, DJ charged toward the tall man, who remained in shadow despite the spotlight overhead.

Milton hesitated. "DJ!"

He squinted up at the aircraft, a menacing mass of black against the white sky. The vehicle grew larger as the machine descended. Artificial wind sent frenzied snowflakes flying in all directions. Despite the whir of the helicopter's blades and the wind screaming in his ears, he heard DJ shout, "My, you're a tall drink of water."

DJ, you fool!

Then the searchlight landed on Milton, and he fled.

Running as fast as he could in the ankle-deep snow, Milton suddenly remembered the vision of the man in the bloody jacket who momentarily had replaced DJ on the bus. Had it been a premonition or simply a hallucination manufactured by his sleep-deprived mind?

He abandoned the question, however, as he turned down one nameless street after another and lost himself in the rhythm of his wheezing breaths and the crunch of snow beneath his feet.

Chapter 16

Vincent hurried through a neighborhood that felt nothing like home in spite of the five months he had lived there. By the time he reached Brady Street, the sun had dropped behind the rooftops of the buildings, casting the sidewalk in shadow.

He spared the other pedestrians an occasional glance—a corporate type coming out of the overpriced coffee shop and a troupe of twenty-somethings with bags from the music store—and wondered what they would do if The Dream came on, causing him to collapse in the middle of the sidewalk. Not wanting to find out, he quickened his pace.

Could Leah be right? Could thoughts about Clementine and Bella be triggering The Dream?

Vincent tried to distract himself. The sign outside of the drugstore advertised Halloween costumes and candy. He recalled with a wry smile how Danny once had chopped up the curtains in his room to make a superhero cape. Surprisingly, their mother had laughed.

Evangeline Pierce hadn't had a problem with Halloween back then, even if there wasn't any money for good costumes. After Clementine was born, roughly around the time his mom got hooked on Catholicism, she tried to convince Bella and him not to let her grandchild celebrate the devil's holiday.

So much for not thinking about Clemmy.

Vincent wondered what his little girl would have looked like at age ten. What costume would she have picked?

No, she'd be eleven now. Funny how I never remember her birthday when it comes around, but I can't forget November 4th, the anniversary of her death.

Fifteen days to go.

His toe caught the lip of the uneven pavement, and he stumbled. To his left, a large window showed the inside of a very narrow building. Vincent had never been inside, but he could see the expensive liquor bottles lined up behind the checkout counter. This was where Jerry had bought his supplies for the night with Paish and her friends.

The beer was gone, but Vincent knew the whiskey bottle was still half full.

That's not going to make things better. Besides, Leah said to lay off alcohol before the sleep study.

His feet took him down the street, around the corner, and up to the brown-and-white house that probably never was home to just one family. At the moment, there weren't any families living in the four-unit building, unless one counted the young couple living in sin in Apartment 1.

The side door was locked, but the door of Apartment 4 wasn't. He went inside. The drone from the TV in the living room confirmed that Jerry was, in fact, home and hadn't absentmindedly left the door unsecured again.

Not that we have anything worth stealing.

After a quick stop in the claustrophobic bathroom, he surveyed the shelves in the pantry. None of the food was his. Hungry, not to mention thirsty for something other than tap water, Vincent conceded defeat to the bad day. He headed for his room, acknowledging Jerry—sitting in his recliner, of course—with an unenthusiastic "hey."

"Hey, wait!"

One foot in his bedroom, Vincent hesitated. "Yeah?"

"Your *wife* called. Twice. She sounded really worried," Jerry said.

First my mother and now Bella. Is there anyone else in my life who'd like to call and tell my roommate how concerned they are for my well-being?

"She said she's been trying to call your cell all day." Jerry frowned. "I thought you were divorced...that you had an *ex*-wife."

Vincent wasn't listening. He reached into his pocket—his empty pocket—and swore. Was his cell back at the restaurant, where he had dropped it during Bella's call? But the missing phone wasn't something he planned to deal immediately. Neither was calling Bella back.

"It can wait until tomorrow. One jump to Valenthor's world was enough for today."

"Huh?" Jerry's face was the definition of bewildered.

"We suspect that thoughts about Bella and Clementine might bring on The Dream," Vincent explained.

"'We'?" Jerry asked. "You and Valenthor?"

Vincent laughed.

So he does *think I'm crazy.*

"No, me and my friend Leah. I met her for lunch today. She's a sleep doctor."

"Oh." Jerry's brow crinkled again. "So when did you have The Dream today?"

"It's a long story." Vincent eyed the laptop on Jerry's lap. "Is that the Master standing by, waiting for a report?"

"No. I'm shopping for my sister's birthday present." Jerry's eyes flicked back to the computer screen. "The world doesn't revolve around you...at least not *this* one."

"Sorry," Vincent said. "It's been a long day. I'll tell you about The Dream tomorrow. I had a nice long talk with Locke."

Jerry didn't say anything. He attacked the keyboard with two index fingers.

Vincent sighed and stepped away from his door. For the first time, Vincent noticed that the ubiquitous joint and ashtray were nowhere to be seen. "What's the matter with you? Are you out of weed or something?"

Jerry looked up and sighed. "No, I just restocked a couple of nights ago. Remember? Paish and her friends were here? I'm just taking a break. Didn't want to risk giving you a contact buzz."

"A what?"

"You know, getting high off the fumes," Jerry replied. "If you apply for a job with the City, they're gonna make you take a piss test. A lot of good me putting in a good word for you would do if you test positive for pot."

Vincent hesitated. "Wait a sec...are you saying the smoke from your joints could affect me without me even knowing it?"

Jerry's eyes were glued to the computer screen. "It's possible."

Vincent didn't know what to say. Was it possible Jerry's secondhand smoke had something to do with The Dream? For that matter, how much damage might young Evie had done to him while partying as an oblivious, soon-to-be parent?

I should count my blessings if blackouts and bizarre dreams are the worst things I reaped from the wild oats my mother sowed.

"Of course, they can't hire you if you don't fill out the application. It's still sitting on the kitchen table," Jerry said.

Is that why he's so cranky?

Vincent turned back to his door. "It's on my list of things to do. Right now, I need to rest...to get some *real* sleep."

"OK…sweet dreams then," Jerry mumbled. The sporadic click of keystrokes followed.

Vincent went into his room and, not bothering to turn the light on, dropped onto his bed.

My pseudo date ended because I fainted while talking to my wife, my stoner roommate is pissed at me for some reason, and my best job prospect is being a garbage man.

Can't imagine why my brain would want to construct a new reality.

Vincent closed his eyes.

Valenthor opened his eyes.

Sunset painted the swaths of clouds in fiery hues. Or was it sunrise? With only a patch of twilit sky visible above—a pocket of light amidst the encroaching treetops—he had no way of discerning east from west. It only compounded the disorientation caused by his sudden expulsion from sleep.

Was I dreaming of Valentine again…lost once more in the day I failed to protect her and her mother?

Valenthor sat up and stiffened when he saw the elf was gone. He scanned the perimeter of the glade, searching for the empty eyes of Locke's mask among the tree trunks. No trace of either companion could be found. He was alone.

Without consciously reaching for it, he suddenly was holding the hammer. The weapon was a far cry from the two-handed broadsword that he had wielded through countless campaigns and which his father had carried before him. Yet the smooth wood of the hammer's haft felt comfortable in his hands. He found what might have been footprints—faint impressions in the sparse, cold grass—and followed them into the woods.

The leaves had begun to bleed autumn colors, and the sweet perfume of decay danced on the cool air. As he walked slowly, warily beneath the canopy, a steady wind shook saplings and older, broader boughs. Red- and orange-tinged foliage rained down around him. He examined the ground but could not ferret out a path.

He stopped, listened.

Underlying the occasional hiss of the wind was the steady burbling of the stream where he had washed his wound. When? That morning? The day before? The memory eluded him, as though his mind recognized the fact but could not recall the experience itself. He wondered if it could be an effect of Locke's elixir.

Could it be that Locke took the elf whilst I slept? Is he an ally or enemy?

Valenthor followed the sound of water for a few yards until the earth began to slope downward. Motes of sunlight speared though the trees and glistened off the shimmering surface. His raw throat choked with thirst, he thought the lazily flowing water looked like a small piece of paradise. He licked his lips and quickened his pace.

Movement out of the corner of his eye sent him diving for cover behind the nearest tree.

The Jötunn, Sir Angus, common bandits—whatever the threat, Valenthor readied himself for battle, tightening his hold on the hammer and mentally preparing to fight for his life. He strained to hear anything above his pulse pounding in his ears.

It took all of his willpower to remain hidden. Instinct ordered him to charge into danger—to take his opponents by surprise and overwhelm them with his ferocity. Several uneventful seconds later, he silently peered around the tree to see what menace waited down by the water.

He stifled a gasp.

The shallow stream could not hide the elf's naked profile. She reached down to cup the water in her hands and then straightened, arching her back and revealed more tantalizing curves. Eyes closed, she poured the water over face. It flowed through her long, honey-blond hair and down the pale, pristine skin of her back. The pink tips of her breasts hardened in response to the chilly bite of the stream.

Valenthor's face burned with something fiercer than bloodlust. With her pointy ears hidden beneath the shiny mane, the elf looked like a human woman—a beautiful, unclothed woman—and his body responded with an intensity that took him by surprise.

'Tis merely a consequence of long span since I have lain with a woman. For the sake of my departed wife, I must look away.

Yet he could not.

She was so unlike his dead beloved, so much slimmer in the belly, taller, and lacking the generous figure of most frontierswomen. Her fair skin glistened like a pearl. The long, golden mane appeared to be the only hair she possessed. So perfect was her form that she scarcely seemed mortal.

Suddenly, she fell into a taut crouch that reminded him of a doe ready to bolt. Or, perhaps, a panther about to pounce. She made no move to cover her nakedness as her eerily bright eyes bore into him from across the distance. Paralyzed, unable to find his voice, he could only wonder what he had done to betray his presence.

The stiffness of her body melted away as quickly as it had come. Slowly, almost leisurely, she walked toward the bank, toward *him*. His face hot with shame, Valenthor looked away. He debated whether or not to make a hasty retreat back to the clearing, but even as he decided to stay and answer for his indecency, the elf silently sidled up to the tree.

"Hail, Valenthor of the Three Rivers. How joyous to see thou are well!" Her voice was as musical as birdsong.

He dared to take a quick glance at her. The oversized black cloak covered all but her hands and face, which were shiny with wetness. Big droplets trickled down through the blond tendrils, caressing her face.

"Well met," he replied guardedly. "Please forgive my intrusion…"

She smiled. "I take no offense. We elves are not ashamed of our natural state. It is said that my people did not learn modesty until they encountered your kind so many ages ago."

Her innocent expression only fueled his guilt. He was on the verge of uttering a second apology when a thought surfaced from deep within his consciousness. Its urgency brought the question immediately to his lips.

"I must know your name, milady."

She smiled thoughtfully. "The language of the Fay is difficult for most humans to pronounce. In your tongue, my name translates to 'fortune' or 'future.'"

Valenthor considered her words. "Fortune…but not all fortune is good, and the future can follow a path either fair or foul."

"Only the Ancestors know for certain," she added.

His scoff would have made Locke proud. "Some humans believe that their fate is guided by the gods. They call it destiny."

"That is my belief as well," she said, her tone grave. "Please, Valenthor, call me Destiny."

"Then I must offer my thanks to you, Destiny, for freeing us from captivity."

"It is I who owe you gratitude," she argued. "You fended off the knights while I recovered from the spell. You might have left me to suffer at the knights' hands."

They stared at each other for a long moment. Again, Valenthor was startled by the power of his desire for her. He wanted to take her in his arms, to taste the sweetness of her lips, to crush her lithe body against his own. Somehow he knew that if he kissed her, she would not reject him.

He turned away, gazing in the direction of the clearing.

"We both are in the debt of another," he said.

He glanced back at her and saw her countenance darken. "You speak of the masked traveler. His tricks have served us thus far, but I fail to understand his motives for aiding us. I do not trust him, Valenthor."

Nor do I, dear Destiny. Nor do I.

"We would do well to keep a careful watch on him," he said. "He says he has no love for the knights or the Jötunn, and he is determined to accompany us on our journey."

Destiny shivered. He suspected it was a reaction to the word "Jötunn" and not the breeze against her wet skin. "I shall pray to all of the Ancestors that we will not have any more use for his protection. But neither will I turn him away. There are many who would twist the prophecy for their own dark ends, and we are a long way from Fay-Lutana."

"Your homeland," Valenthor muttered. "And will your people welcome me as mine did you? What do you expect will happen when we arrive?"

This is madness.

When she would not meet his eyes, he added, "Can you give me even one reason why I should follow you into certain peril?"

Destiny looked up at him, her emerald eyes penetrating his very soul.

"If you give me your trust, Valenthor, I will take you to

your daughter."

Chapter 17

The silver Camry crept down the poorly lit street. Leah peered through the rain-spattered windshield at the line of houses, searching for the number that matched the digits she had scribbled on scrap paper. Staring intently at a white house with brown trim, she jumped when a dark shape appeared outside the passenger-side window.

"Didn't mean to startle you," Vincent said, ducking into the seat next to her. "I can't see the street very well from my apartment, so I was waiting on the side porch."

"No worries," she replied automatically and then frowned. During the two weeks since the "sleep grooming" incident at her apartment, she had decided her relationship with Vincent Cruz needed an injection of professionalism.

She had promised to help him, and she would if she could, even though it would have been easier for everybody if treatment came from an unbiased third party— from someone who didn't blur the lines between physician and friend.

Door-to-door service didn't exactly come standard with the sleep study.

If the test doesn't reveal something concrete, if his condition proves to be psychological and not physiological, I'll have no choice but to refer him to a psychiatrist and wish him the best.

The part of her that had hoped Vincent would provide

her with a mystery to explore—a phenomenon worthy of an award-winning essay— was quickly losing ground to the part that worried she might do more harm than good for the man sitting beside her.

Maybe I wouldn't feel so guilty if I had picked up when Bella called his cell.

"Oh, your phone!" She blindly reaching into her purse. "Sorry I didn't have a chance to drop it off earlier. The past couple of weeks have been crazy. We were lucky there was a cancellation tonight. Otherwise, it might have been months before I could get you in for a poly-somnogram.

"You missed a couple of calls," she added, handing the phone to Vincent.

"Thanks. It was probably just Bella," he said. "My phone isn't exactly ringing off the hook these days."

Leah opened her mouth to say something but thought better of it.

If I want to know about Bella, then I'm just going to have to call her, not pump a patient for information. Not that I'd know what to say to her after fifteen years...and with her losing a child...

"So," Vincent said, "how have you been sleeping?"

She chuckled in spite of herself. "I was about to ask you the same thing. I've been more diligent with my restraints, so I haven't been a threat to myself and others. How about you?"

He was quiet for a moment. "I had The Dream again, but just once. I'm beginning to think you're right about...about how all of this might be because of Clementine."

"Oh?" She glanced over at him, but he was looking out the side window.

"In the dream, Destiny, the elf lady, told me that she's

taking me…taking *Valenthor* to see his daughter."

"I thought Valenthor's daughter had passed away."

"So did I, but maybe it's like you said. Maybe my subconscious or whatever is trying to cope with Clementine's death by constructing a fantasyland where she *didn't* die."

Leah wondered, again, if Valenthor's reunion with Valentine would give Vincent the closure he needed to end The Dream once in for all.

Or will his mind latch onto the fantasy even more desperately?

The turn signal ticked away a handful of seconds before Vincent said, "I just hope I'm not wasting your time tonight, Leah."

"Any answer is better than none, right?" she offered. "Either the PSG will show irregularities or it won't. The data will determine what we do next."

If it's narcolepsy, I'll recommend clomipramine for the cataplexy. The REM suppressors might even stop The Dream once and for all.

And God knows he should probably be on antidepressants anyway.

Vincent turned to her, and she glanced away from the road. Dream or no Dream, the man looked tired.

"I really appreciate everything you're doing…fitting me in and finding a way to pay for this thing tonight," he said.

"Don't mention it," she said, thankful he didn't press her for more details on that final point. A few blocks later, she added, "When you first came to clinic, you mentioned narcolepsy. Are there any narcoleptics in your family?"

"Huh? Oh, no. Not that I know of anyway. I never really knew my father, so I guess it's possible. It's just one of the sleep problems you hear about a lot…unlike what *you* have."

"Cataplexies, the sudden collapses you experience, occur when sleep paralysis is inappropriately activated," she said. "In a way, it's the exact opposite of RBD. When I'm asleep, that protective response doesn't always get triggered, but for some reason it periodically kicks in for you when you're awake."

Leah let her thoughts drift with the swishing of the windshield wipers.

"If it's not narcolepsy," Vincent started hesitantly. "If it turns out I'm just psycho, I'm guessing it's hereditary."

"Why do you say that?"

"Because my mom is crazy."

Leah kept her eyes on the road, her expression neutral.

"She has crazy dreams too," he continued. "Except she doesn't think they're dreams. For instance, she believes an angel came to her in a dream to command her to keep my brother on life support."

Leah sighed inwardly.

I guess there's more than one way to get a patient's family history...

"I never knew you had a brother," she said. "Did he go to Shorewood High?"

"Half-brother actually. And, yes, he went to Shorewood...when he felt like it. He's in a coma now, and if my mother has anything to say about it, he's going to stay hooked up to machines until the Second Coming.

"I think she can't just accept that he is already dead." He took a deep breath. "At first, I thought she wouldn't take him off life support because her church says it's a sin or something. But then one day she finally told me the real reason she wouldn't bury Daniel. An angel had specifically told her not to."

Leah said nothing.

Am I going to hit every red light tonight?

Vincent chuckled. "You don't have to be a shrink to see *she's* delusional."

"People must have said the same thing about the Virgin Mary," Leah said before she could stop herself.

"Huh?"

So much for keeping the conversation professional.

"In both the Bible and the Qur'an, angels deliver messages while people are asleep. John the Apostle apparently dreamed the entire Book of Revelations," she said.

"You believe in that stuff?" Vincent asked, his tone rich with skepticism.

Leah shrugged. "My mother is Muslim, and my father was raised Catholic. I'm not sure what I believe, so I keep an open mind."

Now it was Vincent's turn to shrug. "Well, my mom is not a prophet."

The next few blocks passed in heavy silence, and when they pulled into the parking lot, Leah thought she had never been so relieved to get to work.

Inside the sleep clinic, alone with Leah in a small room with bare walls, a bed, and expensive-looking equipment, Vincent only half listened as Leah explained the procedure. Why bother trying to keep all of the acronyms straight when all he had to do was sleep?

Then again, with so many electrodes stuck to his face and body, he worried that falling asleep would prove challenging.

"I'll be in the next room, monitoring your data and observing you through that," Leah said, pointing to a video camera mounted in the corner of the room.

"How exciting for you."

There was no mirth in her smile. "Good night, Vincent."

"Thanks."

She left, and the lights dimmed. He rolled onto his side. The electrode affixed to his temple itched fiercely, and a pancake might have provided more support than the sorry excuse for a pillow provided. He closed his eyes and concentrated on Bella and Clementine, even going so far as to imagine he was back in his old house on the day Clemmy died.

I haven't had that nightmare since The Dream began. What's the connection?

When sleep did not come, his thoughts drifted back to the conversation in Leah's car. How could she seriously entertain the possibility that an angel contacted his mom? And to compare Evangeline to the Mother of Christ? There was nothing immaculate about either of Evangeline's conceptions.

Just when Vincent had convinced himself he had never been more awake in his life, he opened his eyes to find himself in a room he hadn't seen in nearly twenty years. He sat up quickly and slammed his head on the ceiling.

Cursing loudly, Vincent rolled onto his stomach and slid from the top bunk down to the floor, which was a lot closer than he remembered.

"You better hope Mom didn't hear you say that word."

Vincent rubbed the fast-forming bump on his forehead and locked stares with little Danny, who sat cross-legged on the bottom bunk, reading a comic book.

"What am I doing here?"

Daniel flashed a mischievous smile. He wore his favorite pajamas, which resembled long underwear covered with colorful dinosaurs. "Welcome home, Vince."

"No one calls me Vince anymore," Vincent muttered, but he was no longer looking at Daniel. The Larry Bird poster, the empty terrarium, the mountain of Matchbox cars in the corner—the bedroom was definitely his.

Theirs.

"You were expecting a forest, maybe?" Daniel asked.

Vincent regarded the red-haired eight-year-old suspiciously. "What did you say?"

Daniel stood, tossing *Avengers #1* on his pillow. "I know that elf chick is a hottie and all, but I thought you'd be happier to see me. When was the last time we had a chance to talk?"

I have to get to Valenthor's world so Leah's sleep study isn't for nothing. Maybe if I concentrate…

"I'll refresh your memory," Daniel said. "It was Mom's birthday. You and Bella dropped off her gift, but when you saw I was there, you insisted you couldn't stay for cake."

"There was something we had to do that day," Vincent said, though he couldn't remember what excuse they had used at the time.

"Like what?" Daniel drawled. "You needed a better place to be miserable? Did all holidays become off limits after Clementine died?"

"Fuck you."

The boy's smile grew. "Shhhh! Mom's gonna here you. The walls are very thin. That's not something one forgets easily."

Am I here because I was to Leah about Daniel earlier?

"Why do you want to kill me, Vince?"

Coming from the mouth of a child, the question was more than a little disturbing. "You're already dead, Daniel. Mom just can't deal with reality. She's wracked by guilt because you screwed up your life."

Daniel's eyes narrowed, and his devil-may-care grin disappeared. The new expression made him looked much older. "OK, so I screwed up my life. No arguments there.

And, yeah, Mom made mistakes too, but at least she's trying to make up for it. All she wants is to spend some time with you. Why do you keep pushing her away?"

"Because she's too late!" Vincent spat.

"I think I get it." His brother's one-sided smile returning suddenly. "You want to kill me because it'll kill Mom. You want to punish her because there's no one else left. Clementine is gone. Bella left you—"

Vincent grabbed the boy by his collar, pulling him up to his tiptoes. "You son of a bitch!"

Big grin. "There you go insulting Mom again."

Vincent let go of his little—*too* little—brother. Breathing hard, he said, "You're not real. You're a twisted hallucination my subconscious cooked up to torment me. I'm talking to myself."

"Why do you really hate her?" Daniel asked.

Vincent crossed the room and reached for the bedroom door, but before he could touch the knob, the door opened. He froze.

She looked to be in her mid-twenties. Her blond hair was spiked up in the middle, plastered down on the sides and shaved up the back. The holes in her acid-washed jeans provided an unobstructed view of her knees and more of her thighs than Vincent cared to see. A giant silver cross dangled ironically from one ear. Her blue-shadowed eyes looked alert, for once.

Judging by the zipped-up black leather jacket, Evie wasn't staying sober for long.

"Time for bed, boys," she announced.

"Where are you going?" Vincent asked.

"Out."

Vincent rounded on Daniel. "*This* is why I hate her! Thanks to her, I never knew my father. *This* was my only role model! What chance did I have at being a good dad?"

He fixed his glare on his mother, who crossed her arms and mirrored his frown.

"It's *your* fault my life is so screwed up! It's *your* fault Clementine is dead!"

The door slammed on its own, and he was alone in the room with Daniel.

Adult Daniel.

"OK, so you're pissed off, and Mom is an easy target." Daniel stretched his arms out the length of the bunk and leaned back against the frame. "But we both know that even after you push everyone else away, you still have one person left to hate."

"Just shut up, Daniel."

"Truth is, horrible things happen every day. You made a mistake that morning, but it was an accident, Vince. You can keep on being unhappy, making one bad choice after another, or you can make the best of the time you have left."

"Shut! Up!"

"Clementine died, not you."

He took a swing at Daniel, but suddenly his brother was a boy once more. Young Danny easily ducked under the blow, and Vincent's fist struck the metal bedframe instead.

"You're a bastard," Vincent growled.

Grin. "Takes one to know one."

What is he doing?

Leah stared at the monitor, which showed Vincent sitting up and looking right at her, directly at the camera. And was he talking? When Vincent started waving, she cursed and switched on the lights in his room. A stern voice in the back of her mind told her to stick to the script, to be Dr. Chedid instead of old pal Leah, but even if part of her rankled at interrupting the polysomnography, another part of her was eager to hear what he had to say.

Did he have The Dream?

"What happened?" she asked, approaching the bed.

The artificial light lent Vincent's tan skin a greenish tint. His brow glistened with sweat. "No, not this time."

Leah let out a breath she hadn't realized she was holding. "I didn't think so. You never reached REM, which surprised me. Most narcoleptics enter REM in about ten minutes, but you lingered in NREM for an abnormally long time before waking up."

Vincent stared vacantly across the room. "I was with Danny."

"Pardon?"

"I wasn't Valenthor. I was me…with Daniel back at our old house."

Leah felt her pulse quicken. "Are you saying you dreamed about your brother?"

Vincent nodded. "It wasn't The Dream, but it felt as real as The Dream."

"Was it a lucid dream?" she asked, sounding overeager even to herself. "Did you know you were in a dream?"

He turned to look at her, a puzzled look on his face. "Yeah…why do you look so surprised?"

"Almost all dreaming takes place during REM. Lucid dreaming *only* occurs during REM," she explained.

"So?"

Leah rubbed the back of her neck, a nervous habit she had picked up since she had inadvertently chopped off most of her hair. "You didn't experience REM sleep, Vincent. You lingered in N3, the third stage, for… well…I'll have to double check the readings, but I should have been able to tell if you were having a dream like that. It just doesn't make any sense."

She forced herself to take a breath. "It's too soon to jump to any conclusions. I'll have to get a second opinion, and then there's the chance of mechanical failure. In any case, we should repeat the study and—"

"Leah, just tell me what you're thinking."

"How long did you wait after the dream about Daniel before waving at the camera?" she asked.

"I didn't wait. I just woke up a few seconds ago."

She started to fuss with an electrode on his forehead. He took her hand in his, and their eyes met.

"Please…talk to me," he said.

Old pal Leah it is then.

"If you managed to have a lucid dream in NREM sleep, the instruments didn't detect it," she said. "I was watching pretty closely. I didn't see your eyelids moving at all."

"I don't—"

"If, as the data suggest, you didn't have any dreams, then when you saw your brother, you must have been awake."

Chapter 18

Dawn was a pale orange flirtation on the horizon when Vincent returned to the passenger seat of Leah's immaculate luxury sedan. He pretended to inspect the miniature violin that dangled from the rearview mirror, stealing a glance at Leah as she started the car. Her eyes, underscored by the dark shadows of a sleepless night, had the same faraway look as earlier.

She doesn't really think the machines malfunctioned. Something happened when I was dreaming about Daniel.

While the second half of his sleep study had been uneventful, Leah clearly was preoccupied by the glitch. That worried him. He didn't know much about science—if Bella hadn't done half of his human physiology homework for him, he never would have passed—but he was savvy enough to realize that having dreams while wide awake was very, very bad.

If you're not sleeping, it's not a dream. It's a hallucination.

He buried his questions and stared out the window at a city starting to stir. He knew she would tell him what he needed to know, but first she needed to sort out what, exactly, she knew. In the meantime, he'd do what he had been doing for the past two weeks—wait.

I can't believe tomorrow is already November 4th. Another year without Clementine...

An invisible hand shoved Vincent against the car door,

as the Camry squealed around a corner. He glanced at the speedometer and chuckled nervously.

"You have somewhere you need to be?" he asked.

"Sorry." She let up on the gas but grimaced as a light ahead turned yellow. "I think all the coffee I drank last night finally caught up with me. Is it OK if I use the bathroom at your place?"

"Ah, sure," Vincent said. "But there's never anywhere to park, so just pull in front of the house and put your hazards on."

As they turned onto Arlington Street, Vincent spotted a cranberry-colored Ion parked in the loading zone of the small, fancy Italian restaurant that made the corner smell like garlic every night from 5 to 9. He craned his neck to get a look at the license plate but then lurched forward as the wheels of Leah's car clipped the curb.

"Sorry," muttered Leah, already climbing out of the car.

Vincent got out and hurried to catch up with her. He shot a backward glance at the Ion, but the plates were at an unreadable angle. Pulling his keys from his pocket, he shrugged away the suspicion.

It can't be hers.

As he led the way into the house, a wave of self-consciousness washed over him. The white and black-speckled linoleum of the hall and stairs was dusty and curled. As they ascended to the second level, the stairs creaked irritably beneath their feet. The door to his apartment was more scuffs than paint.

Here's to hoping that the bathroom isn't too filthy.

He inserted his key and tried to turn it, but there was nowhere to go. The door was already unlocked.

"Jesus, Jerry...again?" He pushed open the door. "With a spacey roommate, who needs keys? The bathroom is right there."

"Thank you," she said, scooting into the room and slamming the door behind her.

Vincent sighed and walked over to a kitchen chair. Jerry's bedroom door was closed, which meant he had either gone to bed without locking up, or he was already up and gone. Since it was somewhere around 7 a.m. on a Saturday, he had little hope for the latter scenario.

He was about to sit down when he realized how creepy it would be if he was just lurking in the kitchen when Leah came out of the bathroom. He moved into the living room, debating whether or not to turn on the TV. He never made it to the recliner.

Bella was curled up on the couch with her eyes closed.

The sudden tightness in his chest made it hard to breathe.

That was *her car out front.*

Seeing Bella in the fetal position, her preferred sleeping pose, was beyond surreal. For a moment, he could almost forget the eight years of distance and despair. He wanted to go to her. To touch her and deny the life he had lost. To forget the existence he could not escape.

But the burden of guilt, anger, and regret returned with renewed force.

We haven't seen each other in nearly a year, and she just drops by?

"Why are you here?" he demanded.

Bella jolted upright and blinked dazedly at him. "Vincent? Sorry, I must have dozed off. The door was open, so I let myself in."

"Why are you here?" Vincent repeated through clenched teeth.

Bella stood up, using the arm of the Low Rider for support. "When you didn't return any of my calls, I got worried. Don't you check your messages?"

He was about to offer an excuse about losing his phone in an Indian restaurant, which wouldn't have explained why he didn't use the apartment phone to call her, when he suddenly remembered that Leah was a mere two rooms away.

Christ, all I need is for Bella to find her here and get the wrong idea.

"Well, as you can see, I'm still in one piece," he said, "so unless there's something else you needed…"

Please, Leah, stay in the bathroom!

Bella tucked a loose strand of hair back behind her ear, a habit he used to find sexy. "Regardless of what you might think, I *do* care about you, Vincent. I just wanted to talk face-to-face before…" She sighed. "Tomorrow being what it is, I thought I should stop by. I know how hard that day is for you."

The toilet flushed.

Son of a bitch.

Bella's eyes narrowed. "Is someone else here?"

The sound of water flowing from the faucet filled the tense silence.

"She's just a friend, Bella. She's…she…"

He scrambled to find words that wouldn't make him sound like a cheater or a nutcase. Nothing came to mind.

The pain in his wife's expression filled his guts with ice water. But an instant later, her pale lips tightened, and her eyebrows drew together—tried-and-true warning signs that Bella's temper was on the rise. He knew no tears would come and was relieved.

Anger was an emotion with which he was well acquainted.

*   *   *

Leah considered the ragged, rust-stained towel, then wiped her hands on her slacks instead. She opened the bathroom door and heard Vincent's voice coming from the living room. Figuring he was either on the phone or chatting with his roommate, she decided to peek in and let him know she would see herself out.

She swallowed the unspoken farewell when her eyes met those of Bella Stark.

Bella Cruz!

"Oh!" was all Leah managed to say.

The last time she had seen Bella, they were eighteen and graduating from a high school that had divided them into different cliques. In the dozen years since, Bella had put on some weight, but no more than Leah had. Bella's auburn hair was shorter, the shoulder-length strands streaked with blond highlights. The lines in her face were deeper, particularly those framing her pronounced frown. Her balled fists trembled.

Leah had seen Bella lose her temper on a couple of occasions, and she was immediately reminded of the time in eighth-grade gym class when Marsha Donovan had borrowed her tennis shoes without asking.

Bella had gone off the deep end because someone had taken something that belonged to her. A lifetime later, she was firing that same accusatory stare at Leah.

"I am such an idiot," Bella spat.

Vincent shot Leah an exasperated look before turning back to Bella. "Now wait just a minute. You're overreacting."

"No, no, it's my own damn fault," Bella muttered, scooping up a small handbag tattooed with blue and white flowers. "Honestly, I don't know why I'm surprised."

Vincent rubbed his eyes and sighed. "Bella—"

"And don't worry," Bella added, storming past Vincent.

"I won't waste any more time caring about you. If you don't have the balls to end this marriage, I will."

Vincent flinched but didn't try to stop her from leaving.

The sole target of Bella's fiery glare, Leah finally found her voice. "We're not together, if that's what you think!"

Bella's mouth quivered. Unspent tears glimmered in her eyes. She tried to push past, but Leah didn't budge.

"Don't you recognize me, Bella?" Leah's pulse quickened as Bella cocked her head to the side, regarding her suspiciously. "It's me, Leah Chedid. Vincent came to me for help—"

"*Leah*?" Bella's eyes widened alarmingly. "Why would you do this to me?"

Bella shouldered her way into the kitchen. Leah followed her.

"I'm a doctor," Leah said.

But Bella wasn't listening. Over her shoulder, she shouted, "First I catch you with my cousin, and now you're secretly seeing an old friend of mine? You're a Grade-A asshole, Vincent Cruz."

Bella slammed the apartment door so hard the kitchen cabinets rattled. Leah searched for Vincent. Apparently, he was still where they had left him in the living room. Cursing silently, Leah opened the door and pounded down the stairs after Bella.

Ever the better athlete between them, Bella was already halfway to her car by the time Leah came running around the side of the building.

"Wait!" Leah called breathlessly. "I'm his *doctor*!"

Bella stopped midstride and turned around to confront Leah, who downshifted from a jog to a brisk walk. Leah stopped when she was still a few feet away. She didn't think Bella would hit her, but why take chances?

"His doctor?" Bella shot back. "And what kind of

doctor makes house calls anymore? What, exactly, is wrong with my husband?"

Leah kicked at an orange leaf that the rain had plastered to the street, while her feelings for Bella played tug-of-war with the ethics of her profession. However, there could be no comprise when it came to doctor-patient confidentiality. As much as she wanted to heal Bella's wounded heart, she couldn't give the explanation that would defend Vincent without betraying him.

"Unfortunately, I'm not at liberty to discuss my patients' affairs…" Leah gasped, realizing her error in word choice. "What I mean is—"

"Forget it." Bella resumed the march to her car. "Good luck with Vincent. You'll need it."

Hating herself for not knowing what to do next, Leah simply watched Bella disappear into her vehicle, start the engine, and pull away from the curb. When the car surged forward, Leah backpedaled out of the street.

Leah often had wondered what a reunion with Bella Stark would be like, including what the two of them might talk about if they ran into each other at the grocery store. Nothing in her imagination had come close to reality.

A soft drizzle began to fall, darkening the sidewalk in front of Vincent's apartment. Leah hardly noticed.

Vincent closed the apartment door, which Leah had left open. Then he locked it.

He walked back toward the living room but stopped shy of leaving the kitchen. Numbly, he stared at the cupboard above the refrigerator. A minute later, he opened it. Some part of him heard the knocking and, afterward, Leah calling for him, but another voice was louder.

No matter what you do, your life keeps getting worse.

You might as well just give in to what you really want to do.

He reached for the whiskey.

Chapter 19

Leah scribbled the name of an article and medical journal on a legal pad. College textbooks and other publications she had acquired while researching RBD were strewn about her home office. Some lay open to specific passages, but most of them had been discarded unceremoniously onto a lopsided pile. The half-empty mug of tea on the desk had stopped steaming long ago.

She looked down at the yellow paper and sighed. A measly three sources was all she had to show for the morning's investigating—three articles that may or may not have anything to do with Vincent's condition.

A powerful yawn forced its way out from somewhere deep inside of her. She dropped the legal pad onto the desk. A trip to the public library to search for the journals would have to wait. She needed to sleep, and as intrigued as she was by Vincent's polysomnogram, she knew the real reason she hadn't gone straight to bed when she got home was because she wanted to stay distracted.

I shouldn't have left Vincent's apartment without making sure he was OK. Even if he is a jerk. But what was I supposed to do...break down the door? He was probably embarrassed because of what Bella said about catching him with her cousin.

Not that that excuses his cowardice. If he had followed Bella and me out to her car, then he could have told her about the real reason I was at his apartment.

Leah rubbed her eyes. She had been up all night, but the longer she kept working, the longer she could avoid the memory of Bella's accusing glare.

One more link, and then I'm going to bed.

She navigated back to the search engine, returning to the convoluted query that contained a half-dozen search terms, including "lucid dreaming," "NREM," "phenomenon," and "awake." She clicked the last blue link on the page. Her sigh turned into a snort, however, when the website appeared on screen.

Bold purple script heralded the homepage of the world's first organization for lucid dreamers. Judging by the Clipart crescent moons and copious blocks of colorful text, the Lucid Dreaming Society hadn't updated their site since the '90s.

She scanned down the page and laughed out loud.

Emira looked up at her quizzically.

"Listen to this girl." Leah reached down and scratched the Persian's furry forehead with her free hand. "'The Lucid Dreaming Society connects like-minded people who want to nurture their special abilities and go beyond the traditional limits of the human mind. With proper guidance and practice, some lucid dreamers can evolve to explore the mysteries of shared dreaming and dream telepathy.'"

Emira meowed.

"You're telling me. I guess it takes all kinds."

Like I'm one to judge. I'm either spending my time and money to help the man who cheated on my old friend, or I'm hoping to use him and his affliction to further my career.

Emira purred, and Leah smiled in spite of herself.

"I could be a serial killer, and you wouldn't hold it against me, would you, girl?"

Emira blinked contentedly.

Leah was about to close the Web browser, banishing the poor, neglected webpage back to oblivion, when a quote at the bottom of the page caught her eye:

"If souls can sleep, then why not dream?"
—Dr. Milton Baerwald

Milton Baerwald...why does that sound familiar?

She found his name on her legal pad, jotted next to a study titled "Lucid Dreaming as a Means for Understanding Uncharted Brain Functions and the Essence of Identity." It sounded like pretty heavy stuff. She wondered if Dr. Baerwald had ties to the Lucid Dreaming Society, or had the crackpots taken his quote out of context to make their club sound legitimate?

OK, just one more search, and I'm done.

Leah raised an eyebrow when "Milton Baerwald," a seemingly uncommon name, generated more than a hundred hits. The first link took her to a health-related message board. One of the posts referred to the Baerwald study already on her list. Two other links were for essays that cited the same work. All of the webpages were several years old.

The second page of links connected to other papers by Baerwald—his lesser known works?—and she clicked the first choice, even though the title hinted that the topic had more to do with the philosophical than physiological. After several seconds of displaying the hourglass icon, the browser informed her that the page could not be found. She returned the search engine and tried the next link.

Broken.

She sipped the lukewarm tea and went on to the next link.

Déjà vu.

What the heck?

At the bottom of the list of works was a link to the Lucid Dreaming Society homepage. She rolled her eyes, and then, on an impulse, returned the first page. If she could download "Lucid Dreaming as a Means for Understanding Uncharted Brain Functions and the Essence of Identity" from one of those sites, she wouldn't have to wait until her visit to the library.

She encountered the error screen again and again. Even the pages that mentioned Dr. Baerwald's lucid dreaming article timed out.

Could it be a coincidence? Leah chuckled when she considered the alternative.

I must *be overtired if I'm considering the possibility that someone deleted everything this guy ever wrote from the internet.*

Intrigued in spite of herself, she paged through the search results, skimming over references and even obituaries for individuals who shared the same name as her mystery man. Her spirits sank as the links became less and less relevant. By the time she got to the final page, she had all but given up hope of discovering something of substance about Milton Baerwald.

The very last link, however, took her to the official website of Temple University, where, according to the short bio, Dr. Baerwald taught psychology and neuroscience. There was no picture of the professor emeritus.

She scanned his curriculum vitae, which, while impressive, didn't reveal anything beyond the man's expertise: philosophy, psychology, neuroscience, and, strangely, Norse mythology. His summary of publications and presentations was downright intimidating.

So why can't I find any of his writings on the web?

Leah glanced at the clock in the bottom corner of the

screen. It was half past one in the afternoon.

I really need to get some sleep.

Leah clicked back through the browser's history until she found the first essay that had referenced Dr. Baerwald's work—the only one, she realized, that had actually loaded. She scanned until she found his quote.

"Soul sleep is an ancient and viable theory concerning the state of self immediately following physiological exist-ence. Therefore, when subjects report encountering deceased loved ones in dreams, it is hasty to assume the visitors are merely constructs of the unconscious mind by way of retrieved memories…

"If souls can sleep, then why not dream?"

Or I could call the university.

Leah hits the lockers hard. The crash echoes throughout the locker room, as does her cry of pain and surprise. She tries to get away, but Bella grabs her by her shoulders, bringing her face close to Leah's.

"Why did you steal my shoes?"

Leah attempts to push Bella back, but Bella is bigger and, somehow, older. While she can't look down to see her feet, Leah knows she's wearing her own gym shoes, along with the standard-issue gray T-shirt and matching shorts.

"You're a thief!" Bella shouts.

Leah looks around for help, but the two of them are alone. "I didn't take them!" she insists. "Marsha Donovan did!"

"No," Bella says, "Marsha is my best friend. You, on the other hand, have always been a cold-hearted bitch."

Leah struggles to break away, but Bella's fingers dig harder into her shoulders and collarbones. She pleads for Bella to let her go. She is crying, and Bella is screaming at her. The bell rings.

"Bella, we're going to be late for class…"

The locker room melted away. Leah stared in confusion at the muted rays of sunset streaming through the partially closed Venetian blinds.

Why was I sleeping on the couch in the middle of the day?

The sound came again—a ring tone, not a school bell.

She rolled off the couch and stumbled over to her purse, which hung from the back of a dinette chair. She pulled out her cell. The caller ID didn't display a number. A wrong number maybe? She almost dropped the phone back in her purse but then remembered the incident at Vincent's apartment that morning.

Maybe it's Vincent…or Bella.

She pressed the button and brought the phone to her ear. "Hello?"

"Dr. Chedid?" A man's voice. Not Vincent's.

"This is she."

Pause. "You tried to call Milton Baerwald earlier today."

Memories of fruitless phone calls surfaced suddenly. She had called the number for Dr. Baerwald listed on Temple University's website, but there was no voicemail. Next, she had tried the general office number for the psychology department. Halfway through her rambling message, she had realized it was Saturday. No one would even hear it until Monday.

Apparently, she had been wrong about that.

"Is this Dr. Baerwald?" Leah asked.

Another pause. "No."

"But you got the message I left for him?"

Pause. "How may I help you, Dr. Chedid?"

"With all due respect, Mr…."

"Boden."

"With all due respect, Mr. Boden, I was hoping to speak with Dr. Baerwald. Is there a better number where I can reach him? I promise not to take up too much of his time."

Pause. "I would prefer to collect as much information as possible up front. Milton seldom has as a minute to spare, you see."

Something in the calm—no, cold—voice raised the hairs on the back of her neck. She didn't like Boden, and she sure as hell wasn't going to tell him anything about Vincent. Before she could come up with a suitable response, he spoke again:

"Does this have something to do with his research on lucid dreaming?"

She took a breath and invoked her most professional tone. "I appreciate your assistance, Mr. Boden, but I would be grateful if you could pass along—"

"Are you an acquaintance of Milton's?" Boden asked.

She bit her lip. Who did this guy think he was?

"No, I am not," she replied. "However, I am familiar with his credentials…whereas, I know nothing of yours."

Pause. "I am Dr. Baerwald's colleague and most trusted associate."

"Nonetheless." She cleared her throat. "Please have him give me a call when he can."

Pause. "I'll be in touch."

Then Boden was gone, and Leah could only stare at the phone. Her life had grown much stranger since Vincent Cruz waltzed into her clinic, but nothing—not watching him collapse at the restaurant, nearly stabbing him with a scissors, or being mistaken for the proverbial "other woman"—had unsettled her as much as the phone call from Boden had.

She jumped when her phone went off in her hand. The familiar Lilith Fair anthem immediately alleviated her fear of another conversation with Boden.

"Zaina—"

"Where the hell are you, Leah?" her sister demanded. "Mom and Dad keep asking about you."

The anniversary party…shit!

Grabbing her coat and purse, Leah said, "I'm on my way!"

She was five steps down the hall before she realized she was wearing sweat pants and a tank top.

Chapter 20

Valenthor's breaths were quick and shallow, every gulp of air like an icy blade slashing at his throat. His swift pace, combined with the steady incline, pushed his pulse to a thundering cadence. The fire burning in his muscles vanished periodically, as the mountain gales pierced his sweat-soaked clothes and made him shiver.

All the while, he remained vigilant, surveying the gaps between the evergreens and the dark crannies littering the rocky terrain. Any space that could conceal a giant.

Several steps ahead, Destiny stopped and leaned on a walking staff Locke had fashioned from the bough of a balsam fir. Valenthor tensed, tightening his grip on the hammer. A second passed, then another.

No enemies. She just needs to rest.

Valenthor resisted the urge to approach her. He had had no dearth of questions for the elf ever since she had announced she would take him to his daughter. Yet she repeatedly sidestepped his questions, asking for faith.

Faith in her and in the gods-forsaken Ancestors.

Frustration, anger, a sliver of hope—all of these feelings and more waged war in his mind. He let out a long, slow breath, watching the steam flow snake-like from his mouth. Patience had never been a virtue he claimed as his own. Let the chieftains meet in tents to debate tactics far from the frontlines. Valenthor had ever been more comfortable in the midst of the fray, looking Death full in the face.

"I am impressed."

Locke's muffled voice startled Valenthor, who had all but forgotten the masked stranger. He relaxed his grip on the hammer and turned to Locke for an explanation.

"Whoever veiled this place was a true master." Locke moved past Valenthor to join Destiny at the base of a sheer wall of rock.

Valenthor followed, straining to see what had captured his companions' attention. He saw nothing amiss. In fact, if they had not stopped, Valenthor likely would have pulled himself up and over the ledge without a second thought.

The hole seemed to appear only after Destiny pulled back the brown and barren branches of a shrub. He couldn't decide if the camouflage had been magical or merely a trick accomplished through angles and strategic placements of brush. Before he could ask about opening, Destiny ducked her head and disappeared inside the side of the small cliff.

"After you," Locke said, gesturing at the hole with his staff.

The old injury in his side, caught in a state between scab and scar, protested as Valenthor hunched down. The smell of earth clung to the chilly air. At first, the blackness of the cave's interior was absolute, and he was forced to feel his way along one hard, jagged wall. Then he hit something soft—Destiny, he realized, as soon as he heard her voice. The words, spoken in a near whisper, were impossible to decipher.

Another spell!

No sooner had he come to the realization than a blue-white light enveloped the cave. Locke's eyes must have acclimated to the sudden illumination an instant before his because he was the first to speak.

"A hiding place such as this is worthy of the world's most precious treasures. One should hope to find an enchanted sword, mayhap, or gold and gems enough to acquire an army or two. Methinks the corpse of a small girl is a poor substitution."

If Destiny deigned to reply, Valenthor did not hear her. There was no sound in the entire world. Nothing existed except for the motionless form sprawled out at the back the surprisingly spacious cave. Numbly, he approached his daughter and fell to his knees. His arms reached for the girl. His calloused hands combed through her curly black hair.

Tears spilled down his trembling jaw.

"Valentine!" he sobbed.

A hand on his shoulder. "She has not departed for the afterworld, Valenthor," Destiny said softly, soothingly. "Neither does her spirit dwell in this world."

There was no heartbeat but no stench of rot either. Valentine's shift, stained here and there with dirt and blood, did not cover her chubby arms and legs, which were painfully cold to touch. In the uncanny azure glow, her skin looked like that of someone who had suffered exposure to the elements.

After the Jötunn raid on the Three Rivers, Valenthor had discovered the remains of his wife strewn about the path approaching their home. He had not found any trace of Valentine. His final prayer to the gods was that her body had been among those cast on the communal pyre he and the rest of the returning hunting party had built. Better that she died quickly than be carried away by the giants, he had always believed.

Valenthor had never thought to see his daughter again, alive or dead.

Let alone somewhere in between.

"How is this possible?" he asked, his voice cracking.

"I know not," Destiny said. "The Ancestors showed me this place as I slept. In the dream, I first witnessed the battle that destroyed your home, Valenthor. Then I was soaring far above the world, and I saw the entrance to this cave. I believe the Ancestors brought her here."

If the Ancestors have the power to steal Valentine from the Three Rivers, why did they not do so before the Jötunn attack?

Valenthor wanted to confront the owner of that calm, gentle voice, but he couldn't bear to look away from his daughter. "Why bring me here? Did you believe that seeing her in this state would provoke me to swear vengeance upon the Jötunn? Is this how you would coerce me into fighting your enemies and fulfilling the prophecy?"

"I brought you here because it was the will of the Ancestors," she said.

"Damn your Ancestors!" he roared, shrugging off her hand and turning to face her at last.

Destiny's eyes widened in alarm, but she did not back away.

Locke cleared his throat. Perhaps it was another scoff. "The girl is cursed, Valenthor. Either she was the target of a baleful spell, or the gods interceded so that the Jötunn would ignore her while she feigned death. If the former is true, then your daughter might still be saved."

Valenthor eyed Locke warily and waited for the man to continue.

"You must find the fiend who did this and kill him."

Vincent opened his eyes and groaned. A sliver of yellow light pierced the blessed darkness of his room through the gap between his door and the floor. He heard a woman's voice. He heard his name.

I'm not ready to be Vincent again...just five more minutes, Mom...

He rolled over. Whiskey splashed onto his neck, spilling from the bottle he forgot he was holding. Confident that the bottle had ended up in a more-or-less upright position, he buried his face into his pillow and tried to pass out again.

The three knocks battered Vincent's brain like shotgun blasts.

"Go away," he said, but the pillow swallowed the words. He turned his head, belched, and repeated, "Go away!"

"Dude, I think you should hear this message," Jerry called through the door.

Half rolling, half stumbling out of bed, Vincent gave the f-word more syllables than it had any right to. He kept one hand on the wall to steady himself as he dragged himself to the door. The other hand still clutched the whiskey bottle.

Vincent opened the door and swore again when the searing light from the living forced him to squint. "What's going on?"

"Sorry to bug you, but this sounded like it might be serious." Jerry went to the answering machine and pressed a button.

A mechanical voice said, "Message one, 5:37 p.m., Saturday..."

What time is it now? How long was I out?

"Hey, Vincent. It's Leah. I wanted to check in...again...and, well, I'm probably overreacting, but I just had a very strange conversation. I was trying to reach a professor who has done research on various sleep phenomena, but a man named Boden called back. He was fishing for information. I didn't tell him anything about you, but...I don't know...he gave me the creeps. I don't think it's anything to worry about...just...be careful, I guess. Anyway, I'm on my way to this family thing, but I'll have my phone. Please give me a call when you get this."

The answering machine beeped and went silent.

Leah's words bounced around inside Vincent's head, but he couldn't concentrate on any of them long enough to come up with any kind of meaning.

"Is everything OK, man?"

Vincent saw Jerry look at the whiskey bottle and took a long, defiant gulp. The gesture was undermined, however, by the fury of coughs that followed.

"Just peachy, Jerry." Cough. "Never better."

Jerry frowned. Vincent smiled.

"Dude, I'm getting kind of worried about you."

"Heh, join the club," Vincent laughed. "My mom can be president, and Bella is the vice—"

Bella!

Vincent lurched forward and would have fallen if he hadn't caught himself on the desk. Jerry stepped forward to help him, but something in Vincent's expression must have made him change his mind because he quickly backed off.

"You son of a bitch," Vincent spat. "You left the door open again. Today. This morning. And Bella came in. I came home, and my goddamned wife was lying on the couch because *you* don't know how to use a fucking key!"

Jerry wore a look of absolute astonishment on his stupid face.

"Don't you have enough brain cells left in that hippy-dippy head of yours to remember to lock the door? Now

Bella thinks I'm cheating on her because Leah was here. And I'm not sleeping with Leah. I mean, Leah was there when I was sleeping, but it's because she's a sleep doctor, and I might not have been sleeping anyway. Only Bella doesn't know I'm losing my mind, and you sure as shit better not tell her!"

Jerry backed up until he bumped into his recliner. He maneuvered around it so that the ugly yellow chair stood between the two of them.

"Hey, take it easy. It was just an accident!"

"Where the hell were you anyway?" Vincent demanded. "You're never up before noon on a Saturday. If you had been here, you could have warned me she was her or, better yet, sent her on her way."

"I drove up to Oshkosh for my sister's birthday. We met for lunch." The wrinkles on Jerry's forehead made a rare appearance. "You're pretty wasted. Maybe you should sleep it off."

Vincent's laugh ricocheted off the empty walls of the apartment. "That means *a lot* coming from a junky like you."

Jerry sighed and walked into his bedroom. "Whatever, man."

"Yeah, go light up another joint, Son of Chong!"

Vincent raised the bottle in mock toast to his roommate and brought it to his lips again. But the liquor didn't want to stay down. He made a mad dash for the bathroom and emptied his stomach into the toilet.

When he was certain there was nothing left to purge, he eased back onto his butt, resting his back against the sink cupboard. He wiped his slick forehead with a shirtsleeve while the radiator, toilet, and tub circle him like unrelenting predators. He closed his eyes, but that only made the world spin faster.

Going to be a long night. Better stay close to the toilet.

He crawled over to the bathtub and climbed in. None of positions he tried stopped the incessant storm from rocking his porcelain boat. He cringed at every twist of his guts. He moaned. He shivered.

He prayed for death.

That'd be fitting. She died in the tub too…

The fading light inside the cave made the eyeholes of Locke's mask seem endless. The gods only knew what expression was hidden beneath. Valenthor turned to Destiny. Her eyes shimmered with unspent tears. Her soft lips sank into a solemn frown.

"We must trust the Ancestors to guide us," she whispered.

Valenthor's scoff was even louder than Locke's.

"Bravo, milady. Well played," Locke said. "Prithee forget the phantoms for a moment. You told Master Valenthor from the start that you wanted him to be your Chosen One, to save your homeland. All along, you sought the aid of the living to further your scheme, not the dearly departed. I fail to comprehend why a host of dead elves would care about the soul of one human girl."

Destiny flinched, her customarily wide eyes narrowing into slits. "Still your tongue, scoundrel. This is a holy place!"

Scoff. "One thousand pardons." To Valenthor, Locke said, "We can surmise that the one who cursed your daughter is a friend of the giants. The spell was cast during the Jötunn raid on the Three Rivers. If we can find that band of giants, mayhap we will find your sorcerer."

Valenthor glanced back at Valentine. "What choice do I have?"

"She will be safe here," Destiny insisted.

She took his arm, but he pulled away.

"Have your Ancestors revealed where we might find the Jötunn's war camp?" he asked. "Or shall we wander the wilds slaying giants until we happen upon this sorcerer by chance?"

She closed her eyes—in suffering or supplication, he couldn't say—and wordlessly left the cave.

"Why so morose, milady?" Locke called after her. "Regardless of differing beliefs, your champion has answered your call to battle."

Locke's long coat stirred up the dust as he spun around and ducked under the low arch of the cave's opening. Over his shoulder he said to Valenthor, "This might prove interesting, provided we don't all perish."

Valenthor hesitated, sparing one final look at his daughter, and then followed his companions out of the cave. Silently, he swore to the gods, the Ancestors, and any other unseen power that the next time he looked upon his daughter, she would look back.

The ringing of the phone proved such a stark contrast to the stillness of the cave that Vincent scrambled out of the bathtub, instantly alert and reaching for a weapon that wasn't there. At first, he didn't recognize his apartment, but another shrill chime propelled him through the kitchen and over to the phone.

"Hello?" he asked anxiously.

Silence.

"Hello?" His heart pounded.

"Is this Vincent Cruz?"

"Yeah…Christ, what time is it?"

Pause. "Are you a patient of Dr. Leah Chedid?"

"Yeah. Who is this?"

Pause. "My name is Boden."

The name sounded familiar. He struggled to bring the fragments of memory into focus, but whatever he might have known about the man had been swept away by an undertow of booze. Out of nowhere, he suddenly remembered shouting at Jerry.

Did that really happen? Why were we arguing?

"Are you seeing Dr. Chedid because you are experiencing unexplained dream phenomena?"

"What? Who *are* you?"

Pause. "Have you ever entered someone else's dream?"

"Huh?"

"Has someone else entered your dream?" Boden pressed.

Vincent rubbed at his temples with his free hand. "I don't know what you're talking about. What does that even mean, 'enter someone else's dream'? I have narcolepsy and nightmares because my daughter died."

"Nightmares?"

"Long story. Leah's my doctor. If you have any questions, you can talk to her."

Pause. "I might be able to help you."

Vincent chuckled. "Unless you know an evil wizard who hangs out with the Jötunn, I think you're out of your league, pal."

Silence.

"That's what I thought," Vincent said. "I'm hanging up now."

"Wait, did you say, 'Jötunn'?"

"Have yourself a good night, pal."

Pause. "Do you know Milton Baerwald?"

"Never heard of him. Good night."

"Do you know DJ?" the man asked, but Vincent was

already dropping the phone back onto its cradle.

He looked at his wrist, but he wasn't wearing a watch. It was pitch black outside. That didn't mean much in the middle in the winter. Jerry's light was off.

Vincent dragged himself over to the couch, stretched out, and considered turning on the TV.

He closed his eyes instead.

Chapter 21

Milton tripped and hit the pavement hard. He rolled onto his back, sucking in the bitter-cold air in great gulps. A few lonely snowflakes wafted down from the endless gloom above. Confetti blowing down from a celestial celebration. Litter from heaven.

There was no sign of the black helicopter, no sound whatsoever except for his own panting.

I am alone. Again.

Overcome by exhaustion and despair, Milton closed his eyes. He saw DJ aim his handgun at the tall man, fire, and miss—heard him say, "My, you're a tall drink of water."

The boy is probably dead. Thanks to me.

Shadows had concealed the tall man's face, but Milton was certain he knew him. Was it the same agent who had been chasing him all along? And what name had he used to address Milton?

"Why can't I remember?" Milton groaned, even though he was certain he knew the answer. His pursuers had locked away his memories so that he could not betray their secrets. But unless he could piece the clues together to come up with a working hypothesis before the tall man and his allies returned, Milton might as well surrender and be done with it.

He made a feeble attempt to pull himself up from the sidewalk but did not rise.

DJ was right about one thing. I can't run forever. I

have to catch my breath. I have to think.

Everything had happened so fast after the bus crashed, but he remembered the tall man calling him by a different name. It had seemed so important at the time, but the word was lost to him now, locked behind the same doors that hid the facts he so desperately needed.

Since he couldn't recall what the tall man had called him, Milton focused instead on the van and its peculiar emblem.

That horse had eight legs. I'm sure of it. I recognized it. But from where? A cereal box? A movie? No...a book. A book about mythology! Yes, it was Sleipnir, the gray stallion Odin rides!

Milton's breath caught in his throat. For a moment, he saw the laboratory and the man with the high forehead in the white coat. He stared into the gray-green eyes.

He saw the syringe, the sword.

From somewhere deep in his mind, Milton heard his own voice say, "Odin is chief god in the Norse pantheon. He is associated with wisdom, magic, prophecy—"

"And battle and death," the man with gray-green eyes added.

"Yes, as well as poetry and the hunt," Milton replied. "All of the Norse gods are complex creatures, not nearly as straightforward as their Greco-Roman counterparts."

"And you think I should be Odin, rather than you?"

"It's better this way," Milton said. "Odin was never afraid to get his hands dirty, and before all of this is over, the waters are bound to become murky indeed."

Pause. "Who will you be then, Milton?"

"Borr," he answered. "Odin's father."

Sprawled out on the sidewalk, Milton gasped. The remembered conversation had moved the mental door, nudged it open a little. Desperately, he reached for his memories, eager to take hold of the revelations he had been denied for so long.

But something heaved the door shut once more, allowing only a single memory to escape.

Milton isn't drifting tonight. He isn't even lucid dreaming. Images wash over him, diluted and distant. Since discovering dream drifting so many years ago, he likens such ordinary dreams to subconscious TV shows that seldom keep his full attention. It's not him in the dream, but rather an actor pretending to be him.

But everything changes when the lights start flashing and William Marlowe shows up.

Milton's reflexes kick in, and the scene sharpens. Taking control of the dream feels like flexing a muscle buried deep in his brain. The indistinct surroundings—it might have been a grocery store before—transform, becoming a familiar space. Someplace safe.

Milton watches William warily as he runs his fingers across the spines of the books on the nearest shelf.

"I consider myself as much a scholar as you, Milton, but I don't know how you can enjoy the smell of old books," William says, wrinkling his nose. "So...is this library at Brown or Harvard?"

"Temple, actually," Milton replies. He tries to sound casual, but he has never been able to mimic William's easy nonchalance.

"Ah, yes, I had heard you were still teaching there." William looks around at the stacks on either side of them. "I always preferred Harvard's Psychology Research Library for a nocturnal rendezvous. It was smaller, more intimate."

"What do you want, William?" The question comes out

more forcefully than he would have liked.

William affects a hurt expression, but Milton doesn't buy it. He knows the man doesn't have a heart.

"We haven't spoken since I left the Lucid Dreaming Society eighteen years ago," William says. "I had hoped we could let bygones be bygones."

He unclenches his jaw long enough to say, "It's *your* fault the Society disbanded. If you had taken only Cormac O'Shaughnessy with you, it might have lived on after your resignation, but when you conned Annette into quitting too, it was only a matter of time before the Society dissolved."

Milton takes a breath. "You and I have crossed far beyond bygones."

For a moment, William is at a loss for words. Milton wonders what kind of reception the man expected. Time doesn't heal all wounds, he thinks. Not when the wounds are caused by betrayal.

"I owe you an apology," William says at last. "Many apologies. Can we talk somewhere a little more comfortable? Somewhere with padded chairs and wine? It's your dream. I'll let you choose."

The urge to expel William from his consciousness comes on suddenly and powerfully. He didn't invite William to come into his dream. If it were up to him, Milton would have expunged all traces of the man from his mind long ago, memories included. William's unrelenting obsession with pushing science to its limits—with playing God—had ripped apart the Society, had destroyed Milton's extended family.

Worst of all, William abandoned him.

His emotions get the better of him; the lights flicker violently.

"Please, Milton?" William says quietly. He looks older,

wearier than Milton ever remembers seeing him. Another act? It's Milton's dream, but William has enough control to make subtle adjustments without much effort. William is, after all, one of the most powerful dream drifters on earth. Maybe second only to Milton.

Several more seconds pass while Milton stares into William's dark eyes. Finally, he reaches into his mind, drawing from memory and imagination. The tall book-shelves disintegrate, and the library folds in on itself. High-legged tables, chairs, a circular bar, and a shiny blue piano form out of nothingness.

A moment too late Milton realizes that the lounge is nearly identical to one he and William used to visit in the early days of the Lucid Dreaming Society. Might William have played a part in the choice of scenery? A subtle shaping of the floor plan, an imperceptible tweak in the piano's color? No, Milton suspects the true culprit is his own sub-conscious.

"Yes, this will do nicely," William says cheerfully. He walks behind the bar like he owns the place and inspects the rows of bottles. "What will you have?"

"I'm fine," Milton insists.

William shrugs and retrieves a bottle that Milton recognizes even at a distance. At the base of the long, slim neck is a bold blue circle bearing the profile of a white wolf. It's one of William's favorite merlots—smoky, tart, complex.

In spite of himself, Milton watches as William uncorks the bottle and trickles the deep red wine into a bulbous glass. His movements are graceful and precise. When William sets the bottle down and looks up, Milton quickly stares across the room at the host of empty chairs.

William joins Milton at one of the bistro-style tables. He swirls the wine around in the glass, takes a long sniff, and lets the liquid slide down his throat. All but smacking his lips, he says, "That's quite good."

Milton crosses his arms, waiting.

Across the table, William raises the glass again, but it stops halfway to his lips. He clears his throat. "Annette is not well. She has a brain tumor…aggressive meningioma. The doctors have given her mere months to live."

"I'm sorry to hear that," Milton says, once he is able to speak. Even though Annette Young turned her back on the Society, Milton knows it wasn't personal. She has always been a kind, if naïve, woman.

"Cormac is going to make a power play." William tips the glass one way and then the other, watching the violet waves splash treacherously near the rim with each pass. "Without Annette's support, I won't be able to stop him."

"Stop him from what?"

William hesitates, then swallows the entire contents of the glass.

"Stop Cormac from doing what, William?"

William chuckles dryly. "You know Cormac. One doesn't need a doctorate in psychology to see the man has many unresolved issues. He has never cared about the *science* of what we do."

"But he was useful to you when you wanted to dismantle the LDS from the inside," Milton points out.

William continues, undaunted. "Annette has always brought balance to the group, the superego in opposition to Cormac's id, if you will," William says. "Without her, the others will follow Cormac and his new friend Levi down some very dark avenues, I'm afraid. I won't be able to stop them from rushing headlong into…into…"

"You want me to be your new superego so that you can remain in the middle as the ego, playing the two sides against each other?" Milton chuckles sardonically. "Sorry, Will, but you made your bed a long time ago."

William's eyes blaze. The very air around them grows heavy. Milton grips the edge of the table, presses his fingers against the wood. It's solid. An anchor. His connection to the dream.

If William tries to take control, Milton will fight him.

But William visibly relaxes, and the pressure fades. "This is bigger than my mistakes, Milton. Cormac is reckless. When Annette is gone, it will be only a matter of time before his actions lead to the Order's discovery."

The Clandestine Order for Psychic Exploration.

COPE.

Milton is certain William came up with the name because William was wont to joke that the Lucid Dreaming Society was a support group for those with abilities the rest of humanity could not understand and would not accept. The irony is that William had never been content to merely "cope" with his gift.

"What goes around comes around," Milton mutters. He feels foolish for resorting to clichés and childish antics, but he can't seem to stop taking potshots at his companion. He wants William to suffer because he deserves it.

William sighs. "I need you, Professor."

The words hit Milton hard. Sitting in the piano bar with William—dressed in a stylish and pricey suit, as always—stirs up feelings he buried long ago. For an instant, the past eighteen years never happened. He and his dear friend, his partner in the pursuit of knowledge as well as happiness, are unwinding after a day spent cooped up in a lab.

But the chatter of other patrons is conspicuously absent, and the piano is silent. None of it is real. Not the lounge and not William's apology. Not even Milton's memories of happier times with William, tainted, as they are, by nostalgia.

"You never needed me," he tells William.

"Milton, that's not—"

He raises a hand to forestall the lie. "You already tried to recruit me for COPE back when you left the Society. How was it you described your new club? A group of pioneers exploring uncharted territory with absolute dedication and discretion? As though the members of the Lucid Dreaming Society were just a bunch of oafs whose interest in dream phenomena was so far beneath you!"

William opens his mouth to interject, but Milton presses on. "You and I have never had the same agenda. I am a scholar who wishes to advance understanding of the human brain and its lesser-known functions. You, on the other hand, have only ever been interested in realizing your full potential solely for your own personal benefit. You would hoard knowledge, lording your abilities over those born without similar aptitude.

"My answer is the same today as it was back then. You and your secret society can go to hell!"

William's sudden smile erupts into a laugh. "Wonderful speech, Milton. But for someone who isn't fond of secrets, why ever would you choose to associate yourself with the CIA?"

The temperature in the imaginary piano bar drops fifty degrees. Milton wonders how William could possibly know about his invitation to meet with a representative of the CIA. Milton doesn't know why the agency is interested in seeing him. He wonders if William does.

"I suppose you won't hold anything back," William continues. "You'll tell them all about how you have ventured into the minds of unsuspecting sleepers, probing their unconscious thoughts. I'm sure a national intelligence agency will have no problem with the *full* breadth of your scholarly research. And I'm sure everything you and your new lab partner cook up these days is beyond reproach."

Milton forces himself not to frown because he knows William is gauging his nonverbal cues. He tries to keep his breathing at a relaxed pace. He uncrosses his arms.

"Is that what this is all about, William?" he asks. "You're trying to coerce me into joining COPE so that you won't have to worry about the CIA learning about you and your friends? If you're so worried about Cormac, maybe you should tag along, and we can unburden our souls together."

William takes another drink of wine, sets the glass down, and stands up. "Thank you for the drink and for your time, old friend. I hope, for both of our sakes, this is the last time we meet, either here or in the real world."

William walks away, heading toward the exit. It is a dramatic gesture, Milton supposes, since he could have just as easily disappeared, leaving Milton's dream as suddenly as he arrived.

Before he can stop himself, Milton asks, "What do you mean?"

Across the room, William turns slowly. Whatever fire had flashed from within his deep brown eyes had long since cooled, leaving behind a pair of orbs empty of all emotion. Like the eyes of a serpent, Milton thinks. Cold and predatory.

"Because," William says, "unlike you, I recognize a formidable enemy when I see one."

Milton grunted when something poked him in his ribs.

He squeezed his eyes shut, staving off consciousness, but the dream—the *memory*—was already floating away, wafting into the unreachable recesses of his mind back behind the locked door. He tried to grab onto a piece of the conversation, a name, a face.

Did I dream about Odin?

The uncomfortable pressure in his side returned, and he opened his eyes. A small shape blocked out a corner of the overcast sky above him. He cried out and scrambled into a crouched position, ready to confront the animal.

No, not an animal. A girl who couldn't have been more than three years old looked down at him, neither smiling nor frowning. Her black, braided pigtails swayed in the wind. A dusting of snow clung to her pink nightgown and her bare arms and legs.

"Good God, you must be freezing!" Milton tore off his coat and wrapped it around her, practically drowning her in the fabric. "You're not wearing any shoes. Who let you out of the house like this? Where are your parents?"

The girl shrugged.

"What is your name?"

Her voice was soft, a little shy. "Clementine."

"Why are you wandering the streets all by yourself, Clementine?"

She giggled, bringing a pair of dimples to her pallid cheeks. "Looking for you, silly!"

The familiar twinge of paranoia sent a shiver down Milton's spine. "But you don't even know who I am, child."

"You're Milton."

He took a step away from her. "How…how do you know that?"

"Uncle Danny told me."

Danny? Who the hell is—

"Do you mean DJ?"

She shrugged.

Milton spun around, scanning every direction. They were alone. "Where is Uncle Danny?"

She shrugged again.

"When was the last time you saw him?"

"Before."

Milton sighed. "What exactly did your uncle tell you?"

"You are nice, not a stranger. You will make me safe."

Milton had a few choice words for DJ, but he swallowed them. "We have to get you someplace warm. Do you live near here?"

"Don't know."

Milton took a tentative step forward. "I'm going to carry you. Is that OK, Clementine?"

"Sure."

She was heavier than he had expected. He covered her as best he could with the long coat. She put her thumb in her mouth and lay her head against his chest.

What were you thinking, DJ? How could the safest place for your niece be with a sleep-deprived fugitive?

On one hand, he was furious with DJ for burdening him with the child. On the other hand, it felt good to have some company.

"Don't worry. We'll figure this out," he told her. "I just hope your uncle has a plan."

And I hope he's alive.

Chapter 22

A loud noise from the kitchen wrenched Vincent from a deep sleep to wide awake. He slowly pulled himself into a sitting position, bracing for a dizzy spell or some other symptom of what was sure to be a killer hangover.

Nothing.

He leaned back against the Low Rider's less-than-fluffy cushions and scratched his head.

Didn't I pass out in the bathtub? How did I end up on the couch?

The door to his bedroom was open, and the light was on.

Was I sleepwalking?

Vincent jumped when he heard voices from the kitchen. The man's voice was too low to be Jerry's, and while a woman was doing most of the talking, Vincent couldn't make of out any of her words. From his bedroom came the sound of dresser drawers being opened and closed.

Burglars!

Vincent's gaze darted to the door that led to the suspended porch. He'd likely sprain an ankle if he jumped down to the concrete that comprised his backyard, but there was no other escape route. He forced himself to take a calming breath.

Maybe it's just some of Jerry's friends…Paish, Tara, Marc…

Or maybe Jerry left the damn door unlocked again, and

some crazies wondered in.

Vincent stork-stepped over the coffee table and crept across the living room. He considered grabbing Jerry's lava lamp from its perch atop of the speaker but thought better of it. In Valenthor's world, bashing people's brains in was an effective method for resolving conflict. In the real world, however, Vincent knew he was more likely to get shot than anything.

The hardwood floor protested at his weight at the exact moment he reached the threshold. Vincent froze, wide-eyed. From his vantage, he couldn't see much of the kitchen, only the doorway to the pantry and the bathroom beyond. Which meant that whoever was in the kitchen couldn't see him either.

A tall man wearing a long black coat and dark sunglasses stepped out of the pantry.

Vincent swore and staggered backward. He wanted to lunge for the lava lamp or make a run for the porch door, but all he could do was stare at the pale-skinned man in black, who came no closer.

"Vincent Cruz," said a voice from behind Vincent—from his room.

Vincent whirled around and saw another man in a black trench coat. The newcomer lifted his hands in a placating gesture, but the shiny leather gloves undermined the sentiment.

"What do you want?" Vincent demanded. "We don't have anything worth stealing."

The intruder standing outside of his bedroom looked Vincent up and down. Vincent reciprocated. The man was roughly the same size as Vincent but older, and he had a lot less hair. His dull green eyes somehow made him look smart—or devious.

"We are not thieves," the man said. Then he paused.

"That is to say, we are not after your personal property. I came because you hung up in the middle of our conversation."

Vincent suddenly recognized the voice. "Boden?"

The man nodded. "Please have a seat. This doesn't have to be unpleasant."

Vincent shot a glance at the tall man, who was content to watch him, arms crossed, before retreating to the Low Rider. He chose the cushion closest to the porch door. His heart performed a series of somersaults. He felt light-headed and wondered if he was about to faint.

Boden mumbled something to the tall man that Vincent couldn't hear.

Please don't shoot me. I don't want to die here... alone...

"Is my roommate here?" Vincent blurted out. A pang of guilt prickled his gut as soon as the words left his mouth. If Jerry happened to be sleeping soundly in his bedroom, he wouldn't be for long.

"There is no need to bring Jeremiah into this," Boden replied evenly. He took a few steps closer to Vincent. The tall man remained in the kitchen doorway, blocking Vincent's path to the apartment's exit.

"I need you to tell me everything you know about Leah Chedid and her research," Boden said. "If you can satisfy my curiosity, we will leave you in peace."

"Leah?" Vincent asked. "You don't think she's a terrorist, do you?"

Christ, where did that come from?

"Why would we think that?" Boden asked calmly.

Vincent's pulse found a faster tempo. "I don't know. No reason. I mean, she kind of looks Middle Eastern...but she's not a terrorist. Not that I'm saying all Middle Eastern people are terrorists!"

Shut up, Vincent! Shut up!

Pause. "Her research?"

"Oh, right, she has a condition…rapid-eye something or other. She acts out her dreams sometimes. She's been studying it for a long time."

Boden and the tall man shared a look.

"What about her study concerning *you*, Vincent?"

Vincent laughed nervously. "Me? We don't really know what's wrong with me. I have this reoccurring dream where I'm a warrior named Valenthor, and there's an elf woman who wants me to save her homeland, and a we're traveling with a guy in a mask to save my…to save *Valenthor's*…daughter."

Vincent smiled in spite of himself.

What do you think about that, you Matrix *rejects?*

For once, Boden didn't miss a beat. "Do you recognize anyone from the real world in that dream?"

"No."

"What about the man in the mask?"

"How should I know? He wears a mask!"

For the first time, Boden seemed to lose his composure. His jaw tightened, and his mouth formed a tight frown. The lights in the apartment flickered, and Vincent swore the walls shook.

"Locke can kill knights with a big stick and use magic to hide from the giants," Vincent said quickly. "That's all I know!"

Pause. "Tell me about the giants," Boden pressed, sounding and looking calmer.

Vincent was about to reply when a woman joined the tall man near in the doorway—the owner of the other voice Vincent had heard coming from the kitchen. She matched her accomplices in that she also wore a trench coat. But her bright blue hair, black lipstick and spiky choker made her look badass in a very different way.

"Why don't you just cut the crap, Vinny, and tell us who has Borr?" she asked.

"Syn, return to your post!" Boden ordered, though he never took his eyes off of Vincent.

The woman rolled her eyes. Before she disappeared back into the kitchen, she snapped her teeth at Vincent, as though she would have gladly taken a bite out of his jugular if Boden hadn't been holding her leash.

Once the woman—Syn?—was gone, Boden moved to Jerry's recliner and sat down. "The giants?" he prodded.

Vincent shook his head. "I haven't seen any yet. Locke calls them the Jötunn." The tall man shifted. Or was it a flinch? "Supposedly, they raided Valenthor's homeland and killed his wife and daughter."

For a moment, everyone was silent. Boden's gray-green eyes bore into Vincent. It was as though he were looking directly into Vincent's mind, searching for the truth, for signs of treachery.

"Hey, guys, something is happening in here!" The woman's voice sounded farther away, as though she were calling from the bathroom.

Boden stood up. "Heimdall—"

"I'm on it." The tall man left the doorway.

All of the lights blinked on and off, and the whole apartment began to shake. Vincent clenched the couch cushion, his hands covered in goosebumps.

What the hell is going on?

"Vincent, listen carefully to this question," Boden said. "Do you know who DJ is?"

Elsewhere in the apartment, Syn swore and yelled something about a bathtub. He heard another voice, then, one that sounded like a little girl's. Vincent jumped to his feet, his curiosity overpowering his fear.

"Who is DJ?" Boden asked again, rising from the recliner and grabbing hold of Vincent's arm as he tried to run past him.

"I don't know anyone named—" Vincent stopped struggling.

Does he mean Daniel? Some of his friends used to call him DJ.

The sound of splashing brought his attention back to the present.

"She just appeared in the tub," he heard Syn say. She was standing in the kitchen just out of sight. "At first I thought she was dead, but—"

Vincent gave Boden a shove, knocking him against the speaker and sending the lava lamp crashing to the floor. He burst into the kitchen. The tall man stood with his back to the front door, but Vincent immediately forgot about him when he saw what the woman was holding in her arms.

A steady stream of water droplets pattered against the hardwood floor, falling from the arms, legs, and pigtails of a little girl in a soaked pink nightgown. Clementine lifted her head and smiled at him.

Vincent ran forward, reached out for her. Darkness claimed him.

Valenthor stared into the darkness, searching for whatever had startled him out of a light sleep. A warrior's sleep. Muscles tense, he strained his senses and waited. Was someone out there, or had he been dreaming?

I was dreaming...of Valentine...

Above, a thick cover of clouds smothered out the starlight. He could make out Destiny's silhouette lying on the ground nearby, though not as near him as on previous nights. The elf had said almost nothing to him since their argument at the cave. As he watched her sleep, looking so innocent and fragile, he wondered how he ever could have sided with Locke against her.

Valenthor scanned their small camp but found no sign of the man in the mask. Perhaps he was out walking a wide perimeter, keeping watch for knights, giants, and any other threat the Wild Lands could throw at them.

But why would Locke venture out alone after he had gone to such pains to weave enchantments of protection around us?

Something felt wrong, and Valenthor, the veteran of many battles, had learned long ago to trust his gut. Hammer in hand, he walked toward the trees surrounding the clearing. He cast a look back at Destiny, who stirred beneath the deerskin blanket and murmured something in either the elfish tongue or the senseless language of slumber. He pressed onward.

If an enemy were lurking out there, he would confront it head on.

After several minutes of searching the woods, Valenthor heard the murmur of voices. With as much stealth as he could muster, he crept toward the dim, red-tinged light, taking cover behind the wide trunk of an oak.

Several yards away stood a man with his back to Valenthor. There was no mistaking the threadbare cloak and cowl, the gnarled quarterstaff. Locke leaned on the stick, leisurely, clearly at ease.

"By my measure, a fortnight will pass before our arrival …mayhap less if we do not run afoul of milady's Jötunn patrols," Locke said.

The woman's voice was at once honey-smooth and as raspy as a swarm of bees, like two tongues speaking from the same mouth. "Are you certain the Chosen One will follow you?"

From his vantage, Valenthor could not see the woman, though she appeared to be the source of the uncanny crimson light that had led him to their clandestine meeting. Surely, she was a witch—a witch who commanded the Jötunn.

Small wonder Locke knew so much about Valentine's curse. He has been in league with the sorceress from the start!

Locke scoffed. "Valenthor has seen his daughter. He and the elf will come."

A fire raged inside Valenthor's body. He gripped the hammer tighter. With all of his being, he longed to charge forth and slay the treacherous Locke and the demon woman who had stolen his daughter from him. Yet he knew he was no match for the two of them.

If I am to save Valentine, I must bide my time.

"You had best not be mistaken," said the woman with two voices. "Without the elf and her champion, the prophecy will go unfulfilled."

Valenthor watched as the scarlet light faded. Locke performed a bow in the direction of where the woman had been, turned, and started back toward the campsite. As Locke passed by the oak, Valenthor dropped the hammer and lunged at him, landing on top of him and provoking a groan from behind the mask. The quarterstaff clattered a couple of feet away.

"Traitor!" Valenthor cried.

Locke squirmed, but Valenthor pressed the man's arms against his body and planted a knee firmly in his abdomen.

"Most unfortunate timing," Locke wheezed. "Not that it could have been prevented."

"Who was that woman?" Valenthor demanded. "Is she the one who placed the hex upon my daughter?"

"Yes and no."

Valenthor slammed a fist into Locke's stomach. After he stopped gasping for breath, Locke said, "Events beyond your understanding are unfolding, but if you trust me—"

"Trust you? I do not even know you!"

Scoff. "Whom *do* you trust, Valenthor? The giants plot. The gods scheme. The Ancestors drift through eternity, awaiting the call to arms for the Final Battle. But only I can reunite you with your daughter."

"You have allied yourself with the very witch who cursed Valentine!"

"Not Valentine," Locke said, "*Clementine.*"

Vincent recoiled as his memories came flooding back.

Clementine! I was just with her...before The Dream pulled me in!

Vincent tore off Locke's mask. Daniel Joseph Pierce smiled back.

"You?"

"Surprise," Daniel said, smiling crookedly. "This wasn't how I thought things would turn out, but I suppose it can't be helped. It's better that you're here than with Odin."

Odin? Does he mean Boden? Wait a second...

"You're the one Boden is looking for!" Vincent snarled. "You're the reason he and his henchmen broke into the apartment!"

"Odin and his friends are bad news, Vincent. They are very powerful, and they're dangerous. That's why I had to get you out of there, though I'm not proud of how I managed to do it."

Vincent gasped. "*You* pulled me into The Dream?"

"Guilty as charged. Sorry to have to bring Clemmy into it. I was desperate. We're just lucky Odin and the others didn't follow us."

Even though he was the one pushing all of his weight onto Daniel, Vincent found it difficult to breathe. "I don't understand what's going on. Clementine was there... alive!"

For a moment, Daniel's expression explored unfamiliar territory: sympathy.

"That wasn't really your apartment, Vince. It was just another dream. And that wasn't Clementine either. I had to disguise myself as her. It was the only way I could guarantee that you would end up back here with me."

So Clementine is *the trigger for The Dream.*

"Odin and his lackeys have the ability invade people's dreams," Daniel said. "I'm not sure how they found you, but they're sure to come back, and when they do, I won't be able to help you. So it's very important—"

"It's always been you, hasn't it?" Vincent demanded. "*You* are the reason I started having The Dream in the first place."

"Yes and no."

Vincent's mind flashed back to when they were kids. While Vincent had never been a bully, he had occasionally found himself in the same position, pinning Danny to the floor while trying to force a confession out of him.

Vincent stared hard into Daniel's bright blue eyes. Their childhood arguments had always ended a stalemate. Daniel would say only what he was ready to say. Finally, Vincent relaxed his grip, and the two brothers stood up.

"Please just tell me what's going on, Danny."

Daniel brushed at the wrinkles on his cloak. "It's a long, complicated story, and we don't have a lot of time."

"How are you even doing this?" Vincent asked. "You're in a coma!"

The sarcastic smile returned. "Always sleeping, always dreaming. Guess that's why I was chosen."

"Chosen? What are you talking about? And why does Boden call you DJ?"

Daniel sighed. "The less you know about *that*, the better."

Vincent took a step forward but stopped himself from throttling Daniel. "Only you could manage to find trouble while in a coma. But, you know, I don't even care what you've gotten yourself into. All I want is for The Dream...for Valenthor's world...to disappear. Forever."

Daniel kicked absently at the quarterstaff, which lay on the ground between them. "Can't do it, big brother. We all have our part to play, and I have orders to follow."

"*Whose* orders?"

"You could say I made a deal with devil." Daniel looked up, met Vincent's eyes. "But I've learned my lesson. I'm going to find a way to make it right. You just have to trust me."

"Ah, but I *know* you, Danny. Your Mr. Nice Guy act might fool Mom..." Vincent inhaled suddenly as a realization struck him. "If you can trick me into thinking you're Clementine, it wouldn't be too hard to convince Mom you're an angel."

Daniel looked away. "This is bigger than our family. If Odin has found you, then everyone will be watching you. Valenthor and Locke have to go their separate ways for a while. They're estranged brothers too, you know. Just like our old comic books."

Vincent's expression must have conveyed his confusion because Daniel said, "Don't you get it yet? Valenthor and Locke. Thor and Loki."

"You've lost your mind," Vincent said.

Scoff. "But isn't it nice to know you aren't losing yours?" Daniel's grin vanished. "I *am* sorry about pretending to be Clementine. I promise you'll get a chance to see her again. You just have to trust me."

"You keep Clementine out of this!"

Vincent reached for his brother, but Daniel was quicker. He kicked out his foot, and the staff seemed to jump up into his waiting hands. Vincent stumbled back.

"And if worse comes to worst," Daniel said, "we'll both have front-row seats for the end of the world."

The staff became a blur as it struck the side of Vincent's head with a loud crack.

Chapter 23

Vincent rolled off the couch and crashed to the floor. He curled into a ball, shielding his head from another strike. After a few seconds, he opened his eyes, half expecting to find Locke, staff in hand, standing in the middle of his living room.

Not Locke. Daniel!

His head throbbed fiercely—and not just where the staff had hit him. His stomach rumbled ominously. He must have had worse hangovers, but none came to mind. The next several minutes were measured by the steady throbbing between his temples.

He slung an arm slung across his eyes in an attempt to block out the morning light, tried not to think about anything at all. His plan was foiled, however, when his insides suddenly rebelled, and he was forced to make a run for the bathroom.

With no food in his stomach, it didn't take long for the dry heaves to run their course. He splashed water on his face and returned to the living room, stopping when he spotted the lava lamp standing, undamaged, on the speaker by the recliner.

Boden and his people were never here. Neither was Clementine. It was just another damn dream.

The relentless pounding in his skull made it difficult to sort out which events had happened while he was awake and which had occurred while asleep. The last thing he remembered happening to him in the real world was the argument with Jerry. Then there had been a phone call from Boden too, but he wasn't sure that that actually had happened.

Vincent replayed Leah's message.

"Hey, Vincent. It's Leah. I wanted to check in...again...and, well, I'm probably overreacting, but I just had a very strange conversation. I was trying to reach a professor who has done research on various sleep phenomena, but a man named Boden called back. He was fishing for information. I didn't tell him anything about you, but...I don't know...he gave me the creeps. I don't think it's anything to worry about...just...be careful, I guess. Anyway, I'm on my way to this family thing, but I'll have my phone. Please give me a call when you get this."

Vincent frowned.

That would explain why I had a nightmare about Boden.

He tried to remember what he and Boden had talked about on the phone, just in case it had really happened. He came up with nothing. But details from Boden's dream visit were crystal clear.

Daniel said Boden and his friends can enter dreams. If they did actually come to me in my dream, it was because they were looking for Daniel...only Boden called him DJ for some reason.

But how can any of this be possible?

The bottle of whiskey sat next to the answering machine. The repulsive tang of its contents filled his nostrils. Vincent gagged, but nothing came up.

I'm going nuts. That's the only rational explanation.

He grabbed the whiskey bottle by its neck and looked around for the cap. His search took him to Jerry's bedroom door. He knocked. Jerry deserved an apology for the awful things he had said. But what Vincent needed more than forgiveness was a genuine conversation with a living, breathing human being.

I'll even tell you about the latest twist in The Dream so you can update The Master of All Things Fantasy.

Vincent knocked again. No answer.

The bottle was halfway to his mouth before he caught himself. He set it down and picked up the phone. A primal impulse to call his mother came over him, but he dialed a different number instead.

After three rings, Leah's voice informed him that she was unable to answer the phone and invited him to leave a message after the tone.

"Damn it…uh, sorry, this is Vincent. Something happened last night. Boden called…at least I think so…and I had The Dream again. Daniel…my brother…" He sighed. "It's complicated. I just need to talk to you, Leah. I think something really bad is happening to me. I…I…"

He hung up. Before he could talk himself out of it, he pushed the opening of the bottle against his teeth and swallowed a mouthful of whiskey. It stayed down.

What if Danny isn't dead? What if he really did pretend to be angel so Mom would keep him on life support? But why would he invent Valenthor and Locke and Destiny? Unless he's playing make-believe because he has nothing better to do.

Vincent took another drink of whiskey.

No, Daniel always has a reason. He's always been a schemer, and if he somehow got superpowers…if he really can go into people's dreams…then he'd find a way to profit from it.

Unless he's the one who's lost his mind.

Vincent paced back and forth. If everything Daniel had

said was true, it didn't explain what he meant when he promised that Vincent would see his daughter again. Clementine was dead, not comatose. Perhaps it was a lie he came up with on the spot to keep Vincent from going to the police.

No one would believe me, especially not Mom. She still thinks the whole Daniel-shooting-a-cop incident is just one big misunderstanding.

I'm the only one who's ever seen Daniel for the lowlife he really is.

Vincent took another gulp, then another.

I'm the only one who can stop him.

Suzanne Fortune's fingers hovered above the keyboard. Keeping her eyes fixed on the screen, she tentatively tapped a key with her pinky. Q appeared. She swore under her breath, backspaced, and made another attempt to find the Z.

X showed instead.

With a heavy sigh, she looked down at the keyboard to locate the troublesome key. So close! While it was tempting to revert back to the two-finger, never-look-up-from-the-keyboard method that had served her for countless reports before this one, Suzanne returned to the home keys and looked back up at the screen.

I'll never finish my book if I don't learn how to type faster.

Under other circumstances, Suzanne might have felt guilty practicing typing while on the clock. But for one thing, she would become faster in the long run, which, theoretically, would make her a better receptionist and save the hospital money. For another, she wasn't even supposed to be working that weekend.

She wasn't bitter though. Her husband was on the road, and she didn't have a good reason *not* to take the shift so her coworker could go to a baby shower. Suzanne smiled. She had been to enough baby showers in her life to know she would rather take an extra shift than watch a young mother-to-be spend an hour unwrapping gifts.

Anyway, Sundays tended to be quiet. Not that the coma ward saw much excitement any other day of the week. The nurses station's second-hand radio played a classic Aerosmith song at a handful of decibels, keeping the ghoulish silence at bay. Sometimes she wondered if the patients' odds of waking up would improve if the floor weren't so damn quiet.

Slowly, she typed another line, successfully navigating the QWERTY without a single error. Her self-satisfied chuckle caught in her throat when she caught the reflection of someone else's face in the monitor. She spun her chair around and was confronted by a handsome, if aloof, face.

How can someone so big sneak up on anyone?

"I didn't know you were in today," she said.

Levi cut an imposing figure. The nurse was only a few inches taller than her husband, but somehow he seemed to take up much more space. His frame was muscular but not exactly chiseled. Attractive though he was, Suzanne could never get past the coldness of his dark brown eyes.

"Suzanne." Levi punctuated the obligatory greeting by dropping a manila folder on the stack of files next to her computer. Without another word, without even making eye contact, he turned and walked away.

She watched him go, wondering what strange thoughts percolated behind his mannequin-like expression.

Maybe I could make him into a character...a villain.

She returned to the pile of reports, but it was too late. Her thoughts had already strayed to her private world—an ancient realm of knights, elves, and magic. Progress was slow lately, and though her self-taught typing lessons bore part of the blame, she knew the real reason why the last few scenes had taken so long to write.

She didn't know what was going to happen next.

The squeak of a shoe against the polished floor made her look up. A man was leaning against the counter. His eyes were bloodshot, and by the looks of it, his hair hadn't been acquainted with a brush in days. "Haunted" was the word she would have used to describe him on paper.

And somehow, the man *did* remind her of the reluctant hero in her book.

"Hi, I'm, ah, looking for Danny...*Daniel* Pierce. Can you tell me what room he's in?"

The guy stank of booze.

"Mr. Pierce doesn't get many visitors," Suzanne said. "What is your relation to the patient?"

"I'm his brother. *Half*-brother, actually."

Suzanne sat up a little in her chair. "You're Vincent. Eve's other son."

He looked away. "Yeah, I'm Vincent. Wait a minute. She's not here, is she? My mother, I mean."

"No, not yet." Suzanne had forgotten that by picking up the Sunday shift, she would have a chance to chat with her friend. She looked at her watch. "Mass won't be over for an hour or so."

Eve wasn't kidding when she said she and Vincent had drifted apart since he moved out. I'm sure he would have bolted out of here if I'd told him she was here.

Suzanne pushed the clipboard closer to him. "You'll have to sign in."

He took the pen and slopped his signature on the page.

"It's Room 307," she said, taking the clipboard. "Down that hall and take a left."

Vincent quickly turned around and hurried away. She watched him stagger down the hall—making a valiant attempt at walking a straight line—and almost crash into Levi, who was coming from the opposite direction.

Poor Eve...one son in a coma and the other one drinking his life away.

Suzanne was making a mental note to call her own son after work when Levi's deep voice wrenched her attention back to the present.

"Who was that?" he asked.

"Whuh? Oh, that was Vincent..." She checked the sign-in sheet. "...Cruz. He's here to see Daniel Pierce, his brother."

For the first time in the five months she had known Levi, something akin to emotion flickered across the man's face. Then it was gone. He deposited another file folder on her desk and walked away.

Suzanne wondered what Eve would say, later, when she signed in and saw that Vincent had visited Daniel. The two women had spent many a Sunday afternoon trading stories about their children, and Suzanne thought Eve would be thrilled to learn that Vincent had finally taken the time see his brother.

Of course, if Vincent is still here when Eve arrives, she'll see how drunk he is, which would break her heart.

She recalled Eve saying Vincent used to have a problem with drinking. Apparently, he had fallen off the wagon again. She wondered if her protagonist, also a recovering alcoholic, would relapse before the end of the book.

Suzanne wanted him to redeem himself, but maybe it would add more tension if Valenthor hit rock bottom before he became a true hero.

Not that there are likely to be a lot of taverns in the Wild Lands between the untamed frontier of the human empire and the ancient homeland of the elves.

"Call the police."

At first she didn't recognize Levi's voice—or his face, which was damp with sweat and more animated than she had ever seen it.

"What's going on?" she asked.

"He tried to kill the patient," Levi said, "but I stopped him."

"Who—"

"Vincent," he said. "Tell the police he came to kill his brother."

Suzanne picked up the phone but couldn't decide what came next. At last, her fingers pressed 9-1-1. She looked up, knowing she would need more information when someone picked up and started asking her questions.

What did he mean by "I stopped him"? Are Eve's boys all right?

But her questions, as well as the police's, would go unanswered. Levi was gone. At the end of the hall, the elevator began its descent.

Chapter 24

Though she spent countless hours behind the reception desk, sitting in that very chair, Suzanne felt like an intruder. She had never seen so many people on the third floor. Men in uniforms, wearing gold-and-silver badges that gleamed under the florescent lights, occupied the space around the nurses station and walked the usually quiet hallways.

Her typical, tranquil Sunday morning was a hazy memory, a dream.

She shivered and hugged the knitted sweater tighter against her skin. She had imagined—had even *written*—battle scenes with blood and death. But there was a big difference between made-up warriors fighting for their lives and a real-life man trying to murder his helpless brother.

Valenthor would never sneak up on an enemy and kill his while he slept. Locke, on the other hand...

Suzanne jumped when the elevator pinged. The shiny metal door slid open, and Eve emerged, her eyes big with worry.

God, give me strength!

"Suzie, what's going on?" Eve asked, running up to her. "They wouldn't tell me anything downstairs except that I can't see Daniel because of 'an incident' that took place on the third floor."

Suzanne could see Detective Something-or-other

watching from a few feet away. He was talking to another officer and writing in a small notebook, but she could tell he was listening.

"Is Daniel OK?" Eve asked.

"He's fine, Eve...I mean, his condition is unchanged." Suzanne took a breath and let the words spill out. "Vincent is here. He came to see Daniel. But soon after he arrived, one of the nurses said he tried to hurt Daniel."

"What?" Eve steadied herself against the counter. "That's impossible!"

Suzanne placed her hand on Eve's. "The police are trying to figure out exactly what happened. From what I've gathered, both of your sons are going to be all right."

"I want to see Vincent," Eve said loudly, staring down the crowd of officers. "Where is my son?"

"He's sleeping," the detective said, approaching the desk. His squared jaw line and bright blue eyes reminded Suzanne of a character from one of her favorite cops-and-court dramas. "He's going to wake up to one hell of a hangover, but he'll live."

Eve closed her eyes and dropped her head into her hands. "I knew he was in trouble, but God help me, I never thought he'd do something crazy like this."

Suzanne wanted to say something comforting, but she worried that the detective would ask her to leave if she interrupted. She needed to be there for Eve, so she would keep quiet.

"What kind of trouble?" the detective asked.

"Vincent lost his daughter, my granddaughter, eight years ago...eight years ago *today*, in fact. His marriage is on the rocks, and I'm pretty sure he lost his job. He's just...stuck."

Suzanne's breath caught in her throat. She had forgotten all about Eve's granddaughter, Vincent's daughter. It wasn't something Eve was prone to bring up.

Vincent lost his little girl. Just like Valenthor. And they're both alcoholics who have given up on life. Dear God, did I unconsciously base my main character on Eve's son?

Detective What's-his-name jotted something down in his notebook. "Does Vincent have a history of violent behavior?"

Suzanne tried to gauge the detective's expression. Surely the detective knew Daniel had killed a police officer. What he really wanted to know, Suzanne supposed, was whether violence ran in the family.

Eve let out a shaky sigh. "No, not Vincent."

"Can you think of any reason he would want to harm Daniel?"

Eve looked up. Conflicting emotions pulled at her suddenly colorless face. "Vincent believed keeping Daniel …believed keeping him *here* was a waste of money. We argued about it more than once."

"Argued about keeping Daniel alive," the detective clarified.

Eve nodded. "He said Daniel would never wake up, that he was already gone. But I can't imagine why he would…would… Vincent always looked after his little brother." A big tear traced the curve of her cheek and slid off her chin. Eve cleared her throat. "What did Vincent try to do exactly?"

The detective didn't look up from his notebook. "When was the last time you spoke to your son?"

A short woman in a dark blue windbreaker interrupted before Eve could answer. "Detective, the doctor says there's another drug swimming around with all that booze in his blood…mid-az-o-lam, a fast-acting sedative. And there's a fresh puncture wound in his abdomen, likely from a syringe."

The detective grunted. "Our missing nurse stuck him with a tranquilizer before fleeing the scene." He turned to Suzanne, who wasn't invisible after all, and said, "Does everybody around here walk around with syringes full of sedatives in case the coma patients get rowdy?"

Suzanne resisted the urge to scowl. The detective hadn't been satisfied by her answers—or lack thereof— while questioning her about Levi Nathan.

"What do you mean 'missing nurse'?" Eve asked. "Did anyone here actually *see* what happened?"

"Levi, one of the nurses on duty, told me to call 9-1-1 and say that Vincent tried to kill Daniel. Then he just walked away."

It was like Levi knew Vincent was up to something. Why else would he have followed him into Daniel's room? But how could he have known? And if Levi is the hero in all of this, why did he leave?

"Rest assured, we are doing everything in our power to locate Mr. Nathan," the detective stated.

"But nobody knows what happened for sure," Eve half said, half asked.

The detective added another sentence or two to his notebook. "No, but we will. Soon."

"I want to see my sons," Eve said.

The short female officer shook her head. "Mr. Pierce's room is a crime scene, and Mr. Cruz is still sleeping. The doctors are checking him out. We want to make sure he's healthy before we take him downtown."

Eve's lips trembled as her frown deepened. "Oh God," she whispered.

Another officer called out to the detective, who gave Eve a look that simultaneously said, "Excuse me" and "Don't go anywhere" before he and the short woman disappeared down the hall.

Suzanne squeezed Eve's hand. "Let me get you some coffee."

Eve nodded and wiped the tears from her cheeks. "This is a nightmare. Like the day Daniel got shot all over again. I can't lose Vincent too. I can't…" She started to sob.

Suzanne put the coffee pot down and hurried around the counter. Wrapping Eve in a firm hug, she said, "It's going to be OK, Eve. We'll figure this out together."

Something heavy landed on Leah's stomach—something much bigger than a Persian cat. The sleep mask blinded her from everything except the images of the burglar/rapist conjured by her frantic mind. She could feel the intruder's legs straddling either side of her abdomen. Fumbling with the handcuffs, she tried to keep the panic at bay.

Then her assailant started tickling her.

"What the—?"

She heard a woman giggle, and her terror subsided.

"Bekah, I'm so gonna kick your ass!"

The tickling intensified. Leah, laughing hysterically, writhed under the relentless assault, losing her hold on the cuffs.

"Promise to make me breakfast, and I'll stop," her little sister taunted.

Bekah's fingers dug deep into Leah's armpits, a weak spot her siblings had routinely exploited when they were younger. Leah howled.

"OK, *OK*, I promise!"

The sleep mask was pulled free from Leah's face. Above her, Bekah's pretty, round face stretched into a grin. She wore the same white tank top that had been under her fuzzy lavender sweater the day before. Bucky

Badger scowled at Leah from the borrowed pair of sweat-pants.

"That was payback for all that wine you made me drink last night," Bekah said. "I need to get something in my stomach."

Leah freed herself from the restraints and gave Bekah a shove that nearly sent her bouncing off of the bed. "A hangover? That's what you get for leaving Wisconsin. You've brought shame to your native state." She sat up and felt the beginnings of a headache start to pulse behind her eyes.

No need to tell Bekah about that.

"Anyway," Leah said, "Zaina was the one who kept insisting we order another bottle."

Bekah laughed. "I think she was celebrating a night away from the kids more than Mom and Dad's anniversary."

Leah smiled. It had been a fun evening, even though everyone had given her a lot of grief for showing up late. She couldn't remember the last time all of them were together. After their parents left the restaurant, Leah and her sisters had stayed behind to catch up—and drink.

Leah pulled on a pair of gym shorts that had never seen a gym and made a stop at the bathroom. When she came out, Bekah was waiting for her in the living room.

"So what's for breakfast?" Bekah asked.

"Let me see what I have." Leah went to the kitchen and rifled through the cupboards. Hamburger Helper, tomato soup, cat food. She heard the TV come to life in the next room. She turned to the refrigerator, which mocked her with an almost empty carton of skim milk, low-fat yogurt, grape jelly, and a carton of old Thai takeout.

"I think we're going to have to hit a Denny's," Leah called.

"Jesus!"

"All right, how about Perkins?"

"No, get in here, Leah. This is messed up."

Leah left the kitchen and leaned against the side of the couch, where Bekah sat hunched forward, her eyes glued to the TV. On the screen, a woman with obvious hair extensions and loud magenta lips spoke emphatically into a microphone.

"…are not releasing the name of the attacker, but we have reason to believe he is related to the victim…"

Beneath the reporter's name, the headline read, "Mercy Killing Gone Amok?"

Bekah said, "The one guy is in a coma. They think his brother tried to pull the plug or something."

"Is that St. Mary's?" Leah asked.

"…patient, Daniel Pierce, has been unresponsive for nearly eight months, following a shootout with Milwaukee Police. Pierce shot and killed an officer and was himself shot during a drug raid on the North Side in April…"

"Huh, maybe it's not a mercy killing," Bekah said. "Maybe the brother just wanted to get rid of the black sheep of the family."

The gurgling in Leah's stomach had nothing to do with dehydration. "I think I know him."

"Who, coma man?"

"No, his brother. Half-brother," Leah said.

"You're joking, right?"

Leah walked away without answering. She found her phone at the bottom of her purse. There were three messages. The first one had come in at 6:30 that morning.

"Damn it…uh, sorry, this is Vincent. Something happened last night. Boden called…at least I think so…and I had The Dream again. Daniel…my brother…" He sighed. "It's complicated. I just need to talk to you, Leah. I think something really bad is happening to me. I…I…"

The next message was from an hour later, and Vincent's speech was more than a little slurred.

"It's Vincent again. Daniel is causing The Dream. I'm sure of it. He's Locke, and the little fuck pretended to be Clementine too…today of all days." After several seconds of silence, he continued. "I'm going to stop him. I just wanted to say I'm sorry for what happened with Bella yesterday. I should have told you about kissing her cousin, but I didn't sleep with her. You gotta believe me. Anyway, I'm sorry I got you mixed up in this shit. You don't deserve it. Thanks for everything."

Leah, still keeping an eye on the reporter's dramatic newscast on the television, couldn't bring herself to listen to the message again. It sounded too much like a final confession.

Vincent, what have you done?

"What's going on, Leah? You look like you're going to puke." Bekah stood up and put a hand on her shoulder. She looked scared.

Leah *was* scared.

Before Leah could say anything, her phone dutifully asked if she wanted to hear the next message. She took a deep breath and pressed the button.

"Dr. Chedid, Vincent Cruz has been arrested. It is imperative that he does not tell the police anything… complicated. Do whatever is necessary to get him out of jail. Post his bail. I will be in touch shortly."

Even without the pauses, Leah had no trouble identifying the grave, commanding voice.

"Leah, what is it?" Bekah asked. "Who was that?"

Leah slowly brought the phone away from her ear and mumbled, "Boden."

Chapter 25

The deep creases in Bekah's forehead, combined with her worried frown, only intensified her resemblance to their mother.

"Who is Boden?" she asked.

Leah flicked through the menus on her phone, calling up the recent call list, and was unsurprised to discover that Boden's call had come from a restricted number. She cursed.

"Leah?"

"I don't know who Boden is. It's a long story," Leah replied, dropping her phone back in her purse. "But it looks like I'll have to take a rain check on breakfast."

She started to walk away, but Bekah wouldn't relinquish her hold on her shoulder. "Where are you going?"

"To see Vincent."

"The guy who tried to kill his brother?" Bekah asked. "Are you serious?"

Leah nodded distractedly. "I...I don't know what's going on, but I can't believe Vincent would do something like that. I'm going to the police station."

"Then I'm going with you," Bekah insisted.

"No way," Leah said. "Look, I'll explain everything later, Bek, but right now a friend of mine is in trouble, and I have to help him."

Bekah tightened her grip and she pulled Leah into a hug. "Just be careful, OK? I'll be here when you get back."

Good thing it's Bekah. I never could have talked Zaina out of tagging along.

Leah took the fastest shower of her life, threw on an outfit that adhered uncomfortably to her damp skin, and gave her sister a fake but hopefully reassuring smile on her way to the door. She ran to her car, her teeth chattering.

As the neighborhoods whizzed past her window, the first few drops of rain streaked across the windshield. Her hands squeezed the steering wheel. Her mind raced. She wondered if she could trust Boden. She wondered if she could trust Vincent. But of the many questions spiraling around in her mind, one surfaced over and over again:

What the hell am I doing?

Maybe it was the mystery of it all that had her speeding toward downtown Milwaukee. Vincent's unidentified sleep disorder, his motive for attacking his comatose brother, Boden's identity, and his interest in Vincent— there was no shortage of unknowns. She told herself it was human nature to be curious. And Vincent was a patient, after all.

Bullshit.

Leah rubbed the back of her neck, combing her fingers through the wet strands of hair. Vincent wasn't just a patient or lab rat. And he was more than her old friend's estranged husband. Despite the fact that he tended to treat people like crap, he was her friend, and she wanted to help him.

But I don't love him.

She supposed Vincent fit the profile for her collection of recent ex-boyfriends. After her three-year relationship with Aldrich had fizzled out a week after earning their doctorates, none of her subsequent love interests had been more than diversions, exciting deviations from a dull daily routine. In the end, the guys always turned out to be losers whose lives were going nowhere.

Is that was this is about...just another distraction?

Leah exited the freeway and took the most direct path to where she thought the jail was. She had a vague recollection of going there for a field trip back in grade school, but she suspected it was a hand-me-down memory, an impression her mind fashioned after hearing one of her sisters talk about it so many times.

After two wrong turns, she found it—a strikingly plain structure, especially when compared to the massive and many-pillared courthouse next door. As she approached the police station, her heart started to pound. She thought the building would have made for an intimidating locale for young students.

Then again, Leah's favorite field trip memory involved a visit to the Milwaukee Public Museum, particularly when the day culminated with a stop at the gift shop, where she traded the guts of her piggy bank for old-timey treats. Pulling open the station's heavy door, she doubted anything so sweet was waiting at the end of today's adventure.

She was directed to County Lockup, second floor, where she had to pass through a metal detector. An unsmiling woman in uniform sat behind the reception desk. Age-wise, she could have been anywhere between a rough forty and a lucky sixty.

"Yes?" the woman asked without looking up.

An inhuman sound escaped from Leah's lips. She cleared her throat and tried again. "I'm here to see Vincent Cruz. He was...um...brought here earlier this morning."

The officer didn't say anything for a few minutes, keeping her eyes fixed on a monitor Leah couldn't see. Meanwhile, her fingers stabbed persistently at the keyboard.

Leah was about to repeat herself when the woman asked, "Are you a family member?"

"No, I'm his…" She almost said "friend" but finished with "…doctor."

The woman looked up, arching a narrow eyebrow. "Psychiatrist?"

"No, I'm a sleep specialist."

The officer's eyes shifted back to the computer screen, her fingers dancing an encore performance on the keyboard. "Have a seat. It might be a while, honey."

Leah turned and saw that one corner of the room was lined with the kind of plastic-capped seats usually reserved for bus terminals. Two women sitting next to each other were staring at her.

Smiling self-consciously, Leah sat down, leaving two empty chairs as a buffer between her and the nearest lady, who continued to watch her. There weren't any magazines, so she took out her phone.

I should text Bekah…but what would I say?

"Excuse me."

Leah looked up. The nearest woman, whose hair was too light to be a brunette but barely qualified as a blonde, gave her a ghost of a smile. Pink, puffy skin ringed her eyes.

"Forgive me for being nosey," the woman continued, "but did I hear you ask to see Vincent Cruz?"

Leah nodded warily. "I'm his doctor…and a friend. I specialize in sleep medicine."

An unidentified emotion rippled through the woman's expression. "You must be Leah."

Leah's heart lurched.

Did Boden send her?

The woman must have interpreted Leah's silence as an admission because she said, "Bella told me about running into you at Vincent's apartment. I'm Eve, Vincent's mother."

The complete absence of a family resemblance was astonishing. Leah might not have believed her, except she couldn't think of a reason why the woman would lie.

"Nice to meet you." Leah considered reaching awkwardly across the vacant seats to shake her hand. Eve didn't look like she was going to attempt the same, so Leah kept her hands on her lap.

Eve glanced at the woman seated beside her. "This is Suzanne Fortune. She works at the hospital where Daniel, my other son, stays."

Suzanne smiled politely and said, "Hello."

She looked to be slightly younger than Eve, in her early forties perhaps. Her long blond hair could have used some attention, but Leah knew she was the last person to criticize a hairstyle.

Looking at nothing particular on a far wall, Leah said, "I caught the end of a news report, but I don't really understand what happened…"

Eve scoffed. "No one seems to know. The only eyewitness…other than Vincent…ran off."

"Levi Nathan, a nurse at the hospital, was the one who said he saw Vincent trying to kill Daniel, but no one knows where he is now," Suzanne clarified.

"It has to be a big misunderstanding," Eve said, preempting the very sentiment on the tip of Leah's tongue. "Vincent is *not* a murderer. What possible reason would he have to harm his brother?"

Leah thought back to the second message Vincent had left on her voicemail. She didn't know why Vincent would blame Daniel for The Dream, but since she couldn't mention anything about Vincent's condition, she simply shrugged.

"Was Vincent having trouble sleeping?" Eve asked.

Knowing the question was coming didn't make it any easier for Leah to reply. "I'm sorry, Eve, but I'm not at liberty to discuss anything pertaining to the health of one of my patients."

"Are you sleeping with him?"

Leah nearly fell out of her chair.

"Eve!" Suzanne admonished at the same time Leah gave an emphatic "No!"

Rubbing her eyes, Eve said, "I'm sorry. That wasn't a very Christian thing to say. It's just that I love Bella, who is still my daughter-in-law, and she seems to think you're the other woman."

Eve's eyes locked onto Leah's again. "And I suppose I'm jealous of you too, because you know more about what's going with Vincent than I do."

Leah scratched the back of her neck. Summoning her most professional tone, she said, "I suppose the only thing we can do is sit tight and wait for more information."

Eve leaned back in her seat and crossed her arms. Leah fidgeted with her phone, pretending to do something very important.

The small interrogation room reminded Vincent of the jail cell he had shared with Destiny. But the yellowish-white cinderblocks and oversized mirror would have been out of place in Valenthor's world. Up until recently, they would have been out of place in *his* life too.

Vincent was pretty sure he wasn't dreaming anymore. His hangover felt too real.

"Why did you go to the hospital today, Vincent?" The stiff-jawed detective bore a slight resemblance to Sir Angus. Vincent half expected the man to call him Valenthor.

For a fraction of a second, Vincent considered spilling his guts about The Dream. Everything had seemed to make sense on the cab ride to hospital. If Daniel really did go into their mother's dream in the guise of an angel and if he were orchestrating The Dream, then he deserved to die. And even if everything that had happened last night was only in Vincent's head, that meant Daniel was just a vegetable, after all. No harm in putting him out of his misery.

In retrospect, the logic seemed less than rock solid.

"You haven't seen your brother since spring. Why visit him today?" the detective asked.

If Destiny was here, she could use her magic to tear the wall down.

"As drunk as you were, you couldn't think of a livelier place to party than with a man in a coma?" The detective laughed. "Ever hear of a strip club, buddy?"

"I think I prefer Sir Angus," Vincent muttered.

"What was that?"

Vincent coughed. "Can I get some water?"

The detective leaned back and crossed his arms. "Feeling a bit dehydrated? Yeah, you can have some water. But how about walking me through your morning first?"

Vincent shifted his weight, trying to get comfortable in the medieval torture device posing as a chair. "It's like you said. I was blitzed. I don't know why I went to see Daniel. Must have been feeling sentimental and missed my little brother."

The detective grunted. "Interesting theory. Except your mother said that, by your figuring, Daniel Pierce has been dead since the day he went into that coma. I guess you were paying your respects, huh?"

Vincent couldn't hide his surprise.

"Oh yes, I had a nice, long chat with your mom." The detective smiled smugly. "You two never saw eye to eye on keeping Daniel hooked up to machines. Personally, I'm with you, Vincent. Your brother was a bona fide screw-up. He certainly doesn't deserve all of those visits from your mother or the charity from her church, which keeps him breathing…his heart pumping."

Top-notch care for his body while his mind roams freely…

The detective scooted his chair forward, scraping it against the cold floor and producing a sound like a dying animal. "A lot of guys around here wouldn't blame you for trying to kill him. Pierce is a drug dealer, and he's a killer …twice over, by my count."

When the detective didn't elaborate, Vincent asked, "What do you mean by that?"

The man lowered his voice. "The partner of the officer your brother shot…he blew his brains out a week after the botched drug bust. He must have felt terrible about not being able to save his partner. I saw him the day before he pulled the trigger. He looked like he hadn't slept since it happened." The detective leaned across the table. "*That* didn't make the *Journal*'s front page."

The temperature in the room plummeted.

If Daniel can mess with people's dreams, what would stop him from haunting the man who shot him?

Something shifted menacingly in Vincent's guts. "Can I have that water now?"

The detective didn't blink. "Do you own a red Swiss Army knife?"

"Yeah."

"Did you bring it with you to the hospital this morning?"

"I don't know. I might have."

"What happened when you walked into Daniel Pierce's room?"

I chickened out. Even with half a bottle of whiskey in me and certain he was laughing at me while tormenting me with visions of Clementine, I couldn't kill him. I must have passed out with the knife in my hand.

"Do you remember being attacked?" the detective asked.

Vincent sat up straighter. "Attacked?" What he saw with his mind's eye was more like an impression than a memory. "Now that you mention it, I think someone *did* come up from behind me. I remember struggling against someone who was very strong…struggling for air."

"Do you remember seeing a male nurse on your way into see your brother?"

Vincent started to shake his head. Then the image of a big man in white popped into his head. "I don't know…maybe?"

The detective laughed mirthlessly. "Let me see if I got this straight. You don't know why you went to see your brother because you were shit-faced. A nurse attacks you for no reason and tells the lady at the front desk you tried to kill a man in a coma."

"I guess so."

The detective's eyes hardened. "If that's true, you're one unlucky son of a bitch, Vincent." He stood up suddenly, causing the metal chair legs to screech against the floor again.

Vincent flinched in spite of himself. When the detective walked toward the room's only exit, he asked, "Where are you going?"

Without turning around, the detective replied, "You wanted some water, remember?"

The door slammed, echoing throughout the small room and inside Vincent's head. He ran a hand through his sweat-slicked hair. He felt a gnawing at his insides as he waited for the man to return. There was no clock in the room. Every minute was a piece of eternity.

He had been in trouble with the law twice before—once when he had had to answer those horrible questions the day Clementine died and then his DUI—but he couldn't even bring himself to worry about the detective, the legal system, or anything as mundane as rotting in jail.

Every yawn evoked a fresh wave of panic. Whatever happened to him in the real world could not compare to the deviant delights his half-brother could cook up. Daniel hadn't made another appearance after hitting him in the head with the staff. Then again, Vincent couldn't remember dreaming at all after that.

Next time, I probably won't be so lucky. Will he know what I tried to do to him?

Alone in the small room, Vincent could have sworn he heard Locke's scoff.

Chapter 26

The doorknob turned, and Vincent leaned forward expectantly, surprised at how eager he was to see the detective again.

His drowsiness had escalated into full-blown exhaustion during the eon of solitude. Whatever the detective had planned for the next phase of the interrogation, it was bound to do a better job of keeping Vincent awake than sitting alone in the quiet, empty room.

The detective set a small paper cup on the table in front of Vincent. "You have some visitors. I'll be right outside."

The detective opened the door, and Evangeline and another woman entered the room. His mother took the empty seat across from him at the table. Her companion, an unremarkable woman who nonetheless brought the word "frumpy" to mind, remained standing near the door. The detective left.

Vincent had only a moment to puzzle over the stranger's presence before his mother lunged forward, snatched up his hands, and started to cry. She asked if he was OK, and he nodded, not knowing what else he could or should say.

After another few seconds, she asked, "Vincent, what is going on?"

"I wish I knew," he muttered.

She released his hands and gave him a look so severe it transported him back to his childhood. For the most part,

Vincent had followed the rules, but he had earned a scolding or two throughout the years—usually after Daniel talked him into going along with one of his allegedly foolproof schemes.

"You need to tell me the truth," Evangeline said. "Did you go the hospital to hurt your brother?"

"No."

"Then why were you there?" she asked.

Vincent shrugged, unable to meet her eye. He took the cup and raised it to his lips, greedily swallowing the lukewarm water.

"I know you think Daniel is already gone," she said, "but whether or not he stays in the hospital has never been your decision to make. I have faith—"

Vincent laughed before he could stop himself.

"Yes, *faith*," she continued. Her expression softened. "I know you're angry, Vincent, but punishing Daniel is not going to change anything. You know that, right?"

Vincent's thoughts flashed to the night of the sleep study, the one time Daniel had appeared as himself in one of Vincent's dreams.

"I get it," Daniel had said, "You want to kill me because it'll kill Mom."

That might have been true once, but not anymore. Now I want to protect Mom...from you.

"You can be so blind sometimes, Mom."

She sat back and crossed her arms. "Daniel is *not* dead."

"That's not what I meant," Vincent said, "but since you brought it up, what in the hell makes you think God...or his angels, for that matter...would want Daniel to stick around? He's a murderer!"

Evangeline glanced nervously at the big, two-way mirror on the wall next to them. "Vincent—"

239

"You've never been able to accept Daniel for what he is…a failure and a menace to society." His voice was getting louder, but he didn't care. "You always told yourself he fell in with the wrong crowd, that his friends were bad influences. Well, Mom, I hate to be the one to break it to you, but *Daniel* was the bad influence."

Tears streamed down her cheeks, leaving a glistening trail behind. "Everyone deserves the chance to be forgiven," she said. "Even you, Vincent."

He rolled his eyes.

She'll never be able to see him as anything other than her charming little Danny.

"I hope you never have to learn how wrong you are about him," he said softly.

Evangeline took a big breath. "If you say you didn't go to the hospital to hurt Daniel, then I believe you. But you need help, Vincent. I can put you in touch with a counselor from my church—"

Vincent groaned.

"Fine," she said. "I don't care who you talk to. That doctor lady you've been seeing is here too. Since you obviously aren't comfortable telling your own mother what's wrong with you—"

"What's wrong with me?" The harsh laughter gushed up from somewhere deep inside of him. "OK, Mom, you win. Where would you like me to begin? How about the fact that when I dream, I'm really awake? Or that I lost my job because whatever the hell is wrong with me acts a lot like narcolepsy? Or that I'm clearly losing my mind because I'm seriously considering the possibility that a guy in a coma has the ability to create a fairytale world in which I transform into a barbarian named Valenthor."

Vincent gazed triumphantly at the stunned countenance of his mother. "Aren't you glad you asked?"

"Excuse me, but did you say *Valenthor*?"

Having completely forgotten that there was someone else in the room, Vincent started at the sound of the other woman's voice. The stranger took a couple of timid steps closer to the table. All of the color had drained from her face.

"Yes, when I sleep, I become Valenthor of the Three Rivers," he said, flashing an acerbic smile. "He was a hero once, but after the giants killed his wife and cursed his daughter, he became a useless drunk. Does that scenario sound at all familiar to you?"

Vincent had directed the rhetorical question at his mother, but it was the other woman who replied, "How…how could you know about that?"

"Because that's my life, lady," he shot back. "Whenever The Dream pulls me in, I find myself wandering through forests and mountains on a quest to save my daughter's soul. I hang out with an elf who never stops talk about her ancestors and a mysterious masked man who was tagging along in order to lead us into a trap. Quite an adventure, huh?"

"No!" the woman shouted.

Both Vincent and Eve jumped.

"Suzanne, what—?" his mother started to say.

"How did you get at my book?" The woman—Suzanne—loomed over the table, pressing her fingers so hard into the metal surface they turned white. "*No one* has read any of my writing, not even my husband, and I never told anyone about my characters."

Suddenly, Vincent recognized Suzanne. "You…you work with Daniel!"

Vincent started to laugh. Suzanne shouted something to him, while his mother tried to calm her down, but he couldn't hear any of it above the sounds spilling out of his own mouth. He was vaguely aware of the detective bursting into the room and ushering the two women out.

When they were gone, the detective regarded Vincent warily. "Care to fill me in on the joke, Mr. Cruz?"

Between fits of laughter, Vincent managed to say, "It's not real."

"What isn't real?"

After two great, steadying breaths Vincent said, "You, me, Valenthor…any of this."

Then the dam broke, and the horrible noise could not be stopped.

Leah looked up from her phone—she had finally texted Bekah to let her know that she was OK but that she shouldn't wait for her—when an officer she had never seen before brought Eve and Suzanne back out to the lobby. Eve was saying something to Suzanne, and her tone was far from friendly.

"—can't really think Vincent would break into your house?"

Suzanne, looking dazed, followed a few steps behind her friend. "I don't know what to believe, Eve. How else could he know so much about Valenthor?"

Leah nearly dropped her phone. Boden's words echoed in her mind.

"It is imperative that he does not tell the police any-thing…complicated."

Vincent's mother walked past without a glance. Suzanne looked like she was going to do the same, but at the last second, she made a sharp turn, stopping directly in front of Leah.

"Did he ever tell you about any of his dreams?" Suzanne asked breathlessly. "Has he ever mentioned

Valenthor to you?"

"Why...why do you ask?" Leah faltered.

Eve took Suzanne by the elbow. "Don't waste your time, Suzie," she said, her voice dripping with scorn. "She won't tell you anything. She's a doctor, remember?"

Eve put her arm around Suzanne and began leading her toward the exit.

"Wait," Leah said, rising to her feet. "What happened in there? Is Vincent all right?"

Eve glanced over her shoulder. "You might as well go home. They're not going to let him talk to anyone else while he's here. But don't worry, he's going to see a doctor *who can help him*."

"What do you mean?"

Across the lobby, Eve opened the door for Suzanne. Her mouth trembled as she said, "They're taking Vincent to the County Mental Health Center."

Pulling away from the police station, Leah felt like she was abandoning Vincent. She considered driving to the mental health center but questioned what good going there would do. They weren't likely to release Vincent, a suspect in an attempted murder case who apparently just confessed to leading a double life in a fantasy dream world.

I need to talk to Boden.

Leah glanced at her phone, which lay lifeless on the passenger seat. She wasn't convinced Boden had Vincent's best interest in mind, but he seemed to know something about his condition. If she could get some answers out of him, she might be able to figure out what to do next.

But what if he never calls back?

Since going home felt too much like conceding defeat,

she made an impulsive right turn, squealing the tires. She didn't know what she would find at Vincent's apartment, but it was the only other destination that came to mind. The radio played Wagner's "Ride of the Valkyries," an unlikely soundtrack for what she expected to be an uneventful and altogether pointless detour.

The sun was imprisoned behind a wall of dark gray clouds that threatened heavier rain or possibly snow. She found a parking spot a block away from the apartment and quickly made her way through the cold drizzle, shoving her hands deep into the pockets of her denim jacket.

A young man with two bulldogs was exiting the building as Leah approached. He held the door open for her, which meant she looked respectable enough, despite of her makeup-free face and wind-ravaged hair. Either that, or Vincent's neighbors were accustomed to the comings and goings of unfamiliar people.

She walked up the creaky steps, knocked on the door with the four, and waited. A moment later, she reached for the doorknob to see if Vincent's roommate had left the apartment unlocked again. She jumped guilty back when she heard footsteps on the other side of the door.

The door popped open a couple of inches. A bloodshot eye stared at her from above the chain lock.

"Are you a cop?"

She nearly laughed out loud. "Do I look like a cop?"

"You have to tell me if you are," the man insisted. "I know my rights."

"My name is Leah. I'm a friend of Vincent's."

The eye looked her up and down. Then it disappeared as the door closed again. She was about to protest until she heard the clinking of metal. Vincent's roommate opened the door all of the way.

He was a big guy. His shaggy, sandy-blond hair needed

a trim, but his cheeks and chin were clean-shaven. A parade of Technicolor teddy bears grinned at her from his tie-dyed T-shirt. His eyes looked friendly, albeit sleepy.

"I'm Jerry. C'mon in."

She followed him into the living room, where he took a seat in a recliner. A laptop sat on the coffee table. She took a seat on the couch, her nose twitching. The apartment smelled like someone had broken a bottle of Vanilla Fields all over the floor.

Jerry propped his feet up on the coffee table. "Vincent got himself into some trouble, huh?"

Leah smiled in spite of herself. There was something immediately likable about Jerry. She couldn't recall Vincent saying much about him, other than he sometimes forgot to lock the door. She wondered if the two of them were good friends.

"I don't know the whole story, but, yeah, it looks pretty bad," Leah said. "They took him to the County Mental Health Center."

"That really sucks." An awkward silence ensued. "So…are you guys, like, a couple?"

Her cheeks burned. "No…just friends."

"That's good. He's still married, you know. I only just found out about that. Otherwise, I sure as hell wouldn't have tried to hook him up with Paish." Jerry reached over and typed something on the laptop. "Sorry. Just signing off IM."

"Jerry, did you see Vincent this morning?"

"Nah, I took off last night. Vincent and I had an argument." His drowsy eyes met hers. "He was in real bad shape, drunk off his ass. He was freaking out about how I let Bella in the house. When I left, he was passed out in the bathroom. I figured he'd sleep it off and be fine."

Leah leaned back on the couch and sighed. "He left me

a couple of messages earlier this morning. He sounded shaken up, rambling about his brother, Daniel, and a dream…"

"The Valenthor dream?" Jerry asked.

"Uh…yeah," Leah said cautiously. "I wasn't sure if you knew about that."

Jerry scratched his mop of hair. "He used to give me regular updates. We'd consult the Master, trade theories. It's been a while since Vincent and I talked about anything though."

She leaned forward, her heart pounding. "Wait, who's the Master?"

"A guy online who knows just about everything about the fantasy genre." Jerry stood up and walked out of the room. His words drifted from the kitchen. "We thought he might be able to tell us what Valenthor was supposed to do next…to finish the quest, you know? The Master is a pretty cool dude. He convinced me to give this book about magic and elves and stuff a try. Can't remember the name of it, but one of the author's got my last name."

Jerry returned to the living room, carrying a tube of Pringles. "Want some?"

Leah's stomach rumbled, reminding her she hadn't eaten anything yet that day. She graciously accepted the container, took a handful of chips, and handed it back to him. After the first round of crunching, she asked, "I don't suppose the Master's real name is Boden, is it?"

"I doubt it," Jerry said. "I was chatting with the Master when Boden called before."

She swallowed unexpectedly. The sharp edges of under-chewed chips brought tears to her eyes. "Boden called you?"

"Yeah, a few hours ago." Jerry sucked the salt from his fingers. "He said the cops were on the way to the apartment and that I should get Vincent's back. I erased your message...the one that mentioned Boden...just in case. Otherwise, the only incriminating stuff around here was my own."

"Boden called *you*?" she asked again.

"I know your message said he was creepy and all, but he didn't want Vincent to get into any more trouble than he was already in, so he can't be all bad, right?"

Unless Boden is just trying to cover his own ass...

"And did the police come?" she asked.

Jerry chuckled. "Like five minutes later. I barely had enough time to flush my stash. I didn't let them come in though. Not without a warrant." He jumped up out of the chair, disappeared into the kitchen again. "Want a soda? All I got is Dew."

"Yes, please."

He returned, handing her a cold can and downing about half of his own can before sitting down again. "I didn't even know what Vincent did until after they left and I turned the TV on. Like I said, he didn't leave any clues behind. There wasn't a note or anything saying, 'I'm going to go kill my brother now.' I think the dude might have puked, though. That's why I had to OD on the vanilla air freshener...well, part of the reason."

She happened to spot, at that moment, the little bottle of eye drops next to the laptop. "Are you high, Jerry?"

"Only a little." He hoisted the Pringles container at her. "More chips?"

With a resigned sigh, she accepted.

"So...what do we do now?" Jerry asked.

"There's not much we can do for him while he's incarcerated," she said. "I have quite a few questions for Boden, whoever the heck he is, but I don't have his number, so I'm forced to wait until he calls back."

"How did Boden find you and Vincent in the first place?" Jerry asked, his words garbled by a mouthful of chips.

"I left a message for someone else, and Boden called back," Leah said.

"Then call that number again, and maybe he'll pick up."

From the mouth of a burnout...

She reached for her phone only to realize that she had left it in the car.

"You can use ours, if you want," Jerry offered, indicating the cordless phone on the desk.

With Jerry's permission, Leah also commandeered the laptop. It took but a minute to locate the phone number on Temple University's website again. She held the phone against her ear, her heart thumbing louder with every ring. A voice that wasn't Boden's invited her to leave a message for the psychology department.

Here goes nothing.

"This message is for Boden or Dr. Baerwald or anyone else who can help me. Please call Leah Chedid as soon as possible." She gave her number but then hesitated, debating how much to say on a recording. "I wasn't able to get Vincent out. They took him to Milwaukee County Mental Health Center."

She hung up and responded to Jerry's expectant expression with a shrug. "I guess that's all we can do for now."

"You're welcome to hang out here for a while," said Jerry. "Want to order calzones?"

"No thanks. I should be getting home."

"Will you call me if you hear from Boden?" Jerry asked.

"Of course. What's your number?"

He wrote it down on a sticky note and promised he

would contact her if Boden called the apartment again. They walked to the door. When she turned to say goodbye, Jerry said, "I know it looks bad, but I don't think Vincent is crazy."

"I hope you're right," she said, zipping up her jacket.

"And as for The Dream, well, there's a lot more going on in the brain than we can ever know," Jerry said.

"Does that mean you believe Valenthor is real?" she teased.

Jerry gave her a big smile. "As real as anything."

Chapter 27

Milton's arms and back ached from carrying Clementine for countless city blocks. The frosty gusts of wind and Milton's wheezy breaths didn't seem to disturb her. Aside from an occasional murmur, the girl slept like the dead.

There were no diners and no drug stores, only street after street of dark, lifeless houses. When his arms began trembling uncontrollably, he stopped and leaned up against a wooden fence with flaking white paint. He couldn't go another step, but he couldn't set Clementine down in the snow either.

Damn it, DJ, why did you involve your niece in this?

"Mama and Dada's house!" Clementine started to squirm, leaving Milton no choice but to lower her to the ground. If the contact of her bare feet upon the snowy sidewalk bothered her at all, there was no trace of it in her beaming face. "Let's go!"

"Are you sure this is…hey, wait!" Milton picked up his coat, which Clementine had shrugged off before racing toward the house. By the time he caught up to her, she had already bounded up the steps and was reaching for the door. "Clementine, are you certain this is your house?"

"Uh-huh." She fumbled with the knob, and the door creaked open.

"I think we had better…" Milton swore under his breath as the girl ran into the darkness. He shouldered his way through the entryway. The screen door slammed shut behind him, striking him in the heel.

Milton took a tentative step deeper into the house and shielded his eyes when an end table lamp erupted in light. Clementine jumped up on a couch that might have been fashionable in the 1970s, crossing her legs under her. She certainly seemed at home in the living room, but he would have liked a little more proof they weren't breaking and entering.

Does it even matter anymore? We've been wandering in a snowstorm for, what, an hour...two hours?

"We have to find you some warm clothes and food," he said quietly. "Are you hungry, Clementine?"

"I want pizza pie," she announced, all but bouncing up and down on the couch.

He flinched and waited for the homeowners— Clementine's parents or otherwise—to storm down the stairs, baseball bats at the ready. But no one stirred. He decided to explore the first floor before venturing to the second. The lamplight was sufficient enough for him to traverse the adjacent room, a dining room, without his having to find another light switch. At the far end of the dining room, he found a doorway.

Holding his breath, he turned on the light. A bare light bulb reluctantly blinked to life, casting ghostly reflections across the white tiles surrounding a tub that, strangely, was filled with water. Without knowing quite why, he pulled a rubber duck from the pinkish bathwater.

"Webster!" Clementine, who had silently sidled up behind him, reached eagerly for the toy. He handed it to her. After kissing the yellow duck on the top of its head, she said, "I got a bad owie, Webster."

Before Milton's eyes, Clementine transformed. Water dripped from her drenched skin and her nightgown. Dark blood plastered her bangs to her forehead, trickling down her face in red stripes. He staggered backward until he hit a towel rack.

Clementine looked up at him. "Dada was sleeping, and I wanted to play with Webster."

Speechless, Milton could only stare at the gruesome spectacle. Meanwhile, the light bulb began to dim until it was almost dead before bursting into new light. At once, the blood evaporated, and Clementine was dry again. Humming pleasantly to herself, she skipped past him and, rubber duck in tow, returned to the couch.

For several minutes, he remained in the bathroom, watching her from a safe distance. A furtive glance at the bathtub revealed it was empty. Back in the living room, Clementine lay on her back, holding the toy above her head and quacking merrily.

The same thing happened with DJ on the bus. One moment, the boy was covered in blood, as though he had been shot, and the next, he was fine again. What can it mean?

Milton knew he should go to Clementine and comfort her. But on the one hand, he was afraid the vision might return, and on the other, he was at a loss for what to say. He decided he must not have any children of his own. Otherwise, he would possess enough parental instincts to know what to do.

No children...or do I have a son?

He closed his eyes and concentrated. The conversation replayed in his mind.

"And you think I should be Odin, rather than you?" the man with gray-green eyes asked.

"It's better this way," Milton said. "Odin was never afraid to get his hands dirty, and before all of this is over, the waters are bound to become murky indeed."

Pause. "Who will you be then, Milton?"

"Borr," he replied. "Odin's father."

Infuriatingly, the conversation ended there. Milton tried to follow the memory to see where it led, but the trail took him to the familiar mental block. He didn't bother trying to open the door. He knew it would be locked.

On his way to the living room—vision or no vision, he had to make sure Clementine was all right—he noticed a couple of grocery bags lying on their sides. Much of their contents had spilled onto the small oval table as well as the floor. He picked up a bunch of bananas teetering near the edge.

It's not pizza pie, but it will do…

"Clementine," he started to say, but as he drew closer, he saw her eyes were closed. Thumb in mouth, she cradled the rubber duck under one arm.

Milton covered her with an afghan that had been draped over the back of the couch. The rest of the house needed to be searched. For all he knew, Clementine's parents were upstairs, asleep.

But seeing the girl sleeping so comfortably reminded Milton of how exhausted he was. Ignoring his brain's protests, he sat down at the end of the couch. Almost immediately, his own eyes closed, and he let his thoughts wander.

To his astonishment, the door in his mind abruptly opened.

Milton creeps down the narrow, empty corridor. Every footstep is a sonic boom. The incandescent auxiliary lights above him might as well be searchlights. His eyes dart back and forth at every intersection, expecting to see a stream of agents, side arms drawn, charging toward him to cut off his advance and prevent his escape.

If caught, he expects to be arrested and locked up for

life. Or worse.

He tries to calm down, calling to mind breathing exercises he learned in some psych class or another, but just shakes his head. Either they'll catch me and stop me, or they won't, he thinks. No use giving into panic.

Filled with a new sense of resolve, Milton quickens his pace, abandoning all pretense of stealth. No one is likely to be working in the labs at this hour anyway. And while it has been months since he has come to this part of the Compound, he has no trouble remembering exactly where the serum is stored.

He stops outside of his destination and takes a deep breath.

The door's translucent window is dark; the room, presumably unoccupied. He allows himself a sigh of relief. If someone had been working late in the lab, he doubts he would have had the courage to come back tomorrow. He knows he has to do this now, before he can talk himself out of it.

Milton slides his keycard into the narrow slot. His entry into the lab will be documented in a computer somewhere. Questions will come later. But there is no use worrying about it tonight.

All that matters now is getting his hands on Boden's serum.

A blinking green light and a metallic clicking sound inform him the door has unlocked. He enters, turns on the lights. An electric hum fills the room as, one by one, the computers and equipment lining the walls wake from hibernation.

His eyes linger on a large, padded table at the far end of the lab. He has met several of the test subjects who have lain on the table. Those agents—the valkyries—said the procedure was simple and painless. Milton prays they weren't lying.

He approaches a nearby metal cabinet bearing a number pad and punches in his personalized six-digit code. Nothing happens. He tries again, carefully pressing each button in the proper sequence. His failure is reported by a series of agitated beeps. Then a voice.

"Access to the serum has been upgraded to a higher clearance level."

Milton whirls around, sporting, he is certain, a guilty expression. "Earl, I—"

Boden cuts him off with an upraised hand. "Our last conversation did not sit well with me," he says. "When I first told you about the successful trials of the formula, you could not contain your disappointment. So I had to wonder why, after disapproving of my objective for so long, you were suddenly so interested in the serum's specific chemical compounds, observable side-effects, and the number of test trials completed."

Milton searches Boden's face for a sign of what he will do next. The two of them have been colleagues for more than a decade—first at Temple University and now at the CIA. They have made many wonderful discoveries together while mapping the more obscure areas of the human brain. But Milton recognizes the pain behind his friend's gray-green eyes because these are emotions Milton himself has experienced firsthand.

The anger and hurt from being betrayed.

Milton scrambles to think of a viable excuse for sneaking into Boden's lab, but he has never been a good liar.

"We have always had differing stances on the development of a drug that would grant non-naturals the ability to dream drift," Boden says, "but I cannot believe that you would risk everything to sabotage my work."

Pause. "And did you really think we wouldn't be able

to make more after you disposed of the serum in that safe? Or were you planning to contaminate the supply in order to slow my progress?"

Seeing the face of Boden—his protégé, the son he never had—contorted in rage breaks Milton's heart. Before he can explain, Boden continues.

"In any case, it would be only a matter of time before you were discovered. Did you think they would just let you walk out of here? Project Valhalla *owns* us. Best you never forget that!"

Milton takes a step closer, arms extended in a placating gesture. "I didn't come here to *destroy* the serum. I came here to *steal* it," he confesses.

Boden recoils in surprise. "Steal it? Whatever for?"

Milton sighs. "Because I wish to use it."

Boden runs a hand across his considerable forehead. "There is no telling what affect the serum will have on a natural." Pause. "I can't understand why you would attempt such a thing."

"It's William Marlowe," Milton says at last. "About a week ago, I came across him and his cohorts—"

"The Clandestine Order for Psychic Exploration?" Boden interjects, spitting out the words as though they are a sour taste in his mouth.

"Yes, I believe so, though I recognized only William. They were doing something truly reprehensible, but until I can confirm what I saw, I won't go into details. Suffice it to say, it has more to do with my earliest hypotheses than our current work."

Boden's brow furrows in confusion, but then his eyes widen as he says, "If souls can sleep…"

Milton smiles weakly, confirming Boden's guess. "I've tried to contact William through conventional channels, but he won't respond." Milton takes another step closer to

Boden. "I must stop William, but if I'm going to confront him…and, quite possibly, his allies…then I will need every advantage I can get."

Boden shakes his head and frowns. "What of Project Valhalla? You have allies of your own. Why do this alone?"

Milton sighs. "I had the chance to stop William years ago. He came to me, asking for my help. But I turned my back on him when I might have made a difference. I owe it to William to talk to him, one-on-one, about what I saw before I report it to Project Valhalla. I might even be able to prevent the war for which we all have been preparing."

Pause. "From everything you have told me about William Marlowe, I say you owe him nothing. However, you are not the first person to theorize that the serum might enhance a natural's command of the dreamscape. Yet if you believe you will need an extra…boost when you confront Marlowe, it is all the more reason for you to bring backup. Take Heimdall, at least!"

Milton crosses his arms. "I won't needlessly endanger anyone if I don't have to."

"Only yourself," Boden says, his frown deepening.

"It is a risk I am willing to take. Please, Earl, do this as a favor to me."

Boden remains silent for a long time. "You must swear to me that you will wake up at the first sign of danger, whether from Marlowe or side-effects of the serum."

Milton nods. "I swear."

Boden pushes past Milton, approaching the locked cabinet. "Get up on the table before I change my mind."

Milton doesn't have to be asked twice. Moments later, Boden, wearing a white lab coat and gloves, stands beside him, holding a syringe filled with a milky white liquid. Some of the agents of Project Valhalla have started calling the serum "mead," but Milton thinks there's such a thing as carrying a metaphor too far.

Boden takes Milton's arm and rolls up his sleeve. "So much for not getting your hands dirty," he says, penetrating Milton's skin with the needle. "Perhaps you should have chosen Odin for your codename after all."

The serum spreads like ice water through his veins. Before Milton can say thank you to his dear friend, Boden and the laboratory blur then fade away.

The screen door slammed, and Milton jerked upright. Beside him on the couch, Clementine rolled onto her side but did not wake up. He looked at the front door, where the silhouette of a man blocked out the moonlight.

"Sleeping on the job?" The voice, although somewhat muffled by a peculiar wooden mask, was unmistakably DJ's. "Some babysitter you are!"

Chapter 28

Leah sits on the couch in her apartment, trying to knit, but she doesn't know what she's trying to make, and the purple strands of yarn keep unraveling anyway. When she finally throws the needles and skein to the floor, she realizes that her boyfriend—ex-boyfriend?—Aldrich is there too.

He's shirtless and holding a bottle of whiskey by its neck.

"What are you doing here?" she asks.

Aldrich takes a big gulp of the liquor and smiles handsomely. "I live here now. Did you forget that we got married the day we graduated?"

Now that he mentions it, Leah remembers a courthouse wedding. They wore their caps and gowns. Aldrich must have been living at his old place all of this time, but now they are a family.

"But I don't love you," she tells him.

"You don't have to be in love to make love, baby," Aldrich replies.

He pulls her up from the couch, and they lock lips. He's a better kisser than she remembers. His bare arms and chest are warm under her fingers. He grapples with her shirt and somehow removes both blouse and bra in one move.

She arcs her back, pressing her breasts into him, exposing her neck, which he devours.

"Oh, Vincent!" she moans. When she opens her eyes, Aldrich has been replaced by Vincent Cruz. He kisses her harder. The fireplace she didn't know she had crackles contentedly beside them. She closes her eyes.

Hot air rushes into her ear as Vincent says, "You and Bella have the same soul, so it's OK."

Satisfied by the explanation, she wraps her arms around him and squeezes his unbelievably muscular body. The light from the fireplace grows so bright all she can see is white through her closed eyelids.

Someone clears his throat and says, "So sorry to interrupt, Dr. Chedid."

Leah opened her eyes and gasped. Vincent was gone. A man wearing a long, black coat quickly crossed the room. He averted his eyes as he handed her the discarded white blouse. She quickly took it and pulled it over her head.

"No need to be embarrassed," the man said. "We cannot control where our dreams will take us…well, most of us can't."

She felt like she had just awakened from a dream, and yet she couldn't be awake. The fireplace still sat where her television should have been.

Leah crossed her arms, as though trying to cover up even more. She felt fully exposed under the hard stare of those gray-green eyes. The man smiled diplomatically, but his rigid stance made her own muscles tense.

"Who are—?" Her breath caught in her throat. "Boden!"

He nodded. "Please pardon the unconventional means of communication, but I find this way to be more…direct."

Leah looked around. It was undeniably her apartment, but so many details were wrong. The carpet was the wrong color, portraits of strangers hung next to those of her family members, and then there was the enormous stone fireplace. "You came to talk to me in a dream?"

Boden nodded again.

"How is this even possible?" she asked.

"That is a topic for another time. Suffice it to say it *is* possible, and it is happening to you now. And if you want my help getting Vincent Cruz out of the mental health center, you will answer *all* of my questions to the best of your ability."

Was that a threat?

Before she could respond, Boden walked to the front door and locked it. The act made her feel far from safe.

"Dream drifting is more direct than the telephoning, but not necessarily safer," Boden said, turning back to her. "I have given you no reason to trust me, and for that I apologize. But two people's lives are in jeopardy, Vincent's and Milton's."

"Milton Baerwald? The professor?"

"Yes, the *former* professor." Boden took a long look at the dark corners of her apartment before taking a seat in Emira's chair. "I need you to tell me everything you know about Vincent and his brother, starting with Vincent's recurring dream. Only then will I answer your questions."

Leah considered her options. Sharing Vincent's medical information was a violation of her code of ethics and the law. However, if Boden really could help Vincent, it seemed like a small sacrifice to make.

Besides, what alternatives did she have?

Deep down, she knew the main reason she wanted to give into Boden's demands was because anyone who had the ability to invade people's dreams to have a chat also probably could do other, less pleasant things while he was there.

Leah started at the beginning, telling Boden about the day Vincent walked into the sleep clinic. His face betrayed no emotions whatsoever as he listened to her summation of the past couple of weeks.

"Vincent said he had The Dream again last night… well, two nights ago…but his message was vague. He was upset. He said Daniel was causing The Dream…and he said something about Clementine, his dead daughter. I honestly don't know whether he actually went to the hospital to kill his brother," she concluded.

Pause. "What do you know about Daniel Pierce?"

Leah didn't know whether to be surprised or relieved that Boden wasn't at all shocked by the strange story she had just told him. It was difficult to feel anything except anxious under the man's unwavering stare.

"Daniel is actually Vincent's half-brother," she said. "According to the news, Daniel shot a police officer when they tried to arrest him for drug dealing. He also was shot and ended up in a coma. Vincent said he and his mother fought about whether to keep him on life support…and that his mother believes an angel came to her in her sleep, telling her to keep Daniel on life support." Leah gasped. "It wasn't an angel, was it?"

Boden frowned. "In all likelihood, it was Daniel himself."

"So he can do this too?" She gestured at the man and the replica of her living room. "What did you call it?"

"When two people with the ability come together it is called shared dreaming," Boden said. "When someone enters someone else's dream, uninvited, we refer to it as dream drifting."

"And who, exactly, are 'we'?" Leah asked, her impatience getting the better of her apprehension.

Suddenly, something changed, though it took Leah a

moment to understand that, all around them, colors were fading. Even the flames in the fireplace had lost their luster. In a matter of seconds, the scenery melted into a gray abyss.

Boden remained seated, undaunted by the cataclysm.

She leaped up from the couch, reaching for him. "What are you doing? You promised—"

"—you would help Vincent!"

Leah lost her balance and slammed into something big and unyielding. A vague idea of floating or flying flashed in her mind, but she couldn't grasp it. She righted herself and cried out in surprise at the sight of an armor-clad warrior seated upon a throne made of bones. The man wore a helmet with long, dark horns.

A black-gloved hand reached for her.

She turned to run but was immediately overcome by dizziness. Two torches perched in tall, tower-like sconces on either side of the throne cast a circle of dull light a few feet in all directions. Beyond was absolute darkness. If she ventured too far, she would be swallowed by the void.

"Forgive me, Dr. Chedid. I didn't mean to frighten you," a familiar voice said.

The warrior removed his helmet, revealing the stern countenance of Boden. He made a mild gesture, and a second chair—one made of wood, not bone—appeared in the space before him.

It's only a dream. It's only a dream. It's only a dream.
But it's also real.

Leah's shaky legs took her over to the chair. Heart pounding, she sat down.

"Do you mind if I called you Leah?" Boden asked.

"Sure, no problem." She punctuated her words with a

nervous laugh.

Pause. "Very good. While we are here, it would be more appropriate if you call me Odin." Pause. "The name, my attire, this place…it was all Milton's idea. For as long as I have known him, he has had a fondness for Norse mythology. I had hoped to prepare you better before bringing you here, but your dream was ending, so I pulled you into mine."

Leah scratched the back of her neck. "I was waking up?"

His eyes, which perfectly matched his metallic outfit, narrowed as he thought. "Possibly not. Given the hour, you likely were transitioning into a new sleep cycle. Rather than waste time searching the dreamscape for you again…and risk interrupting another private moment…I took you with me to Valhalla."

He made an almost imperceptible gesture with his hands, and the torchlight intensified. Her claustrophobia didn't abate. So enormous was the chamber that Leah couldn't see its perimeter.

"Think of it as a constant in the ever-changing dreamscape, a static location where my colleagues and I rendezvous," he said.

"It's where you meet before barging into other people's dreams," Leah said, though she immediately regretted her cynical tone.

Long pause. "A fair, if incomplete, assessment of our operations. I know this must be incredibly perplexing, but now that we are in Valhalla, it is safe for me to brief you on the situation as it pertains to you."

"Brief" me? Figures Odin would be a military man.

Boden continued, "Some people are born with the ability to drift into the dreams of others. We call them 'naturals,' and, as far as we know, there are perhaps only five thousand naturals in the entire world, and only a small percentage of them understand what they are capable of.

"As you might imagine, a natural can stir up quite a bit of chaos and confusion in the minds of non-naturals. Invasion of privacy, as you alluded to, is but the tip of the iceberg. Since it is possible for naturals to extract information from sleepers *without their knowledge*, the dream-drifting phenomenon presents a threat to national security. The U.S. government created Project Valhalla to track naturals and use their abilities to defend the population from those who would do them harm.

"In the past few months, the Dream World, dreamscape, humanity's shared unconsciousness...whatever one chooses to call it...has become a battlefield between two factions. Milton Baerwald is a casualty of that war."

When Leah caught up with his explanation, she asked, "Milton is dead?"

Pause. "No. Seven months ago, Milton was ambushed. Since then, he has remained a prisoner in someone else's dream. From what we can ascertain, Milton believes he is awake and running for his life. In actuality, he is fleeing from the very people who want to rescue him...agents of Project Valhalla. Meanwhile, in the real world, Milton is in a coma."

"Just like Daniel," Leah said. "Wait, did you say it happened seven months ago? That's about the time Daniel went into his coma too."

Boden nodded grimly. "We now suspect Daniel is Milton's captor. Who else could maintain a never-ending dream?"

Could Vincent have discovered all of this? Was he trying to stop his brother?

"But why would Daniel do such a thing?" Leah asked. "He's a small-time drug dealer. What is his connection to

Milton...to any of this?"

"That is being investigated as we speak." Pause. "For now, however, I am less concerned with *why* than *how*. We ought to be able to overpower him, but most of the time we cannot even find him in the dreamscape. On the one occasion when agents were able to locate DJ...*Daniel*...he escaped, indicating that he has the ability to maintain the dream that has ensnared Milton while simultaneously hiding in others' dreams."

Leah shrugged. "I'm sorry, but you just lost me."

"I entered your dream earlier. Now you're in mine. I can't leave you here while I drift somewhere else and still maintain control over this dream. I could either bring you along or let you go," Boden explained. "In other words, I couldn't trap you in Valhalla, leave you unattended, and expect you wouldn't eventually wake up.

"When Daniel is absent from the Twilight Realm, my agents should have no trouble manipulating the dream and freeing Milton because Daniel has forfeited his control over that dream."

Leah nearly fell out of her chair at the sound of a new voice behind her.

"That's not entirely true." A dominatrix sauntered past Leah, her high-heeled leather boots striking the stone floor like a hammer on an anvil. She stopped and leaned against the bone throne, her dark leotard-like outfit stretched taught across her generous curves. Her lips, painted blood red, were puckered in a permanent smirk. "When all the gods are in Valhalla, it's a shared dream. Each of us has control to some degree. For all we know, Danny Boy has some friends in the Twilight Realm who keep Borr busy and enforce the rules while he's out messing with his brother."

"Borr?" Leah asked.

"That's Milton. We use code names around here. Can't be too careful," the woman said with a wink.

Boden kept his eyes fixed on Leah as he spoke. "Why are you here, Syn?"

"Heimdall said he can handle Vincent without me...if he's even dreaming tonight. What's this I hear about him being in the loony bin?" Syn straightened up and took several steps closer to Leah. "Besides, I wanted to get a look at our new friend."

Syn was younger than Leah, though it was impossible to discern her age due to the raccoon-like rings around her eyes and jet-black pixie cut. She was part goth, part punk, part fetishist.

In a conspiratorial whisper, Syn said, "You might be powerless here, honey, but I'm a goddess and more than capable of giving you a makeover. You can borrow something of mine. I bet you'd look great in leather."

Looking past the alleged goddess, Leah said to Boden, "You're trying to drift into Vincent's dreams?"

"Not just any dream, *The* Dream," Boden said. "We believe we might have an easier time confronting Daniel there than in the Twilight Realm."

"I don't understand," Leah said.

"That makes two of us," Syn confided.

Pause. "We need to learn more about what Daniel is plotting and whom he is plotting with. The Valenthor dream is our only lead."

"Which is pretty sad when you think about it," Syn said. She pulled out a long dagger from nowhere and ran the flat of the blade up and down the elastic material coating her thigh like a second skin.

"We do not know why Vincent is getting pulled into a dream with a setting so similar to our own Norse theme," Boden continued. "Perhaps Daniel is the one responsible.

Perhaps Vincent is a natural and unconsciously goes to The Dream of his own accord. Regardless, if we are to learn more about Daniel and his agenda, we need Vincent to become Valenthor again."

"So why do you need me?" Leah asked.

Pause. "If Vincent has been secured in a mental health center, it stands to reason the authorities believe he has suffered a mental break. Most of the tranquillizers used at such facilities inhibit REM sleep. We need you to break him out so that he can be sure to dream tomorrow night."

Leah took a few steadying breaths as she looked from the ironclad warrior to his provocative companion. As bizarre as it all sounded, she had no choice but to work with them if she wanted to save her friend. So even though the answer wouldn't change anything, she had to ask the question.

"You said that our dreams have become a battlefield between two forces. Since you work for the CIA, does that mean I'll be working with the good guys?"

Pause. "Project Valhalla falls within the CIA's Directorate of Science of Technology. Our existence is a closely guarded secret. The President of the United States doesn't even know we exist," Boden said. "But as for your question—"

"Only time will tell," Syn said.

Chapter 29

On the other end of the expansive room, an elderly woman whined incomprehensibly. Her childish noises made it hard for Vincent to hear the TV—an old-school model that still had knobs on the front—but her blubbering was only slightly more annoying than the shrill voice of the cartoon character on the screen.

Sitting next to him on the couch, a young woman in flowery pajamas and sporting a hairdo made popular by neo-Nazis stared enraptured at the snowy screen. Her laugh reminded him of the bark of a stray dog he and Danny once tried to sneak into the house.

Vincent looked for somewhere else to go, but the few other patients in the common area were already engaged in conversations with invisible pals. An almost sane-looking guy sat at a round table, playing a one-man game of Sorry. Vincent was weighing the pros and cons of going over and introducing himself when the man popped one of the pawns in his mouth.

He turned back to the TV, where a pink starfish with a head resembling a penis laughed hysterically. Across the room, Vincent thought her heard the words "feather duster" spoken between the old lady's sobs. Beside him, Little Miss Buzz Cut barked so hard she nearly rolled off the couch.

Did Dr. Phillips let me out of my room so I wouldn't feel so isolated or because he wanted me to see how other crazies pass the time?

"Vincent Cruz. You got a visitor, hon."

He twisted around, stretching his neck to see over the back of the brown, scratchy couch. A nurse that had the same body type as his old boss—but none of Darlene's salty attitude—walked toward him, her considerable girth completely obstructing his view of whoever followed her. When she stepped aside, he didn't immediately recognize the woman in the thick-rimmed glasses and navy-blue power suit. His eyes came to rest on the gun holstered at her hip.

"This is Agent Dragsa. She's with the CIA," the nurse told him, speaking more slowly than she needed to. "She wants to ask you some questions."

The nurse shepherded them over to an empty table, walking past the game eater, who surreptitiously shoved another Sorry piece in his mouth.

Vincent started to say something, but his visitor shushed him. Through the no-nonsense spectacles, she watched the nurse as she walked away and then eyeballed the room's other occupants before turning her attention back to Vincent.

"'Agent Dragsa'?" he asked.

"It's Asgard spelled backwards," Leah said quietly. "It must be Boden's attempt at humor."

Vincent didn't get the joke. Then again, he didn't understand what Boden had to do with anything or why Leah was wearing a CIA badge. She removed her glasses, and her expression softened. It was a look his mother had been giving him ever since Clementine died.

Now that he was crazy, Vincent figured he'd start seeing it far more often.

Leah leaned forward. "Vincent, there's a lot I need to tell you...but not in here. We're going to talk for a few minutes. As far as anyone knows, I'm asking you questions about what happened at the hospital. Then we're going to leave. If anyone tries to stop us, I'll flash my badge and tell them you're a threat to national security."

Vincent wondered if the pills were to blame for making her so hard to understand. "I thought the FBI handled internal threats to the country," he said.

Leah gave him an exasperated look. "Yeah, well, let's hope no one else questions why the CIA would be interested in your case. The important thing is to get you out of here!"

"I'm not sure that's such a good idea, Leah," Vincent said. "I tried to kill my brother because of a bad dream. I've got a lot of issues to work through, and Dr. Phillips says I have to let go of my anger before I can get better."

Leah sat motionless for what felt like a long time. Then she started moving her pen across a legal pad. Vincent could tell that she was surreptitiously watching the adjacent table, where the nurse was rescuing the remaining pawns from impending digestion.

In an ultra-professional tone, Leah asked, "And did you recognize the man who thwarted your attempt to kill Mr. Daniel Pierce?"

"No, I never saw the guy before," Vincent answered honestly. "But I think he was blond. And big."

Leah jotted down more fake notes. Meanwhile, two men in gray scrubs forcefully escorted the devourer of games out of the room. The man struggled, sending Sorry cards raining everywhere. The number eight landed on the back of Vincent's hand.

Leah clicked her pen and plunged it into the breast pocket of her blazer. "We have to go. Now."

"But I need help—"

"That's why I'm here," Leah hissed. "You're *not* crazy,

Vincent. There actually is a conspiracy, and your brother is part of it."

Vincent closed his eyes and shook his head. "No. No way. Dr. Phillips says my aggression toward Daniel is a defense mechanism that—"

"What kind of pills are they giving you, Vincent?"

"I don't know. What difference does it make?" he snapped. "For the first time in God knows how long, I'm relaxed. And I'm ready to start dealing with all the shitty things that have happened to me...and the shitty things I've done."

Leah reached into her handbag and dropped a pair of shiny handcuffs on the table. "Put these on."

He reached for them but then stopped. "Leah, I don't think—"

She stood up and, more loudly, said, "We can do this the easy way or the hard way, Mr. Cruz."

Her steely expression was even more alarming than the presence of the handcuffs. Somewhere in the distance, the nurse was talking excitedly, but Vincent couldn't look away from Agent Dragsa.

What if it's not Leah? What if I'm just dreaming *her to look like Leah?*

Leah leaned in and whispered, "Trust me, Vincent."

"Whom do *you trust, Valenthor? The giants plot. The gods scheme. The Ancestors drift through eternity, await-ing the call to arms for the Final Battle. But only I can reunite you with your daughter."*

"Damn it, Vincent," Leah muttered, retrieving the handcuffs, grabbing his arm, and folding the metal around his wrists before he could protest.

"This is bigger than our family." Daniel had said that too.

What if I'm not crazy?

"What's going on here?" Dr. Phillips demanded.

Vincent looked helplessly from one doctor to the other. He liked Leah, but he also liked Dr. Phillips, who didn't dress or talk like a shrink. During their morning session, Vincent had come to appreciate the psychiatrist's insights—and his prescriptions. He didn't want to have to choose between the two of them, so he kept silent and waited to see what would happen next.

Leah pulled at the lapel of her blazer, drawing attention to the badge affixed there. "I'm Special Agent Dragsa, CIA. We have reason to believe that your patient, Mr. Cruz, represents a serious threat to national security. I need to bring him to headquarters for further questioning."

Vincent looked up at Dr. Phillips, who had stopped directly beside him, arms crossed. Dr. Phillips was in his fifties, Vincent guessed, but his bald spot made him look older. So did his glasses, thanks to the lenses' reddish-brown tint.

The psychiatrist scratched his salt-and-pepper goatee. "Vincent was checked in yesterday by the Milwaukee police. He is to undergo a thorough—"

"I am well aware of the situation, Dr....Phillips, was it?"

Dr. Phillips nodded curtly. Red splotches blossomed on the skin beneath his big glasses and on his neck. "Yes, I'm Gregory Phillips. But I didn't catch *your* first name."

"Rebekah Dragsa, Special Agent First Class," Leah replied coolly. "The circumstances are urgent, and I out-rank you and the local law enforcement. So unless you want to become *truly* involved in this investigation, you will step aside. Now."

Leah grabbed Vincent by the shoulder, spun him around, and pushed him toward the room's only exit. He noted that Dr. Phillips did, in fact, step aside in order to avoid catching Leah's elbow in his chest.

Vincent allowed Leah to guide him to the exit. They were more than halfway to the small office he had nicknamed the Nurse's Checkpoint, when Dr. Phillip called out. Leah's fingers dug painfully into his flesh. She turned around. So did Vincent.

"I imagine you'll want to see his file," Dr. Phillips said. "If you can wait just a minute…"

"You've wasted enough of my time already," she told him. "My people will be in touch."

Leah gave Vincent another push, and he resumed his captive's march.

Leah slammed the car door shut and fell back against the seat. Her thoughts racing, her heart hammering beneath the suffocating blazer, she took a few steadying breaths. In the reflection of the rearview mirror, her face was devoid of color.

Did I really just do that?

The past fifteen minutes felt more like a dream than her time with Boden in Valhalla had. When she considered her actions, she felt a wave of nausea ripple through her insides.

From the backseat, Vincent asked, "Are you really a secret agent?"

His voice snapped her out of her trance. She swallowed the metallic taste in her mouth and turned the ignition.

It's not over yet.

"Jesus, Vincent, how doped up *are* you?" She maneuvered the rental car—an extra-shiny black Lexus—out of the parking lot, her eyes flicking back and forth in search of pursuers. When she spotted a mounted security camera, she scrambled for the oversized sunglasses she had bought at a drug store on her way there.

It was all she could do to keep from grinding the gas pedal into the floor.

"Why did you call yourself Rebekah Dragsa?" he asked. "And where did you get that badge?"

Leah winced. Her little sister's name had been the first thing to pop into her head. Using it had only given the police another chance to link Leah Chedid to the false CIA agent.

All they'd have to do is haul me in, and Dr. Phillips would pick me out of a lineup in a heartbeat.

She cranked up the air conditioning, and a rush of cold air washed over, homing in on her damp armpits and chest.

"The badge is real," she replied. "It arrived this morning, along with the gun. Boden sent them." Her heart jumped when she caught sight of a squad car in her rear-view mirror. After several terrifying seconds, it turned out to be a black sedan with a luggage rack. "He works for the CIA, though God only knows why he didn't send a real agent to get you out of there."

She expected him to inquire about Boden and why she was working for him. Instead he asked, "Aren't you going to ask me why I did it?"

"Huh?"

"You're the only person I've talked to since...since yesterday morning who hasn't asked why I went to see Daniel at the hospital," Vincent said.

She glanced at him in the rearview mirror. His eyes were glassy, and he was wearing the standard-issue sweats of a mental patient. He looked years older.

"I'm guessing it has something to do with discovering that your half-brother can barge into people's dreams and take on a variety of forms?"

A gasp from the backseat. "But how...?"

"The messages you left," she said. "And Boden filled in the rest of the blanks…though no one seems to know what he's really up to with The Dream."

Leah did her best to repeat what Boden had told her about dream drifting, Milton Baerwald, and Project Valhalla.

"They think Daniel is keeping Milton trapped in a dream, but Project Valhalla's agents can't get to Milton when Daniel…or DJ, as he calls himself…is around. And they can't find either of them when Daniel is in The Dream. They're hoping they can follow you into The Dream, which is why I had to get you out of the mental health center and away from any drugs that hinder REM sleep."

Several cities blocks came and went in silence. Leah wondered if anything she had said was sinking in.

Finally, Vincent said, "I thought you said I never got to the REM stage that night at the clinic, the time when Daniel appeared as himself in my dream."

Leah allowed herself a small smile.

Looks like he's paying attention after all.

"I didn't have the chance to ask Boden about your polysomnogram, but I did take a closer look at it last night. You *did* reach REM that night, but just barely. According to the instruments, you apparently woke up right after getting there. My guess is Daniel was waiting for you, and the moment you *could* have a lucid dream, he pounced."

She considered the problem further while passing an obscenely slow minivan.

"Maybe the brain always looks like it's awake when someone is visited by a dream drifter," she said. "Or maybe that's something unique to Daniel. If that's his personal MO, that might be why Project Valhalla can't find Daniel and The Dream."

"*Clementine* is his MO," Vincent insisted. "You were right, Leah. He's somehow using my memory of her to pull me into The Dream. I just wish I could figure out *why*."

Leah pulled her foot off the gas when she noticed a squad car farther up ahead. She considered pulling off at the next exit to reattach the rental car's license plates, which she had removed on a whim, but was afraid that if she lost her momentum, she might lose her nerve too.

We're almost there anyway. I'll just hang back...and pray...

"Daniel said not to trust Odin," Vincent said.

"That's Boden's code name," Leah said.

Vincent chuckled. "Yeah, I kind of figured that part out, but do *you*...trust Boden, I mean?"

Leah adjusted her belt so that the gun holster wasn't digging into her thigh. "Yes. Mostly. I believe that he wants to save Milton and win the war in the dreamscape, and in order to do that, he needs our help."

He had better keep his word. Otherwise, we're going to end up in prison.

"A war in our dreams. I'm not sure what to make of that," Vincent said.

"Neither do I," she said, "but if you consider what Daniel has already done...tricking loved ones into believing lies to keep him alive, giving you symptoms of narcolepsy, trapping Milton in a coma...well, I hate to think what else he and his friends can do."

In the mirror, she saw Vincent shift and gaze out the window. After a minute or two, he said, "Daniel also tormented the cop who shot him. The cop ended up killing himself."

Leah didn't know what to say to that, so she turned to a more immediate topic. "You can't go back to your apartment. The police might return with a warrant. And they could come looking for you at my place, since I went to the police station to see you. Hopefully, you'll be safe here."

She flicked the turn signal and pulled into the parking lot of a hotel.

"Leah, I don't…" She heard him inhale a big breath. "I mean, I'm a little light on money these days, and the cops still have my wallet anyway."

She shifted into park and twisted around to look into the backseat. "Don't worry. I'm paying. In cash. And I'm going to get back every penny I spend from Boden and the United States Government."

"Yes, ma'am," Vincent said. "I just can't wait to get these cuffs off."

"You can do it yourself. They're trick cuffs. There's a small release latch down by your wrist." She smiled. "Looks like my RBD came in handy for once."

"What do you mean?"

"I bought those cheap handcuffs before I realized there was more comfortable bondage gear out there," she said. "We're just lucky I held onto those. Most thirty-year-old women don't have spare handcuffs just lying around, you know."

"The freaky ones do," Vincent said.

Leah laughed in spite of herself, but it did little to ease the tension that made her muscles feel stiffer than the second-hand suit jacket.

Chapter 30

The hotel room looked like every other hotel room Vincent had ever seen. There was a bed, a television, a dresser, and a bedside table that undoubtedly contained a Gideon's Bible. A still-life painting of flowers hung in a shiny silver frame above a small table, which contained a laminated room service menu and a chocolaty mint.

Vincent unwrapped the candy and popped it in his mouth. His eyes lingered on the mini fridge tucked under the TV stand. He opened it and considered the tiny bottles of vodka, gin, and whiskey.

"Don't even think about it," Leah said, closing the door and engaging both locks behind her. "Mixing alcohol and antidepressants is not a good idea. Besides, you need to get natural sleep so that The Dream continues."

"I was drunk the last time I had The Dream," Vincent pointed out.

"You also got arrested for attempted murder."

"Touché." Vincent said a silent goodbye to the booze and reached for a soda instead. Taking a seat at the end of the impeccably made bed, he said, "I couldn't do it, you know. Even before Nurse Rambo walked in, I'd already chickened out."

Leah leaned against the table. He spotted her heavy blazer draped over one of the chairs. Her white sleeveless blouse hugged her curves. She smiled reassuringly. "I'm actually relieved to hear that. There must be a better way to stop Daniel. Better yet, if you can get him to come out of hiding, Project Valhalla can deal with him."

"'Get him to come out of hiding'?" Vincent repeated. "What does that even mean? How exactly am I supposed to lead Odin and his buddies to Daniel? I don't decide when The Dream happens. Daniel does. What if I don't become Valenthor again?"

She shrugged. "All you can do is try."

Vincent rolled his eyes. Now that the pleasant cloudiness in his head had started to dissipate, he felt a sarcastic front moving in. "So that's the plan? I stay at this hotel until I have The Dream again or the cops find me?"

"I don't see what other choice we have," Leah said. "With 'the gods' watching your dreams, hopefully, you'll be safe from any more of Daniel's tricks."

"You're assuming Valenthor will find Locke," he said. "When I unmasked Daniel, he said we had to part ways. He also mentioned a final battle with the gods. For all we know, Daniel *wants* Odin and the others to come into The Dream."

Leah sighed and sat beside him on the bed. "I suppose that's possible, but there's really only one way to find out."

"Easy for you to say. You're not the bait!" When she didn't say anything, he frowned and glanced at her. "I'm sorry, Leah. You're just trying to help. You didn't have to spring me from the nut house. You've already risked so much for me."

She smiled and patted his hand. "I guess that makes us both crazy." She started to laugh, but Vincent silenced her with a kiss.

Leah shoved him away.

"Vincent!" she shouted, leaping to her feet. "What the hell?"

His cheeks burned mercilessly. He couldn't lift his eyes from a mystery stain on the beige carpet. "I thought...I thought you liked me. I'm sorry."

"You're married!"

"Barely."

She walked across the room, reaching for her purse, lying next to the hotel's welcome binder. "I should go..."

Vincent summoned the courage to make eye contact. "Hold on a second. Are you planning on talking to Boden tonight?"

"That's entirely up to him, I'm afraid," Leah said. "I still don't have a direct number for him."

Vincent kicked off his tennis shoes—laces-free since his stay at the mental health center—and settled back on the bed. "Well, if he contacts you, tell him to check into the receptionist who works in the coma ward. I'm pretty sure she knows about The Dream. As a matter of fact, she claims Valenthor and the gang are characters in a book she's writing."

Leah dropped her purse onto the table again. "Do you mean Suzanne?"

"That sounds right," he said. "You met her?"

Leah nodded. "At the police station. She was acting strange when she and your mother left. She asked me about The Dream, but I figured it was because you mentioned it, and they thought you had lost your mind."

"Do you think Suzanne is in cahoots with Daniel and that nurse, Levi?" Leah asked.

"It's possible," he replied. "Or he could be screwing with her head too. Maybe we should pay her a visit."

"You're a fugitive, and Suzanne already seemed very shaken up by what you said at the jail," Leah said. "Going to see her would probably be the stupidest thing we could do at this point."

No, I'm pretty sure trying to kiss you was the stupidest thing I could do.

Leah added, "It just doesn't make sense. How can The Dream be from a book someone is writing?"

"Hell if I know, but if Daniel is somehow hijacking her story, she might be able to give me a clue about where I can find him when I return to The Dream. Or…wait a minute…" He stopped suddenly and then blurted, "The Master of All Things Fantasy!"

Leah's brow furrowed. Vincent was about to explain himself, when she said, "The online guy your roommate chats with? What about him?"

"You talked to Jerry too?" Vincent shook his head. "Man, you *have* been busy."

"How can the Master of All Things Fantasy help us?" she asked.

"OK," he said, "this is going to sound insane, but bear with me. If Daniel can manipulate Suzanne's thoughts…not her dreams, but her *thoughts*, and if those thoughts are about a fantasy novel she's writing, then I think we might be in luck. The Master was right about a lot of stuff, including Locke being a relative, come to think of it. Besides, what do we have to lose?"

Vincent reached for the phone on the bedside table, but Leah insisted that he use her cell.

"You might be here a while, and we wouldn't want the police to check Jerry's phone records and find the hotel's number," she explained.

"Are you sure you're not really a spy?" He dialed the apartment, and Jerry picked up on the second ring.

"Hello?"

"Jerry, it's Vincent. I need you to do me a—"

"Vincent! Are you OK, man?"

A pang of guilt soured Vincent's stomach.

After I treated you like shit, you still care.

"Yeah, I'm fine at the moment. But I need a favor. Do you still keep in touch with the Master of All Things Fantasy?"

"Uh…yeah."

"Can you see if he's online?"

"Uh…no."

"Why not?"

Jerry's sober tone scared Vincent nearly as much as his words. "Some guy broke in here, Vincent. He trashed the place and took my laptop."

"What?"

Leah leaned in closer to Vincent, putting her ear near the phone. "What's going on?"

Jerry continued, "I didn't leave the door open either. He must've jimmied open the lock, and when I walked in, he grabbed the laptop and ran for it. He was a big guy, bigger than me. Light blond hair."

Levi?

Vincent swore.

"What's going on?" Leah asked again.

Vincent told her.

Leah grabbed the phone from him. "Jerry, did you save the history of your correspondences with the Master? Did you ever go in and delete your chat history?"

Vincent didn't hear Jerry's answer, but whatever he said made Leah curse.

"What's the matter?" Vincent asked.

Leah handed the phone back to him and said, "If Levi didn't know all of the details about Valenthor and The Dream before, he does now."

* * *

After cycling through the dozen channels on the hotel TV, Vincent settled on an ultra-late talk show he'd never heard of. He dropped the remote on the bedside table. The clock displayed 1:14 in blood-red digits.

He was procrastinating, and he knew it.

On the TV screen, the young, blond actress laughed a little too forcefully at the host's quips. She was awfully thin, except for the parts that had been engineered otherwise. Vincent supposed she was attractive in a glammed-up-Hollywood sort of way. He started getting hard, which reminded him that there were other options for fending off sleep.

What is it about hotel rooms that makes a guy think about sex?

His thoughts turned to the unsuccessful kiss with Leah. He hoped she would dismiss the episode as a side effect of Dr. Phillips's pills, but the answer was much simpler. Leah was attractive, and Vincent was lonely. Aside from Jeremiah Weis, loyal roommate extraordinaire—and his mother, he supposed—Leah was the only person who cared enough to help him.

If he had given into the temptation to take their relationship to the next level, was that such a big deal?

A piece of a conversation he had had with Daniel more than a year ago interrupted his thoughts.

"It is *a big deal, big brother, because you're married to a great girl, and the woman you chose to cheat with is her cousin."*

A commercial came on, injecting the room with a high-octane sales pitch from a local car salesman. He reached for the remote and muted the TV.

Kissing Bella's cousin had been an accident. A stupid accident. He had run into Sheila at a bar, and they both had been sloshed. His and Bella's sex life had been struggling for survival ever since Clementine's death. And Sheila definitely started flirting first...

"You have to tell her, Vincent. Things will only get worse if you don't."

Vincent had told Daniel he would keep the kiss a secret to spare Bella any more pain. It wasn't as though they slept together, though Vincent knew it could have come to that if he had let it. Regardless, he had hated himself for betraying Bella.

Sheila's conscience was made of weaker stuff, however. She called Bella in tears two days later and confessed. A week later, Vincent moved in with his mother.

"I guess I should have listened to you, Danny," Vincent muttered.

In retrospect, Daniel was much better at giving advice than taking it. Maybe it was always easier to fix other people's problems than cleaning up one's own life. Vincent had long ago given up on trying to talk his brother into walking the straight and narrow. His words never seemed to sink in.

I guess I should have kept trying, but how was I to know you were going to shoot a cop?

The talk show came back on. Vincent left it muted. He knew the real reason he hated Leah's—no *Boden's*—plan was because he didn't want to have to face Daniel again. What if Daniel's friends were waiting for him to fall asleep? What if the Project Valhalla agents couldn't protect him?

What if Daniel knows what I tried to do to him?

Vincent let out a long yawn. He couldn't stay awake forever. Cursing out loud, he turned off the TV and the lamp, flooding the unfamiliar room with darkness.

OK, let's get this over with.

He closed his eyes and surrendered to sleep.

*   *   *

Eyes closed, Valenthor heard a rustle in the underbrush and felt a shadow fall upon him. He rolled onto his side, wrapped his legs around whoever had sneaked up on him, and twisted. The would-be assailant came crashing to the ground. Valenthor threw himself onto the enemy, trapping the opponent between his body and the forest floor.

Trapping *her* against his body…

Destiny's startlingly green eyes stared wildly into his. Her breath was hot on his neck. Her soft, pink lips opened in surprise, but no words came out.

Valenthor scrambled off of her and extended a hand to help her up. "Pray forgive me. I knew not it was you."

The elf, who looked shaken but no worse for her fall, accepted his hand. She gasped, however, once she got to her feet. "What has happened to your head?"

At the question, he became aware of the rhythmic bursts of pain surging through his skull. Valenthor carefully traced the large, sticky knob protruding from just above his right ear and considered his surroundings. Above him, the crooked boughs of ancient trees creaked menacingly. The sparse vegetation below glinted with frost.

Locke's mask stared up at him from several paces away.

Daniel!

Something shifted in Vincent's mind, like a switch being flipped. He felt his own consciousness come flooding in, burying Valenthor's perceptions beneath a sudden rush of stark awareness.

A simple spectator of The Dream no more, Vincent said, "Locke jumped me. He's been working with the giants all along." He was reminding himself as much as updating the elf.

Destiny exclaimed something in her native tongue that sounded far from friendly. Coming closer to him, she said, "Be still, Valenthor. I will call upon the Ancestors to tend your wound."

Dream or no dream, the pain sure feels real.

Vincent regarded her suspiciously but then bent down so that she could reach his head. He winced when she touched the spot where Locke's staff had made contact. Strange, silky syllables spilled out of her mouth. Vincent drew in a deep breath when the throbbing faded and was replaced by a faint warm sensation.

"Thanks," he said. "If that works for hangovers too, you're my new favorite drinking buddy."

Destiny stared blankly at him.

"Look, I don't know about elves, but when humans drink too much…um…ale, they tend to regret it the next day," he explained.

She folded her hands and said, "It is my hope that you will not again become a slave to your sorrows once your quest is over."

My quest…

"And which quest might that be? Freeing the soul of a girl who looks like Clementine from a curse? Saving a bunch of elves from extinction?" He walked over to where Valenthor had dropped his hammer before tackling Locke and picked it up. "The only thing I care about now is finding my brother…finding Locke."

Destiny frowned, and worry lines formed like cracks across her flawless skin. "I confess I know not how to track the rogue. Moreover, we depended upon Locke's magic to lead us to the Jötunn army."

"Are you trying to tell me that after all of this, you can't take me where I need to go?" Vincent demanded.

The elf wilted under his glare. "I shall pray to the

Ancestors for guidance."

"Fuck that! I don't have time for any more goose chases, Destiny!" He studied her face intently. "Or is there somebody else in there? Suzanne, maybe?"

"I do not understand," the elf said, tears welling up in her eyes. "Mayhap the bump on your head has addled your thoughts."

After several more seconds of staring into her wide, innocent eyes, he said, "No, you're just a mindless puppet, and Daniel is pulling your strings." Vincent looked up at the sky and shouted, "How about a little help, Boden? I found my way back to The Dream. Now what?"

Silence.

"What about you, Daniel, are you and your friends around here somewhere? Do we really have to bother with all of this Valenthor bullshit?"

Destiny started to cry, and Vincent sighed.

I guess I don't have a choice. The only way to keep moving forward is to go along with it.

"I'm sorry, Destiny. That was out of line." He wandered over to the Locke's mask and scooped it up. Clearing his throat, he said, "I vow that Locke shall not have the last laugh. As the gods are my witness, we will find a way to defeat him."

Destiny's face veritably burst with excitement. "You possess his mask!"

"So? I mean, how does that help us?" he asked.

"The mask is a personal artifact belonging to the man we seek," she said. "With a blessing from the Ancestors, the mask will lead us to its owner."

Vincent chuckled but stopped short of rolling his eyes.

Nice touch, Suzanne...or Daniel...or whoever.

In the most stoic tone he could muster, Vincent proclaimed, "Locke has a considerable head start. We had best get moving."

Chapter 31

Vincent heard the battle before he saw it—the savage clang of weapon against armor, the bestial screams of the dying.

Wait a second, how did we get here? We only just started walking!

He followed Destiny to the last line of trees and peered out at the open plain. Beside him, the elf stifled a cry and clasped onto his arm. He knew the gentlemanly thing to do would be to comfort her, but he couldn't wrench his eyes away from the carnage.

Metal-clad knights carrying shields and swords traded blows with creatures that resembled men in shape, if not size. The Jötunn towered over the men, striking the knights down with clubs, spears, and in some cases their bare hands. They wore ragged animal hides that left much of their hairy skin exposed. Their frenzied assault mangled steel, pulverized bone, and sent human warriors flying around the battlefield.

Although Vincent was confident that, only seconds ago, he and Destiny had been alone in the woods where Daniel jumped him, he also had a hazy memory of a long hike. It was as though time had fast-forwarded through the uneventful portion of their trek and resumed its natural speed at the first sign of action.

I guess regular dreams jump around a lot too. So do books, for that matter.

But even though Vincent knew Valenthor's world was just a figment of *someone's* imagination, he couldn't shake the visceral effect the sights and sounds of the battle had on him. In the clearing ahead, a handful of knights fought back-to-back against forty giants, the least of which stood a good four feet taller than the largest knight. The spray of blood, the lifeless stares of the fallen were all too real.

Vincent swallowed the bad taste building at the back of his mouth.

"We must help them," Destiny announced.

"Must we?" Vincent asked. "Unless Locke is in that mess...and I sure as hell don't see him...I think we're better off avoiding them."

She immediately released his arm. Her solemn—no, sanctimonious—tone matched her expression perfectly. "Your kinsmen face certain death at the hands of those vile beasts. We must intercede, Valenthor, because it is the right thing to do."

"Kinsmen? Have you forgotten that it was knights who arrested us when we first met? And if memory serves, Locke and I were forced to kill a few of them during our escape," Vincent said.

Destiny crossed her arms. In one hand, Locke's mask glowed with a faint blue light. "I will take you no further unless you intercede."

This doesn't even make any sense. Why does she give a damn about the knights?

Vincent sighed and hefted the hammer up so that the wooden haft rested against the hollow of his shoulder. "I guess it wouldn't be a very good story if we scurried away, huh?"

"I will pray for your protection," she said solemnly.

"That's it? You're going to *pray*?" he asked, incredulous. "Can't you throw some fireballs or something?"

She shook her head. "Such destructive incantations are sent from the Dark Ones, not the Ancestors."

"Fine, whatever," Vincent muttered. He considered his only weapon. In the comic books, Thor's hammer shot lightning. But Valenthor was no god. He was a washed-up warrior who fought his demons at the bottom of a cup.

We never would have escaped from the village if Locke hadn't shown up.

If Daniel hadn't interfered...

"You won't let the giants kill Valenthor now, will you, little brother?" he mumbled. "I'm the Chosen One after all."

He thought he heard Destiny gasp, but when he looked at her, her eyes were closed, and her mouth formed words heard only by her gods.

Fuck it.

Vincent raised the hammer above his head and charged toward the fight. If worse came to worst—if he died in battle—he figured he'd just wake up back in the hotel room. He might lose his chance to find Daniel, but maybe, just maybe, The Dream would end.

He slammed the hammer into the spine of the nearest giant. It pitched forward, falling to its knees with a roar. Vincent immediately barreled into the next one, falling into the rhythm that had carried Valenthor through many battles. His feet performed a strange yet familiar dance. His muscles reacted without his conscious direction.

In a matter of seconds, he was covered in blood, shouting with every swing of the hammer. Dodging, striking, shoving—he slowly cleaved a path to the struggling knights. When they saw him, the knights fought harder, forcing the giants to fall back or risk getting skewered.

Vincent felt the tide of the battle turn in the men's favor. He saw it in the faces of the remaining Jötunn, which watched him—watched the Chosen One—warily. He let out a heartfelt laugh that was more Valenthor's than his.

Out of the corner of his eye, he saw a knight crumple to the ground. Before the giant could raise its club for a second strike, Vincent leaped over the fallen knight and drove his shoulder into the creature's flank.

The giant staggered back and spat out what Vincent could only assume were curses. It swiped at Vincent's head with the gnarled weapon. Vincent dropped into a low crouch. The wind from the club's arc ruffled his hair. He thrust the hammer forward and heard a sickening crunch as the metal head smashed the giant's groin.

Before Vincent could turn back to the injured knight, two more giants closed in on him. One of them swung an ax, a crude tool with a stone blade, grazing Vincent's back. He felt no pain.

After completing a series of complex maneuvers that sent the ax wielder and its companion crashing to the ground, Vincent turned to confront the next foe, but there were none. Bodies of men and giants alike lay strewn about the field. Only Vincent and two of the knights were left standing. The cold breeze carried the metallic tang of blood.

Someone grunted behind him, and Vincent spun around, ready to bash another giant's brains in. However, the voice belonged to a third knight, who climbed unsteadily to his feet and removed a badly dented helmet.

Sir Angus regarded him grimly. "Valenthor of the Three Rivers, you are an unexpected savior, to be sure."

"Small world," Vincent managed to say between gulps of air.

The two men locked stares, and for a moment Vincent feared the knight would pick up where they had left off after the jailbreak. But then Sir Angus wiped the flat of his sword's blade on a dead giant's shirt and sheathed his weapon.

"Thee and thy ally in the mask slew my men," Sir Angus said. "What little honor I possess precludes me from taking thy life, as thou hast saved ours today. Let the gods judge thee for thy sins, for I cannot."

"What's that supposed to mean?" Vincent asked.

The knight's visage twisted into a scornful smile. "Whilst my brothers-in-arms and I hunted for thee and the fugitive elf, the Jötunn ravaged the town. That which we were duty-bound to protect was burned to the ground. Those whom we had sworn to defend were slaughtered."

Sir Angus retrieved his shield from the where it lay half-concealed under a dead giant. "Henceforth, my remaining cohorts and I are dedicated to ridding the world of as many Jötunn as the gods allow so that we might atone for our failure before we too partake of our final rest."

"You're on a suicide mission," Vincent stated.

Sir Angus did not appear to hear him. Looking past Vincent, eyes narrowed, the knight said, "Lo! Here approaches the self-same she-elf who instigated this chain of tragedies."

Sir Angus's two men muttered to each other as Destiny tiptoed through the corpses. "Valenthor! Ancestors be praised!" she sang, but her breath caught in her throat. "You are wounded!"

Even as the words left her lips, Vincent felt a burning down the length of his back. The muscles in his arms and legs began to throb, and his lungs burned with every ragged breath. The sight of his blood-soaked hands made his head spin and his stomach lurch. He wanted to drop the heavy hammer and sit for a moment, but a guttural voice from nearby caused even the stalwart Sir Angus to start.

Vincent couldn't muster the strength to raise his hammer. Sir Angus pulled his sword from its scabbard and leveled the tip at the throat of a giant that lay on its side.

The Jötunn was in bad shape. Blood stained most of its ugly face a brownish red. A tiny stub was all that remained of one ear. The giant's sinewy body was riddled with gashes and contusions. Its tattered leather jerkin, bearing the silhouette of a howling wolf, was soaked with dark blood and pungent sweat.

"What say thee, knave?" Sir Angus demanded, pressing the point of his blade against the giant's neck.

The giant ignored the weapon, ignored the knight entirely, and stared daggers at Destiny.

"I think he hates elves even more than you do," Vincent said.

"Where is thine army?" Sir Angus shouted at the giant.

Still glaring at Destiny, the giant croaked out another sentence—nonsense to Vincent, Sir Angus, and the other two knights. But Destiny must have understood because she moaned softly and closed her eyes.

"You speak giant?" Vincent asked her.

She gave a quick nod. "Our tongues share a common root, as do our people."

How convenient.

"What did it say?" Vincent asked.

Destiny wiped away a tear with the back of her hand. "He declares the damnation of the Fay is nigh. Two days hence, the Jötunn will plunge all of the nations into eternal darkness."

"And if worse comes to worst, we'll both have front-row seats for the end of the world." Daniel's words.

"Command the beast to reveal the position of the Jötunn war camp," Sir Angus ordered.

Destiny looked to Vincent, who shrugged. When at last she spoke, she formed her words slowly, carefully. A grimace accompanied the harsh sounds, as though each syllable left a bad taste in her mouth.

The giant's terse reply needed no translation.

"Answer yon she-elf, else I shall hew thee in twain!" Sir Angus shouted. The tip of his blade drew a trickle of blood from the beast's neck.

"Ask him about Locke," Vincent said suddenly.

She did. The giant, clutching at a gaping hole in its belly, deigned not to reply.

Vincent looked away. "OK, ask if it knows anything about a woman who talks with two voices...I think she commands the Jötunn," Vincent said.

No sooner had Destiny translated Vincent's question, than the Jötunn's yellow-stained eyes bulged. Vincent swore he heard the giant say "hell," but he didn't recognize any of the other words. The giant's voice, eerily quiet, made Vincent shiver.

Destiny, fair-skinned at the best of times, managed to grow even whiter as she translated. "Death's daughter walks among the mortals." Fresh tears spilled down her cheeks. "Valenthor, the Final Battle truly draws near!"

Sir Angus sneered. "'Tis naught but a fairytale to frighten brats."

"Nay," the elf said, "a prophecy that must be fulfilled."

"It matters not," Sir Angus said. "We venture whithersoever the Jötunn venture. Force the fiend to divulge where the Final Battle will be waged."

Destiny shook her head. "I know where we must go."

"Well?" Vincent pressed.

She was trembling now. "To Yggdrasil, the holiest of temples."

"Can you take us there?" Vincent asked.

Destiny hesitated, then whispered, "Yes."

Without warning, Sir Angus lunged forward, sliding his sword into the helpless giant's neck. A fountain of blood spewed from the wound. The creature died with a gurgling wheeze.

When Vincent was certain he wasn't going to throw up, he rounded on the knight. "What the hell did you do that for?"

"Stay thy pity, Valenthor." Sir Angus returned his blade to its sheath. "Anger will serve thee far better in what we face ahead."

Chapter 32

Vincent blinked, and everything changed. Destiny, the knights, the dozens of dead bodies, and even the sun disappeared, replaced by a canopy of constellations that stretched across the cloudless sky. Several feet away, the flames of a small campfire danced wildly, making one half of his face uncomfortably warm while leaving the other side as cold as a gravestone.

He sat up suddenly, his heart racing.

Does Valenthor always wake up in a state of panic? Whoever's directing this show needs a new trick.

Vincent looked around the campsite. The three knights, still wearing their heavy armor, lay motionless on the other side of the fire. Sir Angus had insisted on lighting a fire, arguing that the likelihood of freezing to death without one eclipsed the risk of attracting more Jötunn.

How can I remember that when I wasn't there? Did I lose control to Valenthor in between the conversation with that giant and now? Or did the conversation about lighting a campfire not really happen...like when a memory in a dream becomes real the exact moment you think of it?

It suddenly occurred to Vincent that something was very wrong. One didn't light a beacon in enemy territory without keeping watch, and all three knights were sleeping soundly. Up until a few seconds ago, Valenthor had been too.

Then he noticed Destiny was gone.

Vincent reached for his hammer and peered into the dense blackness that ringed the meager firelight. Although he hoped the elf had gone to answer nature's call, he suspected something more sinister—something more *significant*—was occurring.

Which means it must be time for me to wander off and find out what happened to her.

Quietly, he slipped away from the snoring knights, heading in the same direction that the elf had been leading him for the past few days, first while following the magical pull of Locke's mask and, later, while following her inner compass to Yggdrasil. Apparently, that's where Daniel had been headed all along.

Vincent didn't question where the vague memories of the long, exhausting hike with Destiny and the knights came from or how he was able to use the stars to orient himself. In some ways, The Dream was like any other dream. Logic took a backseat to momentum.

If I keep moving forward, eventually I'll find Daniel. He'll make sure of that.

After several minutes, Vincent's eyes adjusted to the starlight, and he could make out more and more features of the landscape. The rocky terrain presented enough natural obstacles to keep him stumbling. Since he had survived the battle against the Jötunn, he wasn't too worried about walking off a cliff. Valenthor was the hero of the story. Vincent was beginning to think he was invincible.

Nonetheless, he jumped and nearly lost his balance altogether when Destiny's voice came out of nowhere:

"It was foolish of me not to ensnare you in the same slumber spell as the knights."

Vincent saw her an instant later, standing on a rocky outcropping and looking as though she herself were made of stone, a majestic statue whose beauty alone might have drawn him onward except for the severe expression on her face.

She carried no weapon, but that didn't mean she wasn't dangerous. The three unconscious knights were evidence of that.

Just what I need, another plot twist.

"So why didn't you cast your spell on me?" Vincent asked, daring to take a step closer.

"If the Jötunn discovered you, I did not want your sleep's hold to be so strong that you could not hear their approach," she replied.

Vincent took another step toward her. "I can understand why you wouldn't want to stick with the knights. Sir Angus is an asshole. But that's no reason to ditch me too."

The hardness of Destiny's countenance crumbled, and her sudden sadness was so palpable Vincent stopped mid step. Her stern expression returned an instant later. "Our paths must diverge here, Valenthor. You cannot follow me to Yggdrasil."

"What the hell are you talking about? *You* came to *me,* remember? *You* asked *me* to save your homeland, and I followed you because you convinced me I could save my daughter. What makes you think I'm going to give up now?"

Her jaw stiffened, but she didn't look away. "The Ancestors entrust only the high priests to preserve that most hallowed of shrines. No human has ever beheld the holy sanctuary of Yggdrasil. Your presence would defile it."

"The world is about to end, and you're worried about breaking the rules?" Vincent exclaimed. "If you and I have a shot at stopping Daniel...at stopping Locke and the Jötunn, then your gods should be *grateful* we're dropping by."

Destiny looked away. Vincent wanted to grab her by the shoulders and shake some sense into her—or shake the truth out of her—but a battle was raging inside of her, and he didn't want to give her a reason to lash out with her magic.

Finally, she said, "My people have known of the prophecy since the dawn of the ages. As has been foretold, the Dark Ones, those vile spirits who corrupted the Jötunn and wrought evil in the hearts of men, have finally returned to enslave the mortal races. If their conquest is to be thwarted, the Chosen One must reach Yggdrasil with all haste to summon the Ancestors to unite in battle against the armies of evil."

Sensing that the danger had passed, if only for the moment, Vincent approached her. Speaking with as much calm as he could muster, he said, "But you said the Ancestors came to you in a dream and told you all of this was about to happen months ago. That's why you came looking for Valenthor in the first place, right?"

When she didn't reply, he added, "What I can't figure out is why you were so surprised when that giant confirmed that it's all going down in a couple of days. What has changed?"

Destiny looked away, but not before he saw the glint of a teardrop on her cheek. "The prophecy also says a sacrifice will be demanded…a noble soul that will open the Heart of Yggdrasil and call upon the Ancestors to defend the realms. From a very young age, I was taught the mysteries of the Ancestors, and during my earliest lessons, I learned that the Ancestors' advent will take place only after the royal priestess willingly gives her life for her people."

She took a steadying breath. "I am the eldest daughter of my people's sovereign ruler."

It took him a moment to connect the statement to her earlier explanation.

"Wait, you're a princess?"

She nodded.

Chalk up another point for the Master of All Things Fantasy.

Destiny reached for his hand. Her shimmering eyes bore into his as she said, "You see, Valenthor, *I* am the Chosen One, not you."

Vincent opened his mouth, but no words came out.

She continued, "When the Ancestors told me that the time of the prophecy was upon us, I was terrified of what I must do. And so they revealed to me another way to fulfill the prophecy. They showed me your daughter, and then they also showed me a worthy substitute for the required sacrifice. You, Valenthor."

Vincent tried to pull away from her, but her small, delicate hands held his with a strength that surprised him.

"You brought me along so that I could die in your place?"

Her betrayal hurt more than Vincent would have expected, considering she was a fictional character. He wanted to push her away from him, but something deep inside insisted on patience and compassion. At last, he asked, "So what made you change your mind?"

Destiny's hand trembled. "I am ashamed of my cowardice and my deception. I beg your forgiveness, though I deserve it not." She stifled a sob and said, "The reason I cannot allow you to die in my place is because …because I have come to love you, Valenthor."

Again, Vincent was at a loss for words. Her big green eyes contained so much raw emotion that all of his anger and frustration disappeared. With her honey-blond hair blowing in the wind and her breasts heaving with each rapid breath, Vincent was awestruck by her beauty—no, her perfection. The sudden urge to kiss the elf nearly overwhelmed him.

Destiny drew closer, taking his other hand in her own. His desire grew stronger, intolerable.

Why fight it? The Dream always gets its way...

Vincent pulled the elf to him, crushing her slender body against his own. He kissed her deeply. Her lips tasted like an exotic fruit, sweet and enticing. Not even the snow-flake-laden gales could cool his burning skin.

When the kiss ended, Destiny whispered, "I am so afraid."

"Don't worry," Vincent replied. "This story is bound to have a happy ending."

He gently guided the elf down to the flat-topped rock, cupping her head with his calloused hand. The fine golden strands of hair tickled his cheek as he devoured her neck and pulled open her shirt. She let out a moan and dug her fingernails into his back.

Then their lips met once more. Daniel, dream drifters, and the end of the world couldn't have been farther from his mind.

The world whizzed by at a nauseating speed, and when Vincent's vision could focus again, he was back on his feet, standing beside a fully-clothed Destiny, who was staring at something with an expression of absolute horror. The sun had returned. So had the knights.

Vincent followed Destiny's gaze to a humongous castle that resembled an oversized church. Its tall towers were dwarfed only by the ring of jagged mountains that fenced in the valley from all sides. But his eyes didn't linger on the architectural marvel because at that moment, thousands

—maybe tens of thousands—of Jötunn were throwing themselves at the castle's defenders, which could only be the elves.

One minute I'm about to make love to a gorgeous elf princess and the next I'm facing a war to end all wars? When I figure out who is in control of all this, I'm going to punch them square in the face.

In the distance, giants fell by the score, but Vincent knew it was only a matter of time before they breached the castle. There were simply too many of them.

"Alas, Yggdrasil," Destiny moaned.

Yggdrasil? This castle is the elves' holiest of temples? There's no way we're going to be able to fight our way through the Jötunn army to get inside.

"We're too late," said Vincent numbly.

"Nay," Sir Angus said with a broad smile and a wild gleam in his eyes. "Let us lend our swords to a battle that will beget legends untold. Anon, we die with honor!"

"If this is the Final Battle, who is going to be around to talk about it afterward?" Vincent wondered aloud.

Sir Angus raised his sword, and his men followed suit. "Come, Valenthor, we shall bathe the earth with the blood of our foes!"

Vincent looked from the fanatical knight to the Jötunn hoard. Arrows rained down from the castle walls. The giants retaliated with catapults that launched huge balls of fire. Battle cries and the screams of agony echoed off of the mountains.

It would take a certified miracle to make it in and out of that mess alive, and I'm not even the Chosen One. But if Destiny is the Chosen One, maybe I'm supposed to protect her while she makes a run for it.

Maybe I'm here to die after all.

"Wait!" cried Destiny. "There is another way."

Oh, thank God!

"I know of a hidden route that will take us to the Heart of Yggdrasil," she said.

Sir Angus stabbed the blade of his sword into the ground. "Bah! I came here to slay giants, not cower behind the gates of yon elfish stronghold. Choose thy course wisely, Valenthor. The gods demand atonement for our sins. Let not this witch lure thee away from redemption's path."

Vincent let the handle of the hammer slide from his grip and crossed his arms. "Not gonna happen, pal. But do enjoy your suicide run."

Angus wrenched his sword from the ground. Vincent braced himself for an attack, but it never came. "Damn thee, Valenthor," the knight snarled. "Damn thee to hell!"

As the three knights turned and ran toward the battle-field, Vincent almost pitied Sir Angus. Sure, he was a pain in the ass, but it wasn't Sir Angus's fault he was a two-dimensional cliché. He was only doing what he thought was right.

Maybe it's impossible to change who we really are.

"We must hurry, Valenthor."

Destiny offered him her hand, and he took it un-questioningly. With his other hand, he clenched the hammer. The gears were turning. The game pieces were in place. One way or another, the ordeal was coming to a close.

As he followed Destiny along an invisible path among the evergreens, Vincent knew that if he tried, he could remember everything that had happened since he and Destiny had started fooling around, but he didn't bother to harness the pseudo memories. In the end, it didn't matter if Valenthor and Destiny went all the way or how they came to join up with the knights again.

What came next was important. Every fast-forward brought him closer to Daniel.

And this time I'll be ready.

Destiny stopped in front of an enormous tree with a trunk that must have been five yards thick. Its branches stretched twice as tall as the neighboring trees. Vincent wondered why he hadn't noticed it earlier. Was it another of the Ancestors' enchantments or a convenient shortcut courtesy of The Dream?

The elf lay a hand on the knotty bark and spoke a handful of words that raised the hairs on Vincent's neck. A faint green glimmer flowed between the deep furrows of the bark and formed the unmistakable shape of a doorway.

"A secret passageway," Vincent laughed. "Who'd of thunk it?"

Destiny stepped through the opening, and Vincent hurried after her before the bark could reappear and separate them. While Valenthor was duty-bound to protect the elf, Vincent had a more practical reason for staying close by her side. If he lost her, he would have to figure out what to do all on his own.

The interior of the passage smelled like Christmas and was dimly lit by a dull yellow glow. As they walked, logic told him there should have been a spiraling staircase or something, that it was impossible for them to walk yard after yard inside a tree that, while gigantic, was nowhere near big enough to account for their unerringly straight course.

He told logic to shut up.

After walking maybe a mile through the wood-lined tunnel, Vincent noticed a brighter light up ahead. The air grew warmer the closer they came to it. Then the path ended, and Vincent found himself inside a space about the size of his kitchen and living room combined. The walls were carved with a million tiny symbols that reflected the light from a golden ball that levitated in the center of the room.

The sphere's light was inexplicably comforting and filled him with a deep contentment he couldn't comprehend. The feeling was both simple and complicated, like when he was a kid and found joy in just lying in the warm grass under the bright summer sun. Vincent couldn't take his eyes off of the thing.

Dazedly, he approached the orb, reaching out for the source of the awesome light.

"No!" Destiny's cry echoed off the walls. "I alone must touch the Heart of Yggdrasil and add my inner light to the holy reservoir!"

Vincent snatched his hand back, as though pulling them from the gaping jaws of a wild beast. He reluctantly looked away from the sphere and asked, "You're really going to touch it? Like Sir Angus, you're going to throw your life away?"

"I have no choice," she whispered.

Vincent said the words before he quite realized what they meant. "Unless I really am the Chosen One and the reason the Ancestors brought you to me was because you are supposed to survive this, not me."

Scoff.

Vincent and Destiny spun around to confront Locke, but without the mask to conceal the fair skin, intense blue eyes, and tangle of red curls, there was no Locke—only Daniel. His brother. His nemesis.

"So the Heart of Yggdrasil isn't even inside the temple," Daniel said. "Tricky, tricky."

"You followed us!" Destiny gasped.

"Technically, you followed me to Yggdrasil's hidden vale, but once you got here, I knew you'd lead me right to the secret talisman." Daniel tapped the bottom of his staff against the smooth wooden floor as he walked up to them. Vincent took a step in front of Destiny, holding the hammer across his chest.

"But don't let me interrupt." Daniel flashed a crooked smile. "I think you were arguing about which one of you gets to die first."

Chapter 33

Tap. Tap. Tap.

A thick fog filled the small chamber. Destiny and Daniel vanished. A second later, even the brilliant Heart of Yggdrasil faded from sight. Completely blind, Vincent focused on the sound of Daniel's staff rapping against the smooth wooden floor.

Tap. Tap. Tap.

Vincent tried to shout his brother's name, but no sound came out. He was paralyzed. He was alone.

This isn't one of Daniel's tricks. I'm waking up!

"No!" Vincent yelled, a pillow muffling his voice. He rolled onto his back, blinking in confusion at the unfamiliar room. Then the memory of his ride with Leah from the mental health center to the hotel slammed into his brain like a runaway semitrailer. A thin line of sunlight framed the large, curtain-covered windows beside the bed.

How long have I been sleeping?

Knock. Knock. Knock.

So much for the do-not-disturb sign.

"Vincent, are you in there?" The voice on the other side of the door was unmistakably Leah's.

Swearing under his breath, he dragged himself out of bed and scooped up his only clothes from the floor. He performed a ridiculous jig across the room while pulling on the pants, and he managed to worm his head and one arm through the appropriate shirt holes before yanking open the door.

"Oh," a visibly surprised Leah Chedid said. "Are you just *now* waking up?"

Vincent wrestled with the uncooperative shirt until he got his other arm in place. "Yeah. What time is it, anyway? Did I miss breakfast?"

"And lunch too," Jerry said, following Leah into the hotel room. He dropped a grease-soaked brown bag onto the small table by the TV.

The pungent smell of fast food filed the room. Vincent's stomach rumbled.

"I tried calling your room this morning, but you didn't answer. I thought maybe you left...or worse." Leah took a big breath. "The police came by my place after I left here yesterday."

"What did you tell them?" Vincent asked. He pulled a heaping container of curly fries from the bag and a sandwich wrapped in foil.

"I lied," Leah replied with a nervous laugh. "I told them the reason I went to the police station to see you was because you're one of my patients and I saw you on the news. I said I hadn't seen you since the sleep study."

Vincent swallowed a mouthful of cheeseburger. "Did they believe you?"

Leah shrugged. "They didn't arrest me, but they had plenty of questions about the 'family emergency' that has kept me home from work. It's only a matter of time before they connect me to Agent Dragsa. All they'd have to do is check my credit card, and they'll see that I rented a Lexus yesterday and returned it just a few hours later."

"The cops came back to the apartment too." Jerry stole one of Vincent's fries. "They had a warrant, and they asked a bunch more questions about you...if I knew why the CIA might have an interest in you and if I'd had any contact with you since the hospital. Don't worry. I didn't mention anything about the break in or my stolen laptop."

Vincent took another bite of cheeseburger and digested their news. He noticed Leah was holding a white plastic bag. He swallowed an uncomfortably large wad of food and asked, "What's in the bag?"

"Some of your clothes." She handed him the bag. "I think it's time to check out, Vincent. You have to keep moving...at least until Boden can straighten everything out."

"Boden!" Vincent snapped. "Did you happen to talk to him last night?"

Leah frowned. "No."

"Yeah, well, neither did I," he said, tossing the plastic bag on the bed. "I had The Dream again. I was in Valenthor's world for a very long time, and Boden never showed up."

"What happened?" Leah and Jerry asked at the same time.

In between bites of burger and gulps of cola—it seemed like weeks since he had had a decent meal—Vincent gave them a summary of last night's adventures.

"If I could've stayed in The Dream for just five more minutes..." he concluded with a shrug.

Leah cocked her head.

Jerry said, "Sorry, man" and snagged another fry.

Vincent sighed. "That wasn't supposed to sound like an accusation. It's just frustrating. I was so close...but I still don't know what I'm supposed to do with Daniel now that I've found him. The Dream seems to be coming to end, but I'm no closer to figuring out what Daniel is up to."

Jerry and Leah exchanged a look.

"What?" Vincent asked.

"About The Dream..." Jerry wiped his hands on his

pants. "…The Master of All Things Fantasy had some dire predictions about where ol' Valenthor is headed."

Vincent cringed at the sudden cramp in his stomach. "If the nurse-burglar stole your computer, how were you able to talk with the Master?"

"We used my computer," Leah said. "The bottom line is the Master thinks the story is going to end with the Final Battle."

"He said the Jötunn are from Norse mythology," Jerry interjected. "So the Final Battle might end up being Ragnarök, which the Master described as a big war between the forces of good and evil. The Viking version of Armageddon."

The Ancestors versus the Dark Ones…

"Basically," Jerry continued, "they all kill each other, and the world resets. Almost everybody dies, Vincent, maybe even Valenthor."

Vincent dropped the sloppy remains of the sandwich into the garbage. He took the bag from the bed and headed into the bathroom.

Through the door, he heard Leah say, "You can take a shower if you want. We don't have to leave this very second, but we shouldn't stay too much longer."

Vincent used the toilet, quickly changed his clothes, and splashed some water on his face. The man looking back from the mirror looked vaguely familiar. He opened the bathroom door.

"I'm not going to run, Leah. If I can't get answers from Daniel, I'm going to talk to the one person who might be able to tell us what happens next."

Leah's frown reappeared. "I've already told you I have no way of contacting Boden."

"Not Boden. *Suzanne.*"

Leah's eyes widened, and her mouth dropped open.

"Vincent, no. I don't think Suzanne Fortune has a clue what Daniel is doing in The Dream. And if she told the police anything *you* said about her book, they might have her house under surveillance."

"I don't care," Vincent said. "Maybe Boden *can't* interfere because The Dream isn't even a real dream on Suzanne's end. It's a book. We know Daniel has stolen her story, so if nothing else, Suzanne will be able to tell me what happens to Valenthor and Locke. At least I'll know what I'm walking into the next time I'm in The Dream."

Leah was already shaking her head. "Maybe Boden and his men were just waiting for Daniel to show up before they made their move."

Vincent placed his hands on her shoulders. Their eyes locked. "Leah, I'm going to talk to Suzanne. I don't know where she lives, but I know where she works. I'll go back to the hospital if I have to, but together maybe we can find another way."

Leah, her face filled with worry, waited a moment before she said, "OK. If that's what you want to do, I'm with you. But if we could wait until Boden gets in touch again, we can ask him to find out where she—"

"Got it!" Jerry shouted, holding up the phonebook. "Rick and Suzanne Fortune, Menomonee Falls."

Leah shot Jerry a withering look.

Vincent couldn't help but smile. "Nice one, Jerry. Now let's get out of here."

From the passenger seat of Leah's car, Vincent watched Jerry ring the doorbell of the brown, square home of Suzanne Fortune. Leah stood behind Jerry and a little off to the side. It was anyone's guess whether Suzanne would be more likely to open the door to a complete stranger or the possible accomplice of a fugitive. They were gambling on the former.

Vincent held his breath and waited. The driveway was empty, but Suzanne's car could be in the garage, he reasoned. Or maybe she didn't even own a car and took the bus to work.

Please be home!

He gasped as the door opened, and Suzanne's face peered out from the small space she allowed between the door and its frame. Vincent slid slower in his seat, trying, but failing, to read her lips. Moments later, when Leah stepped up to the door and motioned toward the car, Vincent's heart pounded with an enthusiasm that rivaled the bass of any suped-up sound system.

Even from a dozen yards away, Vincent saw the parade of emotions marching across Suzanne's face.

She's not going to let us in. Unless...

On a whim, Vincent opened the glove compartment and rifled through its contents—a stack of maps, a couple of pens, tire gauge, tampons, an official CIA badge, and a black handgun. He picked up the gun and stuffed it inside his jacket.

Someone tapped on the window, and Vincent jumped.

"We're good to go!" Jerry's voice was muted by the glass. He gave Vincent two thumbs up.

Vincent slammed the glove compartment closed and got out of the car. "What did she say?"

"Not much," Jerry said. "She seems kind of skittish, so just stay chill, OK?"

Leah and Suzanne had already vanished into the house. Vincent followed Jerry up the front stairs and into the living room, where the two women stood in heavy silence, obviously waiting for him.

"Your mother is worried sick about you, you know,"

Suzanne said softly.

Vincent managed a smile. "Yeah, I'm sorry about that. With any luck, all of this will get sorted out very soon. That's why I'm here actually."

Suzanne forced a smile back. "Right. Please have a seat, everyone. Um…can I get you all something to drink?"

"No th—" Leah started to say.

"Got any Dew?" Jerry asked.

"Yes," said Suzanne. "I think we do. Let me go and check…"

As soon as she left the room, Vincent and Leah glared at Jerry.

"Well, she asked!" he said defensively.

Vincent sighed and took a seat next to Leah on a well-worn sofa. Jerry, naturally, gravitated to an oversized Lay-Z-Boy recliner—the couch potato king trying out a new throne. The four walls of the living room formed a gallery of nature paintings of deer, ducks, and fish, along with a collection of family portraits of Suzanne and, Vincent assumed, her husband and son. The young bride in the wedding picture bore an unmistakable resemblance to Destiny.

The house smelled like cooking of some kind, though Vincent couldn't identify the dish. A giant cuckoo clock marked the passing seconds with loud, mechanical clicks. He was just about to wonder out loud about what was taking Suzanne so long, when their hostess returned.

"I looked everywhere, but I guess Cory drank the last Mountain Dew. I hope Diet 7UP is OK," she said, handing Jerry the bottle and a coaster.

"Sure, no worries," Jerry said.

Suzanne sat on a matching loveseat opposite of the couch so that she faced Vincent and Leah. "So…"

"Mrs. Fortune," Vincent began, searching for words that wouldn't put his sanity under immediate scrutiny. "I know you must find all of this very strange. I'm not going to pretend I understand what is happening to me, but if you can answer a few questions, I promise we'll be out of here before you know it."

"First, tell me how you know about my book." Suzanne's voice rose at the end of the statement, making it sound more like a question.

"Fine," Vincent said. "For the past few weeks, I've been having a recurring dream about...well, about Valenthor...about *being* Valenthor. And Daniel, my brother, is Locke. Now this is going to sound crazy, but I have to ask it...have you had any contact with Daniel?"

Suzanne looked more than a little confused. "Contact?"

"Conversations," Vincent prompted. "Maybe you read your book out loud to him or something?"

"No," she said. "No one has ever read my book."

Here goes nothing.

"Have you ever talked to Daniel in a dream?"

Suzanne looked from Vincent to Leah to Jerry and then back to Vincent. "I have no idea what you're talking about."

"OK, OK." Vincent rubbed his eyes. Despite the twelve-plus hours of sleep he had gotten last night, he didn't feel at all rested. "But it can't be coincidence that Valenthor and I have so much in common. He lost a daughter. I lost a daughter. He has a drinking problem... and I've been known to throw back a few. Are Locke and Valenthor related too?"

Suzanne nodded. "Half-brothers." Her leg jerked up and down nervously. "I think...I think I might have unconsciously based Valenthor on you. When I first met your mother, she talked a lot about you and Daniel. But I didn't do it on purpose, and everything else is made up."

"Except for what you took from Norse mythology," Jerry said.

Suzanne flinched. To Vincent, she said, "But that doesn't explain how you know anything about my—"

"I want to see it," Vincent said.

"What?"

"I want to see the book," he said.

Suzanne's face became an alarming shade of red. "I don't let anybody read my writing, not even my husband."

"Please?"

"No!"

Vincent clenched his teeth.

We don't have time for this!

Leah must have sensed he was losing patience because she said, "Please, Suzanne. We're not here to critique your work. If Daniel is using themes and characters from your book…"

Vincent stood up, pulled the handgun from his inside jacket pocket, and aimed it at Suzanne. Her yelp was echoed by a gasp from Leah and a "Dude!" from Jerry.

"Give me the book now!" Vincent ordered.

Oh God, what am I doing?

Eyes bulging, Suzanne rose shakily and walked to the end table under the cuckoo clock. She picked up and opened a laptop.

"I haven't p-printed it out or anything. I only just finished it last night. The ending j-just sort of poured out of me…"

"Vincent." Leah said his name in the same way a person would address a stray pit bull as "nice doggy." "What are you doing?"

Ignoring her, Vincent said, "Open the book file and set the laptop on the coffee table."

Suzanne obeyed, and Vincent sat back down. He kept the pistol pointed at Suzanne, who continued to stand, trembling, in the middle of the room.

"Destiny's Story" was spelled out in bold letters across the top of the screen. The first line under that read, "It all began with a dream."

Vincent scrolled down to the bottom of the file and then backtracked until he found the start of the last chapter.

THE ANCIENT AND MYSTICAL TEMPLE OF YGGDRASIL LIES IN A GREAT VALE BORDERED BY HIGH, TREACHEROUS MOUNTAINS. SUNLIGHT GLINTED OFF OF ITS SILVER SPIRES. DESTINY NEVER FAILED TO BE AWED BY THE BEAUTY OF THE PLACE, BUT THE MAGNIFICENT ARCHITECTURE OF THE MASSIVE STRUCTURE WAS AS PRACTICAL AS IT WAS ARTISTIC. EVEN FROM A DISTANCE, THERE WAS NO MISTAKING THE TOOTH-LIKE CRENELLATIONS AND MURDER HOLES INTERSPERSED AMONG THE STAINED-GLASS MURALS AND MAGNIFICENT SCULPTURES OF OVERSIZED ELVES.

YGGDRASIL WAS AS MUCH A FORTRESS AS IT WAS A CHURCH, FRIENDLY YET FOREBODING.

THE SURPRISINGLY LUSH FLATLAND SURROUNDING THE TEMPLE WAS ACCESSIBLE ONLY BY A LONG AND WINDING VALLEY, A NATURAL CORRIDOR THAT AT TIMES FEELS MORE LIKE A TUNNEL AT ITS NARROWEST POINTS. THE LOCATION OF BOTH THE TEMPLE AND ITS ENTRANCE ARE A CLOSELY GUARDED SECRET, KNOWN ONLY BY THE ELITE MEMBERS OF ELVES' PRIESTHOOD.

THAT IS, UNTIL NOW.

DESTINY LED HER DEAREST VALENTHOR AND THE KNIGHTS THROUGH THE HIDDEN PATH. THE JÖTUNN HADN'T BOTHERED TO POST SENTRIES, AND ONLY THE BODIES OF THE SOLIDER ELVES REMAINED AS EVIDENCE THAT THE FAY HAD WATCHED THAT SECRET ROAD. CONCEALED BY A COPSE OF HARDY EVERGREENS, THE PARTY GAZED UPON THE JÖTUNN HOST. THE WAR CAMP FORMED A GLOOMY RING AROUND THE TEMPLE. EVEN AS THEY WATCHED, THE ELFIN DEFENDERS REPELLED THE THOUSANDS OF BESIEGERS WITH FLAMING ARROWS AND VATS OF BOILING OIL.

"ALAS, YGGDRASIL!" DESTINY CRIED.

VALENTHOR FELL TO ONE KNEE BESIDE HIS LADY LOVE. "VERILY, WE ARRIVE TOO LATE!"

Vincent looked up from the screen, as much to give his eyes a rest from the reader-unfriendly font as the agonizingly unhelpful words.

Who would willingly read a whole book like this?

From his regal recliner, Jerry sat up straight and asked Suzanne, "Did you call the five-oh?"

Vincent raised the barrel of the gun, which had drooped while he was reading, and listened. The sound of sirens, which he had dismissed as background noise a moment ago, seemed to be getting louder. He jumped to his feet.

"Just tell me how it ends!" Vincent shouted.

"Does Valenthor die?" Jerry asked.

Suzanne, her forehead slick with sweat, didn't say anything at first. Finally, she said, "I knew from the beginning that Valenthor was going to die. He had to do something heroic so he could forgive himself for not being there when his wife and daughter needed him the most."

Destiny was right. This never was Valenthor's story.

The wail of sirens grew louder.

"Vincent, we have to go!" Leah announced, suddenly standing beside him.

It's too late…

Vincent let the gun fall to his side. To Suzanne, he said, "Does Valenthor get to see Clementine at least?"

"Who?" Suzanne asked. "Do you mean Valentine?"

But Vincent couldn't reply. The second he spoke his daughter's name, the room started to disappear. The Dream's pull was stronger, more urgent than ever before. He didn't struggle against the undertow.

Chapter 34

Milton sprang up from the couch and squinted at the silhouette in the doorframe.

"DJ?" he asked hoarsely.

"Yes," the other replied, his voice muffled by a mask with big, dark eyeholes. "But you might as well call me Daniel now."

When he stepped out of the shadows, he lowered his hood and removed the mask. A pair of penetrating blue eyes replaced the empty sockets. A long knotty stick held Milton's gaze until he noticed the bloody wound in Daniel's abdomen.

"My God, what did they do to you?" Milton asked, remembering the tall man from the white van.

"Nothing yet." Daniel looked down and poked his index finger into the bullet hole. "Oh, this? It's an old wound. You must've been expecting me to look beat up."

The boy isn't making any sense. He must be in shock.

On the couch, Clementine stirred restlessly and mumbled something unintelligible in her sleep. Daniel knelt beside her. "Thanks for taking care of her, Milton. I owe you one."

Milton rounded on him. "What were you thinking, getting your niece involved?"

Scoff. "Not my call, Milton. *She* came to *me*." Daniel rose, a wistful smile on his face. "We'll let her sleep for now. I've got a big surprise in store for her...if all goes according to plan."

"Daniel, you've been shot—" Milton sucked in a breath through his teeth. When Daniel moved his hand away from the wound, the black sweatshirt was whole and clean again. The stick also seemed to have evaporated into thin air. Milton staggered back a few steps and almost tripped over a table. "Who *are* you?"

"Who am I?" Daniel gave him an amused look. "I'm a scoundrel and a schemer, your captor and co-conspirator. The lock and key."

"I have no idea what you're talking about."

"That's because you've forgotten that this is all a dream," Daniel stated.

"Impossible!" Milton argued.

"No…" Daniel's dingy jeans and hooded sweatshirt transformed into a dark brown cloak. "…it's not."

Milton stumbled backwards and rammed the back of one leg into the low-standing coffee table. He fell onto it and stared up at Daniel, who looked like to his old self again.

"How are you doing that?" Milton asked.

Scoff. "You know how. You're one of the pioneers of dream drifting. You just have to remember."

Milton shook his head. "I told you before…I *can't* remember."

"That was before, Milton, and it was my fault. *Partially* my fault. I didn't want you to remember everything too soon, or you'd figure out that you've just been asleep this whole time. But you *have* been remembering…through dreams…dreams within a dream."

Milton started to argue, but when he went back to the door in his mind, he found it wide open. The scenes from the dreams—his memories—poured out: meeting with the Lucid Dreaming Society officers about the ethics of dream drifting; his last encounter with William Marlowe before he, Milton, and his protégé Earl Boden agreed to work for the CIA; draping their top-secret research in a Norse theme; talking Boden into injecting him with the serum so he would have the strength to confront William and his allies.

Only it wasn't enough. They were waiting for me...

Milton launched himself at Daniel, grabbing him by the front of his sweatshirt. "You ambushed me!"

"Whoa, take it easy. I wasn't even there," Daniel protested. "I got dragged into this after they'd already monkeyed with your memories. They said all I had to do was keep an eye on you and make sure your friends from Project Valhalla never reached you."

Daniel tried to pull away, but Milton tighten his grip on the sweatshirt. "How long have I been asleep?"

Daniel's shoulders raised in a clumsy shrug. "You were here before me. As best as I can tell, I've been in a coma for seven months."

Milton, suddenly numb, let go of the boy. "Seven months? I've been in this dream for more than *seven months*?"

Anger surged through him, but he suppressed the startling urge to tackle Daniel.

I need answers, and once I get them, I will wake up and report back to Boden.

He swallowed the lump in his throat and asked, "Why have you done this to me?"

"At first, to save my own skin," Daniel said matter-of-factly. "I would have died...*should* have died...except a dream drifter made me an offer I couldn't refuse. And since I had some unfinished business of my own, I agreed to be your babysitter."

"*Who* made you the offer?"

Scoff. "You're thinking it was your old chum, William Marlowe? Could be. But who knows? Anybody can be anybody in the dreamscape."

Clementine lashed out violently and then was still once more.

Daniel looked at her and gave a lopsided frown. "My niece told me it was a woman who'd been bugging her. When Clementine found me, that's when I knew I had to do something. It's bad enough that dream drifters can fuck with the living, but to harass a dead little girl? Talk about despicable."

Milton's breath caught in his throat. "You can't mean...Clementine is *dead*?" he whispered.

If souls can sleep, then why not dream?

Daniel nodded. "Milton, what exactly did you see that made you want to confront Marlowe in the dreamscape? What are they doing to the dead?"

"Not the dead, the *dying*." Milton took a steadying breath, as the memory surfaced without any resistance whatsoever. "I saw members of COPE following the soul of someone dying en route to his eternal rest. I believe COPE is searching for a way to circumvent death...to go on living *here* instead of succumbing to soul sleep. Or, more precisely, if dream drifters can roam the collective unconscious while alive, then perhaps they can do the same, lucidly, after they have passed."

"Hmm," Daniel said. "So they want to live forever. If you call this living."

Milton's thoughts raced in a hundred different directions. Question upon question assailed him, but he pushed them aside except for the most immediate among them. "Daniel, why did you choose to end this charade now?"

Daniel smiled mischievously. "Plato said, 'The virtuous man is content to dream what a wicked man really does.'

Maybe he meant that while everyone has a dark side, they should be judged by their actions, not their thoughts. Or maybe it means deep down, even the best of us is capable of doing some really shitty things when we think we can get away with it. No one should have the power to pick through someone else's thoughts.

"The more I learned about what you and your friends can do...what *I* can do, the more I knew I had to stop you. All of you. So I've been playing one side against the other in hopes that you'd destroy each other...or at least be too busy duking it out to mess with innocent people."

Daniel reached into the waistband of his pants and pulled out his silver pistol. Milton tensed. Before he could decide whether to fight back—even though it was Daniel's dream, Milton was confident he could overpower the boy in a one-on-one battle of wills, Daniel reversed his hold on the weapon and handed the gun, handle first, to Milton.

"You're letting me go?" Milton asked.

"After I watched your memories, I realized you're one of the good guys, Milton. You tried to keep the Lucid Dreaming Society in check back in the day, and I'm guessing the only reason you joined the CIA was because you knew they were going to investigate dream drifting anyway and you wanted keep an eye on them and make sure they didn't abuse it. Hell, you probably even use your turn signal when nobody else is around. Take the gun."

Milton did so, albeit reluctantly. The gun felt heavy and awkward in his hand.

"I'm letting you go because you have to stop the people who actually believe they're gods." Daniel bent down and kissed Clementine on the top of her head. "I've tried to keep this place hidden from both Project Valhalla and COPE, but once my old friends realize I betrayed them, it won't take them long to find me. We'd better go."

"Shouldn't we just wake up?" Milton asked.

Scoff. "I wish I could. Maybe you could, but I have a much more interesting destination in mind."

"Where?"

Daniel let out a full-blown laugh. "You wouldn't believe me if I told you."

The stillness of the sleepy house was shattered by a cacophony of screams and the shriek of metal splitting metal. Milton fell into a crouching position, covering his ears while staring, agog, at the war raging around him.

A man with pointed ears crashed to the ground beside him, his bronze helmet cleaved cleanly in half and his face obscured in thick red blood. The creature's horror-stricken eyes met Milton's. Then he said something in a language that sounded like Old Norse and promptly died.

All around him, the elves—at least Milton assumed that was what they were supposed to be—were falling back, shields raised to fend off the blows of the hundreds of half-naked brutes that towered nearly twice the height of an average man. The elves ignored him as they retreated to the safety of a massive bastion made of white stone.

Out of desperation and fear, Milton raised Daniel's gun, only to find that it had become a shiny silver dagger.

What the hell is happening?

Milton scrambled after the fleeing elves, but something big and solid clipped him in the shoulder, jarring every bone in his body.

He hit the ground and rolled uncontrollably for a several yards. When the world stopped spinning, he saw a giant standing over him, club raised. He tried to tell himself it was only a dream, but reason alone couldn't quell the instinctual terror gripping him.

The club came down quickly.

Milton closed his eyes. An instant later, a horrible, gurgling noise made him open them again. The point of a long blade disappeared back into the giant's gut. The behemoth fell first to its knees and then onto its face. Behind the giant, a knight with a bloody sword and a long mustache stared quizzically at him.

"Who art thou and what are thy intentions?" barked the knight.

Not a real person...just a mannequin...

"My name is Milton Baerwald, and I haven't the faintest idea why I...look out!"

The knight reacted instantly, bringing his sword up to block the barbed spearhead speeding toward his spine. Milton barely breathed as he watched the knight square off against the giant, swinging his sword in wide arcs. After a few narrow escapes—the spear passed perilously close to the knight's unprotected face on one exchange—the knight drove his blade into the giant's knee. The beast howled and fell forward.

With a final swing of the sword, the giant's head flew from its shoulders.

But two giants were there to take its place. As the knight struggled against the newcomers, Milton noticed for the first time that two other men in suits of armor fought nearby. At some point, Milton must have risen to his feet again because he felt his knees go weak when one of the other knights collapsed under a club the size of a small tree trunk. A moment later, the one was cut down by a giant's ax.

None of them are real...but whose dream is this?

The knight closest to him cried out. Milton noted the newly dead giant at his feet, but one of the beast's companions let out a roar of sadistic delight as the knight staggered backward. His breastplate was crumpled, as, presumably, were the bones beneath. To his credit, the knight still clutched his sword. The red-strained tip jerked erratically as he tried to maintain his balance.

Suddenly, the knight shouted, "Gods, receive my soul this day!" and flung himself blade-first at the giant.

The humungous club struck with a hollow thud, launching the knight into the air. The man hit the ground twenty feet away.

The giant turned its attention to Milton.

This is a dream. I can do anything.

Milton held out the gun-turned-dagger and concentrated. The blade stretched out until reaching what he supposed was a respectable length for a sword. At the same time, his 21st century clothes faded to gray and grew as hard as steel. Though the strain was enormous—greater than any battle of wills he had ever waged—he produced a shield for his other hand.

The giant's jaw dropped.

"I don't know whose nightmare this is, but I'm taking over," Milton said.

The giant continued to gape, but Milton realized it wasn't looking at him but *beyond* him. The scene went silent, as giants and elves ceased fighting and, one by one, turned to look in the same direction. Milton turned around slowly.

Perhaps a mile away, an enormous tree burned with bright golden flames. He had to shield his eyes when a beam of light shot from the topmost branches straight up into the sky. Thunder shook the earth. The clouds hanging over the valley turned gold, then red.

"Ragnarök," said a guttural voice from behind him.

Milton shot the giant a skeptical look. "You're joking, right?"

An ear-splitting keen swallowed his last word and made the hairs on his neck stand up. Spectral figures soared down from where the golden light had pierced the clouds. Many of the phantoms looked like people, but others resembled animals boasting exaggerated fangs and claws as well as extra appendages.

He stood there, staring, for what seemed like days.

Ragnarök...literally "the destiny of the gods." Daniel, you have one twisted sense of humor.

"Milton!"

Hearing the familiar voice in such a foreign place made the situation seem even more surreal. Milton tore his eyes away from the heavenly host and found the speaker. The knight who had spoken to him earlier—the man who had sped like a golf ball across the battlefield—ran toward him. While the blood-spattered armor remained, the mustache was gone. The man's gray-green eyes were un-mistakable.

"Is it really you, Earl?" Milton asked.

Boden, an astonished smile on his face, said, "I was about to ask you the same thing."

Milton laughed, unable and unwilling to hide his relief. "I suppose this makes you my knight in shining armor."

The other man's smile faded, and his eyes made a quick sweep of their surroundings. "To be honest, we weren't expecting to find *you* here. But since you are...and you remember who we are...I advise a hasty retreat. The enemy might be close by."

"William?" Milton asked.

Pause. "We're not entirely certain who is in charge."

Beyond Odin—and never had Boden's code name seemed more appropriate—the two other fallen knights climbed to their feet and hurried over to them. One of them was noticeably taller than he had been before. The other had grown long hot-pink hair and breasts.

"Heimdall! Syn!" Milton exclaimed.

Syn wrapped him in a hug. Their armor made the embrace more than a little awkward. "It's about friggin' time you recognize us!"

Odin, a long spear in hand, cleared his throat. "You have to wake up, Borr, before Daniel Pierce and his cohorts return."

Milton shook his head. "Daniel isn't a threat. He's the one who let me go."

Before he could say more, the ground began to rumble, and a giant crack zigzagged across the valley. Hundreds of hunched, dark-skinned monsters poured up from the hole.

The black elves.

"This really is Ragnarök," Milton said. "But whose dream are we in?"

"It's not a dream at all." Syn pulled a stiletto out of a sheath in her high-heeled boot and sent it spinning at a charging black elf. The improvised dart buried itself hilt-deep in the creature's throat. "We're in a novel."

"What?"

Odin stretched out his hand, and five lightning bolts shot from his fingertips, scattering a group of the dark, misshapen creatures. "There is a lot to explain, but this is not the place for a debriefing."

"To Valhalla then?" Heimdall suggested.

"No!" Milton shouted, surprising even himself by the intensity behind the word. "The mastermind behind all of this must be here somewhere."

The three of them ducked as a dragon covered in irides-cent green scales swooped low over the battlefield. The wyrm belched a ball of swirling flame at the castle, melt-ing the alabaster walls. Some of the elves fell from the parapets. Those that didn't escape in time were reduced to ash that rained down on the combatants below.

Odin dispatched a giant with the long, barbed spear. "We must retreat and regroup!"

Milton could barely hear him over the latest peal of thunder—a growl not from the sky, but from somewhere deep beneath their feet.

"No," Milton yelled back. "I want answers!"

Where are you, William?

Something humungous and white shot out from a pit near the castle. Taller and taller it grew, looking almost like an albino beanstalk. When it reached the height of the tallest tower, the rounded tip wrapped itself around the crenellations. Two cold black eyes looked down at Milton.

"What the hell is that?" Syn asked.

"Jörmungandr," Milton gasped. "The Midgard serpent. It's long enough to encircle the world, and it kills Thor at Ragnarök, according to the legend."

Syn drew another short blade from her boot. "Speaking of Thor, where *is* Vin—?"

"Heimdall, stay with Borr," Odin ordered. "I will return to Valhalla and summon the valkyries."

The deep voice of Jörmungandr shook the air. "Milton Baerwald is here! Stop him, Fenrir!"

The biggest wolf Milton had ever seen emerged from the fog-like shadow that had washed over the valley. Claws bared, jaws slavering, it leaped at Milton.

"No!" Odin shoved him aside, taking the full brunt of the wolf's attack.

Fenrisúlfr slays Odin during Ragnarök. But this isn't real. Fenrir and Jörmungandr might be dream drifters, but none of us can die here.

A small voice in the back of Milton's mind reminded him that he had been ambushed once before. Could the wolf and serpent render his friends comatose as well?

Heimdall, suddenly clad in armor of the purest white and clutching a rod with the head of ram, maneuvered himself between Milton and the wolf, which pinned Odin to the ground. "We're not prepared for this, Borr," Heimdall said. "Might revenge wait for another day?"

"This isn't about revenge!" Milton snapped.

Syn tried to close in on the wolf's flank, but the beast lashed out with its hind legs and sent the woman tumbling into a band of black elves, which immediately started slashing her with cleavers and knives.

Meanwhile, Odin had managed to heave Fenrir off of him, but not before one of the wolf's immense paws scored a hit. Claws ripped through the armor and flesh beneath. Odin swore but brought his spear to the ready, preparing for the next attack.

The wolf let out a growl that sounded too much like a man's laugh.

"Heimdall, *you* get the reinforcements!" Odin ordered.

"Wait!" Milton shouted.

"The virtuous man is content to dream what the wicked man really does."

Is this a test of my moral fiber, Daniel? Or were you hoping we dream drifters would fight this battle through to the end?

Milton let his weapon, which had shrunk back down to the size of a dagger, fall to the ground. "Everyone, retreat to Valhalla!"

"No arguments here!" Syn said, rejoining them.

The relief was clear in Odin's expression. He and Heimdall had forced Fenrir back, but the wolf circled them, waiting to strike. If they were going to flee, it was now or never.

Milton concentrated on the image of Yggdrasil. The tapestries lining the wide corridors. The way the flickering light from the torches made the shadows dance around the Great Hall. The flagstone floors. The faces of his friends.

"Nooooo!" Jörmungandr's deafening cry was underscored by Fenrir's howl.

As the apocalypse began to disintegrate all around him, Milton caught a glimpse of a small Asian child standing alone on the battlefield, witnessing the pandemonium without expression.

William?

Chapter 35

Vincent struggled against the darkness, frantically trying to orient himself. The sensation was much like falling, as though a vortex had appeared in Suzanne's living room and sucked him into a vacuum.

But he knew where he was going and who would be there.

He felt the warmth from the Heart of Yggdrasil on his face before he saw the small wooden chamber. The instant Daniel came into focus, Vincent lunged at him. Daniel was quicker. Up came the staff, striking Vincent directly in the solar plexus. Vincent fell back, gasping for breath, and watched helplessly as Daniel grabbed Destiny's wrist.

Daniel pulled the elf toward him, spinning her around so that she faced Vincent. He held the staff against her throat, pinning her body against his. Tears welled up in Destiny's eyes.

Vincent suppressed another series of coughs and, ignoring the pain in the center of his chest, straightened into a mostly upright position. "You want to kill her?" he wheezed. "Go ahead. She's not real."

"She's real to Suzanne," Daniel said. "But you're right. Threatening a two-dimensional character from a wannabe writer's secret novel is pretty pointless. Now if she were the love of your life, *that* would make for an interesting situation."

Instantly, Destiny's terrified visage became his wife's.

Wearing the elf's medieval clothes, Bella looked like she was dressed up for a Halloween party. Her expression of absolute confusion changed to that of suspicion when she recognized Vincent.

"That's not really her...is it?" Vincent asked, his voice breaking.

Daniel ignored the question. "Then again, maybe you don't love Bella anymore. It's been more than a year since you kissed her cousin and she kicked you out." Daniel's lips curled into a one-sided smile. "I mean, it's not like she's the last woman you've seen naked."

Bella disappeared. A panicked-looking Paish took her place.

"What the fu—?" Paish started to say, but Daniel pulled the staff tighter against her windpipe, cutting off her air.

Daniel clucked his tongue. "A pierced-up coed? Really, Vince?"

"Why are you doing this?" Vincent considered the weight of the hammer in his hand. Would Daniel really kill Paish if he rushed him? *Could* he kill her?

"Ah, but she was just a fling," Daniel continued. "At least your latest crush is closer to your age."

Vincent inhaled sharply.

No, not her...

He watched helplessly as Paish's pale skin darkened to olive. Her blond hair became shorter, straighter, and black. Leah's panic-stricken eyes stared into Vincent's.

"Nice to meet you, Leah. Wish we could have met under better circumstances," Daniel said.

Vincent swallowed the sickening taste in his throat. "That's...that's not really her."

"Vincent," Leah started to say.

"Shut up!" Daniel yanked the staff up higher, forcing Leah's head and neck into an unnatural position and eliciting a yelp of pain from the woman. "Of course, it's her. I brought her here the same way I brought you. Didn't Odin tell you? I'm a dream drifter."

Damn your poker face, Daniel!

"You're bluffing," Vincent said.

Scoff. "Quite the gamble you'd be taking. Have you forgotten that the good doctor suffers from a disorder that causes her to act out her dreams? Something tells me she's not safely handcuffed to her bed right now."

"How could you know?"

"I've been in your head, big brother."

Quiet strangling sounds escaped Leah's lips, and Vincent couldn't avoid looking at her any longer.

I'm so sorry I got you into this.

He wondered what Jerry and Suzanne were thinking back in the real world, what they would do if Leah began stumbling around uncontrollably or if she started choking on nonexistent blood?

What will the police do if she refuses to put her hands where they can see them?

Vincent dropped the hammer. The resulting crash echoed through the small chamber. "What do you want from me?"

Daniel's expression grew serious, and Vincent felt more afraid than ever.

"I want you to make a choice," he said softly. "I promised I would reunite you with Clementine, and I'm finally in a position to do that. But you have to choose whose life is more important, Clementine's or Leah's."

The room began to teeter, and Vincent braced himself against the altar that held the Heart of Yggdrasil.

"Watch out for that sphere," Daniel cautioned. "The elf was right. Whoever touches it dies. Now, if I understand Suzanne's story, Locke doesn't want either Valenthor or

Destiny to touch it. One of them is the Chosen One, after all, so if either of them touches the Heart of Yggdrasil, the barrier between worlds opens and the gods, Ancestors, or whatever will return to fight the Dark Ones. Since Locke is hoping for a one-sided battle, he would offer Valenthor his daughter's soul if he, Valenthor, lets Locke kill the elf princess. Then the two of them can walk away from the sphere."

"What do *you* want?"

"I'm getting to that," Daniel replied. "We have to stick close to the script, or this won't work. Anyway, I'm making the same offer. Just say the word, and I'll kill Leah. Then I'll take you to Clementine. You'll be able to see her whenever you want."

No. He can't really do it. He's lying, like always.

But what if he isn't?

Vincent swallowed hard. "Clementine...will she...live in this place? Would I have to come here, as Valenthor, in order to spend time with her, as Valentine? Or...would we be able to go anywhere I can dream of?"

Leah groaned, but he refused to meet her eyes.

"Only one way to find out," Daniel said.

Vincent wiped his eyes and let out a wordless cry of pure frustration.

He's insane. There's no other explanation.

Maybe it runs in the family.

This has to end.

Now.

Vincent breathed a shaky sigh, "I'm sorry, Leah. But if there's a chance I can see my daughter again... For all I know, he'd kill you anyway." Vincent clutched the edge of the altar and bowed his head. "Just make it quick, Danny."

"Wait, what?" Daniel asked. "*Really?*"

Here goes nothing!

Vincent let out a roar that would have done Valenthor proud, lifted the Heart of Yggdrasil above his head, and threw it at his brother. The sphere struck him in the side of the head. Daniel fell. The room erupted into an inferno of golden light. Invisible flames blistered the skin on Vincent's hands, burning every place that had made contact with the orb.

He pushed the pain aside and tried to take a step toward Leah, but then an intense light burst from a crack in the sphere, and he was completely consumed.

Vincent was pretty sure he was dead.

The cold void was a shocking contrast to the heat of the destroyed Heart of Yggdrasil. A dull whiteness permeated everything around him, an effect that made him question whether he was actually seeing at all. He rubbed his eyes. The fact that he had eyes—and hands to rub them— seemed to suggest his continued existence.

A voice behind him said, "It's always snowing here. Just like the day she died."

Daniel wore a pair of blue jeans and the black hoodie that had been a staple component of his wardrobe throughout high school and for years thereafter. There was no sign of Locke's ragged coat. Or his staff.

Vincent tackled Daniel.

They landed in heap, producing a deformed snow angel beneath them. Sitting on top of his brother's stomach, Vincent lost control. His fist slammed into Daniel's nose once, twice. He lost count.

When Vincent finally stopped, he realized he was crying.

Daniel turned his head, spit a mouthful of blood into the snow, and laughed. "Why does our quality time always end in a fight?"

Struggling for breath, Vincent asked, "Where...is... Leah?"

"You called it, Vince. She was never here."

Vincent considered landing a final blow.

"Go ahead and hit me some more if it makes you feel better," Daniel said. "It won't change anything. This is just a dream, remember?"

Daniel's broken nose straightened. The spattered blood evaporated.

Vincent climbed to his feet. "*Why*, Daniel? What is the point of all this?"

Daniel pulled himself up but stayed sitting in the snow. "You had to believe that Leah's life was in your hands. I'm glad you chose to save her. I'll admit, you had me going for a second there." He raised a hand to forestall any interruption. "The truth is, you act like your life ended the day Clementine died. And since I found myself in a unique opportunity to help you have a revelation, I took it."

Vincent eyed his brother warily. "What revelation is that?"

"That you can't bring her back, and even if you could find a way to cheat death, you shouldn't." Daniel stood up and brushed the snow off the back of his pants. "Everybody dies, Vince. It sucks, but it's true. And contrary to your recent experiences, we only get *one* life. Don't throw it away out of some misplaced sense of guilt."

Vincent looked away, hot tears spilling down his cheeks. "I always thought I'd do anything to get my daughter back, and there was a part of me that did want to trade Leah for Clementine." He let out a long sigh and watched his breath drift into the chilly air. "And if I actually believed you could do what you promised, I just might have let you kill Leah."

"No, you wouldn't have," Daniel insisted. "Deep down, you're a good guy. You just have to let go of the past and let yourself have a future."

Vincent shot Daniel a skeptical look. "So you did all of this to teach me a lesson?"

"Well, that's not the *whole* story," Daniel confessed. "Like I said before, this thing is bigger than our family. But I'm done messing around with false gods. I feel bad about having used Suzanne's imagination for a hideout, but I had to find a place off of everyone else's radar that I could get to easily. Anyway, neither of us will be going back there, and what all of those other dream drifters do while Suzanne's story comes to an end is their business. She'll be none the wiser."

"The Dream is finally over, then?" Vincent was surprised at how conflicted he felt about the possibility.

"It's over for you. Valenthor just died, taking Locke with him. Guess he was the Chosen One, after all."

"But he wasn't able to save his daughter…"

Daniel shrugged. "Well, he did kill Locke, who presumably cursed Valentine in the first place. That's my theory, anyway. So I'm guessing Valentine will wake up, and Destiny will find her, and the two of them will live happily ever after in a brave, new world. A happy enough ending."

Vincent grunted and kicked at the snow.

"But that's not *your* ending," Daniel added, stepping over to Vincent's. "I promised I'd bring you and Clementine together, didn't I?"

Daniel stretched out his arm and pointed to a building that Vincent hadn't noticed until that exact moment. His legs gave out, but Daniel caught him. The old house looked exactly as Vincent remembered it.

"Come on, Vince. She's waiting for you."

*　　*　　*

The screen door slammed, and Clementine sat upright.

"Dada!" she shouted, leaping off the couch and running over to him. Vincent fell to his knees and caught her. He wrapped her in a tight hug.

"Clemmy...oh, Clemmy," he muttered, half laughing, half crying. Somehow he knew it really was her. "I'm so sorry, baby. I should have been there for you...shouldn't have fallen asleep....oh, God..."

Clementine patted his back. "It was a accident, silly."

Vincent buried his face in her hair and sobbed. He had no idea how long he cried. The only thing that mattered was Clementine's warm body against his and the sound of her high-pitched voice still fresh in his ears.

After a while, Daniel cleared his throat. "Sorry to interrupt, but you could wake up at any moment, and there's still something I have to tell you."

It took all of Vincent's willpower to pull away from his daughter. Unwilling to break contact, he picked her up, cradling her against his chest. "How did you manage this?"

For once, Daniel's smile held no trace of sarcasm. "I wish I knew. She came to me. I think she's a dream drifter too, and I think she's been looking for you."

All those times I had the recurring nightmare about the morning she died...was that her trying to reach out to me?

Daniel mussed Clementine's hair. "When she found me, I promised her I'd bring you here so the two of you could say a proper goodbye."

Vincent squeezed his eyes shut. "I don't want her to go."

"She needs to go back..." Daniel glanced at Clementine. "...back to sleep, and you need to get back to your life. This is no place for her, especially with the war in the dreamscape heating up."

Clementine tucked her rubber duck, Webster, under her chin and said, "Dada, I'm scared."

"Me too, Clemmy."

Daniel gave the rubber duck a big squeeze, and Clementine giggled at the drawn-out squeak that followed. "What did Uncle Danny tell you, huh? I'm going with you, so you won't be alone. And before you know it, we'll all wake up, and you'll see your daddy again."

"And Mommy too?"

"Yes, Mommy too," Vincent replied.

"Can I bring Webster?"

Vincent swallowed the lump in his throat. "Sure thing, kiddo."

Seemingly satisfied, Clementine squirmed out of his arms and skipped over to the middle of the living room, where she started dancing to music only she could hear. Watching her filled Vincent with more pain and joy than he thought one person could endure.

To Daniel he said, "Thank you...for this."

"It was the least I could do." Daniel was also watching Clementine, who launched into an off-key rendition of "Oh My Darling, Clementine"—a former Cruz Family favorite.

"What about you, Danny?"

"I just told you." Daniel pulled up his hood, covering his tangled mess of red hair. "I'm going with her."

"To die? Can't you just, I don't know, wake up?"

Daniel's sigh metamorphosed into a chuckle. "You better believe I tried. But, you know, I got what I had coming. And since I'm not coming back, I'm hoping you could to do a couple of favors for me."

"Anything," Vincent promised.

"Mom is going to need you to be there for her when…when I go." The mischievous smile returned. "I *am* her favorite son, after all."

Vincent laughed in spite of himself. "Yeah, sure."

"That means you have to be nice to her, even though she's a flawed human being like the rest of us," Daniel added.

"Can I tell her about you? About…this?"

Scoff. "The woman believes in miracles, but this might be kind of a stretch."

Across the room, Clementine, holding Webster out in front of her and spinning in circles, sang, "Drovy ducklings in the water, any morning jusset nine."

"Vincent, I didn't kill that cop."

Daniel was looking out the window, where big, puffy snowflakes wafted through the yellow streetlights.

"A week before the shooting, I got busted for carrying," he said. "To get a lesser sentence, I agreed to help them flush out a bigger fish. I wore a wire…just like on the TV shows…except a million times scarier."

Daniel took a deep breath. "Somebody fucked up. The next thing I know, bullets are flying, and I get tagged. But I never fired a shot. It's not like they let me take my piece."

"Then how did the reporters get it so wrong?" Vincent asked.

Daniel spun around, his eyes blazing. "Because the pricks lied to them! Their little sting operation blew up in their faces. A cop was dead, and a witness in police custody was in a coma. Why *not* pin it on me?"

"I believe you, but…" Vincent ran a hand through his hair. "A detective told me that the partner of the cop who was shot that day killed himself a week later…that he hadn't been sleeping well…"

Daniel winced and looked away. "Yeah, that was me. I wanted revenge, and I got it. But it didn't make anything better." He sighed. "I truly regret tormenting that man. I was no better than those other jerks who think it's OK to play God with people's lives."

"So you want me to set the record straight about the shooting," Vincent concluded.

"I don't give a damn what the public thinks, but there is someone who needs to know the truth…"

Clementine threw Webster in the air and didn't come close to catching him. The duck bounced off the carpet and settled next to Vincent's shoe. Her voice climbed to a volume that bordered on yelling.

"Oma darlin', oma darlin', oma darlin', Clementine. You were lost in gone f'rever. Dead for sorry, Clementine."

Once Daniel finished explaining exactly what he wanted Vincent to do, Vincent pulled him into a bear hug. "I'm sorry I wasn't a better brother, Danny. I should've been looking after you, not the other way around."

"Don't worry about it," Daniel said. "I know I'm a bastard. Then again, so are you."

Vincent laughed and wiped away a tear. "So this is it."

Daniel flashed a lopsided grin. "Yep…unless Suzanne finds a way to bring us back for the sequel."

Epilogue

Vincent loosened his tie and unfastened the top button of his shirt. He looked around and decided he was, hands down, the best-dressed customer in the diner that morning.

His booth was flanked on one side by three college guys who took turns exchanging enthusiastic recounts of last night's revelries. By the looks of their breakfast selections, they were attempting to keep hangovers at bay with equal parts caffeine and grease. Behind Vincent sat an unremarkable elderly couple who spoke Russian when they spoke at all. An oldies radio station piped in "Puff the Magic Dragon."

Thumbing through the oversized, laminated menu, Vincent contemplated ordering the Belgian waffles but decided not to tempt fate. He couldn't afford to pay the dry cleaning bill if he spilled syrup on his suit.

"There's my favorite former fugitive," Leah said, approaching his table. "I almost didn't recognize you without the T-shirt and jeans."

He looked down at the black coat and maroon tie. "I haven't put this on since Clementine's funeral. Would've been nice to have a happy occasion to wear it to between then and now."

Leah smiled sympathetically as she removed her stylish, knee-length coat, which was covered with rapidly melting snowflakes. She shuffled into the seat across from him. "I'm sorry I'm going to miss your brother's funeral."

"It's probably just as well," Vincent replied. "You being there might raise some awkward questions."

"If Suzanne comes, you mean?" Leah asked. "*You're* the one who pulled a gun on her. By the way, what does your mom think of all of this?"

"They told her the same thing they told the cops and everyone else…'Vincent Cruz, Leah Chedid, and Jeremiah Weis were working under the auspices of a classified, government-sponsored project in the interest of national security.' Whenever Mom presses me for details, I tell her I'm not allowed to talk about it. Mostly, I think, she's just relieved it's over."

A waitress of indeterminate age refilled Vincent's coffee and poured Leah some decaf. After they placed their order—a Greek omelet for Vincent and crepes for Leah—Vincent realized he had lost the thread of their conversation.

"So…your message said you're flying out East this afternoon…" Vincent prompted.

"Yes," Leah said. "I'm finally going to meet Boden face to face."

"What? Look, I know Boden saved our asses after the cops arrested us at Suzanne's place, but we don't owe him—"

"I'm going because I *want* to." Leah emptied a pink packet of artificial sweetener into her cup. "Boden wants to compare notes, but I also think he's going to offer me a job."

"With the CIA?"

Leah took a sip of her coffee, grimaced, and reached for another sweetener. "Boden said Project Valhalla could benefit from my expertise in sleep phenomena, especially RBD."

"And you're gonna take the job?"

Leah shrugged. "Maybe. Before you came along, my professional development had sort of stalled out. I was bored. Working with Boden and Dr. Baerwald could prove very rewarding, and I have to admit I am eager to learn more details about Project Valhalla."

Vincent conjured up a mental image of Leah Chedid in a dark suit and black sunglasses, packing heat. He chuckled. "Well, you already have the badge."

They drank coffee quietly for a few minutes. Then Vincent said, "They tried to get his body...Daniel's, I mean. Someone, supposedly from the hospital, called Mom to see if she would consider donating his body to science. I wonder if it was Boden or Levi who called."

"What did your mother say?"

"She said she wanted a real Catholic funeral *with* a body. But it still took a long time to get the coroner's report, which is why the funeral is more than a week late." Vincent sighed. "I can't remember the exact lingo, but basically the coroner said his brain just shut off at about the same time I woke up with Jerry in a jail cell."

Leah reached for Vincent's hands and gave them a squeeze. "If Boden fills me in on anything that pertains to you and Daniel, I'll be sure to pass it along to you."

"Unless it's classified," Vincent argued.

She smiled slyly. "Far be it from me to break the rules."

Their breakfast arrived a moment later, and they ate in silence, lost in their own thoughts. Vincent couldn't decide how he felt about the idea of Leah moving away. On the one hand, he would miss her. On the other, it would be easier to stop thinking about her if she wasn't around.

He flinched when Leah asked, "Do you think Bella will be at the funeral?"

After swallowing a forkful of hash browns, Vincent replied, "She said she would be."

"You talked to her?"

"We've had a couple of conversations since Danny died. Bella always had a soft spot for him. I suppose everybody did but me." He took another bite. Leah continued to watch him. Eyes on his plate, Vincent added, "I don't know what's going to happen. Neither of us has filed for divorce yet, but I don't see us getting back together. Maybe we could be friends again though."

"Well, talking is a good first step," Leah said.

"It sure beats sulking." Vincent attempted a smile. "I'm also waiting for a call back from Jerry's boss. I figure any job is better than sitting around the apartment feeling sorry for myself."

Leah wiped her mouth with a corner of her napkin and asked, "Are you going to be OK, Vincent?"

So many questions...you would've made a good shrink, Leah.

"The funeral will be all right. I already said goodbye to Daniel...and to Clemmy. I'm going to get a new job, and Mom loaned me some money, so I won't get evicted. Things are looking up."

"No more dreams?"

"Valenthor is gone. May he rest in peace. The only dreams I've had lately are the run-of-the-mill variety. Half the time I don't even remember them. Which is nice."

Leah looked at her watch. "I have to get to the airport. I'll try to touch base soon." She scooped up her coat and dropped a twenty-dollar bill on the table. Before Vincent could protest, she said, "You can get the next one. Take care of yourself."

"You too. Guess I'll see you around."

Over her shoulder, she said, "Maybe in your dreams."

*　　*　　*

Idling at a red light, Vincent glanced down again at the address on the napkin. Not that he needed the reminder. He doubted he would have been able to forget Daniel's last request if he wanted to.

The light turned green. He gently coaxed Jerry's boxy, old sedan to a shaky twenty-five miles per hour. He supposed it was only appropriate that he should be driving a bona fide ghetto cruiser. The farther north he went, the more rundown the neighborhoods became. The North Side's graffiti and barred-up windows reminded him of his childhood, back when Danny invented the game Spot the Crack House. Only later, when plywood replaced kicked-in doors and busted-out windows, would they know who was right.

Vincent shook his head and smiled.

Part of him had hoped the drive to the North Side wouldn't be necessary. But there had been no surprise guests at the funeral. He must have been glancing around a lot because both his mother and Bella had asked him if he was looking for someone in particular. He hadn't told them. Not yet.

He slowed down once he reached the street written on the napkin. The house numbers looked back from cookie-cutter apartment complexes that might have seen better days but probably not. When he found the number he was looking for, he pulled into a vacant spot in the crater-filled parking lot. The Buick gave a final belch and went silent. Vincent sighed.

No backing out now. A promise is a promise.

The hallway of the apartment building reeked of cigarette smoke. A steady thump of electronic bass rattled the door of one of the units. Vincent stopped at Apartment 8 and knocked. Several seconds later, the door opened a little. A dark brown eye with long mascara-black lashes peered at him from just above the chain.

"Who're you?"

"My name is Vincent Cruz. I think maybe you knew my brother, Daniel."

The eye narrowed. "I don't know no Daniel Cruz."

"Not Cruz…Pierce," Vincent corrected. "We're half-brothers."

The door closed, and the chain jangled. Then the woman threw open the door. A cascade of jet-black braids framed a pretty face that regarded him suspiciously. She was short and, judging from the beach-ball bump under her pink tank top, very pregnant.

"You're Dan's brother?" she asked. Vincent couldn't decide if the hint of accent was Hispanic or Hood. She looked him up and down, her eyes lingering on his suit. "You must've come from the funeral, huh?"

"Yeah…" He shifted his weight from one leg to the other. "Can I come in? I have something I need to tell you."

She crossed her arms awkwardly above her bulbous belly and scowled. "Unless you're here to tell me Dan left a fortune for me and his kid, you got no business here." She stared him down. "That's what I thought. That asshole was no good to us alive and no good dead either."

She started to close the door, but Vincent reached out and held it open. "Chloe, wait. I promised Daniel I'd tell you the truth about what happened to him. Please just listen. Then I'll go."

Her shiny red lips remained fixed in a frown, but she let go of the door.

"I know Daniel swore to you he was going to stop selling drugs," Vincent began, "and he didn't…at least not as soon as he should have. Daniel got arrested for possession with intent to sell. The cops said they would cut him loose if he went undercover to help them nab his supplier. It all went to hell, and Daniel got shot, hit his head, and went into a coma."

Vincent took a deep breath. "But Daniel never shot a cop, Chloe. The only reason he was there was because he wanted a clean slate. He wanted to be there for you and the baby."

Chloe's expression didn't change, but after a few seconds, a pair of tears trickled down her cheeks. "Are you for real?"

"He didn't want his son or daughter to grow up thinking he was a bad guy."

Chloe sniffed and wiped at her face with the back of her hands. "Dan *was* a bad guy. But he was a good guy too. God, I miss him so much sometimes."

She started to cry, and the next thing Vincent knew he was holding her, patting her back. The hard bulge of her belly pushed against his abdomen. Her body shook with each sob.

He wished he knew more about her—how she and Daniel had met, how long they had been together before she got pregnant, what she did for a living—but at the moment, all that mattered was that she was family.

Sniff. "I think a part of me was hoping he'd wake up from the coma and come home like nothing happened. We were going to try to make it work. I don't know what I'm gonna do now."

"We'll figure it out," Vincent said. "You're not alone. That's my niece or nephew in there, you know."

She pulled away and looked down at her stomach. "Niece," she said. "I'm having a girl."

If Sin Dwells Deep

An excerpt from
Book Two of
The Soul Sleep Cycle

Available now from
ONEMILLIONWORDS

Prologue

For the Wolf, tracking his prey was almost as thrilling as the kill itself.

False leads. Dead ends. So many places his quarry could hide. Sometimes the trail took him in endless circles or, worse, a straight line that never seemed to decrease the distance between hunter and hunted, no matter how far he ran.

But obstacles only heightened his excitement, delaying the exquisite moment that distracted him during the day and consumed him at night.

Her scent suddenly filled his nostrils, and the Wolf picked up speed. The scenery on either side of the path became a blur. All the easier to pretend he was surrounded by trees. The ground, a forest floor.

As the smell of vanilla intensified, he remembered how she looked back then. The store-bought blond curls framing a flawless neck. Those smirking lips, so red and shiny. The biggest tits in school, teachers included.

Her passably pretty face, soon to be smeared with blood...

Momentarily lost in his hunger, he felt the trail grow colder. The wind roared in his ears, drowning out his own growl of frustration. Reluctantly, he slowed, forgetting the pleasure ahead and focusing only on his memory of her.

He concentrated. He sniffed. The pull returned—subtle at first, then stronger.

Changing course, he allowed himself a brief grin. He'd enjoy the hunt while it lasted. It would be over all too soon.

Now that he was getting so close to her, he couldn't keep from sprinting. As the imaginary trees vanished and he plunged headlong into more vivid surroundings, he pushed himself even faster. Only when he heard the sound of applause did he stop to assess his surroundings.

The edge of an enormous room. Warm air instead of the coolness of his false forest. Above, a constellation of big, blinding lights. Ahead, the cheers of a crowd. Her sickeningly sweet perfume.

Squinting against the glare of the stage lights, he cautiously flanked the front row of spectators. He wasn't surprised to see their faces were practically blank. A hint of a mouth. The suggestion of eyes. A bump that would form a nose if he stared at it long enough.

He didn't bother. His prey wasn't among the dummies.

Beyond the studio audience, a semicircle of camera men surrounded an immaculately clean kitchen. All lenses were aimed at a woman behind a waist-high counter, dumping ingredients one by one into a tall, shiny pot.

The moment of discovery always took him back to that fateful hunting trip with Uncle Bob. When the buck had stepped up to the stream to drink, unaware of him and the mortal danger he represented, he'd nearly lost his nerve. But in the end, he did himself—and his uncle—proud. His first kill was clean. The animal never knew what hit it.

Drunk from the power only a predator can know, he watched her. His pulse raced. He grew rock hard.

The buck had never seen who killed it, but she would.

As the woman delivered lines about proper measurements to the cameras, he studied her. The years since high school graduation had etched deep lines upon her fleshier face, grooves that even a thick coat of stage makeup couldn't hide. Hidden beneath a loud floral-print blouse, her once-glorious rack sagged down to a belly made doughy by too much food, too many beers, a bunch of kids, or all the above.

Seeing the former heartbreaker in such sad shape filled the Wolf with perverse joy. She and her stuck-up friends had laughed in his face when he had finally mustered the courage to ask her to the prom. "Little boy," she had called him. The next day, the Queen Bee and her two drones had filled his locker with shaving cream.

She had thought herself superior to him, but as he watched the pitiful woman stir the pot with a wooden spoon, he promised to prove her wrong.

He'd show her he was the man of her dreams, whether she liked it or not.

Teeth clenched tightly, *painfully* together, he looked back at the audience. With a little concentration, two of the women in the front row started to resemble the woman's high school friends—the stupid bitches who had latched onto her like a pair of remoras because they couldn't achieve popularity on their own. They had laughed on cue whenever their leader insulted other students.

They would die first.

A voice in the back of his mind urged caution, warning him of the dire consequences he'd face if he got caught. The words belonged to a woman, one he hated even more than Queen Bee.

But the Wolf had come too far to turn back. He craved vengeance. Hungered for blood.

He dropped to his knees and placed his hands on the smooth cement floor. The transformation was instantaneous and painless. One moment, he was a man, and the next, a fine—if massive—specimen of *canis lupis*.

He crouched, his new muscles trembling with unspent power beneath a pelt of long black fur. Then he pushed off with his massive paws, leaving gouges in the floor.

A living shadow, he cleared the distance to the studio audience in a single leap. The claws of one foreleg had already sunk deep into his first victim's neck and shoulder before any of the mannequins reacted. Drone Number One's scream was quickly echoed by others. The Wolf reared up on his hind legs and struck again, a brutal blow that reduced her face to bloody strips of skin and cartilage.

As the lifeless body slumped to the ground, chaos filled the studio. Queen Bee's other friend tried to run with the rest of the crowd, but the Wolf pounced. He threw his full weight at her back, sending her sprawling into the aisle. She let out a pained gasp when he landed on top of her.

He considered rolling her over so that he could watch her expression as he eviscerated her. But he had grown bored with killing dummies a long time ago. Tonight's target had to be someone real.

A quick glance over at Queen Bee revealed an expression of pure terror. If he didn't hurry, she might run or wake up, and while he loved a good chase, he couldn't wait another night for satisfaction.

For the Wolf, tracking his prey was almost as thrilling as the kill itself.

Almost.

Available in paperback and for Kindle at Amazon.com.

Also available from ONEMILLIONWORDS

Praise for The Renegade Chronicles

"David Michael Williams transports you to a world where
you never know what is going to happen!
Sit down and hang on!"

"Fantastic!"

"I couldn't put it down. The books are action packed and
full of mystery, magic, and a dash of romance."

"A great big step into a world that keeps you pleasantly off
balance by feeling uncannily familiar and strange at the
same time."

"I hope we haven't heard the last from these
characters…I'm craving more!"

**Available in paperback and for Kindle
at Amazon.com.**

Acknowledgments

First and foremost, I want to thank my wife, **Stephanie Williams**, for all of her support throughout this project. *If Souls Can Sleep* wouldn't have happened—*couldn't* have happened—without her. She has the dubious role of reading the worst of my writing (first drafts), pointing out what's broken without bruising my ego too badly, and putting up with me when my skin isn't as thick as it should be.

They say one of the greatest contributions to a book's commercial success is the cover art. If that's true, then you're holding a future best-seller in your hands. I couldn't be happier with what designer extraordinaire **Mary Christopherson** created for *If Souls Can Sleep*. And I'm eager to seeing what she conjures up for the sequels!

I'm a firm believer that he who proofs his own work has a fool for a client. Fortunately, I know **Dusty Krikau**, who has a keen eye for wayward words and misplaced punctuation. She has my undying gratitude for delving into such a stylistically strange manuscript and saving me much embarrassment.

Finally, I would like to thank these members of the Allied Authors of Wisconsin, who were exposed to *If Souls Can Sleep* in its earliest form, chapter by chapter, month after month. It's a testament to your acumen and investment in my success that you were able to provide cogent criticism to such a nonlinear narrative.

Marilyn Auer	**Alexia Lamont**
Bill Binder	**Maureen Mertens**
Jack Byrne	**Roberta Bard Ruby**
Mark J. Engels	**Fern Ramirez**
John D. Haefele	**Tom Ramirez**

Photo: Jaime Lynn Hunt

David Michael Williams has suffered from a storytelling addiction for as long as he can remember. With a background in journalism, public relations, and marketing, he also flaunts his love affair with the written word as an author of speculative fiction. His books include the sword-and-sorcery trilogy *The Renegade Chronicles* and *The Soul Sleep Cycle*, a dreampunk series that explores life, death, and eternity.

David lives in Wisconsin with the best wife on this or any other planet and their two amazing children.

Visit his website at david-michael-williams.com.